The Lost Saint

BREE DESPAIN

EGMONT

EGMONT

We bring stories to life

www.breedespain.com

First published by Egmont USA 2011
This edition published in Great Britain 2011
by Egmont UK Limited
239 Kensington High Street
London W8 6SA

Text copyright © Bree Despain 2011
Jacket and interior design by J DRIFT DESIGN
Jacket photograph courtesy Jose Torralba 2009 / Getty Images
Published by Egmont USA and used with permission

The moral rights of the author have been asserted

ISBN 978 1 4052 5679 7

1 3 5 7 9 10 8 6 4 2

A CIP catalogue record for this title is available from the British Library

Printed and bound in Great Britain by the CPI Group

In loving memory of Mildred Coy Rane.

I don't know how much you cared for my fantastical stories of werewolves and demon hunters, but you were always supportive and proud.

I miss you daily.

Your granddaughter,
Bree

Consequence

"Do what he wants, and you might survive," a harsh voice said into the boy's ear before he felt a sharp blow to the kidneys. He fell forward onto the concrete, his arms splayed out in front of him.

"So this is the one who tried to get away?" another voice asked from the shadows. It was a deeper, older, more guttural voice. Almost like a growl. "This isn't a clubhouse, boy. You can't just decide to stop playing and go home."

The boy coughed. Bloodstained saliva dribbled from his mouth. "I wasn't . . . I didn't . . ." He tried to push himself up onto his knees, but a kick from behind sent him sprawling forward again on the ground. His mind raced, replaying what he'd done to get himself to this place.

This place.

They'd said he could call this place home. They'd

said they were his friends. They'd called him their brother.

And that was all it took. That was all he'd wanted.

But this place wasn't home. . . .

"You belong to me," the man said as he stepped out of the shadowed alcove. "And that's why you'll tell me what I want to know."

This place was a prison. And these people were not his family. . . .

The man the others called Father towered over the boy, glaring down at him with glowing, yellow, murderous eyes. "Tell me!" the man roared, and slammed his booted foot down on the ring on the boy's extended hand, grinding into it with his heel.

The boy screamed—but not because of the searing pain he felt as the fragments of the ring sliced into his flesh, and his tendons ripped away from the splintering bones in his fingers. He screamed because he knew that for what he'd done, everyone he'd ever loved, everything he'd left behind, was going to die.

CHAPTER ONE

The Sky is Falling

"You can do this, Grace," Daniel said between sharp breaths. "You know you can."

"I'm trying." My fingers trembled as I tightened them into fists.

It was the pain of the transition that always surprised me—no matter how prepared I thought I was. It started as an aching sensation deep inside my body. Pooling in my muscles, making my shoulders shake and my legs throb. My biceps felt like they were on fire.

"Come on, Grace. Don't quit on me now."

"Shut up!" I said, and took another swing.

Daniel laughed and countered to the left. My blow missed his mitt entirely.

"Agh!" I stumbled forward, but Daniel caught me before I fell and pushed me back up. I gritted my teeth and rocked back on my heels in the grass. I was *supposed* to be more agile than this. "Stop moving around."

"Your opponent"—Daniel panted—"isn't going to stand still and just let you hit him." He held his boxing mitts out in front of him, welcoming a new attack.

"He would if he knew what was good for him." I jutted forward with a combination of a hook and a jab, which Daniel deflected with his mitts. He spun out of my way, and my next swing went wildly into the air.

"Gah." I shook my head. My moonstone necklace bounced against my chest. It felt warm against my already flushed skin, pulsing with heat.

"You're pushing your punches too much. Save your energy. Quick jabs. Send your arm out with a snap and then bring it back immediately."

"I'm *trying*." The pain in my muscles mounted. But it wasn't from fatigue. It was my powers. My "abilities," as Daniel called them. They were always lingering there, just out of reach, whenever we trained. And if I could just push through the wall of fire that stood between them and me, I could grab on to my powers and use them. Own them.

I cringed as the crescent-shaped scar on my arm throbbed and flared. I dropped my arm and tried to shake out the pain.

"Arms up," Daniel said. "Rule number one: Never drop your guard." He smacked me lightly on the shoulder. It was meant to be a playful hit, but the pain in my scar shot through my arm like electricity.

I glared at him.

"You're getting annoyed," Daniel said. That wry grin of his played on his lips.

"You think?" I sent another combination into his mitts. Three jabs and a hook. I felt a surge of power through my body—finally—and the last punch flew faster and harder than I expected. Daniel missed deflecting it, and my fist slammed into his shoulder.

"Whoa!" He jumped back and shook out his shoulders. "Rein it in, Grace. Don't let your emotions have too much control."

"Then why are you *trying* to annoy me?"

His smile edged from wry to devious. "So you can practice balance." He smacked his mitts together and gestured for me to attack him again.

I could feel my powers pulsing through me—finally in my grasp. I laughed and bounced back several feet. "How's this for balance?" I asked with a smile, and faster than I could think, my body went into a spin kick that landed squarely in one of Daniel's outstretched mitts.

Daniel grunted and stumbled back. His knee wobbled and gave out from under him, and he went flying backward toward the ground.

"Oh no!" I lunged for him and caught him by the arm. But it was too late to stop him from falling, and I toppled with him onto the grass.

We landed side by side on the lawn. I was momentarily

stunned—hitting the ground had knocked the wind, and my powers, right out of me. Daniel rolled onto his side and moaned, startling me back into reality.

"Oh no, I'm sorry!" I sat up. "I wasn't thinking. My powers kicked in and I . . . Are you okay?"

Daniel's moan turned into a half laugh. "That's not the kind of balance I was talking about." He winced and pulled off his mitts and tossed them aside.

"Seriously, are you okay?"

"Yeah." Daniel leaned forward and rubbed his knee. He'd trashed it pretty badly when he fell from the parish's balcony a little less than ten months ago. And since I'd cured him of the werewolf curse right after he fell, he'd lost his superhuman powers and had to wait for it to heal like any other regular person. Even after spending weeks on crutches and doing a regimen of physical therapy, he still had a lot of trouble with his knee. "Beatin' up on a gimp. What would your daddy say?"

"Ha-ha." I made a face at him.

"Seriously, though. You're getting good." He groaned and lay back into the grass, tucking his arms behind his head.

"Not good enough."

It took almost an hour of intense sparring before my powers even started to manifest, and once they kicked in, they lasted only, what, like thirty seconds? That was the thing about my *abilities*. They came in spurts whenever *they* felt like it—totally uncontrolled by me. My wounds healed over more quickly than those of a normal human, but I still couldn't draw on that power the way Daniel used to be able to. I couldn't heal myself on my own terms. I'd get bursts of speed or agility, like my body had a mind of its own—like when I kicked Daniel just now—but I usually couldn't control *when* it happened.

After Daniel's doctor gave him the go-ahead to be active again, we started training together three nights a week—when I wasn't grounded, that is. We'd go running, try out some parkour moves, box with mitts like we did tonight, practice trying to hear and see long distances. But even though I was notably faster and stronger than I had been even a few months ago, it was beginning to seem like, no matter how much I tried, I'd never be able to use my powers the way I wanted— instead of them using me.

Daniel sighed. He pointed up in the sky. "Looks like we quit just in time. Meteor shower's started."

I looked up as a shooting star streaked through the dark, clear night above us. "Oh yeah. I almost forgot about that."

Daniel and I had planned on tracking the meteor shower after tonight's training session. We were supposed to count how many meteors we saw in a thirty-minute period for an extra-credit science project at school.

I knew it bothered Daniel that Principal Conway

wouldn't even consider letting him graduate last year—
he'd missed way too much school during the years he'd
spent on the run from the curse that used to plague his
every thought. But I, for one, was happy he hadn't left
for college yet. And with his attending summer school,
doing some extra credit, and testing out of a few classes,
we'd get to graduate *together* next spring.

"I'll get the light," I said after I pulled off my glove
wraps. I flexed my fingers, stretching out my sore knuckles as I crossed the yard behind Maryanne Duke's old
house. I flipped off the porch light, grabbed my hoodie,
and headed back over to the lawn. With my sweatshirt
draped over my chest like a blanket, I took in a deep
breath of autumn air and melted into the cool leaves of
grass next to Daniel.

"That's six," I said after a long moment.

Daniel grunted in agreement.

"Oh! Did you see that one?" I pointed above my head
at an especially bright star that glistened through the
sky until it fizzled into nothing.

"Yeah," Daniel said softly. "Beautiful."

I glanced at him. He was lying on his side, staring at
me.

"You weren't even watching," I teased.

"Yes, I was." Daniel flashed me another one of his
wry smiles. "I could see it reflecting in your eyes." He
reached out and brushed my cheek with his fingers.
"One of the most beautiful things I've ever seen." He

hooked one of his fingers under my chin, drawing my face closer to his.

I looked away from his deep, dark brown eyes, surveyed the curves of his muscles under the thin running shirt he'd worn for our training session. Then my gaze flitted to his shaggy hair, which had settled into a nice golden blond over the summer—all the dark had finally washed out. I followed the lines of his jaw and then rested my gaze on the curve of his smiling lips. It wasn't his devious smile anymore, but the one he saved for moments like this—the one that meant he was truly happy.

He was still warm from our sparring match, and I could feel the heat radiating off his body only a few inches away. Drawing me to him. Willing me to close the gap between us. I looked back at his eyes, loving the feeling that I could get lost in them forever.

It was moments like these when I still couldn't believe that he was even here.

That he was still alive.

That he was *mine*.

I'd watched him die once. Held him in my arms and listened to his heartbeat fade away into nothing.

It happened the night my brother Jude lost himself to the werewolf curse—just days before he left a note on the kitchen table, walked out into a snowstorm, and disappeared. The same night Jude infected me with the powers that taunted me now.

The night I almost lost everything.

"There goes another one." Daniel leaned in and touched a kiss just beside my eye. He trailed his lips across my cheek and down my jaw, sending a tingling sensation through my body with the deliciousness of his touch.

Daniel's lips came to my mouth. He brushed them softly there at first and then pressed gently. His lips parted, and he mingled them with mine.

My legs ached as I pulled him closer—finally closing the distance between us.

I didn't care that we were out in the yard behind Maryanne Duke's old house. I didn't care that we were supposed to be tracking the meteor shower for class. Nothing existed outside his touch. There was nothing under the falling stars except Daniel and me and the blanket of grass underneath us.

Daniel jerked his head back slightly. "You're buzzing," he whispered against my lips.

"Huh?" I asked, and kissed him.

He pulled away. "I think it's your phone."

I noticed the buzzing, too. My cell phone in my sweatshirt pocket.

"So what?" I grabbed the front of his shirt playfully and pulled him closer. "They can leave a message."

"It could be your mom," Daniel said. "I just got you back. I don't want to lose you for another two weeks."

"Damn it."

Daniel smirked. He always thought it was hilarious when I swore. But he did have a point—about my mom, that is. She had only two modes since Jude left: Zombie Queen and Crazed Mother Bear. It was like her own personal brand of bipolar disorder.

I'd left for the evening before she got back from seeing Aunt Carol off at the train station, so I wasn't sure what mode she would be in, but if it was of the overbearing sort, I could possibly be grounded again just for the act of not answering her calls on the second ring.

I sat up and dug into the pocket of my hoodie, but I'd already taken too much time, and the call ended before I pulled out my phone.

"Crap." I couldn't take another two weeks of not seeing Daniel outside of school. I flipped open my phone to check the missed call info, mentally crossing my fingers that it hadn't been my mother, but what I saw made me cock my head in confusion. "Where's your phone?" I asked Daniel.

"I left it inside. On my bed." Daniel yawned. "Why?"

I stood up, still staring at the display on my phone. A dark feeling crept under my skin. My hair stood up on the back of my neck, and my muscles tensed in that way they did when my body sensed danger. The phone started ringing again in my hand. I almost dropped it.

"Who's calling you?"

"You are."

I fumbled with the phone and almost dropped it again. I pushed the Answer button. "Hello?" I asked tentatively as I put it to my ear.

Silence.

I looked at the screen on my phone to make sure I hadn't missed the call or accidentally hit the Disconnect button. I returned it to my ear. "Um, hello?"

Still nothing.

I looked at Daniel and shrugged. "It must be some weird kind of flyaway." I was about to hang up when I heard something on the line. It sounded almost like a hand covering the receiver.

"Hello?" My skin tingled. Goose bumps pricked up my arms. "Who's there?"

"They're coming for you," a muffled voice said over the phone. "You're in danger. You're all in danger. You can't stop them."

"Who is this?" I asked, panic rising with the tension in my muscles. "How did you get Daniel's phone?"

"Don't trust him," the trembling voice said. "He makes you think you can trust him, but you can't."

Daniel reached for the phone, but I shook him off.

"What are you talking about?" I asked.

"You can't trust him." The voice on the line seemed suddenly clearer—like the hand muffling the receiver had moved out of the way—and the familiarity of it made my heart nearly stop. "Please, Gracie, *listen* to me this time. You're all in danger. You have to know that—" The voice cut off with a clatter, like the phone had been dropped, and the line went dead.

"Jude!" I shouted into my phone.

ABOUT TEN SECONDS LATER

"Wait!" Daniel called after me as he tried to push himself up from the ground.

But I'd hit the button to call back Daniel's cell, and was off the grass and across the back patio before it even started ringing. I could hear his ringtone faintly playing a metal guitar version of "Moonlight Sonata" from his apartment in Maryanne's basement. I felt a burst of supernatural speed and, in a matter of seconds, flew around the house and down the cement stairs that led to the apartment.

The old yellow door was slightly ajar. My palms suddenly went sweaty. Daniel was normally a bit compulsive about keeping his door locked. The hinges groaned as I pushed the door open a little farther.

"Jude?" I called into the studio apartment. The phone had stopped ringing, and the apartment was dark, but I could see a pair of Daniel's Converse lying on the ground next to a crumpled pile of laundry. The sofa bed was pulled out but the blanket was missing, and the sheets were halfway off the thin mattress.

"Gracie, wait." Daniel appeared at the top of the

stairs. "That may not have been your brother on the phone."

"It was him. I'd know his voice anywhere." I was absolutely, upon threat of death from my father, not allowed to enter Daniel's apartment with him alone—but I took a step into the doorway anyway. "Jude, are you here?"

"That's not what I mean." Daniel limped down the steps. "I mean, Jude may not have been *your brother* when he was calling. He may have been under the influences of the wolf."

Once again, Daniel had a point, and I shivered at the reminder of the things my brother had done before while under the control of the wolf. The crescent-shaped scar in my arm twinged, as if to punctuate the memories. But still, if Jude *was* here, I needed to know. My heart sped up as I took a step inside the apartment.

"Jude?" I flicked the light switch a couple of times. Nothing happened.

My footsteps kept time with my heartbeat as I walked deeper into the dark room. Apprehension tightened in my muscles. Tingling pain spread through my tendons. My body was preparing for something—flight or fight.

I passed the sofa bed, inspecting the crumpled sheets for the phone Daniel said he'd left there. Daniel opened the bathroom door and cautiously eased inside the tiny room. I heard the opening and closing of cabinets, and then the rustling of the shower curtain.

The tingling pain spread to my fingertips, and I tightened my hand around my cell phone. I hit the Redial button once more. I could hear the ringing through my end before the metal tone of Daniel's phone began. The noise was soft at first, but then it rapidly got louder and closer.

My body whirled on instinct toward the sound. I landed in a crouching position, ready to pounce. A small growl escaped from my lips.

"Whoa, Gracie!" Daniel said. He stood in front of me, his hands up in a defensive position, and his cell phone clutched in one of his fists. "It's just me. I found my phone in the shower."

I lunged at him and threw my arms around his neck. "Holy crap, I thought you were . . . were . . ." I held my breath and pressed my moonstone necklace to my chest, letting anxiety slowly drain out of my body. I don't know exactly what I'd thought was behind me. A werewolf with a phone in its jaws? I felt positively ridiculous now.

"It's okay." Daniel brushed his fingers through my hair. "Nobody's here."

"But someone *was* here," I said. "Unless you have a habit of talking on the phone in the shower."

"Try using your powers to tell if it was Jude," Daniel said. "Use your senses like I taught you."

I didn't have much hope that it would actually work, but I took a deep breath, held the air in the back of my mouth, and tried to let it fill my senses like Daniel had explained to me at least two dozen times in the last few months. I was supposed to be testing the air for hints of my brother, trying to sift out a faint familiar taste or smell beyond Daniel's almondy scent and the tang of oil paint that always filled his apartment. I let my breath out in a long, frustrated hiss.

Daniel gave me a hopeful look.

I shook my head. I'd failed again.

"It's okay," Daniel said. "It'll come. It just takes time." That's what he *always* said.

"Yeah, I know." I hoped he wasn't going to launch into his usual speech about how it takes balance, and how I'm doing great so far, and how most Urbat take *years* to develop their powers. "Besides, I don't even know if I remember what my brother smells like, and I certainly haven't ever tasted him before."

Daniel smiled. *Lecture averted.*

I took his cell phone from him and used my *human* eyes to inspect it for clues. The face was cracked, like it had been dropped, and I was surprised it still worked. I checked the time and the number of the last call made from the phone. "He definitely called me from this." I shuddered. "He was right in here while we were just outside."

"What did he say?" Daniel asked.

"He said I was in danger. That we were all in danger.

He said, 'They're coming for you,' and that I couldn't stop them. And he said that I couldn't trust someone else . . ." I bit my lip and hesitated. "I don't know, but I think he meant you."

Daniel crossed his arms in front of his chest. "Sounds like his feelings toward me haven't changed." A look of concern settled in his dark brown eyes.

I wondered if he was thinking the same thing as me—that maybe Jude had other intentions for breaking into the apartment. Maybe Jude had thought Daniel would be here alone and vulnerable? But that didn't make any sense. If he had wanted to attack Daniel, my presence certainly wouldn't have stopped him. It hadn't stopped him before.

"Did he say anything else?" Daniel asked.

"No. The call cut off. I think he dropped the phone. He seemed nervous. Maybe his hand was shaking." *Or maybe he'd been about to go through the change.*

"Do you think he was messing with you?" Daniel asked. "Maybe this is just some kind of twisted game to him. He never wanted us to be together in the first place."

"I don't know." I looked down at the phone in my hands. "I guess it's possible. But it doesn't make sense that he'd come back here just for a practical joke. I think he's got some other motivation."

Maybe it was my new wolf instincts taking over

again, or maybe it was just some kind of sibling connection, but something deep down told me that Jude was right . . . we were all in danger. I just didn't know if *he* was the one we were all in danger from.

CHAPTER TWO

Benefit of the Doubt

Daniel insisted on following me home on his new—to him, anyway—motorcycle. I drove slowly as I navigated the few miles between my house and Oak Park, scanning the streets as I went. I slowed every time I came upon a pedestrian, which wasn't often, since it was after ten o'clock.

I dialed Dad's cell phone over and over, but it kept going straight to voice mail. What was the point of his finally getting us all cell phones so we can stay connected if he always forgot to charge his? "Call me," was the message I left each time. Considering how much energy he'd put into looking for Jude over the past few months, I didn't want to just tell Dad on his voice mail about his being back. That was the kind of thing you sprang on someone in person, preferably when they were standing—okay, sitting—right in front of you.

Chaos was the only word that could describe the scene that met us when I opened the front door to my house. The ten o'clock news blared from the family room, like someone had turned it up to full volume to hear the anchorman speaking over the sounds of James's wailing as he thrashed in Charity's arms on the stairs. It looked like she was trying to haul him up to his bedroom, but the toddler flailed so hard they were both in danger of falling down the steps.

The vibration of the sound suddenly burst tenfold inside my head. I winced and clasped my hands over my ears. Great time for my superhearing to decide to pay me a visit. "What's going on?" I called over the din. "I put James to bed two hours ago." I'd made sure James was tucked in for the night and Charity was started on homework before I'd left for the evening. It was the least I could do with Dad being gone.

"I don't know. He woke up screaming about an hour ago," Charity said, narrowly missing getting smacked in the face by James. "I finally got him calmed down, but then he started freaking when I tried to take him back to his room. I think maybe he had a nightmare that there was something at his window."

I exchanged a look with Daniel. He nodded. What James had seen at his window might not have been a nightmare.

"Arg, James! Stop!" Charity yelled as James arched his back in her arms and kicked his legs. She nearly lost her grip and almost dropped him down the stairs.

"I'll take him." Daniel slipped past me in the doorway and pulled James out of Charity's arms. "Calm down, Baby J," Daniel said, and bounced him on his hip. James quieted almost immediately and wrapped his trembling arms around Daniel's neck. Daniel was still his mighty hero, and James, in his footie pajamas, looked so tiny wrapped in Daniel's strong arms. I couldn't help remembering the way Daniel had caught him when he fell off that forty-foot cliff in the woods behind our neighborhood.

"How about I read you a story?" Daniel asked, and nuzzled his nose against James's cheek.

James nodded and wiped his puffy, red eyes.

"How about that *Wild Things* one? I like the kid with the wolf suit." That was James's favorite book—a present from Daniel when he turned two six months ago.

James shook his head. "Nah, too scawey." His chin quivered. He must have really had a fright.

"*Winnie-the-Pooh*, then?" Daniel swung James onto his shoulders and looked at me. "I'll put James to bed."

"Thanks," Charity and I said in unison.

I watched Daniel trot up the stairs, talking to James in his best Eeyore voice—which sounded more like Marlon Brando, if you ask me. How could anyone *not* love him? And why would Jude still think he couldn't be trusted?

"Finally," Charity grumbled. "I've got like three more pages of math homework to do."

"I'm sorry. I wouldn't have stayed out so late if I'd known."

"It's okay." Charity traced the grain on the oak banister with her finger. "You're not the one who should be dealing with James anyway." She glanced down the entry hall toward the family room. "Do you think you can get Mom to turn it down? I really need to concentrate."

"So it's Zombie Queen mode again?"

Charity nodded.

I should have known better than to think a day with Aunt Carol would have made Mom feel any better. Carol liked to come out to "help" every once in a while when Dad was gone, but her snide remarks about how our Divine little family wasn't so perfect after all got old really fast.

"Wonder how long it'll last this time," Charity said, and headed up the stairs.

I sucked in a deep breath and made my way to the family room. James had stopped crying, and I could even make out a trill of his laughter coming from his bedroom, but the TV volume was still up at full blast. My ears throbbed as I got closer to the set. I picked up the remote just as the newscast started in on a new story.

A reporter stood in front of a police line outside a jewelry store called the Family Jewels that I'd passed more than once while in the antiques district of the

22

city. "Two jewelry stores were hit in broad daylight in the last two days," the reporter said, "but with no eyewitnesses of these bold crimes, the police are left scratching their heads. Employees at both stores claim to have been knocked unconscious before seeing anything, and both stores were completely vandalized and robbed of all their merchandise in a matter of minutes. Security cameras failed to pick up anything at either scene, and authorities speculate that the cameras were somehow disabled before they were able to capture anyone on film."

The screen cut to a plump anchorman with puffy hair sitting behind a desk. "Wow, Graham," the anchorman said. "These robberies sound frighteningly familiar, don't they?"

"Yes," the reporter said. "These two robberies may be related to a string of other bizarre and unexplained thefts and attacks in the city, which we've reported on in the last few months. But it seems the police are just as baffled as everyone else."

"Hmm," the anchorman said. "Perhaps we should all be worried that the Markham Street Monster has turned to a life of organized crime. . . ."

I turned down the volume, cutting off the anchorman chuckling at his own lame joke. I never did find any kidding about the Markham Street Monster funny—especially now that I knew the truth about it . . . or *him*, I guess I should say. Mom didn't protest my messing with the volume. She just stared at the footage of bystanders being interviewed about the mysterious robberies. Her eyes flicked from face to face in the crowd. I knew who she was looking for.

"Mom?" I picked up the empty wineglass and the bowl of cold tomato soup off the coffee table in front of the couch. "You didn't eat. Do you want me to make you something else?"

Mom shifted slightly so she could see the TV past my legs.

"Dad said I should call Dr. Connors if you stopped eating again."

She didn't even blink.

Every ounce of me wanted to tell Mom about Jude's calling. That he'd been right here in Rose Crest. That I'd talked to him. That while she was busy watching the news for any sign of him, he may have been right outside her other son's window.

But it was that last thought that stopped me. I didn't know why Jude had come back. I didn't know what he wanted. I didn't know if he was more monster than human now, staring into the windows of the people he'd once called his family. And I didn't know if he'd even come back again after tonight. What I did know was that it was best not to say anything to Mom—at least for now.

She reached for the remote and clicked the volume up a few notches. I took her bowl to the kitchen sink and dumped out the contents, watching the red of the congealed tomato soup slip down the drain. I rinsed the bowl and then started in on the rest of the dishes, filling the sink with the hottest water possible. I don't know why, but I liked the way heat swallowed my hands as I plunged them into the scalding water and scrubbed the dishes. Mom's Zombie Queen mode always made me want to feel something extra—like I was feeling pain for both of us.

I prayed silently while I scrubbed a pot that Mom wouldn't see anyone on the news she thought looked like Jude. She'd get all worked up, call Dad, and make him go looking in whatever city or state or even country she *thought* she'd seen him in. And Dad would go, even if he'd already been gone for almost two weeks, because maybe *this* time it really was Jude. Maybe *this* time he'd find him and bring him home.

I'd been just as hopeful as Mom the first time she thought she'd seen Jude on the TV. I'd waited with her by the window all night long while Dad was gone looking for him. But when Dad came back—alone—it felt like Jude had left all over again. Mom didn't eat for an entire week—that is, until she thought she saw Jude in the background of a CNN newscast about an industrial fire in California. But that didn't pan out, either, and Mom only got worse the longer Dad was gone.

The third time he left to follow one of her wild leads—

a bear attack in Yellowstone, where a dark-haired boy supposedly saved a young girl from being killed—I got angry. I'd stood in front of the door, my arms crossed, unwilling to let Dad leave. But he took my hand and sat me down on the porch. "You know the story of the Good Shepherd, don't you, Grace?"

I shook my head, even though I did. I was too upset to speak.

"The Bible says that a good shepherd, even if he has one hundred sheep, if he loses but one of them in the wilderness, he must leave the other ninety-nine behind to go looking for that one."

"But doesn't that mean he's basically throwing the rest to the wolves?" I asked.

Dad sighed. "It's what I did for Daniel—helped him no matter what. It's what *you* did for him. Now we owe that to your brother, too."

I couldn't argue with that.

Dad squeezed my fingers. "Besides, I'm leaving the rest of the family in capable hands," he'd said, then he got up and left.

But I didn't feel very capable right now. I mean, what was I supposed to do when the lost sheep found us and the Good Shepherd wasn't here? And what if the sheep wasn't a sheep at all?

What if he was the wolf?

I'd almost emptied the sink when Daniel came into the kitchen. "James is finally down." He brushed my arm and then picked up a towel and dried a saucepot.

"Thanks," I said, and handed him a newly washed cup.

He frowned at my reddened skin. "You should take better care of yourself."

I looked at my hand and then closed my eyes, concentrating on erasing the pain. I waited a few seconds, but when I opened my eyes, my skin was just as red and tender. I wasn't surprised.

"I should get my mom to bed," I said, and dried my hands on my pants.

"Do you want me to stay here? Just in case Jude . . . comes back. I can sleep on the couch."

As much as the idea of Daniel's spending the night made me feel better, almost as if my dad were here, I knew it couldn't happen. "That might push my mom over the edge," I said.

"Hmm. Good point."

"Then again, maybe that wouldn't be such a bad thing. Getting a reaction out of her would be almost worth it." I was glad I wasn't going to be grounded for coming in after the ten o'clock news had started, but as much as I hated Mom hovering over my every move when she was in a Crazed Mother Bear manic state, it was still preferable to the zombie zone she was in now.

Daniel's devious grin slid across his face. He took my hand gently in his and brought it up to his lips. The look in his eyes as he kissed my reddened knuckles made my knees ache, and for a moment I wished we were still lying in the grass together.

"Not a good idea," I whispered, and pulled my hand out of his. If Mom did come to her senses, I'd be grounded for the rest of my life.

"As you wish," Daniel said, and picked up another cup to dry. "I'll help you finish this up before I go."

I sighed. I knew the house would feel empty and cold the moment he left. Every sound would make me jump. Every minute would drag on for a year until I finally fell asleep. "I wish my dad were here at least . . . but I doubt he'd be able to protect us, either."

Daniel frowned and put down the cup. He shifted his weight from his bad leg to his good one.

A wave of guilt washed through me. "I didn't mean you." I put my hand on his shoulder. "I didn't mean to say that you couldn't protect us anymore. I was talking about me, I swear."

"It's okay. I know I can't, Grace. It's kind of a side effect of losing my powers."

"But you're still strong. You could—"

"No." Daniel finally looked back at me. "But you

can . . . someday. I promise. You'll get the hang of it. . . ."

"I have a feeling *someday* isn't going to be soon enough. I think Jude called me because he needs my help." I looked down at my stupid red hands that refused to heal. "But I'm not strong enough to do anything."

"Grace, you're the strongest person I know. You'd have to be to save me the way you did. You *can* be a hero like you wanted." He lowered his voice and glanced back at my mom on the sofa, as if he was worried she might actually be paying attention to us. "You have all this power just beyond your fingertips, and we'll figure out how to reach out and grab it for good. All you need is a little more time and patience and balance, and we can make it work. Maybe we've been pushing it too hard to begin with. Maybe we need to ease into it more. Take more time with your lessons . . ."

"What if we don't have more time? What if Jude is right? What if somebody really is after us?" For the first time I really let that fear sink in—the weight of it trying to pull me under. "What if I need my powers right now?"

Daniel grabbed a fistful of his shaggy hair and tugged at it in frustration. "I don't understand what you want me to say, Grace. What do you want me to do? If you want me to train you faster, that's not going to happen. You know that wouldn't be safe. I'm not going to let you lose yourself to the wolf."

"I'm not going to lose myself to the wolf, Daniel. That's not what I want . . . Gah, I don't even know what I want! A way to stop time, maybe. A magical way to make my powers come faster. I don't know."

"I don't know, either." Daniel picked up a bowl from the counter and then set it right back down. "I still think Jude was just messing with you, Grace. The wolf is probably getting a real kick out of tormenting the people he *loved*." Daniel put an extra emphasis on the past tense.

But I didn't want to believe that. Daniel still loved me when he was taken by the wolf. He still wanted to find a way to come back to our family. I wanted to believe the same thing about Jude now. I had to give him the same benefit of the doubt. Deep down I wanted to believe that he called me tonight not out of some sick joke, but because he *needed* to warn me. He still wanted to be my brother.

"You didn't hear the concern in Jude's voice," I said. "I think it was a cry for help."

Daniel shook his head. "I wish I could track him down for you. Find out what the hell he wants, or stop this person, or whoever is supposedly after us. But I'm not the one with the superpowers."

"And apparently neither am I," I grumbled.

He looked at me, his dark eyes laced with sadness, but he stayed silent. We both did for a few long minutes. Mom was listening to a different station's evening newscast recorded by the DVR, but they were playing an almost identical account of the story from earlier. Invisible bandits. Terrible crimes in broad daylight. Even a similar joke about the Markham Street Monster turned to a life of organized crime . . .

"Do you regret it?" I finally asked Daniel. It was the question I'd held back for months now. The question that came into my mind each time I watched Daniel struggle to keep up with me when we ran, or nursed his knee after a sparring match. "Do you regret that I cured you? It must be hard not to have your powers anymore." And it must be hard for him to watch me not figuring out mine. Like whenever I struggled as he tried to teach me a new painting technique, and I could feel him itching to grab the brush and just do it himself— but he never did. Good teachers don't do that.

"No," Daniel said. "Sometimes I miss my powers. But I never regret what you did for me. I'm here because of you. I'm a whole person again. I could never go back to that place I was in again—I could never deal with having the potential of becoming a monster again. I think I'd rather die . . ." Daniel trailed off. He hesitated for a moment and then said, "Do *you* regret it? Do you regret being there to save me?" From the sound of his voice, I knew he'd been holding that question back for a while, too.

I looked down at the sink. The suds had died into a murky film on the water. "Sometimes I almost wish that

I could go back and stop Jude from infecting me with the werewolf curse. But I always stop myself, because I know if it meant being there to save your soul, I wouldn't risk changing anything about what I did that night. That part I don't regret. That part I would never trade for anything. Saving you, curing you. That part I'd get infected a thousand times over for." I made a swirl in the film on the surface of the water with my fingertip. "I just wish things had turned out differently with Jude, you know? I wish I knew what to make of him coming back." I sighed. "I just wish that if I'm going to be infected with these powers, that I knew how to use them properly, you know? Use them to help Jude now."

I turned away from Daniel and reached far into the murky water and pulled the drain. I'd wanted the water to be hot on my skin, but it had cooled considerably during our conversation. I felt warmth on my shoulder and realized that Daniel had placed his hand on my arm, right over where my crescent-shaped scar hid under my sleeve. I hadn't realized that it had been stinging with pain until I felt his soothing touch. He kept his hand there for a moment and then pulled it away and started drying dishes again.

Daniel stayed until after we finished cleaning the kitchen and Mom had drained the DVR of all the other stations' news programs she'd recorded. I said good-bye to Daniel at the door, and the second he left, the house felt empty, just like I knew it would. I locked all the doors and windows and then turned off the TV and told Mom to go to bed. When I was alone in my room, I tried calling Dad again. It went straight to voice mail.

"Jude was here, Dad," I finally told the machine. "Right here in Rose Crest. Come home. Please." I listened to the emptiness on the other line until the voice-mail recorder beeped and cut off the call.

With my phone still in my hand, I checked the lock on my own window and noticed a faint light inside the Corolla. I'd left it parked beside the curb in front of the house. I peered through the blinds and saw Daniel curled up in the backseat of the car. From what I could tell, it looked like he'd nodded off while reading a book.

This evening hadn't gone so smoothly with Daniel— not at all like I'd pictured it when Daniel suggested we watch the meteor shower together. But seeing Daniel outside my house, knowing he was there, made me feel safe and warm, like nothing could possibly ever tear us apart.

I flipped open my phone and sent Daniel a text: *I love you.*

As I crawled into bed, my phone beeped with a message back from him: *Always.*

And then, thirty seconds later, another, which said: *Be patient. We'll figure it out. Maybe when your dad gets back, he'll know what to do.* Then another text: *I believe in you.*

Then, almost a full two minutes later, like the idea had suddenly crossed his mind for the first time: *Please don't go looking for Jude on your own, ok?*

Ok, I texted back.

It wasn't like I'd even know where to start looking.

CHAPTER THREE

Shattered

MORNING

I wasn't surprised when Daniel was gone the next morning. He always worked an early-morning shift at Day's Market before school on Fridays. But I figured he'd be a wreck from sleeping in the backseat of the Corolla all night.

Debbie Lambson, the part-time housekeeper Dad had hired to keep an eye on James—and my mom—while Charity and I were at school, was already at the house making breakfast when I came downstairs. I grabbed a couple of her muffins off the kitchen counter and headed out to the drive-through at the Java Pot. I picked up two coffees to go and then made a beeline for Day's Market in hopes of catching Daniel before he took off for school.

I knew something was wrong even before I saw the police tape barring the entrance to the parking lot behind the market—the sheriff's patrol car was parked out front, the OPEN sign whose neon usually blazed above the glass doors was dark, and a small group of would-be customers stood gesturing a few yards off from the store.

Tension pricked under my skin as I pulled up behind the patrol car. I couldn't help thinking about that night a little less than ten months ago when there had been a very similar scene here. On that same terrible night when I'd almost lost Daniel.

The scar on my arm flared, and the pain of my powers tingled into my muscles. I clutched my moonstone and shook off those terrible memories. A more immediate problem stood in front of me now.

I left the tray of coffee cups in the car and headed up to the storefront. The thing that struck me the most was how strangely clean the glass of the front door seemed. That is, until I realized the door was actually missing. Shards of shattered glass littered the ground just inside the doorway. I hesitated for a moment, unsure if I was allowed to enter, but no one tried to stop me, so I stepped through the gap. I heard voices near the cash registers—or where the cash registers should have been. One lay smashed on the ground, and the other two appeared to be missing altogether. Mr. Day slumped on a stool while talking to Chris Tripton, another early-morning employee, and Daniel stood nearby with a broom.

It looked like Day's Market had been the epicenter of an earthquake that somehow hadn't touched the rest of town. Most of the shelving had been knocked over like a giant set of dominos, it's demolished contents scattered everywhere. Spots on the floor were slick with soup oozing out of crushed cans. Basketball-sized holes pocked the walls, and the Halloween display in the center of the store looked like someone had taken a bulldozer to it.

"What happened?" I asked Daniel when I caught his attention. "It looks like a hurricane swept through here."

"Might as well." Daniel leaned his weight into his broom. "Somebody ransacked the place last night. They emptied out the registers, tore the safe out of the wall in the back office, and trashed just about everything else."

"Holy hell," I said.

Stacey Canova came up to us with an empty box in her arms. "The strange thing is," she said, "they destroyed everything else, but took every last bag of chips and can of beer in the place."

"What? Does the sheriff think it was teenagers?" I asked her.

"Only if they make teenagers with superpowers these days," a voice said from behind me.

I reeled around to Mr. Day. "What was that?" I blushed and crossed my arms behind my back, as if I had something to hide.

"Whoever did this had to be superfast, and strong as a bull. It would take a forklift to knock over one of those aisles. And they got in and out of here in a matter of minutes. I locked up and headed home last night, but I was barely a few blocks away when I realized that I'd left my garage key in the back office. I turned around and came back to the store and found all this. I was gone five minutes tops. And there's nothing on the security cameras." Mr. Day indicated the cameras in each corner of the store. "Looked them over with the sheriff last night. They just go black. And these are battery powered, so it's not like cutting the power to the whole building would do anything. None of you scrawny Holy Trinity kids could have pulled this off."

He turned to Chris Tripton. "I'm telling you, it had to be those invisible bandits from the city. Either that, or the Markham Street Monster has turned to a life of larceny." Mr. Day sounded just like the news reporter from last night, only he wasn't joking.

Stacey rolled her eyes but then shook her head when she saw Mr. Day glaring at her.

Daniel looked down and swept up some broken glass into a pile with his broom.

According to the "official" story, wild dogs had attacked Mr. Day's granddaughter Jessica and were responsible for the other attacks in town last winter— Maryanne's mutilation, James's going missing, and then what happened to Daniel, Jude, and me at the parish—but Mr. Day had been a die-hard believer in the Markham Street Monster ever since.

"Either way, this town is in trouble. I bet I'm just the first of many. Someone—or something—with that much power isn't going to stop at one store. Mark my words: Rose Crest is going to hell in a handbasket unless somebody can do something."

The phone rang from the back office. It had a strange, tinny echo. It must have been damaged. "Local paper got ahold of the story." Mr. Day grumbled. "They keep on calling. Won't be surprised if we end up with reporters from the city picking through the place like vultures later today. I could be ruined, and they think it makes a great headline. Thought I'd never have to deal with those buzzards again since they got tired of the story about Jessica's death. Now they'll want to pick at her dead bones some more with all of this." He was trying to sound gruff and annoyed, but his voice had a high-pitched catch to it, and I noticed a puffy redness to his eyes.

The phone kept ringing, and Mr. Day stalked toward his office. "You two get on to school," he said, pointing back at Daniel and me.

"But we can help," I said.

"You kids got college applications coming up soon. Don't want you messing up your grades because of this. But I expect you back here after school," he said to Daniel, then grabbed the receiver of the ringing phone on his desk. "Hello!" he practically shouted into the phone before he shut the office door behind him. Mr. Day really didn't deserve this—especially after what had happened to Jessica.

"I guess we should head out, then." Daniel handed his broom to Chris. "I'll be back right after my last class."

"We'll still be here," Chris said, sounding like he wished he had an excuse to take off, too.

Daniel took my hand and we headed toward the non-existent door, but after about four steps I noticed something sticking to the bottom of my shoe. I let go of Daniel and reached down and peeled some kind of plastic card from the heel of my boot. I flipped it over. It was a plain white card with a small logo on the front that said THE DEPOT and a magnetic strip on the back. It reminded me of my frequent buyer's card for the Java Pot that they swiped each time I bought something.

Daniel stopped and looked back at me. "What've you got?"

"Looks like a membership card or something. You ever heard of a place called The Depot?"

Daniel shook his head.

I held up the card. "This could be a clue, don't you think? Maybe the person who did this dropped this card."

"Hmm, could be, I guess." Daniel looked like he didn't put much stock in that idea.

Stacey made a snorting sound from behind me. "You sound like one of those Scooby-Doo kids," she said. "Don't get your hopes up, though. Customers drop crap like that in here all the time. We've got a whole box of lost-and-found stuff in the office, but hardly anyone ever comes to claim anything. I'd just chuck it in one of the trash piles."

I flipped the card over again. Rose Crest hosted only a handful of businesses, and none of them were called The Depot. *It probably is just trash*, I thought, but I tucked it into the pocket of my jacket instead of throwing it away.

Daniel raised his eyebrows at me, but he didn't say a word.

FIVE MINUTES LATER

Daniel left his motorcycle at the market and hitched a ride with me in the Corolla. It rattled and groaned the few blocks to school, as if telling me that it didn't plan on making it through another winter. Hopefully, Daniel could keep it running for a while longer, considering money was tighter with Mom not working anymore and the extra expense of a housekeeper. I wondered how much longer Dad could afford to keep paying Debbie— let alone even think about buying a new car.

I parked in my usual spot near the parish, and then we started across the school parking lot together. Daniel sipped his coffee and made an appreciative grunt. His face looked gaunter than it had in a while, and his shaggy hair was tussled more than usual. He ate the cinnamon muffin I'd given him in three huge bites, and then cleared his throat.

"He's got a point," Daniel said. "What Mr. Day said—it would take someone with a lot of special abilities to pull this off in that short amount of time. A superpowered teen, perhaps?"

I held up my hands. "I'm innocent, I swear. Unless I ransack stores in my sleep . . ."

Daniel smirked, but it lasted only a second. His face was straight and serious when he said the name I'd been trying to deflect with my humor: "Jude. It makes sense, don't you think?" Daniel asked. "He was in town last night. He went to Maryanne's house, and he was probably outside James's window. It makes complete sense that he'd go to Day's next."

"What, like he's taking a tour of all the places . . . ? Oh." I stopped right in front of the main doors of the school, suddenly knowing what Daniel was getting at. Maryanne's house, James's window, Day's Market. These were all the places where the wolf had caused him to lose control last year. He'd mauled Maryanne's frozen body as she lay dead on her porch, then he'd gone through a window at my house and stolen Baby James to make it look like he'd been carried off into the forest, and then he'd left Jessica's body in the Dumpster behind the market where Daniel worked—all in an effort to frame Daniel as the monster.

"You think the wolf is making him revisit the places of his past crimes? But why? And do you think Jude's really capable of doing all that damage over at Day's by himself?"

"Excuse me," a high-pitched voice yelped from behind us.

I turned slightly and saw my former best friend, April Thomas, standing there. She trembled in that cocker-spaniel way of hers like she did when she was excited or frightened or experiencing pretty much any other emotion. It was one of the things that I'd always liked best about her.

"Excuse me, Grace," she said again, her voice all shaky.

"Yeah?" I asked, feeling a rush of mixed emotions: resentment that she hadn't wanted anything to do with me in the last ten months, and joy at hearing her voice actually speaking my name.

April looked at me for a long moment, twisting her finger in one of her springy curls. Her mouth twitched, like she was trying to figure out how to form the words to something important she wanted to say.

But all she finally did was shrug and ask if she could get by me through the door. "Don't want to be tardy," she mumbled, and brushed past me when I stepped aside.

I watched her disappear into the throng of students

in the main hall until Daniel lightly nudged me through the door.

"You know what worries me the most, Grace?" Daniel asked as we approached our lockers in the senior hall.

"What?" I gave him a quizzical look, still thinking about April. *Did she really want to say something to me?*

"What you said just a minute ago about Jude not being capable of ransacking Day's Market by himself . . . Well, Jude may or may not have been involved in what happened, but whoever *did* do this couldn't have been acting alone."

Chapter Four

Bombshell

It hadn't taken long after Christmas vacation and school starting up again for people in our neighborhood to notice that Jude was gone and that Mom wasn't exactly acting like her usual Martha-Stewart-meets-Florence-Nightingale self. By the end of the first week of school in January, the whole parish knew that something was off with the Divines, and Dad decided that he should make some sort of statement to his parishioners. He'd wanted to tell the truth. At least the version of it that didn't involve werewolves—my own mother didn't even know *that* much, and considering her fragile mental state, it was probably for the best.

"All I want to say is that Jude was troubled and ran away," Dad had explained to us. "And we'd appreciate everyone's patience while our family adjusts."

But Mom wouldn't allow it. She hated the idea of

people judging her parenting, thinking anything ill of our family.

"So what do you want us to do?" Dad had asked her.

"We lie," she said.

"To the entire town?" I asked.

"Yes." She rocked back and forth in her chair and stared at the TV set. "He'll be home soon. We'll find him. Nobody will know anything was ever wrong."

So that second Sunday in January, Dad fed the "official" story to Rose Crest—lied to everyone right over the pulpit. According to what my mother wanted him to say, Jude had gone to live with Grandma and Grandpa Kramer in Florida, because they needed help around the house after Grandpa's back surgery—and Dad would occasionally be flying down to help, too.

But people aren't stupid. They were bound to notice that Jude had been gone for almost ten months without coming home to visit once. And that his disappearance coincided with a mysterious "dog attack" inside the parish that had put Daniel in the ICU for a week. They were bound to notice that Mom could barely make it through one of Dad's sermons, with that fake grin plastered on her face and her eyes completely glassed over. They were going to notice that Dad was "flying down to Florida" to help his in-laws more often than he was home some weeks.

Which meant people were also going to talk.

I knew it wasn't possible to come completely clean

about everything that had happened in the last year, but on top of knowing the secrets of the underworld and lying to everyone about my brother's disappearance, I also had to hide the fact that I could *hear* what people said about my family and me behind our backs. Another less exciting perk of having superhuman hearing that decides to kick in at the most inconvenient times.

Most people are genuinely nice, you know. But some people were nice only to my face, and I could hear them whisper about my family when they thought I was well out of earshot. They liked to speculate about how Jude must have been on drugs, or how he possibly ran away to join a cult. Or maybe he was at one of those schools out west where they make messed-up kids hike through the desert without enough water.

"I always knew that kid was too perfect to be for real. I bet they were all getting high in the parish that night," I heard Brett Johnson—one of Jude's *friends*—whisper once when I was a good block away from him and his girlfriend.

I knew people called my mom crazy when they thought I couldn't possibly hear them.

Only slightly less annoying was the stuff people at school would say about me. I'd always been used to people watching me, judging me, because I was the pastor's daughter. But now I was pretty much the school pariah when my back was turned—which is apparently what happens to you when the captain of the school hockey team gets arrested and then kicked out of school for assaulting you. I mean, seriously, I had no idea HTA was so fanatic about hockey until I got blamed for us losing our chance to win State last year. Never mind the fact that Pete Bradshaw was the one who attacked *me*.

And I couldn't even react, because normal people aren't supposed to hear what others say about them when they're two rooms away. So I have to admit that when my superhearing decided to act up at school today, I felt only *slightly* guilty that the masses had a whole new topic of juicy gossip to chew on.

News spread quickly about what happened at Day's Market, and the speculations about the culprit only heightened when my second-period gym class was cancelled because it was discovered there had been an attempted break-in at the school through one of the gymnasium windows.

And by third period, rumors flew like spit wads across the halls when it was announced that all religion classes were cancelled, too, because Mr. Shumway, the religion teacher, hadn't shown up for school.

Some people claimed that Mr. Shumway was missing, but as I walked by the main hall I overheard one of the secretaries *inside* the principal's office say that Mr. Shumway had up and quit first thing this morning. But that didn't make any sense at all since Mr. Shumway had been teasing our class with some big surprise for the last two weeks, and he was supposedly going to tell us the details today. I was almost ready to believe the guy about fifty yards down the hall from my locker who said he heard that Mr. Shumway had "seen something" connected with the break-in. And it had freaked him out so bad he refused to come back to the school.

There was so much chatter, in fact, that by the time I got to fourth period all I could do was lay my head on the art table and clamp my hands over my ears.

"That bad?" Daniel asked as he slipped into the seat next to mine.

"Blech. This whole not being able to turn on and off my superhearing whenever I want is getting to be way too nauseating. Oh, and remind me not to walk past the boys' locker room when my hearing is acting up. For a bunch of Christian guys, they sure have dirty mouths."

Daniel laughed. The vibration made me want to pound my forehead against the table.

"Sorry," Daniel whispered. He cleared his throat. "So do you think Jude may have had something to do with the attempted break-in at the gym?" he asked as quietly as possible. "Coach Brown says he thinks whoever did it must have been after the computers in the lab next door. But my guess is that Jude went there after Day's."

I lifted my head just as April Thomas flitted past our table and headed for her spot in the back of the room. Her eyes flicked in my direction for a quarter of a second, but then she went straight to the table she shared with Kimberly Woodruff without making any other acknowledgment that I was even alive. I remembered not too long ago when she and I shared a table together—last year, when we were the only juniors allowed in Mr. Barlow's AP art class. Back before Daniel returned to town and April started dating my brother and everything got weird between us.

"What do you think?" Daniel asked.

I didn't want to believe it, but it would make sense that Jude would go to the school after Day's, considering that's where he went the same night he planted Jessica Day's body behind the market. He'd gone to the gym looking for Daniel at the Christmas dance.

I was about to comment on Daniel's theory when someone behind me said, "Hey, guys!" so loud I jumped in my seat.

Daniel and I turned in our chairs to see Katie Summers, the new transfer student from Brighton, standing there with a handful of charcoal pencils tied with a bright orange ribbon, which looked surprisingly like a bra strap. It matched perfectly with the funky handmade headband in her blond A-line bobbed hair. "Wow, Grace, your hair looks great today. You should wear it up all the time. It's totally quirky."

Coming from most people, that might sound like a backhanded compliment—especially since I'd worn my hair up in a messy ponytail because I hadn't bothered to do anything else with it this morning—but from someone like Katie, who brought her tofu sandwiches and organic wheatgrass juice in a varying collection of vintage lunch boxes, *quirky* seemed like a good thing.

"Um, thanks," I said. Considering my own best friend didn't even talk to me anymore, I always found it surprising when anyone at school other than my teachers or Daniel actually made an effort to engage me in conversation. "You look awesome, as always."

Which she did.

Katie was one of those naturally beautiful people who could wear a dress made out of a dyed blue potato sack to a school picnic—which she *had* back in September— and still look drop-dead gorgeous.

"You're too sweet." Katie turned her cobalt blue eyes on Daniel. "Hey," she said. "Thanks for letting me borrow your charcoal pencil last week. I so wouldn't have finished my project on time without you." She held out the bundle of pencils with her many-ringed fingers and offered it to Daniel. "This is for you."

"Really? Thanks, Katie." Daniel's cheeks tinged with pink, and he seemed extra careful not to touch the bra-strap-resembling ribbon. "You barely used my pencil, though. You didn't need to get me these."

"Anything for my hero," she said, and smiled at him.

I liked Katie, I really did. She didn't treat me in a hands-off manner like most everyone else at HTA lately. And I'd never once heard her say anything bad about me behind my back. But what I didn't like about Katie was the way she smiled at Daniel. Not to mention the way she always asked his opinion about her latest projects—which were always as stunning as she was. Her parents had moved to Rose Crest during the summer just so she could be in Holy Trinity Academy's advanced art program.

Daniel's cheeks got pinker.

I kicked him in the shin. A little too hard.

"Ow. So not necessary," he said, but gave me a sarcastically devious smile.

"Talk to you guys later," Katie said. "I think today's the big day, don't you?"

Ugh. I laid my head back down on the table and listened to her shoes glide across the linoleum floor toward a table on the other side of the room. The big day was the last thing I even had the energy to think about right now.

AFTER LUNCH

But the bombshell dropped right after fifth period started.

AP art was a two-period class with a lunch break in the middle. And when Daniel and I came back from grabbing a bite to eat, Mr. Barlow asked us to come into his office. Everyone had been speculating about when the big announcement was going to happen because

Mr. Barlow had been acting weird for the last couple of weeks. He'd loom over our tables while we worked, watching our every brushstroke, making it impossible for me to paint a straight line—and causing me to lose what little hope I had that the big day was going to hold anything but disappointment for me.

Which was why I was more than shocked when I realized Barlow wasn't just inviting *Daniel* into his office at the moment.

April was already in there. She crossed her arms in front of her chest and looked away when I entered. Katie Summers sat next to Barlow's desk, looking a bit green but still excited. She smiled and waved at Daniel when he followed me into the office.

Mr. Barlow shut his office door behind him. He took a stack of large white envelopes from his desk and passed out one to each of us. April turned hers over and practically yelped. I flipped mine over and felt my heart speed up. I slid my hand across the sapphire-blue embossed logo of the Amelia Trenton Art Institute.

This really was the big day.

And I was included?

"As you know," Mr. Barlow said after he'd taken his seat behind his desk, "Trenton is a very competitive school. HTA has one of the few art programs in the Midwest from which Trenton will even consider students. To keep up the reputation of our program, I hand select the students from my AP class each year who I feel are best suited to apply for the program. There are only four applications to go around this year, and each of you is holding one."

Daniel took in a deep breath beside me, as if savoring the moment.

I just plain couldn't breathe.

"The application is due in a month. You will need to take photographs of your best pieces to make a portfolio of your work, get two letters of recommendation—I will provide one of them for each of you—and write two personal essays. You must mail the package by the date on the application, or you will not be considered. This is your one chance for Trenton, people—don't blow it."

April shook like a happy puppy. Katie hugged the application to her chest. Daniel wrapped his arm around me and gave my shoulders a squeeze.

"We did it, Grace," he whispered, and kissed the side of my head.

"Don't start celebrating yet." Barlow clasped his hands on top of his desk. He usually did that when he was about to deliver the catch. "Trenton usually accepts only one HTA student a year—occasionally two." His eyes flicked between Daniel and me. Then he looked at April and Katie. "I chose you four because you have a real shot. Do your absolute best with the applications, and maybe we'll set a new record this year." He stroked his handlebar mustache. "Now get out of my office and get back to work."

"Good luck, ladies!" Katie said after we left the office. "Daniel"—she put her hand on his arm—"I want to make sure my painting is just right for my portfolio. Do you mind looking over it for me? Everyone knows you're the best."

"Um. Yeah. Sure." He gave my shoulders another squeeze and then followed her to her table.

I drifted over to my chair and sat there for a moment, staring at the Trenton packet in front of me. I'd convinced myself that there was no way Mr. Barlow was going to give me an application; besides my recent unsteady hand, my grades had taken a real dip last winter—what with finding out my true love was a werewolf, and my brother's wreaking havoc all over town.

Daniel talked about Trenton on a daily basis. What it would be like for the two of us to go there together. He wanted to be an industrial designer—to make functional art that people could hold in their hands and that would change the way they lived their lives—and it was one of the reasons he came back to Rose Crest. Besides looking for a cure for his werewolf curse, that is. It was his dream for us to go off to college together. Leave behind curfews and the sideways glances of everyone in town. Escape the memories of his terrible father, which haunted him each time he had to walk past his old home in order to get to mine.

Katie erupted into laughter on the other side of the

room. I glanced over and saw Daniel grinning in that wry way of his as he pointed at something in her painting. Obviously, he'd just made some sort of joke—but my superhearing had faded away sometime during lunch, so I didn't know what he'd said.

But Katie was right about him: Daniel was the best. We all knew he was the shoo-in for Trenton. It didn't matter that he should have graduated last year. He'd all but been promised a spot in Trenton by one of the admissions counselors if he graduated from HTA. The real competition was between April, Katie, and me to see who got a possible second spot at the art institute.

My odds seemed slim. I mean, April was killer with pastels, and Katie was better at acrylics than anyone else in the class. But then again, even though charcoal had always been my specialty, with Daniel's tutelage I was really getting the hang of oils. I'd gotten two A-pluses from Barlow this semester, and he saved those only for projects he thought were truly special. And Barlow had said it himself: he wouldn't have given me this application if he didn't think I stood a chance.

As the shock wore off, I felt tears well in the corners of my eyes. I brushed them away. This was a happy moment, but I'd never been a fan of crying.

Daniel left Katie's table. He smiled at me as he carried his application back to our table. Even without superpowers, I could hear Lana Hansen and

Mitch Greyson whispering from the table behind us. Apparently, Mitch had an issue with a couple of Barlow's choices for the applications. I shrugged and picked up my Trenton envelope and tucked it into my backpack for safekeeping.

Chapter Five

Helpless

Our last-period class was cancelled because of the whole not-having-a-religion-teacher thing, and since I'd already spent an hour in study hall instead of gym class earlier in the day, I headed over to the market with Daniel to help out with the cleanup.

I was surprised by how little it seemed had been accomplished while we were gone, but then as we dug into it, I realized just how devastating the destruction was. Almost every window had been broken; there were gaping holes in the walls; and every single shelf and display had been emptied and most everything smashed. It seemed like it would take a week to sort through it all to find what was salvageable.

Daniel talked excitedly about our Trenton applications at first—showing his to Mr. Day and Chris, and telling me which of my paintings I should submit for my portfolio—but as the hours dragged on, he grew quiet and sullen like everyone else and just concentrated on clearing one foot of space at a time. The sun had long set and the Dumpster was overflowing when Mr. Day told us to go home for the night. I would have kept cleaning, but I was thankful for the reprieve—my back ached, and I could barely put one foot in front of the other.

Daniel and I picked up the last of the trash and went out the back door into the parking lot.

"I don't think we can fit one more thing in this Dumpster," Daniel said. "Let's try the one at McCool's."

Day's parking lot butted up against the lot of the new pub. I hefted my box of trash in my arms and followed him over to their Dumpster, trying all the way to will my superstrength to kick in, since the box of broken glass I carried felt more like it was full of bricks.

"You think the store will survive?" I put the box down on the asphalt when we got to the Dumpster, and stretched out my arms.

A group of guys horsed around by the back exit of the pub only a few yards away. Their loud bursts of laughter seemed so unnatural compared to how I felt at the moment.

"Don't know," Daniel said as he flung one of the bags into the Dumpster. "Insurance will only cover so much, and if we don't get it up and running soon . . . A place like this can't survive long with that kind of lost revenue."

"It's not fair, you know. I mean, why would Ju—I mean, why would anyone want to target Mr. Day that way?"

"Maybe it's because he employs freaks," a familiar voice said.

I turned around and saw Pete Bradshaw strutting toward us from the group of rowdy guys. A thin line of smoke wafted from the cigarette between his fingers. Apparently, he'd taken up smoking since he'd been kicked out of HTA—that, and grown a nasty little goatee. Daniel swore under his breath as Pete walked right up to us.

"First that Mooney retard, and now *you*." Pete waved his cigarette too close to Daniel's face.

"Back off, Pete," I said.

"You gotta expect it. You hang with trash, and sooner or later somebody is going to trash you."

Pete always tried to pick a fight whenever we ran into him. He had a pretty big chip on his shoulder, since being kicked out of HTA meant he lost his hockey scholarship and his dad refused to pay for anything other than community college.

"Yo, Pete?" one of his friends called from the group near the exit. "This place blows, man. Didn't you say you know a dude who can get us into The Depot?"

The Depot? I stuck my hand in my jacket pocket and fingered the plastic card I'd found this morning at Day's.

Pete glanced back at his friend. "Yeah, Ty. You want

to announce that a little louder to rest of the world?"

"Whatever, let's go."

"Good thing for you I've got better places to be." Pete flicked his cigarette at Daniel's feet. He turned back toward his friends and started to walk away.

Daniel let out a small sigh.

Pete liked to talk the talk, but he usually found an excuse to walk away when Daniel didn't react to his goading. And I knew I should just let him keep on going, but I couldn't stop myself from doing what I did next.

"Wait, Pete," I called after him.

"What?" Pete looked back at me.

"What are you doing, Grace?" Daniel whispered. "Let him go."

I shook my head. "The Depot? Where is it?" I asked Pete.

He laughed. "*You* want to go to The Depot?"

"Can you just tell me where it is? It's important."

Pete laughed even harder. His friends all watched us now. He took a step toward me. "And what do I get in return for this bit of information? Or are you looking to ditch this piece of trash here and come party with a real man?"

"It was just a question, Pete. Do you have an answer or not?"

"And I asked you what the answer was worth."

"Shut it, Bradshaw." Daniel stepped up next to me. "Just forget she asked and leave."

"Or what? Mooney ain't around to mess people up for her. And what can you do?"

Daniel clenched his fists at his sides, but he didn't move.

"That's what I thought," Pete said. He turned slightly, like he was about to leave again, but then he suddenly lunged at Daniel and shoved him hard. Daniel stumbled back and fell over the box of trash I'd left by the Dumpster.

"No!" I yelled, and ran to Daniel.

I tried to help him stand, but he waved me off. His face twisted into a terrible wince as he pushed himself up from the asphalt. A red slash painted his forearm, and I gasped when I saw a shard of bloodstained glass sticking out of the box where Daniel had fallen.

"Oh my . . . Are you okay?"

At the same time I heard someone from the group of guys call to Pete. "You need some help?" The guy named Ty and another one of Pete's friends approached from the group.

I expected my body to tense, acknowledging the danger surrounding us, and my powers to seep into my muscles with that aching, familiar pain—but nothing happened. *Crap*, I thought. This was no time for my powers to hit the Snooze button. I needed them now.

"You going to fight?" Pete stepped up in front of Daniel. His two friends flanked us on both sides. "Or you gonna let me use you as a punching bag?"

"Better me than Grace," Daniel said, gripping his bleeding arm.

"How do you know she's not next?" Pete asked as he pulled back his fist.

"Stop!" I lunged at Pete, but Ty caught me around the waist. I tried to summon my supernatural strength as I kicked at his legs, but he just laughed. I felt like a rag doll when he pushed me aside.

I hit the brick wall of the pub and was momentarily stunned. Then I heard a smacking noise, like fist on face, and then something large stumbled over my feet. I looked down, expecting to find Daniel, but it was Pete who'd hit the ground right in front of me. I heard a louder thud and grunt, and Pete's unnamed friend fell to his knees beside me, doubled over. Ty threw his hands up and backed away as fast as he could.

Pete moaned and wiped his bleeding nose. "You are a freak," he said to Daniel as he slowly stood up. "Come on," he said to his injured friend. "We don't have time for this trash. Let's go." He spat a bloody loogie on the asphalt by my feet.

"You better watch your backs," Pete called to us before he and the other two rejoined the group of guys. Their loud laughter echoed off the buildings around us as they took off down the street.

Daniel stood next to the Dumpster, his back to me. His shoulders heaved as he breathed in and out, and he clenched his hand over the wound in his arm.

"That was . . . awesome," I said. "Who needs super-powers when you can fight like that?"

"Is that all you ever think about?" Daniel asked. "Damn superpowers?"

"What?" His words stung, but I guess I deserved his reproach for making light of the situation. I came up beside him and put my hand on his shoulder. "I'm sorry. I shouldn't have said anything like that. You're hurt. Let me see your arm. Are you okay?"

"No," Daniel said, and shook off my touch. He pressed his injured arm against his chest so I couldn't see his wound. "I need to go home."

"You probably need to go to the hospital. I'll drive you."

"No, I don't want you to." He stumbled toward his motorcycle in the Day's Market lot. "I just need to go home."

I followed after him. "Are you in shock? You can't drive a motorcycle like this. You probably need stitches."

"I'll be fine." He climbed onto his bike, his arm still pressed into his chest.

"Damn it, Daniel. Let me help you."

"You've *helped* enough already," Daniel said, and kicked his bike to life. He twisted the throttle with his good hand, then flew out of the parking lot before I could respond.

He didn't even look back to see me standing there,

my arms at my sides, not knowing what on earth had just happened.

What did he mean by saying that I'd *helped* enough already?

I hadn't been able to *do* anything.

HEADED HOME AGAIN

I sat in my car in the parking lot for a good ten minutes, debating whether or not I should follow Daniel home to make sure he got there all right. And then force him to go to the ER to get his cut checked out. But he'd been so adamant about not wanting me to help him that I worried he'd only get angrier if I showed up uninvited. Perhaps it was best to let him cool off. Maybe call him in a couple of hours to make sure he was okay.

But a creeping thought kept bothering me as I started my car. Was Daniel just pissed at me for causing that fight with Pete, or was it possible that he didn't want my help because he thought I didn't have enough control over my powers to handle the sight of his blood?

I turned on the car radio, trying to drown out my guilty thoughts, and listened to the news report on the local Rose Crest station. They were discussing the attempted break-in at the school and how it might relate to Day's Market. The reporter speculated that the burglar must have been scared off somehow, because nothing was missing from the school. But, of course, the school's security cameras were blank.

I flipped off the radio and discovered my phone ringing deep within my backpack, which I'd left in the car all afternoon. What kind of calls could I have missed? What if Jude had tried to contact me again?

I looked at the display and sighed with relief.

"Hey, Dad," I said into the phone. "You got my messages?"

"Yes." Dad sounded so tired, and I could barely hear him over the din on his end of the phone. "Tell me what happened?"

I told him all about the phone call from Jude, trying to recount it word for word. Then I told him about how Jude had been in Daniel's apartment in Maryanne's basement.

Dad was silent for a moment. "All this searching for him, and he was practically in our own backyard," he finally said. He sounded angry, shocked, and relieved all at the same time. "Anything else? Have you heard from him again?"

"No." I hesitated for a moment. I wasn't sure if I wanted to share Daniel's theory with Dad, but I knew I shouldn't hold anything back that might help find Jude. "Nothing definitive, anyway, but I think he may have actually been in our backyard." I told Dad about James's seeing something at his window, then the ransacking of Day's Market, and the attempted break-in at the school.

"Daniel thinks it's Jude." I was just pulling into our

driveway, and I decided to sit in the idling car until I was done talking to Dad—I didn't want anyone to over-hear our conversation.

"That's a logical conclusion," Dad said. "It makes sense."

"Does it? Why would he do those things? Why is he back?"

"I don't know, Gracie." He sighed, and I heard some announcer's voice in the background. He must have been at an airport or a train station. "I really don't know."

"Are you on your way home?"

"No," he said. "I don't know when I'll be back."

"What? But Jude was here. Why aren't you com-ing—?"

"I need to go. It's the last call for my train. I'll explain later, but I don't know when I'll be home."

Anger surged inside of me. Dad was gone all the time, and I'd thought it was because he was desperately looking for Jude—looking for a way to make our fam-ily whole again. But maybe it was us he was trying to stay away from? Why else wouldn't he come home now? Right now when we needed him most.

"Fine. Just don't forget where you live in the mean-time," I said.

"I'm sorry. I'll come home as soon as I can." Then he called to someone else on his end, "Yes, that's my bag. I'm coming." He cleared his throat and spoke back into the phone again. "One last thing, Gracie. You are not, under any circumstances, allowed to go looking for Jude on your own."

I made a scoffing noise. It would have been a laugh if I hadn't been so upset. I just found it funny and annoying at the same time that Dad would say the same thing as Daniel. Like they thought I wasn't capable of *not* going out and looking for Jude.

"Just don't, Gracie. You aren't prepared for what you might find. . . ." He sighed heavily into the phone. "And we've already lost one child. Your mother would never survive if you left us, too."

LATER

Mom was asleep on the couch when I finally went inside, the evening news playing in the background. I didn't bother to wake her and went straight up the stairs. I was more than exhausted, drained of everything, and I could barely keep my eyes open. I was halfway to my bed when Baby James started crying in his room. It was a whimpering, frightened whine, growing louder and louder. I pushed his door open and looked in on him. He sat in his toddler-sized bed, rubbing his eyes. With the light from the hallway, I could see big, fat tears running down his red-splotched face.

"It's okay." I dropped my backpack in his doorway and scooped him up in my arms. "It's okay, Baby James."

"Not baby," James said through his sobs. He was only two and half and was already starting to resist his family pet name.

"You're right. You're a big boy, huh?"

James nodded and cuddled close into my shoulder.

"Did you have another bad dream?"

"Yuh." He trembled in my arms.

"It's okay." I curled up with him in his tiny bed and brushed my fingers through his brown curls. "It's okay. I'm here. I'll protect you . . . I promise."

James smiled through his tears and patted my face. Within a few minutes his breathing became heavy and deep. His eyes closed, and he fell fast asleep with his fingers wrapped around a fistful of my hair.

I watched his chest rise and fall, thinking about everything that had happened in the last twenty-four hours, knowing that something terrible was trying to tear apart my little world. The crimes of the city were spreading to my hometown. Jude had been here, staring in at our little brother with his silver, glowing eyes. I didn't know Jude's intentions, and I didn't know how he was connected to what had happened at Day's or at the school, but all of this made it feel like the sky was about to come crashing down on us at any given moment.

I thought about what Daniel had said about his believing that I could be a hero. And I wished beyond all wishes that he were right—that I had the ability to keep the promise I had just made to James. I wished I really were capable of protecting everyone I loved.

I glanced over at my backpack in the doorway, remembering my Trenton application tucked inside of it. James snored slightly next to me, looking innocent and helpless, but what would he be like if I hadn't been here to quiet his cries?

And that was when it hit me: even if I beat out April and Katie, even if Trenton decided to let both Daniel and me in, I still couldn't go.

Any possibility of my going to Trenton, or to college at all, had been destroyed the day Jude ran away. What with my dad always gone looking for him, and Mom's manic-depressive state. And wouldn't Mom just get worse when I went off to school? Who would watch over Baby James? A part-time housekeeper wasn't the same as a mother or a sister. And how could I leave Charity with all this to deal with on her own? She was the smart one in the family—practically all she ever did was homework—and it wouldn't be fair if I ruined her future by taking off just like Jude.

Trenton was everything Daniel wanted, and everything I couldn't have.

And I hated Jude for taking it away from me.

CHAPTER SIX

The Way We Were

I woke up stiff and sore from a cramped sleep in James's toddler bed around four thirty in the morning. I slipped out of his room, hoping he'd sleep another couple of hours, and crawled into my own bed. But I tossed and turned, and no matter how much I tried, I couldn't block out the dream that had woken me in first place.

What was strange was that I had dreamed of a happy memory: the weekend Daniel, Jude, and I went fishing with my dad at Grandpa Kramer's cabin about five years ago. Daniel had been living with us at the time, and I dreamed about how he used to tease me, and how I'd eat up every second of his attention. And how Jude had declared that he was happy that Daniel was part of our family now—and how he hoped that was the way it would always be.

It was a dream about the way things were once, and

the way they should have always been—but it haunted me like the worst of any nightmare.

I finally got out of bed and went to the stack of Masonite boards next to my desk. I pulled out one painting at a time until I found the one I'd been working on the night Jude ran away. It was a picture of Jude from that fishing trip to Grandpa Kramer's pond. I'd fallen asleep at my desk while working on the painting, and was awoken several hours later by my mother's screams. She'd found Jude's note on the table, the one that said he was leaving, and her mental state had not been quite solid since.

I set the painting on my desk and looked it over. The background was there, and I'd roughed in the basic colors for Jude. I'd been practicing a new technique Daniel had taught me, trying to distract myself while I waited for news from the hospital about his condition. But when I found out Jude had left, I couldn't bring myself to finish the project. Maybe I was just waiting for the right moment—waiting for him to come back.

I opened my desk drawer and pulled out a rubber-banded bundle of photos. I found the snapshot of Jude I'd been working from and put it on top of the painting. Then I flipped through the rest of the pictures until I found the one I was looking for. In it, Daniel, Jude, and I all sat on a boulder by the pond. Our half-eaten lunches sat on our laps, and our arms were wrapped around one another's shoulders. Jude made a gesture with one of his hands—three fingers extended. I'd almost forgotten about that. It was the sign we made up that spring for our little pack: THREE MUSKETEERS FOREVER.

I pulled that photo out and held it for a while.

Last night I'd decided I couldn't go to college because of everything that was happening. Last night I thought I hated Jude. But now I knew the real reason I couldn't go to college, the real reason I couldn't leave home: because I'd promised myself that when Jude came back, I'd be here to help him the way I'd helped Daniel.

Everyone kept telling me not to go looking for Jude. Like it was the one thing they expected me to do. Maybe that's because they knew that's what I *should* be doing?

I didn't have enough control over my powers to physically fight anyone yet—what happened yesterday with Pete and his friends proved that—but that didn't mean I couldn't try to find Jude. I could still help him. Maybe if I got him to come home. Figured out how to help him get his life back, the way I'd helped Daniel—the way I promised I would—then maybe Dad would stop leaving, and Mom would level out, and maybe my family would be like it had been in my dream. The way we'd all wanted it to be forever.

And then maybe, just maybe, I could even start thinking about going to college. About having a future of my very own.

CHAPTER SEVEN

What April Knows

SATURDAY AFTERNOON

I stood outside the old hardwood door, my hand perched just above the weathered wood, unsure if I had the nerve to go through with this plan. Something that had happened yesterday kept playing out in my mind all morning, pushing me in this direction until I was standing on this doorstep. But I didn't know if I was ready for the answers I might get if somebody actually answered the door.

I knew I'd promised not to go looking for Jude on my own. But I hadn't planned on going alone. I'd have Daniel with me. At least, that had been the original plan.

Only Daniel wasn't answering his phone. I'd called him three times, to no avail. I wondered if his phone had been damaged more than we'd originally thought and had finally petered out, so I decided to go over to his place to tell him my idea.

However, I was halfway there when he finally called me back.

"I'm sick," he said, his voice sounding distant.

"It's probably because you wouldn't let me take you to the hospital. You've probably got an infection."

"I *did* go to the hospital. I've got the stitches to prove it. And I probably picked up some bug while I was there."

"Oh." Suddenly, it felt like he was blaming me for his illness. "I can bring you some soup. I'll be there in a few minutes."

"No," he said a little too abruptly. "Leave me alone."

"What?" My voice caught a bit in my throat.

Daniel sighed into the phone. "Sorry. I don't know what . . . I don't know if I'm contagious. Just stay away, okay?"

"But there's no one there to take care of you," I said. "When was the last time you were even sick anyway?"

That was one of the few benefits of being an Urbat—I hadn't even had so much as a sniffle in the last ten months. Daniel probably hadn't been sick a day in his life in the last eighteen years. A common cold might knock him flat.

"I can take care of myself."

I sighed. "Just tell me you aren't trying to avoid me on purpose. Are you still mad at me for what happened with Pete?"

"No, Gracie," he said. "I was never mad at you in the first place. I just feel like sleeping all day. And you know you're not really supposed to be inside my place. I mean, what could you even do to help me?"

I still felt terrible about last night, and it made me feel worse that he wouldn't let me help him now. But if that's the way he wanted it, I wasn't going to force myself into his apartment.

"Okay. But call me if you need anything."

"Yeah. Okay. Bye."

"Oh, and I have something to tell you—" I said, but Daniel hung up before I even finished. I thought about calling him back and telling him my plan, but since he was so sick, I didn't want him thinking he had to come along.

I might not have been able to stop Daniel from getting hurt, or help him feel better now, but I was tired of standing idly by. I needed to *do* something before I went crazy. I tucked my phone into my bag, turned the car around at the next light, and headed to the place where I was now.

Trepidation filled me as I stood outside the door, but I wasn't going to let it stop me from getting answers. I mean, we used to be best friends. What's the worst she could do anyway: slam the door in my face? I knocked and waited almost a full minute before the door opened.

"Hey," I said.

April looked at me for a long moment, like she was *actually* contemplating slamming the door. But then she crossed her arms in front of her chest and said, "Hey." She waited another few seconds. "What do you want?"

"Jude," I said. "I need to find him, and I think you know where he is."

A FEW MINUTES LATER, UP IN APRIL'S BEDROOM

"You know where Jude is, don't you?" I asked April as soon as she shut her bedroom door behind us.

April glanced sideways at the computer on her desk and then looked back at me. "I have no idea what you're talking about. I don't know anything about Jude being back."

"Then how did you know he's back?"

"Because . . ." Her gaze shifted toward her computer again.

"You overheard my conversation with Daniel yesterday morning, didn't you?"

April looked down at her hands.

That was the thing that had been bugging me all morning. The way April had been acting yesterday, I was pretty sure she'd overheard what Daniel and I had said about Jude's being back. And she seemed only mildly surprised. Then it seemed like she'd wanted to tell me something important, reconsidered, and now was trying to hide that something from me.

"Jude called me from *inside* Daniel's apartment. He was back here in Rose Crest two nights ago, but you already knew that, didn't you?"

"He called *you*?" April folded her arms and leaned against her desk, the top of which was littered with beads, what I assumed were fake gems, metal charms, and what looked like fishing line. There were even a pair of little pliers and a large magnifying glass. "I don't believe that."

"Why? He's *my* brother."

"Because you're the reason he left."

"I know." I couldn't help rubbing the scar that hid under my sleeve. I'd always figured Jude left because of what he did to me.

"After what you did to him, I'm surprised he'd ever want to talk to you again." April put her hands on her hips. "I know I didn't."

"Wait, what *I* did to *him*?" I asked.

All this time I thought April had been avoiding me because she was still freaked out by all the things she saw in the parish that terrible night, but it was really because she blamed me for Jude's leaving?

"He told me he left because you betrayed him for Daniel," April said. "Daniel tried to kill your own brother, and you still sided with that stupid dog boy. You and your dad act like Daniel's some sort of angel, but he's really just a wolf in sheep's clothing." April picked up a purple bead from her desk and held it between her thumb and forefinger. "I know what Daniel is, Grace. And I know what he did to Jude."

Dog boy. Wolf in sheep's clothing.

"How?" I asked. I wondered just how much Jude had told her about what had happened—or at least *his* version of it.

"Jude always called him a monster. At first, I thought he was being metaphorical. But then I saw Daniel turn from a wolf into a person in the parish, when you pulled that knife from his chest. I'm not completely stupid. It didn't take a lot to figure out that he's a werewolf."

"Was," I corrected her. "He's been cured. And I've forgiven him for the things he did while he was under the influence of the wolf. If Jude had been capable of that, then he wouldn't be where he is now."

April stared at the bead she held in her fingers. She bit her lip.

"Do you know about Jude, then?" I asked tentatively. "What *really* happened to him?"

"He's a werewolf now, too. Because of what Daniel did to him. Jude said he was going through changes, and I figured it out on my own. You've always treated me like I was dumb or something. You've never given me enough credit, but at least Jude does. He trusts me."

Whoa. Maybe I hadn't given April enough credit. She knew my family's secret, and still she was standing here talking to me? And I'd always thought that Jude's interest in April was based purely on rebounding from his emotions—but if he'd been in contact with her since he left, then maybe I'd been wrong about their relationship. But the most important part of that thought was that April had been in contact with Jude.

"So you have talked to Jude since he's left?" I asked.

April used her finger to roll the bead around in the palm of her hand.

"I know you care about him, April. I care about him, too. I think he's in trouble, and all I want to do is bring him home."

"He has a new home," April said. "He told me that he found a new home, and a new family who wouldn't turn their backs on him the way you did. But the way he talked about them . . . I don't know, Grace. They sound dangerous. Not like a real family at all. I wouldn't be surprised if they were involved in what happened at Day's Market."

I put my hand over my mouth. What had my brother gotten himself into?

April placed the bead carefully on the table and then looked up at me. "I knew he was in the city, but I honestly didn't think he'd come here."

"So you've known all along where Jude is, and you haven't told anyone? Do you know how hard my dad's been looking for him?"

"I haven't known *all along*," she said. "He sends me emails every once in a while. I can't respond to them or anything. My messages just bounce right back."

I nodded. I used to send a daily email to Jude at his school address, asking him to come home, but I gave up after a while when my messages kept bouncing back to me. "And he told you where he is?"

"No, he never said anything about his location. But I think I've traced him."

My eyebrows went up involuntarily. "You know how to trace emails?"

"No. But I do know how to trace blog comments. Check this out." April sat on her desk chair and wiggled her computer mouse. Her screen came to life and she logged on to the Internet. "In addition to the emails, I started to get some random, anonymous comments on my blog a couple of months ago. After a while I figured out it was Jude."

"Your blog?" Jude had been hiding from everyone in his family, yet he'd had time to comment on April's blog? *I* didn't even know she had a blog.

"I design jewelry"—April pointed at the stuff on her desk—"and sell it on a blog." She pointed at her computer. There was a blog pulled up on the screen with pink swirls around a banner that said APRIL SHOW- ERS JEWELRY and then pictures of rings, necklaces, and bracelets.

"I didn't know." But now that I thought about it, whenever I saw April lately, it seemed she had a new necklace or bracelet. They were beautiful. "I guess that kind of happens when somebody stops talking to you."

April shrugged. "Anyway, like I said, I started getting these anonymous comments on my blog, and they all seemed like they were from the same person. Like when I posted a pic of this necklace." She clicked on a picture of a tree-shaped pendant. It was the same necklace she wore now. "I got this comment." She scrolled down a bit and hovered the cursor over the comment. "I don't know how this could be from anyone other than Jude. It's the last thing I've heard from him."

I leaned over her shoulder and read the comment.

Anonymous said:
Beautiful. This looks just like the walnut tree outside my old house. Sometimes I wish I could see it again from the porch swing where we used to sit together. But that won't ever happen again, will it? Not after what they did to me.

My heart tightened in my chest, and I looked away from the words. The first two lines had sounded so much like the old Jude, but the rest stung too much to read again.

"I don't know if you noticed, but that comment had a time stamp of three a.m. on September twenty-fifth. Three weeks ago." I heard the click of a mouse and when I looked back at the screen, she was on a new website. "This is my stat counter. It shows where my blog visitors come from." She clicked on something else, and it pulled up a list of times and dates and locations. "You can see from this that the only person who visited my blog at three a.m. on September twenty-fifth was located in the city."

"Wow, that's really possible to see?" I fingered my moonstone necklace. It always pulsed with a warm vibration. To me, it meant hope. But then I let go of the pendant and sighed. "But Jude could still be anywhere. The city's a big place."

"Ah, but it gets better than that. I can drill it down even more and actually see the IP address of the visitor and the server he's using."

"Seriously?" Apparently, there was a lot I didn't know about April these days. She used to have zero interest in computers, and now she was talking about tracing IP addresses and servers? "How did you learn to do all this?"

"You know Avery Nagamatsu—Miya's older brother? The one who's studying to be a software programmer?"

I nodded.

"I went with him to a couple of frat parties over the summer to make it look like he had a girlfriend. And in exchange, he helped me set up a blog for my jewelry business and showed me how to do all this so I could see where my customers were coming from. But it has its added benefits for tracking down rogue boyfriends."

"Huh." Well, I'd always known the girl had gumption.

April made a few more clicks with her mouse. "Usually,

the server name is too vague to really tell me anything, but Jude's just happens to belong to a business."

April pointed at a name on the screen. I almost gasped when I saw it.

"'The Depot,'" I read out loud. "Do you know what that is?"

"I've been asking around," she said. "I couldn't find out anything at first. Not even anything on the Internet that wasn't in a locked forum. But then I was at that old movie theater in Apple Valley with Miya and Claire the other night. And you know that stoner-looking guy who works at the concessions stand—the one who always wears those gamer hats?"

"Yeah."

"Well, I was buying some popcorn when I heard that kid going on about some new club he was dying to play at—a place called The Depot."

My mouth popped open. "Did you find out anything else?"

"Yeah. I had to give him ten bucks, but he finally told me that The Depot is like this superexclusive emo-gamers' nightclub in the city. And for another twenty bucks he gave me the address."

She opened her drawer and pulled out a folded-up piece of paper.

"What . . . really?" I reached for it.

April pulled it away. "I don't know if I should tell you where Jude is."

"Why?"

"Because if I tell you, then you'll go tell Daniel or your dad, and they'll go down there and just scare him off. If he wanted *them* to find him, then he would have contacted them . . . not me."

"Not *us*. Jude contacted me, too."

April looked down at the folded piece of paper. She turned it over in her hand a couple of times and sighed. "I don't know if this will even do you any good. You can't just walk into The Depot. I told you, it's, like, superexclusive. Not even the kid who gave me the address had actually even been inside yet. You have to have a special keycard or you can't even get in the door."

Keycard? I stuck my hand in my jacket pocket and pulled out the plastic card I'd found at the market yesterday. "You mean like this one?"

April's jaw dropped. "How did—?"

"You've got the address. I've got the card. We can do this together, or not at all." I took a step toward her. "What do you say?"

"Okay." April stood up. She shook in that excited-nervous way of hers. "But we're going to need makeovers."

I almost dropped the keycard. "We're going to need . . . what?"

CHAPTER EIGHT

The Depot

THAT NIGHT

Yeah, so this is pretty much the dumbest thing I've ever done, I thought as I listened to the weird *vroom-vroom* noise the borrowed pair of vinyl pants I wore made as I walked. The sound was so distracting that I didn't see the crack in the sidewalk, and stumbled in the high-heeled red leather boots April had insisted that I wear.

April caught me by the arm before I fell. "Those are hard to walk in, huh?"

"The pants or the boots?" I grumbled. "Seriously, why do you even have vinyl pants?"

"They're for my Halloween costume. I'm going as Lady Gaga." She pointed to the pink sequined top she wore with a denim jacket and a black miniskirt. "This goes with it."

Great, I was headed to a nightclub for the very first time in half a Halloween costume. I wrapped my arms around my waist, trying to cover up my bare midriff. This lacy red top was far too short for my taste, but April had forbidden me to wear my wool jacket over it because she said it would ruin the "ensemble."

And not only was I dressed like a pseudohooker, I was also walking down a street only two blocks away from Markham—the worst neighborhood in the Midwest—after dark. *Yep, this definitely ranks on the list of the stupidest things I've ever done.*

April looked down at the paper in her hand and then did a full circle, looking at all the buildings on the street. "This is supposed to be the address, but this doesn't look like a nightclub to me."

I'd been so distracted by my ridiculous clothes, and the prospect of getting mugged and/or solicited by a total stranger, that I hadn't even paid attention to the architecture around us. I looked up at the building we stood in front of. It was long and wide, with boarded-up windows and a huge chain wrapped around the handles of the decrepit double doors. I could feel a slight vibration under my feet. "Isn't this that abandoned train station they're always talking about on the news? How it needs to be demolished?"

April shrugged. "All I know is that I'm going to punch that stoner kid in the 'nads if he doesn't give me my twenty bucks back. He totally ripped me off."

I took a couple of steps closer to the building. The vibration in the ground got stronger, rumbling through the soles of my shoes and up the pointy four-inch heels. Another two steps closer and I could feel the vibration in my ears now. Music—coming from somewhere nearby. Underneath us, perhaps? If it weren't for my powers, I probably would have missed it.

"No," I said. "I think we've found it. The Depot? Train station? Makes sense, doesn't it?"

"I guess," April said. "But this place is totally boarded up."

I motioned to April as I followed the musical vibration around the side of the building and down the narrow alley between the train station and an equally abandoned-looking warehouse. *Stupid, stupid, stupid,* I kept chanting to myself with every quick step, but if this was the only way to track down Jude, I wasn't going to turn back now. The sounds of a screeching car and a shouting man back out on the street made me pick up my pace until I came to a metal door on the side of the building. It looked far more modern than the chained-up doors out front. The vibration was strong from behind the door, and I could even pick up the faint rhythmic pulse of techno music.

"I think this is it."

"Are you sure? This doesn't look like a club entrance. I mean, shouldn't there be bouncers or something?" April's earlier courage seemed to have washed right out of her. The pale look on her face made it seem like she'd been half anticipating/half hoping we wouldn't be able to get into the club without fake IDs. A consideration I hadn't even thought of until now.

I tried the handle, but a bolt in the door stopped it from opening. Then I noticed a keypad next to the doorway with a small red light. "I think all we need to get into the club is the keycard." I pulled the card out of my pocket—a harder feat than it sounds when your pants are made out of vinyl—and swiped it through what looked like a credit card reader. The light on the keypad turned green, followed by a loud clicking noise as the bolt in the door unlocked.

I pulled on the handle. The door slid open, and a wave of pulsing music flooded the alley. "You ready?" I asked April.

"I guess so. . . ." She straightened her miniskirt. "I mean, yes," she said with only a hint of a tremble in her voice. "Let's do this."

Just inside the doorway was a long staircase. I grabbed on to the railing and prayed I wouldn't slip in my high heels as I navigated my way down the cement steps. At the bottom we went through an open doorway and entered the club. It buzzed like a hive with gyrating people, flashing lights, pulsing music, wafting fog from a dance floor in the middle of the room, and flickering plasma TVs as big as cars extended from cables attached to the ceiling. Groups of guys, mostly in their early twenties or younger, crowded around the TVs. They cheered and shouted while playing video games that mostly involved shooting, speeding cars, and almost-naked women. The gaming crowd was dotted with a few girls—dressed just as scantily as the ones on the screens. But mostly the only females in the place crowded around the bar on the far end of the club, or partied on the dance floor in corsets and leather getups that put my attempt at a tough-girl outfit to shame.

The guys who filled the expansive room were a weird mix of hipsters and Goths. I'd never seen so much nasty facial hair, so many tight pants, piercings, and tattoos in one place. I couldn't help thinking of the party I'd happened upon at Daniel's old apartment on Markham Street—the one that had sent me running scared into the night—only this was twenty times worse. This was definitely the kind of place I always imagined the adults in Rose Crest were trying to keep us away from when they told us stories about the Markham Street Monster.

"There's the Wi-Fi station," April said. Her voice still shook a bit. "That's gotta be where Jude contacted me from." She started toward a group of narrow metal tables with rows of bolted-down laptops on the far left-hand side of the club, slightly removed from all the commotion.

"What are you doing? I thought the plan was to stick to the shadows?"

"*You're* supposed to stick to the shadows. Keep an eye out for your brother, maybe ask around. I'm the bait." She fluffed her curls and plumped her pink lips.

"If Jude's here, then I want him to see me. We'll lure him out into the open."

"I'm not so sure that's a good idea." Even from our spot in a dark corner, I could tell we were drawing more attention than I cared for. I knew April had been going for sexy with her choice of outfit, but her denim jacket and pink-sequined tank stood out like a neon HELLO, I'M CLUELESS AND VULNERABLE! sign in this sea of black leather and piercings.

And vinyl pants or no vinyl pants, I'm sure I looked just as poseresque as she did.

"If Jude's here, then the person he's most likely to approach is me. Just stick to the shadows and keep an eye out." April sauntered over to the Wi-Fi station. With a flourish, she swept her blond curls over her shoulder and sat at the computer. I cringed at how innocent she looked, sitting there out in the open.

I decided to stay close to the perimeter, circle the room, and keep one eye out for Jude and the other eye on April. I made it once around the whole club without making eye contact with anyone, but then realized that I probably *did* need to ask around if I planned on finding anything out about Jude. I stood in a corner for a minute, working up my courage, and then noticed someone I actually recognized among a group of guys at one of the gaming stations. Under their tattoos, most of the guys looked like they couldn't be much older than me, and the one sitting with a wireless game paddle off to the side of the group looked all too familiar.

Pete's friend . . . the one he called Ty. I glanced around me, wondering if that meant Pete was somewhere nearby—he was the last person I wanted to run into in this place—but it seemed like Ty was here without him. I knew the guy had thrown me against a brick wall the night before, but I hoped he was still freaked enough by Daniel leveling his friends that he wouldn't give me any trouble if I tried to question him. Besides, he seemed relatively docile compared to most of the guys at his gaming station.

Ty frantically pushed buttons on his controller and chanted, "Come on, come on," under his breath, so he didn't notice me sidle up behind him. I was about to tap him on the shoulder when the tattoo-painted guy next to him shot straight up and started screaming obscenities at the screen.

"Who just killed me?" he roared.

Ty dropped his controller on the metal table in front of him and tried to scramble out of his chair, but the angry gamer grabbed him by his jacket and yanked him up so hard his feet dangled just above the concrete floor.

"Did you just kill me?" the gamer shouted into Ty's face.

"I'm sorry, man." Ty's voice quavered. "I've never played this game before."

"Who let this newb in here?"

The gamer threw Ty against his chair. It tipped

backward and almost knocked me over. I hopped out of the way just in time. The gamer kept screaming at Ty and then shoved another guy who hadn't even been involved in the argument. If this was how they felt about new people around here, then I needed to get away fast before an all-out brawl broke out. I turned to dash from the scene, but I'd taken only a few stumbling steps in my stupid heels when I ran straight into what seemed to be a flannel-covered brick wall.

"Whoa, there. You okay?"

The brick wall speaks?

I took a slight step back and looked up to see that I'd smacked right into the chest of a guy wearing a flannel shirt. He looked down at me with wide green eyes.

"I'm sorry," I said, and took another step back. "I didn't see you there."

But really, I didn't know how I hadn't noticed this guy before. I mean, if I thought *I* stood out here, how had I not noticed someone like him in a place like this? While the current fashion statement in the club involved ink and an abundance of black, this guy wore a green flannel shirt, light blue jeans, and a large bronze antiquey-looking belt buckle that resembled a Texas marshal's star. He had wavy hair the color of milk chocolate that stuck out from under the edges of his blue baseball cap, and his tan face was completely free of weird markings or bad facial hair, unlike most of the guys here. I looked down, expecting him to be wearing cowboy boots, but instead he had on a pair of gray Nike running shoes—otherwise, he would have looked like he'd sauntered right in here off a ranch or farm or something.

He gave me a friendly smile—making his tanned, chiseled cheeks dimple—and he wrapped his warm fingers around my elbow. "A pretty girl like you should be more careful in a place like this," he said, and pulled me farther away from the fight that brewed behind me.

"Yeah. Um. I know. Sorry."

His large, callused hand was still on my elbow. His words—*pretty girl like you*—finally sank into my brain. I bit my lip as heat rushed into my cheeks. I wanted to excuse myself and run off to hide in the bathroom or something.

The guy's smile widened, and it struck me that there was something about him—perhaps the shape of his mouth, or the tone of his voice—that seemed inexplicably, yet comfortingly, familiar. Like the first wafting scent of warm caramel-apple pie on Thanksgiving Day after a full year of not having tasted it. I realized then that for the same reason this guy stood out like a sore thumb in this place, he was probably the only person here I'd actually feel safe asking about Jude. "Hey, can I ask you something?"

He let go of my elbow. His green eyes flicked in the direction of the shouting gamers only a few yards away and then rested back on my face. "Sure thing, love."

"Have you . . . Ahh!" I clasped my hands over my

ears as a burst of pain exploded in my eardrums and my hearing magnified ten times. The vibration of the blaring music was excruciating, but mixed with the chorus of shouting players and the sound effects from several different video games going on all at once, it was downright nauseating. "Never mind." I winced and backed away.

"Are you okay?" The sound of his voice so close made my eardrums throb even more.

I waved him off and retreated to an empty corner. I took in ten deep breaths and concentrated on filtering the barrage of sounds like Daniel had tried to teach me. After a long moment, I was finally able to separate the music blasting from the stereo system from the beeping and wails of the video games, and then the lower noises of human conversation. People discussing their strategy for taking on the next level of a game, a guy trying to convince a girl named Veronica to go home with him, the guys at the gaming station I'd been near still shouting at one another, someone else asking where he could "score some smack."

And then suddenly the shrill sound of a female voice shouting: "Stop it! Leave me alone!"

I whirled toward the voice, knowing instantly it wasn't just a sound effect from one of the games. I'd been distracted and taken my eye off April, and now she wasn't sitting at the Wi-Fi bar anymore. She was standing, trying to push away a guy in a leather jacket who had her by the wrist. Another guy stood behind her, his fingers in her hair. April tried to turn around to push that guy away, but the one in the leather jacket pulled her in tight against him. She shrieked. The noise sliced into my ears.

My legs ached with power, and I bolted across the room in a matter of seconds.

"Let's dance," the guy said to April, crushing her against him.

She shrieked again. The sound almost split my eardrums this time. Which was good, actually, since it meant my powers were still working—at least for the moment.

I strode up to the guys and said in my best faux I'm-not-scared-at-all voice, "Let her go."

The two guys looked at me and laughed. The one who had his fingers in April's hair let go of her and smiled at me. He was a young guy, maybe nineteen, but one of his teeth was missing, and the others were yellow—probably from years of smoking, gauging by the smell of him. But there was another, underlying scent in the air that kept my arm hairs standing on end. Something I couldn't quite place. My muscles twitched as the guy approached me.

"Looks like our little bird brought a friend. How many *dances* do you think we can get out of them?"

"At least three," said the one holding April.

"Gross!" April kicked him in the shin, but he just laughed.

These guys were ticking me off—more so even than Pete and his nasty friends—and I was happy that my powers were pooling in my muscles, searing under my skin. I was in no mood for playing the part of the damsel in distress.

"I like this one's hair even better," the yellow-teethed one said, and he reached his large, dirty hand toward one of my dark curls.

I felt a tiny pop of power as I swung my arm up and smacked his hand away before he could touch me. The guy looked stunned for a second. He shook his hand like I'd actually hurt him. Then he smiled even bigger. "This one's got some real fight in her. I like that."

He reached for me again, but before I knew what I was doing, my fists were up in the boxing stance Daniel had taught me. I knocked the guy's hand away again and bounced back on my heels. When he came at me for a third time, my muscles flared with heat. I swung my leg and my high-heeled foot landed a perfect round-house kick in the guy's stomach. I felt the sheer power in the movement, but I was still surprised when he went flying back. He collided with his friend. The leather-jacketed dude let go of April, and the two guys landed in a heap in front of the docking station.

I grabbed April's arm. We were about to turn and run when I felt an iron-hard hand grip my ankle. The hand tugged on my leg. My pointy heel slipped out from under me. I let go of April and toppled backward, slamming back-first onto the concrete floor.

The noise and the motion of the lights suddenly came to a standstill, like time had stopped. All I could feel were a crushing pain around my ankle and April's grasp as she tried to pull me up. My powers were gone. I'd felt them dissipate the second I hit the ground. I shook my head, and my vision and hearing improved a bit.

The pain eased on my ankle, but then it moved up to my knee. Maybe it was because my powers were suddenly gone, but the crushing force of his grip felt practically superhuman. The guy kept me pinned by the leg as he leaned over me—his yellow teeth and rotten breath only inches from my face. He raised his fist. "Why you little bi—"

"*STOP!*" someone shouted. But it wasn't a scream. It sounded like a command.

The yellow-teethed guy let go of my leg almost instantly and backed away.

"Well, if it isn't the Good Samaritan," his friend said. "What do you want?"

"These girls are with me," the commanding voice said, "so get the hell out of my sight, now!"

Yellowed-teethed guy scrambled a good ten feet away, and his friend mumbled something like, "Whatever. Have fun with 'em," and disappeared into the crowd of gawkers that had formed around our little altercation.

I was still confused, shocked really, when I realized

someone else leaned over me now, holding his hand out to pull me up. I could barely see him at first with all the flashing lights and fake fog, but when I finally focused on his face, I gasped.

I didn't know who I'd expected to have come to my rescue—maybe Daniel had secretly followed me here, or perhaps even Jude had come out of hiding when he saw his sister and girlfriend in distress—but I certainly hadn't expected the boy in the flannel shirt to be the one who'd saved me.

CHAPTER NINE

Talbot

OUTSIDE THE CLUB

The next thing I knew, I was being pulled through the throng in the club toward the exit, April following close behind. People practically jumped out of the flannel-shirt guy's way in order to let us through. It wasn't until we were up the stairs and outside in the slightly fresher air—and I realized that the guy was holding me by my hand—that I got my bearings enough to react.

"Where are you taking us?" I tugged my hand from his grasp, expecting him to keep it imprisoned in his, but he let go without hesitation.

"To your car," he said. "I assume you drove a car here. You don't seem like the girls who live nearby, and I'm guessing you're not the public-transit sort."

I hugged my arms around my bare stomach. I'm sure that only reinforced his assumption that we didn't belong here.

"We're the Corolla at the end of the street." April pointed in the direction of my car, parked near the only working meter we could find. "We drove all the way from Rose Crest." April sounded all breathless, and I couldn't help noticing her smiling at the guy in an all-too-friendly way.

"April," I snapped. I gave her a look that was supposed to say, *We don't know this guy from Adam, so don't tell him where we live!*

"What?" she whispered, *not quietly.* "The dude just saved our lives . . . *and* he's cute."

For some reason, heat flushed into my cheeks. I couldn't deny the guy was attractive—in a down-home boy-from-the-farm sort of way, with his milk-chocolate-brown wavy hair, dimples, green eyes, and massive forearms that made it look like he'd spent hours baling hay. Even his flannel shirt and faded jeans screamed Clark Kent—without the superpowers, that is.

But it certainly didn't *mean* anything that I'd noticed all of those things about him, right? And it especially didn't mean I should trust him right away.

"I think we're good from here," I said to him. "Um, thanks for your help."

"No way. Those guys are going to be pissed," he said. "I'm not letting you out of my sight until you're driving far away from here."

"Really, it's like two blocks to the car. You can go now."

"Grace, you're being rude," April said. She swooped

in and grabbed Mr. Flannel by the arm and pulled him toward the car. "I'm April, by the way. Thank you for helping us. What's your name?"

"Talbot," he said, looking back at me as if checking to make sure I was following. Which I was—begrudgingly. "Nathan Talbot, actually. But I go by Talbot. My good friends call me Tal."

"Well, Tal," April said, "I'm glad you were there to help us out. We would have been toast without you."

"Toast?" Talbot asked. The twang in his voice made it sound like he was thoroughly amused by April's friendliness. "What are you girls doing here anyway? Doesn't seem like your kind of scene."

They were too far away for me to kick April in the shin before she could share any more information about us. "We're looking for Grace's brother. His name's Jude Divine. He's missing, and we think he may have been hanging out at that club."

Talbot stopped and turned back toward me. I almost ran right into his chest again. "Really?" he asked. "What does your brother look like? Maybe I can help."

I looked up at him. He grinned down at me with a friendly smile that made his dimples extra pronounced. Something about him put me on edge—made my heart beat faster when he looked at me. Maybe it was the way everyone else in the club had seemed a little bit afraid of him.

Talbot put his hand on my shoulder. "You can trust me."

And there it was: the shape of his mouth or the tone of his voice—something I still couldn't place—caused a wave of warm familiarity to ripple through my body. That same feeling had made me want to trust him in the club, so why not trust him now? He'd saved us from those guys, after all.

"I don't know for sure what my brother looks like anymore," I said. "I haven't seen him in almost a year." I remembered how much Daniel had changed physically in the three years while he was gone. Jude could look like anyone these days—especially if he was trying to hide. I pulled out my cell phone and scrolled to the very first photo I'd taken the day I got it—the day before Jude ran away. I'd snapped a picture of Jude as he looked at the moonstone ring Dad had given him.

I handed the phone to Talbot. "It's kind of hard to tell in that picture because he's looking down, but Jude's, like, seven inches taller than me, and he has a lot squarer jaw. He had short, dark brown hair the same color as mine the last time I saw him. And we've always had the same nose and violet eyes."

"Hmm." Talbot held the phone up next to my head. He bit his lip while he studied the picture on the phone and then my face. I couldn't help but stare back at him.

It was then that I realized that despite the dimples, he had a more mature fullness to his face than most teenage guys I knew. If I had to guess, I'd say he was probably about twenty-one or twenty-two years old. Talbot reached out and brushed my hair off the side of my face as if to help him see my profile better. He took a small step closer and studied me for another moment. I held my breath for every second of it.

"Nope, sorry. Haven't seen him," he finally said. He handed back my phone, his warm fingers brushing against my skin. "I'm pretty sure I'd remember eyes like yours."

Heat crept into my cheeks again. I dropped my gaze and stepped away.

"Well, we're here." I motioned toward the Corolla about twenty feet away. "Um, thanks for your help back there."

"Yes, thank you, Tal!" April looked like she was about to spring a bear hug on the poor boy.

Talbot held up his hands. "No problem. It's what I'm here for."

"Good-bye!" April waved at him while I dragged her to the car.

"Hey, Grace Divine?" Talbot called after me.

I glanced back at him. "Yeah?"

"See you around."

"Okay," I said, but I don't know why—it wasn't like I was ever going to see him again.

"You should so totally go for him!" April blurted out as we pulled away from the curb.

"What are you talking about?" I checked my rearview mirror and saw Talbot standing like a sentinel on the sidewalk. He wasn't kidding about keeping an eye on us until we were driving away. "I already *have* a boyfriend."

"Okay, I will concede to the fact that Daniel is wicked hot, but Tal is like a delicious new treat, don't you think?" April trembled in that excited way of hers. "Did you see how those other guys practically *ran* away from him?" She squealed and sank into her seat with a dramatic sigh.

"Um, *you're* welcome to make a move on the boy, if you want. I can turn the car around so you can get his number."

"No!" April sat straight up. Her eyes were wide, as if horror-struck by the very idea. She could be a flirt sometimes, but she usually cowered like my old cocker spaniel when it actually came to something real with a guy. "Don't you dare! Besides, he only had eyes for you." She jabbed me in the arm. "Grace Divine," she said in a deep voice, imitating Talbot, "see you around."

Heat swelled in my face, and I turned my head away before she could see me blush. It didn't mean anything, and the last thing I wanted was for her to tease me about it.

Just when I thought April had already forgotten our purpose for going to the club in the first place, she sighed again and stared out the window. "Anyway, Jude is the only guy I care about."

We were stopped at a traffic light a good three blocks away now, and Talbot had faded from my rearview mirror. I looked straight ahead through the windshield and noticed a long line of motorcycles parked outside a bar called Knuckle Grinders. One of them—a black-and-red Honda Shadow Spirit—reminded me of Daniel's bike.

"Yeah, I know what you mean," I said. "I've already got the best guy out there."

April made an uncomfortable noise and shifted in her seat. After a second she asked, "Do you think Daniel's really changed?"

The light turned green, and I drove through the intersection. I took one last glimpse at the Honda outside the bar. It sure did look a lot like Daniel's bike. But there was no way he'd coincidentally be at a bar only three blocks from where I'd been at The Depot. There was no way he'd even be at a bar at all. Besides, he was home sick in bed. "What do you mean?" I asked April.

"All the stuff Jude told me about Daniel—the things that he did. Who . . . what . . . he used to be. Don't you worry about him just going back to the way he was before?"

"I know he won't," I said. "It's physically impossible—he's been cured of the wolf curse that turned him into a monster in the first place."

"But the other stuff. You know, the stuff he was into before he even turned into a werewolf. Jude said he got real messed up before then. Drugs and drinking and fighting and stuff."

"That was all still the influence of the wolf. He was born with the curse. The wolf was always there, driving him to make bad choices." At least that was the way I thought about it. I guess it was possible that Daniel had made some of those decisions on his own. But that didn't matter anymore. "I know he wouldn't go down that road again. We sacrificed too much to save him. He'd never turn his back on that . . . on me."

"My mom says people never really change." April kept staring far out the window. I wondered if her mom was referring to April's dad, who'd walked out on them a few years ago.

"If you really believed that, then you wouldn't have come with me to help find Jude."

"I guess not." She was quiet for a moment. "But I still don't think you should trust Daniel as much as you do."

"Hmm," I said, and let silence fill the space between us in the car.

For a while this evening it had felt like we were friends again. I'd missed the way April and I joked around, and the way she drooled after guys and acted like an overexcited puppy most of time. With everyone at school treating me like last week's gym socks, my mom checked into Hotel Alternate Reality, Dad leaving all the time, and me trying to keep Charity in the dark about everything, when Daniel wasn't around, it felt like I had no one to talk to. I could handle the weird stares from people and the whispers behind my back, but I hated the silence that filled so many hours of my day. Not that it was quiet—especially when my super-hearing kicked in—it was just that very few people talked *to* me these days, rather than just about me.

And I missed my best friend.

We were about ten minutes out of the city when I decided to break the silence. I didn't want quiet anymore. "Those two guys were nasty, right? I can't believe what happened."

April perked right up. "Dude, the way you kicked that guy was awesome! Claire and Miya will never believe it . . . not that I would tell them about it, though. I mean, everyone would freak if we told them about going to The Depot."

She smiled at me like we had this great secret. It made my heart feel lighter.

"Where'd you learn how to do that?" she asked.

"I've been training with Daniel."

"Training? What for?"

My heart suddenly felt heavier all over again, because

I realized that April might know about Daniel and Jude, but she didn't know about me. She didn't know that I was infected with a curse that could possibly turn me into a monster. And I didn't know if I should tell her the truth. It was a pretty big deal to swallow.

What if the truth scared her away just when I was starting to get my best friend back?

But then I remembered how April had accused me of not giving her enough credit. She'd come with me tonight even when she knew how dangerous Jude could possibly be. Part of my heart still stung from the way she'd turned her back on me for the last year—but maybe that wouldn't have happened at all if I'd just been honest with her from the moment Daniel came home.

I stopped at another red light and put the car in park. It was time to lay it all out on the line. "There's something I have to show you." I pushed my sleeve up to my shoulder and exposed the crescent-shaped scar on my upper arm.

"What is that?" April's face went white. "Have you been . . . been . . . ?"

"Bitten."

"God. Daniel bit you? How can you still—?"

"Daniel didn't bite me. Jude did. He attacked me right after he turned into a werewolf."

April looked away. She played with one of the sequins on her shirt. "What does this mean? You're not a werewolf yet, right?"

"No. I've been infected with the curse, but I'm not a wolf yet. And I never will be if Daniel and I can help it. He's training me so I can use my powers to help people. But yes, there is the potential of me becoming a monster."

A car honked from behind us, and I shifted back into drive. I looked at April for her reaction, almost afraid she'd bolt from the car now that she knew the truth. She was quiet until we'd driven through the intersection, and then she leaned in real close to me. "Are you serious?" she asked. "Are you telling me you've got superpowers? 'Cause that'd be pretty much made out of awesome." She grinned at me and shook in her excited, trembly way.

"Um. Yeah. Kind of. I mean, I'm just learning how to use them, and they're kind of fickle—but they came in handy tonight, didn't they?"

"Heck, yeah, they did!" April squealed. "Did you see the look on that guy's face when he hit the ground? Seriously, that was the coolest thing ever. He was all like, 'Come here, defenseless little girl,' and then you were like, '*Bam!* Take that, suck-face! I've got superpowers!'"

I laughed. "Um, you're kind of forgetting about the part where he knocked me down and was about to take my face off."

"Yes, but that's why the universe created boys like Talbot. Those other guys practically peed their pants when they saw him."

"Yeah, didn't you think that was kind of weird? I mean, what was a guy like Nathan Talbot doing there, anyway? He didn't exactly mesh with the crowd."

"*Tal*," she said, emphasizing the nickname he'd told her his friends used, "is probably a DD."

"A what?"

"Part of the designated-driver program at the university. He's probably like the resident adviser for one of the dorms. I bet he could get those guys kicked out of school for being tools. That's probably why they backed off, but it's still cool the way he swooped in to save us like that."

I cringed. I absolutely hated that someone had had to "swoop in" to save me. I had abilities, and if only I could figure out how to use them the right way, I wouldn't need some random guy to come to my rescue.

April giggled. "And it doesn't hurt, either, if your knight in green-and-blue plaid just happens to be hot."

I laughed. "You know, just because a guy looks nice and seems nice . . . doesn't mean he *is*." I'd learned that all too well with Pete Bradshaw last year.

"Oh. My. Gosh." April shouted so loud I slammed on the breaks, thinking we were about to hit a dog or something. But April bounced in her seat with the craziest smile on her face, like she'd just thought of the best idea since nail polish. "Okay, sorry to segue away from the hotness that is Talbot, but I have to ask: if you're gonna be a superhero, can I be your sidekick?"

"What?" I gaped at April, hoping she was kidding—but of course, she wasn't.

"Dynamic Duo," she crooned, waving her finger between me and her.

"Um, I'm pretty sure sidekicks have to have super-powers, too," I said gently, sorry to break the news to her.

April's crazy smile faded. "Oh, yeah." But then she popped up in her seat again. "Okay, but that doesn't mean I can't be your Alfred."

"My Alfred?"

"You know, I can, like, help you design gadgets and stuff. Oh!" Her eyes went wide. "I can design you outfits for crime fighting!"

"I'm just in training, April. I don't think I need—"

"Oh, come on, Grace. It would be perfect for my Trenton portfolio. I want to get into their fashion design program, and Katie already has more experience than I do. Please?" April made puppy-dog eyes at me and clasped her hands together.

I couldn't help laughing. "Okay. Sure. But no spandex."

April yelped with joy and threw her arms around my shoulders as I drove. I really had no need for super-hero costumes or gadgets of any kind, but I guessed this meant we really were best friends again. "At least something good came out of tonight," I said out loud.

April let go of me and sat back down in her seat. We

were just pulling into her neighborhood. "So are you going to tell Daniel about what happened tonight?"

"Good question." Except I wished she hadn't brought it up. Any joy I'd felt in the last few minutes faded away as I thought about having to tell Daniel that I'd broken my word to him and gone looking for Jude on my own. And even if I hadn't technically been alone . . . I wasn't sure I was up for the reaction I'd get when I told him I'd almost gotten maimed in the process. Not to mention that because April and I had caused such a scene at the club, we'd probably ruined any minute chance of finding Jude through that lead.

And I didn't know why, but for some reason I felt uncomfortable telling Daniel about Talbot's coming to my rescue. Like maybe he'd worry there was something between this new guy and me when there totally wasn't.

"I will," I said to April before she got out of the car. "Eventually."

Chapter Ten

Barriers

SUNDAY MORNING

Church was cancelled for the second week in a row because Dad was *still* gone. He'd been gone for two and a half weeks straight now—his longest trip yet.

When Mom first started sending him out to look for Jude, he'd always made it a point to be back for Sunday services. I mean, it was bad enough when he missed teaching his Wednesday Bible study class. This was our livelihood, after all.

However, lately, his trips had gotten longer and longer, and today made the fifth Sunday he'd missed in the last twelve weeks, and the third time he'd forgotten—or hadn't bothered—to make arrangements for someone else to cover for him and give the sermon.

Mom woke up in one of her overbearing manic states, and she made Charity and me call every single one of the parishioners to tell them church was cancelled, and to apologize on my dad's behalf—even though *she* was the reason he'd left in the first place. But the thing was, the list of families to call kept getting shorter each time Dad missed a Sunday.

People used to come from all over Rose Crest and Oak Park, and even parts of Apple Valley, to hear the gospel from Pastor Divine. But more and more of Dad's once loyal parishioners were defecting to Pastor Clark over at New Hope—and every time Dad missed a sermon there were rumblings about the parish needing a new pastor.

The more sympathetic folks I called suggested that Dad bring in a junior pastor who would always be on call to substitute when he was gone—and perhaps pick up teaching the religion classes at the school, since Mr. Shumway had quit. But a couple of the more frustrated and rude parishioners grumbled about needing to replace Dad altogether, even if the parish had been in the hands of the Divines for the last three decades. I wondered if they would still feel the same way if I came right out and told them Dad was gone because he was looking for Jude.

I hung up from the last call, expecting to feel drained, but all I felt was anxiety. That was because there was one number I'd dialed seven times without getting an answer—Daniel's.

Why wouldn't he pick up the phone?

He's probably just sleeping, I tried to tell myself. *If*

he's still sick, then he needs rest and I shouldn't bother him.

However, tension tingled in my muscles every time my mind drifted to the image of that motorcycle that looked like his parked only a few blocks from The Depot. *But it couldn't have been his bike, could it? What would he have been doing in the city?*

No, it wasn't Daniel's bike. He was sick in bed—that's what he said, anyway.

I mean, why would he lie?

I tried to read a book for English class for a while and then tackled the mountain of chores Mom forced on Charity and me even though it was Sunday. But no matter how much I tried, I couldn't shake the restlessness in my body. I wanted out of my house. I wanted to go to Daniel.

I wanted to run.

That was one of the things I still hadn't gotten used to in all of this being-infected stuff—the need to run. I'd never been a runner before. In fact, our tenth-grade gym teacher dubbed April and me the "turtle twins" because we always came in last during the daily mile: April because she didn't care for sweating, and me because I didn't care for running. But now I often craved a good run, and I knew I wouldn't be able to relax all day if I didn't pound out the aching in my muscles on the pavement—and check on Daniel in the process.

Mom was dressing James in his jacket for an evening trip out to the senior center to visit Mrs. Ludwig and a couple of the other widows from the parish (one of Dad's Sunday tasks) when I came downstairs in my running clothes and shoes.

"Where do you think you're going?" she asked.

"I really need a run, Mom. I've finished all my homework and cleaned all the bathrooms and organized the laundry room, like you asked." More like *demanded*, but whatever. "I won't be gone too long, I promise."

The pinched look on her face convinced me she wasn't going to let me out of the house. But she snapped the last button on James's jacket and hooked her purse on her shoulder. "Very well, then. But do not go too far from home," she said. "It will be dark soon, and you never know who's out there these days."

"Okay." I didn't tell her I was planning on running all the way to Oak Park, and slipped out the door before she could change her mind.

I stopped at the walnut tree and rested my hand against it while I stretched my quads, then started out in a light jog. All day long, I hadn't been able to stop thinking about what had happened the night before. I'd had my powers in my grasp, reined them in for once, and used them for a moment. I'd sparred with Daniel time and again, but actually using my powers to really fight that guy off and protect someone I cared about was absolutely exhilarating.

And I wanted more.

I was a mile from home when the familiar aching of my powers began to well inside my body, pooling in my muscles, making my shoulders shake and my legs throb. I increased my speed to a flat-out sprint.

The sun was sinking behind the hills of Rose Crest, and I knew Mom would want me to turn back toward home. But I couldn't stop thinking about how frustrating it had been when my powers had dissipated last night and I'd had to rely on someone else to come to my aid. If I'd had better control, then I could have taken those guys on without any help. And even more frustrating was the realization that I really *did* need my powers if I was going to find Jude. Last night's debacle had proven that to me.

I concentrated on the pain engulfing my body. Tried to embrace it. Tried to will my legs to run faster and harder than ever before.

But nothing happened.

I couldn't break through whatever barrier stood between me and my being able to use my powers fully.

LATER

My legs were about as stable as putty erasers when I jogged into Daniel's neighborhood, toward Maryanne Duke's old house. I'd been hoping to be able to share good news with Daniel—tell him how I'd finally gotten a handle on my speed and agility—but instead my shoulders sagged with frustration. I didn't understand it. Why had I been able to use my powers last night, but not right now? What was the difference?

But my frustration shifted into curiosity as I approached Maryanne's house and saw Daniel out front, strapping down a duffel bag on the back of his Honda Shadow.

"Hey," I called as I jogged up the driveway.

Daniel crouched and adjusted one of the straps holding down his bag. "What're you doing here?"

"Checking up on . . . Um, just stopping by to say hi." I gave him a slight wave. "So, um, hi."

"Hi." Daniel scratched at the bandage on his forearm, then tested the hold of a second strap that secured his bag. He hadn't even looked at me yet.

"What's going on?" I fingered the zipper on his duffel. "Are you going somewhere?"

Daniel grunted, but before he could answer we both turned at the sound of a car pulling up in the driveway behind us. Not just any car—the sheriff's patrol truck. Daniel stiffened and straightened up. His dark eyes finally flicked in my direction for half a second and then returned to his duffel bag on the back of his bike. He stepped in front of it as Sheriff Ford and Deputy Marsh got out of the truck.

"Hello, there, sir," he said to the sheriff. "Is there a problem, or something I can help you with?" He sounded like someone who'd been pulled over for speeding many times—which I didn't doubt. Daniel had always had a thing for moving fast. But the pale look on Sheriff Ford's face made me pretty sure he had something much more serious than traffic tickets on his mind.

"What's wrong?" I asked.

"Either of you know a Tyler Whitney?" Ford asked.

"No," Daniel said. "Pretty sure I don't."

"Well, I have a witness who says you do." He pointed at the bandage on Daniel's arm. "Someone says you got into an altercation with Tyler and a couple of his friends the other night."

"Wait. Tyler?" I looked up at Daniel. His expression was like stone. "I think he means Pete Bradshaw's friend Ty." *The one I saw at the club last night.* "This is totally bogus," I said to the sheriff. "Because if they're pressing charges, then you should know that Daniel and I were minding our own business when they approached us. Daniel only acted in self-defense."

"Grace," Daniel said, a warning tone in his voice.

"What? They should know the truth."

"Looks like you got pretty hurt," Deputy Marsh said. "You weren't looking for a little payback, were you? Didn't track Tyler down and try to teach him a lesson for messing with you? Maybe went a little too far?"

"What?" Daniel stared Deputy Marsh right in the eyes. "I have no idea what you're talking about. Did something happen to this Tyler kid?"

Sheriff Ford cleared his throat. "He's dead."

My stomach lurched. "What happened?"

"His roommate, a Pete Bradshaw"—Sheriff Ford consulted his notepad—"found him outside their apartment this morning. Looks like he was jumped in the parking lot and beaten to death sometime during the night."

"Pete told us you had an altercation with him two nights ago," Deputy Marsh said. "He said you'd be looking for revenge."

"That's insane," I said. "Daniel would never attack anyone." Well, at least not the new, werewolf-free Daniel. "Pete's a total liar. He'd say anything to get Daniel in trouble."

"I assure you, sir, I had nothing to do with this," Daniel said to the sheriff, sounding much calmer than I did.

"You two have quite the history with Mr. Bradshaw, as I recall." Deputy Marsh glared at Daniel. "Perhaps you were looking to settle an old score with Pete, but went after his roommate when you couldn't find him. You must have been angry when the charges were dropped in your girlfriend's case, considering the only other witness died. Most guys wouldn't take it lightly if their girl was attacked by a classmate who got off without even a slap on the wrists. Perhaps the fight from the other night was the final straw."

"Marsh," the sheriff snapped. Ford liked Daniel a

lot more than his deputy did, and he had a lot of respect for my father. Either that, or they were doing a great job at playing good cop/bad cop. "I'm not at liberty to discuss the details, but we have reason to believe that Tyler's death may have been connected with the burglary at Day's Market, but since you had an altercation with Tyler and you work at Day's, we need to ask you a few questions. We can do it here or at the station."

"Wait, now you're blaming him for Day's Market, too?"

"We're not blaming, just investigating."

Anger roiled in my stomach. Pete and his stupid accusations were making a fine mess of our lives. If Tyler and the market were connected, then this probably had more to do with his being at The Depot last night. *Gah! Of course. The Depot!* Those gamer guys had looked like they wanted to skin Tyler alive for messing up their game. What if they'd followed him home and decided to mess him up in return?

"Tyler likes to hang out a place called The Depot . . . in the city. Maybe you should—"

Daniel shot me a weighted look.

Deputy Marsh's thin eyebrows perked into arches. "So you're aware of Tyler's whereabouts last night? That's interesting. His friends were supposed to meet him at a place called The Depot, but he wasn't around when they got there. Were you two following him?"

"Um . . . no." Crap, how come everything I said

made Daniel look guiltier? How could I tell them what I saw at the club without letting them know that I'd been there myself? It would only make it sound like I was following Tyler. "I'm just saying that I've heard it's a dangerous place, and if Tyler went there and stepped on the wrong toes . . . like messed up someone's video game, they might be mad enough to take it out on him."

"You think Tyler was killed over a video game?" Deputy Marsh asked.

"It's possible," I said, but I didn't sound like even I believed myself at this point. I really probably should just shut up.

"We'll look into it," Ford said. "But in the meantime, I have to ask you, Daniel, about your whereabouts last night."

Daniel tensed beside me. I could almost feel the stress radiating off his body. He'd seemed so calm until this moment. I looked at him, waiting for his reply.

"I was here," he said slowly, deliberately, "watching TV."

"Between the hours of ten p.m. and one a.m.? What did you watch? Times? Channels? Any specific commercials you can remember?"

"Um . . ." Daniel's fingers twitched next to mine. I wanted to grab his hand to calm the tic before the others noticed it—but that would probably be just as noticeable. "I don't recall anything specific."

"Really," Deputy Marsh asked, "nothing at all?" He put his hands on his hips and puffed out his chest like he was preparing to grab Daniel and haul him down to the station. The cocky smile on his face made it seem like he'd enjoy doing it, too.

Daniel took a slight step back, his fingers still twitching. "I'm sorry. I really can't remember."

I stepped forward. "What he means is that he was distracted. We were here . . . together. The TV was on, but we weren't exactly, you know, watching it." I blushed even though I wasn't telling the truth, but hopefully it would blend in with the red splotches that always painted my neck whenever I lied.

Daniel gave me a look like he was surprised by my acting abilities—but hopefully grateful.

"I stayed until about two a.m. Daniel just didn't mention it because, you know . . . you won't tell my dad, will you?" I asked, wringing my hands. I didn't even have to *act* that part. "Please?"

Sheriff Ford cleared his throat. "And you're sure you were here with him the whole time, alone?"

I nodded.

"Very well, then." Ford slipped his notepad into his pocket. "That's all I needed to know."

Marsh's shoulders dropped, though the cocky smirk stayed on his face. He indicated the duffel bag strapped to Daniel's bike. "I hope you're not planning on leaving town anytime soon."

"No, sir," Daniel said quietly.

"We'll be watching you," Deputy Marsh said.

Daniel and I stood side by side and watched the two officers climb into the truck and drive away. Daniel's fingers twitched even after they were gone. I grabbed his hand before he could turn away.

"So tell me," I said. "Where *were* you last night?"

A FULL SIXTY SECONDS OF SILENCE LATER

The longer Daniel went without speaking, the more my muscles tensed. I could feel that familiar aching inside of me—like I did when I knew something was wrong. It was that same feeling that made me want to fight or run.

Daniel tugged at my grasp on his hand. I was squeezing it tighter than I realized. His fingertips were bright red.

I let go of his hand. I felt a rush of guilt as he rubbed his fingers and then the bandage on his forearm. I was sure I'd aggravated the pain of his stitches. But that guilt edged into anger. *Why should you feel guilty when he's the one in the wrong?* a foreign voice said inside my mind. I shook myself. I don't know why I'd even thought that. There was no excuse for causing someone pain.

"Why won't you tell me where you were last night?" I asked. "It should be a simple question."

Daniel scratched behind his ear and looked off into the twilight that surrounded us now. "I said it already.

I was here. Watching TV."

He's lying, said that foreign voice inside my head. *You lied to the cops for him, and he pays you back with more lies.*

I took a step back. Why was I hearing a voice inside my head that didn't even sound like my own? But it pointed out the blaring truth.

"I just lied to the cops for you, Daniel. Don't you think you owe me an explanation as to why I needed to?"

"I never asked you to lie." Daniel shoved his hands in his pockets. It was like he didn't know what to do with his twitching fingers. "I don't owe you anything."

"You don't?" My voice cracked with anger. "After all we've been through?" *After everything you've done for him!* that voice said. "I saved your damned soul—quite literally—and you think you don't owe me a simple explanation as to where you were last night? What the hell were you doing?"

"That's not what I meant." Daniel dropped his shoulders and looked up at the sky. "I just . . . can't."

"Can't what? Tell me? Trust me?" I practically shouted at him. It was like I couldn't control the volume of my voice.

"Please, Gracie. Just be patient with me. I need you to stay out of it. Give me some space."

"Some space?" Fire burned under my skin. I shook with anger and surging power. Something was wrong.

Most definitely wrong. *Fight or Flight,* that voice whispered inside my head. But a small, rational part of my brain didn't want to lash out at Daniel, so I did what felt like second nature to me now. "Have all the space you want," I said, and ran.

"Wait, Gracie!" Daniel shouted as I bolted down the driveway. "Damn it, that's not what I meant."

But I kept running—even when I heard the roar of Daniel's motorcycle behind me. I picked up my speed. He shouted my name, told me to stop. But I couldn't. Power seeped into every cell of my body, pushing me faster. Daniel pulled up beside me on his motorcycle. I could hear him calling me, but I veered up onto the curb and cut through several yards and weaved in between houses where he couldn't follow.

And even though I knew I'd shaken Daniel, I didn't slow down. The crescent-shaped scar on my arm flared like crazy. I picked up my already sprinting pace. I ran faster now than I could have ever dreamed of only a few months before. But I willed myself to go even faster.

My legs screamed for more speed.

I needed it.

Craved it.

My feet picked up momentum like lightning under me. The night was dark now, but as the blood pulsed into my face, I felt a burning pressure behind my eyes. I blinked and suddenly my vision was clearer, sharper, almost as if the night had brightened. I could see just as well as if it were dusk on a cloudy day.

But the thing was, I didn't need to see. My feet knew where to go on instinct. They landed in just the right places, narrowly missing the cracks and potholes in the uneven streets. They found the easiest path between the headstones and overgrown bushes in the graveyard on Faraway Boulevard. And with every lightning-quick step, the pain and anger inside of me melted away, replaced by a feeling of sheer exhilaration.

Freedom.

Abandon.

Like how I'd felt the first time I ran with Daniel in the forest. Back when he was the one who had to pull me along. Back when I was only human. It had felt wonderful then . . . like nothing I'd known before. But this was so much more than that. Not merely energy transferred from someone else. This came from inside of *me*. This was *my* power. And no one could take it away from me.

I tilted my head back, taking in the glow of the glistening sliver of a moon rising in the night sky as I ran, and let that feeling of power wash through me. Tingling warmth spread up my arms and legs and into my chest. *You're in control now,* that foreign voice reassured me as I ran.

I'd finally broken through the barrier.

CHAPTER ELEVEN

Stranger

AN HOUR LATER

The moon peeked over the steeple of the parish as I sprinted down Crescent Street. It was a Sunday, and a school night, and most of Rose Crest had gone to bed. I'd passed only a couple of cars on the street, and the parking lot for the school and the parish was empty. It felt exhilarating to have gone so far, done so much, while most of the town was tucked in bed at home. And I still couldn't believe that I'd run full tilt for so long, using all my powers at the same time without losing my grip on them. Part of me wanted to go back to Daniel's—tell him the good news, see the look of pride on his face. But then I remembered why I'd started running in the first place, and my heart sank with sorrow.

I slowed my pace to a jog. I had only a few more blocks until home, and I wanted to cool down. But then

I noticed something strange about the parish as I went past: the lights were on.

It was late, and Dad was still out of town. I knew it was possible that the lights had been left on at some point over the weekend, but a feeling—kind of like an extra sense—told me that someone, or something, was inside the building.

But who would be in there at this hour?

My thoughts immediately went to what happened at the market, the report about the attempted break-in at the school, and Daniel's speculation that Jude was revisiting the places of his past misdeeds. First Maryanne's house, James's window, Day's Market, and then the school. Wouldn't the logical next place be the parish—the final place he'd go? The place where he'd ultimately turned into a werewolf, the place where he'd attacked me, infected me, and where he'd tried to kill Daniel?

I didn't want to believe that Jude was trying to cause damage and terror on purpose. But if this *was* his final stop on his tour of his past crimes, then this could be my only chance to find him—especially since my only other lead hadn't panned out.

I slowed my pace even more as I approached the parish, and I tried to will my heart to stop pounding so loudly. I listened as closely as I could over my disobedient heartbeat, concentrating on far-off noises: the sound of a car on the empty evening streets, a song whistled by another person somewhere down the block, the chirp of the crosswalk meter.

I followed another sound, a rustling noise, like boxes or objects being moved around, down the alley between the parish and the school. At first I thought the noise came from my father's office. I hesitated for a moment outside the door in the alley, but then I realized the sound came from somewhere deeper inside the parish. I slipped around the side of the building to another door in the back. It was the entrance to the small caretaker's apartment that had been unoccupied since Don Mooney died. Dad hadn't rented out the apartment again, and it had been left untouched since the day we heard about Don's death.

My ears picked up a rattling from behind the door. It sounded like a stuck drawer being forced open. Suddenly, I wasn't thinking about rescuing Jude anymore. I was thinking about the destruction caused at Day's Market. All the anger I'd felt today filled me again. *Someone might be trying to do the same to your father's parish,* said that voice in my head. *Starting in your friend's old home.* I wasn't going to let someone get away with that—even if that someone was my own brother.

That rumbling anger surged through me. Clutched at my heart like a clawed hand. Before I could stop myself, I burst through the doorway into the room.

A tall man whirled around in front of Don's desk. Something silver flashed in his hand. My feet and arms were not my own as I flew at him. A look of shock crossed his face as I knocked the knife from his hand and hit him in the chest with the butt of my hand. He flew back and slammed against the wall, and then landed on top of the desk. I jumped on top of him and grabbed him by the throat.

"How dare you," I snarled. "How dare you try to steal my friend's things?" I raised my fist above the man's face, ready to smash it into his nose if he so much as made a false move.

But the man didn't struggle. He just stared up at me. My breaths heaved in my chest, and my hand trembled with rage as I held my fist above his head. But I couldn't help staring back into his steel-blue eyes—eyes that seemed familiar, like I'd gazed into them before. The man seemed young, mid-twenties maybe, but something about his eyes seemed absolutely ancient—like he'd seen enough of the world to fill a dozen lifetimes.

My fingers twitched against his throat. I could feel his pulse in my hand, steady and sure. Something foreign and hateful inside my head told me to squeeze. *Punish this man for invading this place.*

But did I really want to do that?

A smile slid across the stranger's lips. It seemed as ancient as his eyes. "Hello, Grace," he said, sounding somewhat strangled.

At the sound of my name, the power clutching my heart eased a bit. I gasped at the sight of my hand gripping his throat. But I didn't let go. I couldn't until I knew what this man was doing here. "How do you know me?" I demanded.

I looked the man over for the first time. Or what little I could see of him, since I was straddling him, pinning his arms down with my knees. He had longish auburn hair and a short trimmed beard. He was tall, almost as tall as Don Mooney—whom I always thought of as being as big as a grizzly—had been, but slim. He wore black from head to toe, which had made him seem sinister at first. But then, a horrible realization dawned on me as I noticed the white square notch in his black collar— a pastor's collar, like the one my dad sometimes wore when he was working.

"Oh, no!" I let go of his throat and scrambled off him as fast as I could. I clutched at the moonstone pendant that hung from my own neck. I let its warm, calming strength wash through me. "I'm sorry, Pastor. I'm so sorry." Heat seared my cheeks. "I don't know what came over me, Pastor . . . I just . . . just . . ." I let my sentence trail off. How could I possibly explain what I had just done to this man?

I mean, I had attacked a pastor—in a freaking church! My anger had been replaced by embarrassment, which quickly edged into shame.

"I'm sorry," I said again. Could I possibly apologize enough? "I saw you in here with that knife . . ." I pointed at the silver dagger, lodged in the ground with its handle sticking straight up in the air. A small scrap of fabric had fluttered to the ground near the knife when I'd knocked it from the man's hand. It was Don's infamous knife—the one that I'd plunged into Daniel's chest. The one I'd used to break the curse. I'd found it in the parish a few weeks later, brought it here to Don's apartment, and left it with his things, where it belonged.

"I thought you were a burglar. I thought you were trying to steal that knife." The knife was ancient, made of very pure silver, and I always figured it could fetch a nice price with the right buyer. But pastors don't break into churches and steal stuff. There had to be some other explanation.

The man smiled again, and with a quick movement he reached down and picked up the scrap of cloth and then wrapped it around the hilt of the silver knife and pulled it out of its sticking place in the floor. He looked at the dagger with appraising eyes, like a collector inspecting an antique. "How can I steal something that already belongs to me?"

"What?" I looked at him again—the body of a young man with the eyes of an ancient seer. I noticed the way he gingerly held the knife in his hand, careful to keep the scrap of fabric between his skin and the knife. I could think of only one reason that this man would be afraid to touch silver.

My muscles tensed immediately as the thought took

root in my brain. This man *wasn't* a pastor. This man wasn't even human. Then another thought surpassed those, and my body trembled with fear. *They're coming for you. He makes you think you can trust him, but you can't,* Jude's voice echoed in my head.

"I'm sorry," I said, backing away toward the door. "I need to go." I bumped into a chair and tried to steady myself without looking too frantic. I didn't know what I'd been thinking coming into this room in the first place; I was no match for this man. I might have fought a couple of punks at a nightclub last night and run at full capacity without faltering this evening, but that was nothing, I realized now. No matter what kind of power I could summon, it was nothing compared to what he could do to me. This man was dangerous. This man was a werewolf.

This man was—

"Gabriel!"

"What?" I whirled around toward the open door.

Daniel stood there, his mouth hanging open. He dropped his motorcycle keys in the doorway and lunged for the man with the knife. But it wasn't an offensive strike. The man grabbed Daniel by the arm, and the two embraced. It was a quick hug, but a hug nonetheless.

"Daniel, my boy!" The man clapped him on the back. "You're looking much better since Christmas. Although I was hoping to see you without any bandages."

Daniel shook his head. "You have no idea how much I need to talk to you right now."

I glanced away from the two.

"Always glad to be of service."

I shifted from one foot to the other and cleared my throat.

They turned toward me. "Grace," Daniel said, "this is Gabriel."

"Gabriel the Angel?" That was how I'd always referred to him in my head, because of the statue of him in the Garden of Angels.

"*Angel*, huh? Sounds like Daniel's been making up stories about me." Gabriel's lips edged up in an ancient, friendly smile.

"I'm sorry to sound rude, but why are you here?" I couldn't help asking. And how had Daniel followed me?

"Because I brought him here," my dad said as he came through the narrow doorway into the already crowded room. "Gabriel came to help us."

"You're back!" I sprang at Dad the way Daniel had lunged at Gabriel, and wrapped my arms around his middle. As mad as I'd been at him for being gone, I couldn't help feeling a rush of relief that he was here. "I thought you didn't know when you were coming back."

"I didn't," Dad said. "I wasn't sure how long it was going to take to track down Gabriel and convince him to come to Rose Crest."

"But why didn't you tell me that's where you were headed in the first place?"

"Because I didn't want either you or Daniel trying to come after me."

"Why?"

"Because hunting down a werewolf pack and visiting their den without an invitation is a dangerous and fool-hardy endeavor. Especially for a human," Gabriel said. "Your father is lucky he's good with words. Sirhan, my alpha, was quite intrigued by his stories."

I let go of Dad and turned back toward Gabriel.

"Your father was also lucky that I was already hoping to pay you a visit," Gabriel said. "I've been wanting to meet you, Grace."

"Me?"

"You're gaining quite the reputation in my pack. They call you the Divine One."

"The what?"

"It's a silly name, yes. But they can't help being fascinated by you. In the four thousand years since the first Urbat succumbed to the curse, nobody has ever cured someone the way you cured Daniel."

Gabriel clapped Daniel on the back again, but this time Daniel dropped his gaze to his feet. Red flushed his face. I didn't know why he'd be embarrassed by the notion that he'd been saved. But then again, sometimes I wondered if he still thought he wasn't worthy of it. Or maybe he just didn't want to look me in the eye. We were still in a fight, after all.

"They think you're something quite special, Grace." Gabriel crossed the distance between the two of us and took my hand. He held it for a moment and then bowed his head. The gesture felt like something from centuries ago.

I was the one blushing now. I glanced at Daniel to see what he made of this "Divine One" idea, but he was still staring at his feet. I looked back at Gabriel. "And you? Do you think I'm *special*?"

Gabriel gently let go of my hand. "I'm here to find out."

It was then that the idea hit me. With Gabriel here, I finally had the chance to reach my full potential. I had someone with the same abilities as me who could really teach me how to use them. No offense to Daniel or anything, but it was hard for him to show me how to use powers that he didn't have anymore. I mean, I'd outrun him even when he'd been on a motorcycle. But Gabriel had been using his superpowers for more than eight hundred years. And he was the one who thought it was possible for the Urbat to reclaim their blessings—to use their powers to help the world. Or at least that was what he'd written in those letters to his sister Katharine.

Using my powers to run this evening had been amazing. But now that Gabriel was here to help, my becoming a hero actually felt possible.

Dad cleared his throat. I'd all but forgotten he was still there. "Let's move this gathering to my office so we can discuss what to do about Jude. It's time to figure out how we're going to find him."

A FEW MINUTES LATER, IN MY DAD'S OFFICE AT THE PARISH

Gabriel sat in one of the cushiony chairs in front of my dad's desk. It was so strange how he looked so young yet so old at the same time. And even stranger to be standing here listening to him talking for the first time when I already felt like I knew him so well. Reading the book of letters he had written to his sister all those centuries ago made it seem as if I'd looked into his soul. I was practically bursting to tell him my idea about wanting him to train me.

"Grace?" Dad said. His tone of his voice suggested he'd had to say my name a few times before getting my attention.

"What?" I pulled my gaze off Gabriel and looked at my dad.

He raised his eyebrows above the rims of his glasses. "I just asked you to tell us about the phone call from Jude."

"Oh." I told them about the call and what Jude had said about someone coming for us. "He also said that I couldn't trust someone."

"Sounds like Jude may still have it out for Daniel," Dad said. "He still thinks we shouldn't trust you." Dad looked at Daniel. He sat in the far corner, picking at the white bandage on his arm.

"What else is new?" Daniel mumbled. It was the first thing he'd said since we'd left Don Mooney's apartment.

"I think the more significant part of the conversation is that Jude said that there was someone *coming* for you," Gabriel said. "Do you have any idea what he means?"

"Not a clue." I shrugged. "Daniel thinks he's just messing with us, but I don't think he'd come back here just for a sick joke."

"Depends on how far gone your brother is. The wolf can make you do all sorts of sick things." Gabriel pulled at the pastor's collar around his neck. I wondered if he was thinking about Katharine—the sister he'd killed after he became a werewolf. "But I think it is safe to assume that you are all in danger if Jude is anywhere near here."

"Which means we need to find him soon." Dad leaned forward in his chair. "And we're going to need a proper plan of attack. I think it's only logical to assume that Jude may have contacted other people from his past. I'd like you to find a way to bring the subject up with April. Find out if she's heard anything from him."

"I already have," I said.

"And?"

I told them about my visit to April's house and what she told me about her blog and tracking Jude's IP address. "It was for a club in the city. They have a Wi-Fi bar there that he must have used. Get this, Daniel, it's called The *Depot*." I looked at Daniel, but he didn't even glance in my direction. Whatever temporary good mood seeing Gabriel had put him in was apparently gone now. I cleared my throat and turned to my dad. "I found a card for the club in the mess at Day's Market."

Dad sat up a bit. He must have recognized it as a clue, the same way I had—unlike Daniel, who had originally scoffed at the idea.

"Hmm," Daniel said from his corner. I glanced back at him. His eyebrows knitted together as he scratched at the tape on his bandage. "I've been asking around about the place. Not good stuff."

"Who did you ask?" I gave Daniel a pointed look that he didn't see. "Is that what you were doing last night?" But if that were the case, why wouldn't he have just told me?

Daniel ignored my questions and looked at my dad. "Maybe you and I should go down there tonight and ask around. I don't want Grace to go."

"Um . . ." I hesitated. "I kind of already did."

"Grace!" Daniel and my dad bellowed at the same time.

"Do you have any idea what kind of people—not to mention *nonpeople*—hang out there?" Daniel asked, looking at me for the first time. Except it was more like a glare.

"Well, I do *now*."

Daniel almost cracked a smile, but he shifted it quickly back into a look of annoyance. "I thought I asked you not to go looking for Jude on your own."

"I know. But you were sick, or so you *claimed*, so I didn't want to bug you." Except Daniel didn't look sick at all. Not even earlier when I was at his place. "And April said she knew where it was, and I had the key-card, so we kind of teamed up."

"Whoa, you took April with you? Grace, do you have any idea how—?"

"Spare me the lecture, okay? It was stupid. I should've known better. We could have been killed. . . ."

"What? Are you okay?" Daniel asked, his voice suddenly softer. It was the first time he'd sounded like my boyfriend all evening. "Did someone hurt you?"

"No." I looked away from his concerned gaze, trying to hide the red lie on my neck. I definitely didn't feel like bringing up what happened with those two guys and Talbot now. "The point is that I went down there and asked around and found nothing. It's probably been weeks since he's been there."

"And any chance of finding him through that club has probably been lost," Gabriel said.

I groaned. "Don't remind me."

"I still want to go down there and see what I can find," Dad said.

"You can't get in without the keycard." I gave him a sheepish grin. "And I think I kind of dropped it while I was there." I hadn't been able to find it since Talbot dragged us out of there.

Dad made a grumbling noise.

"I've got some contacts," Daniel said. "I'll ask around again. See if I can get a new card."

"Can you think of anyone else Jude might try to contact?" Dad asked me.

I shook my head.

"Hmm." Dad rubbed his temples, like he was trying to ward off a headache. "I'm going to have to mull this over a bit more before we come up with a plan B. In the meantime, we need to figure out what to do with you, Grace."

"What to do with me?"

"I don't want you running off all half-cocked again. If I can't trust you to use your head, then maybe you need to be grounded. No more unauthorized visits to the city. Pull back on your training and hit the books again for a while."

"What? No!" I'd been surprised when Dad had been supportive of the idea of my training in the first place. I knew he felt guilty that he hadn't told Jude what was happening to him. So when I finally told Dad that I had been infected, he said, "Knowledge is power," and gave me all of his books on werewolf lore. He even bought me some books on karate and self-defense. I think he hoped they'd help me develop my abilities without losing control like Jude. Not that you can really learn how to fight from a book, but that was just the way Dad operated— anything important could be found in a book, as far as he was concerned.

But why would he try to take that away from me now? Especially with Gabriel here to train me?

"Dad, you can't do this. Not now. I'm just starting to be able to really tap into my powers. I ran at full speed for almost an hour and a half this evening. And last night I . . ." I let that thought drop before I said too much.

"What's all this?" Gabriel asked. "You've been *training* for what?"

Gabriel! Yes, he was the one who could help me convince Dad.

"Daniel and I have been working on developing my superpowers. We think I can become a Hound of Heaven, like what you wrote about the Urbat. How these powers are meant to help people. How they can be a blessing and not a curse. Daniel's been trying to teach me how to use my abilities, and I'm just starting to figure it out, but now that you're here, you can teach me everything you know. You can help me finally tap into the power. If you train me, then you can help me reclaim the Urbat blessings, just like you told your sister you wanted to do in those letters."

Gabriel stood up from his chair. He tugged on the pastor's collar and cleared his throat. "No, Grace. I think it's a terrible idea. Training is the last thing someone like you should be doing."

I took a step back. That wasn't the response I'd expected. "But you saw me fight a few minutes ago. I'm getting stronger and faster. I mean, you saw what I'm capable of . . ."

"Yes, Grace. I saw exactly what you're capable of. And that's why I won't train you. Daniel should have never started in the first place. What you did back there was lose control. You wanted to hurt me. I saw it in your eyes."

"Yes . . ." I felt tongue-tied by frustration. Gabriel was basing his entire summation of my character on that one incident. He didn't really know me. "But that's never happened before. And it won't happen again. It was one brief lapse . . . I can do this—"

"One brief lapse is all that it takes, Grace. Do you have any idea how close you were to losing yourself to the wolf? All you'd had to do was squeeze."

Dad shot up from his chair. I didn't know what he wanted to do, but he hesitated and glanced between Gabriel and me, obviously realizing that he'd missed something before coming into Don's apartment. Daniel sat frozen like a statue in his chair, staring at the floor.

"Daniel, tell them. This was your idea in the first place. You're the one who convinced me that I could become a hero. You know I can do this." Daniel owed me this, and I tried to get that across in my tone of voice. After all that crap in his driveway, and whatever secrets he was keeping, *this* was his chance to make up for being a jackass. "Tell them."

Daniel took a deep breath. He didn't look up at me. "I'm sorry, Grace," he said sternly. "But I think they're right."

"What?"

My lips trembled. I should have been angry, but all I felt was hurt. Tears stung behind my eyes, but I forced them back. Bursting out crying right now wasn't going to convince anyone that I was the pinnacle of control. I couldn't look at Daniel anymore.

"But you said I was special," I said to Gabriel, trying one more time to get through to him. "Isn't that why you wanted to come here? And isn't this what you wanted? Isn't this what you told Katharine you wanted to do? Find a way to help the Urbat use these powers for good? Fight the good fight?"

"I wrote those letters eight hundred and thirty years ago, Grace. I *used* to think that these powers could be used for good. I don't believe in fighting anymore. I don't use my powers if I can help it." Gabriel stepped toward me. "You *are* special, Grace. I can tell just by hearing how badly you want to save your brother. But that's why we can't lose you to the curse." He reached for my hand again.

I pulled it away. This person standing in front of me wasn't the Gabriel I'd expected—the Gabriel I'd imagined meeting someday. This wasn't the Gabriel I'd gotten to know through those letters.

I didn't know this man at all.

"You *can* help people, Grace," he said. "But not in the way you're thinking. There are other ways to be a hero in this world. That I *am* willing to teach you if you'll let me."

I let out a long breath between my teeth. "Fine," I said, even though I felt far from it. I just didn't want to talk anymore. How could the three people who were supposed to help turn their backs on me?

Dad tapped his desk with his knuckles and sat back down in his chair. "I need to get some work done here. But the three of you should get to bed. You've all got school in the morning."

"All of us?" Daniel asked.

Gabriel tugged on his collar.

"Meet Pastor Saint Moon, junior pastor and your new religion teacher," Dad said. "Gabriel will be taking over Mr. Shumway's religion classes and covering for me at the parish if I need to leave again."

"He's the new religion teacher?" My mind couldn't really wrap itself around the idea of an eight-hundred-something-year-old Catholic monk turned werewolf teaching religion classes at a Protestant private school for teenagers. But the part that bothered me was that my mental decision to never talk to Gabriel again wasn't going to work if he invaded my school life—and especially not if he was going to be my freaking teacher.

"This'll be interesting," I said, a little too much sarcasm in my voice.

"I agree." Gabriel grimaced. "But do I have to wear this stupid collar? Makes me feel like a dog on somebody else's leash."

"Get used to it," I said.

"Grace," Dad snapped, with a very knock-it-off tone. "You should get home. Daniel, will you see Grace back to the house?"

I glanced at Daniel and crossed my arms in front of my chest. I wasn't in the mood to go anywhere with him, but I'd already learned it was of no use to protest this sort of thing.

"Actually, sir"—Daniel got up from his chair—"I really need to speak with Gabriel—alone. It can't wait any longer."

Dad glanced from Daniel to me, as if noticing the tension between us for the first time. "Very well." Dad picked up a book and put it in his bag. "I'll finish up here as quickly as I can and then she can go home with me."

Daniel nodded. He picked up his duffel bag and motioned for Gabriel to go with him outside. He didn't even glance my way before leaving.

Gabriel put his hand on my shoulder. "We'll become fast friends yet, Grace." He gave me an ancient smile. His eyes crinkled with age in his otherwise smooth, youthful face. "You look so much like Katharine, you know. At least what little of her I can remember." He tapped his forehead and then let go of my shoulder. He followed Daniel out of the office.

"I'll just be a few minutes," my dad said.

I nodded and leaned against the door Gabriel had just closed behind him. I held my breath and concentrated as hard as I could, listening beyond the thick metal door. My ears burned only slightly—it was getting easier to call on this power—and then I heard Gabriel's voice.

"What is it, my boy?" he asked Daniel. They sounded like they were a good twenty feet from the door.

"I don't know," Daniel said. His voice was even farther away now. From the sound of it, they were walking toward the back of the parish. Probably back to Don's apartment. I assumed that was where Gabriel would be staying. "I'm not sure what—"

"Gracie," Dad called from his desk.

I jumped. It sounded like he'd screamed into my oversensitive ears. I shook my head, and my super-hearing dissipated.

"Go call your mother and tell her you're with me. I imagine she was expecting you home a while ago."

"Oh. Yeah." I hesitated for a moment and tried to

hone in on Daniel and Gabriel's conversation again, but then a sneaking voice filled my mind. *Already using your powers for ill? Spying on the person you love? Good for you.*

I clutched my hands to my head and stepped away from the door. How could I let myself think such disturbing things?

CHAPTER TWELVE

Good Samaritan

SCHOOL, THE NEXT DAY

Pretty much everyone was in a flurry about the new religion teacher on Monday. Considering the median age of teachers at HTA was well over forty, having such a young (if only by appearance) new teacher was *something* to talk about.

"I hear he's cute," April said as we walked to senior religion studies—the last class of the day.

I was glad for her company, since Daniel and I were apparently avoiding each other today. Or at least I was, considering the fact that I'd chosen to sit next to April in the back of the art room since her tablemate was out sick. April had spent most of art class sketching out costume designs for me. Even though I didn't much care for wearing a violet-purple cape with a big sequined *WG* (for Wolf Girl!) on the back, I didn't have the heart to tell her I'd been grounded from training—and if Daniel, Gabriel, and Dad had anything to say about it, I'd never have a need for any of her designs. But now I almost wished April would go back to the subject of optimal crime-fighting footwear, because debating the finer points of Gabriel, or Pastor Saint Moon, or whoever he was supposed to be, wasn't exactly something I wanted to do.

April sighed as we walked through the classroom door. "Yep, he's cute all right. Actually, I think *handsome* is more the word for him, don't you think? Cute implies a certain boyishness, but . . ."

I leaned in close to her ear. "You know he's, like, an eight-hundred-and-something-year-old werewolf, right?"

"What?" April asked about ten more questions in a single breath, but I have to admit I tuned her out.

Gabriel stood next to Daniel's desk. They both looked over a piece of paper in Daniel's hand. I knew I could switch on my superhearing—it really was getting quite easy to control that power—to overhear what they were saying, but I didn't like the idea of using my abilities to spy on Daniel. I also knew I could probably just walk right over there and ask what they were up to. I usually sat next to Daniel anyway. But I honestly wasn't ready to talk to either of them yet. And since Daniel hadn't made any effort to try to talk to me since last night, let alone apologize for lying about his whereabouts and then turning his back on me, I pulled a babbling April to the opposite side of the room.

"Hey, Grace," Miya Nagamatsu said after I sat down in front of her.

"Hi." I smiled at her. Mostly because her presence meant April stopped asking me questions about Gabriel's were-status.

"We never see you around anymore."

I shrugged. That was the thing about when April and I stopped being friends. It was as if we'd had an unspoken agreement that she'd get to keep all our other friends, like Miya, Claire, and Lane. They usually ate lunch together at the Rose Crest Café while I stayed back in the art room to work with Daniel and sometimes Katie Summers. Only today, Daniel had taken off as soon as the lunch bell rang, so it was just Katie and me working on our paintings—and she'd definitely been less talkative without Daniel around.

"Yeah," said Claire. "We miss you."

"Thanks, guys."

"Did you and Daniel break up or something?" Miya pointed at Daniel across the room. "You guys are usually glued at the hip."

As if on cue, Daniel looked up at me. Our eyes met for a moment, and he gave me half a smile. More sadness laced his expression than I'd expected to see. It made my heart feel hollow.

What is *going on with him?*

"No," I said to Miya, "I just felt like a change today." But I suddenly felt the urge to close the distance between

Daniel and me. Yes, Daniel had lied, and he hadn't backed me up when I needed him, but he was obviously going through something. I hated myself for being stupid and petty and not being there for him now.

But just then Katie Summers slipped into the empty desk next to Daniel, where I usually sat. She leaned over and asked Daniel a question. He took his eyes off me and answered her.

The bell rang. I begrudgingly turned my attention to Gabriel as he introduced himself to the class. He wrote the words *Pastor Saint Moon* on the dry-erase board at the front of the room. I wondered why he used that name. It was his sister's married name—not his.

"I'm new to Rose Crest, but I imagine some of you knew my uncle, Donald Saint Moon. Though most of you probably knew him as Don Mooney."

I almost let out a short laugh. The idea that Don had been Gabriel's *uncle* was somewhat amusing—it was more like he was his great-great-great-multiplied-by-ten grandnephew.

"I want to jump right in where Mr. Shumway left off. Who remembers what you discussed last week?"

Katie's hand shot straight up. "We had just started a discussion on the parable of the Good Samaritan. We read the scriptural account the last time Mr. Shumway was here."

"Grace"—Gabriel turned toward me—"can you tell us what you know about the Good Samaritan?"

"What?" The only thing I could think of at the moment was how the guy in the leather jacket had called Talbot the Good Samaritan when he'd stopped the fight in the club. The image of Talbot leaning over me as I lay on the ground—offering his hand to help, fog swirling behind him—flashed in my mind. I pushed the mental picture out of my head. It was a stupid thing to think about, and surely not what Gabriel had meant.

"Can you summarize the story for us?" Gabriel asked.

"Oh yeah, sure."

"Stand up so everyone can see you."

I stood. "A Jewish man had been robbed, beaten, and left for dead on the side of the road. Two wealthy men of his own people saw him and did nothing because they were scared. But when a Samaritan—who the Jews hated—saw him, he took pity on the man and brought him to an inn and paid to make sure he was nursed back to health."

"And what does that mean to you?"

I thought about it for a moment. "It means that if you have the ability and the opportunity to help someone, but you don't do anything just because you're scared or it's inconvenient or something, then maybe you're just as bad as the people who caused the problem in the first place."

"Good analysis," he said. "Thank you."

I was about to sit back down, but something about

that explanation bothered me. "So doesn't that mean if you have the *abilities* needed to help someone, then you should do it? I mean, the Good Samaritan could have just kept on walking like everyone else. But he chose to do something instead. That's what makes him a hero. He didn't let *fear* hold him back."

"Yes, but the Samaritan also didn't try to hunt down the bandits and fight them. He helped the wounded man through charity and compassion. Violence and fighting are not the answer."

"But what if you're at war? What if it's a battle between good and evil? Shouldn't you 'fight fire with fire'?" I looked at Daniel, because that was how he'd described the reason for God's creating the Urbat in the first place. In the battle against the devil and demons, God had created His own warriors to protect humankind. He'd imbued them with the essence of the most powerful beast in their highland forests—ancient wolves—in order to "fight fire with fire." I looked back at Gabriel. "When you're at war with someone evil, then it's totally different, right? Sometimes you have to use extreme tactics to protect the ones you love?"

Gabriel cleared his throat. "Believe me, Grace. I've been to war. That's not a place you want to go."

I didn't know what to say in return, so Gabriel and I just stood there, staring at each other for a moment, until Claire asked from behind me, "Were you in the Middle East?"

Gabriel blinked and looked at her. "I'm sorry, what?"

"The Middle East? The war? My brother's in Iraq."

Gabriel took a step back. "Oh, yes. I've been to the Middle East."

"What's it like?"

"I don't remember. It was a long time ago." His voice was soft, and I wasn't sure he said it loud enough for anyone other than me to hear.

I sat down in my chair and opened my notebook.

"How about we move on with the lesson?" Gabriel said to the whole class. "I understand that you've all been discussing gospel principles, but I'm a firm believer in moving past talk and actually *acting* on the lessons we're supposed to learn. Practice what we preach, so to speak. And according to what Mr. Shumway had planned for the next few weeks, it seems like he was a man of like mind." Gabriel went to the board and wrote in large letters: *Senior Religion Studies Project.*

"Mr. Shumway had plans to institute a new requirement for all seniors who wish to graduate this year. He wanted each of you to fulfill an intensive community-service project before midterm break. I think it's a brilliant idea, and I plan on carrying out the arrangements he's already made."

I sat up straighter. This must have been the big surprise Mr. Shumway had teased us with before he quit.

"Before the break?" Chris Conway, the principal's

son, stopped drawing flaming skulls on his notebook. I was surprised he'd been paying attention for once. "There's only two more weeks until midterms. That's impossible."

"It's not impossible, and I will be letting you out an hour early from school every day to report to your different projects."

"Can we do anything we want?" April asked. "I could make jewelry for the kids at the children's hospital."

"Actually, Mr. Shumway already arranged your projects for you. We'll be working with a group called the Rock Canyon Foundation."

"They own the shelter in the city, right?" I asked.

"Very good, Grace."

"I'm sorry, but there's no way my parents will let me work at the shelter," Katie said. "They don't let me go into the city ever since those invisible criminals started running around."

"That's why we'll be splitting into two groups. One group will be staying close to home. Mr. Shumway had originally planned for this group to volunteer with the Rock Canyon Foundation at their senior center in Oak Park. However, I'm going to make a modification to this. I assume most of you have heard about what happened at the local food market? I hear the proprietor needs help getting the store up and running again. There's more cleanup and some light construction to do, and I imagine they could use a fund-raiser and a few free man-hours in the next few weeks.

"Daniel Kalbi will be heading up that group since he already works for Mr. Day. Those of you who aren't allowed to travel, or who have work directly after school, will be in that group. Mr. Shumway had already contacted each of your guardians for permission and divided the class into two groups. Daniel has the names of those of you who will be staying in Rose Crest."

Daniel waved the slip of paper he'd been looking at with Gabriel.

"Daniel, you'll need a co-captain."

I started to raise my hand, but I swear Gabriel deliberately ignored me. "The young lady sitting next to Daniel, what's your name?"

"Katie Summers," she said. "I'd be happy to co-captain."

"Good," he said. "Help Daniel pass out instructions to each of the people on his list."

Just perfect, I thought. I raised my hand again. "I'd like to be in the Day's Market group. I've already helped with some of the cleanup."

"Actually, Grace"—Gabriel finally paid attention to me—"Mr. Shumway specifically named you as the captain of the second group, and I agree that you'd be the perfect fit. Your team will be working with the Rock Canyon Foundation as part of their Good Samaritan project. You'll be split into pairs and assigned a driver, who will take you around to their various projects in the city and the neighboring towns. Anything from delivering food for Meals on Wheels, working at the Boys and Girls Club, helping the elderly with household tasks . . . whatever they need. This group will really be getting out there and serving the needs of the community."

"This is bogus," Chris said. "My dad will never let us go off campus like that."

"Actually, your father will be helping oversee your group today. And I think you'll make a good co-captain for Grace."

Even more perfect. I doubted Chris had done a single school assignment in the last three years. The only reason he hadn't been kicked out of HTA was because his dad was the principal. I could just picture myself doing all the work on my own.

I was about to protest and insist on being in Daniel's group, but I realized this might be the perfect opportunity to look for Jude in the city again. Maybe I'd be able to sneak away at some point—stake out The Depot, more incognito this time, or some of the other surrounding businesses.

"Okay," I said. "So when do we get started?"

ON THE SCHOOL BUS

Gabriel hadn't been kidding about Mr. Shumway's having made all the arrangements already. He had permission slips signed by all of our parents, and we were set to get working immediately.

Half the class went to the market with Daniel and Gabriel, and the rest of us got on a school bus with Principal Conway. I thought we wouldn't be getting started at least until the next day, but Gabriel said that the project was actually supposed to start last Friday, so the Rock Canyon people were eager to get us working. I didn't have a problem with this sudden development, since it meant that I'd be able to get to the city sooner than expected.

Only Principal Conway informed us that we would be meeting the Good Samaritan group at the rec center in Apple Valley. Just a few of us would even be going into the city at all—depending on our driver's agenda.

I passed out the stack of papers Gabriel had handed to me just before I got on the bus. He'd already paired everyone up, with Chris and me working together, just as I'd feared. When the bus pulled up to the rec center, we all filed out into the parking lot and were met by a line of vans marked with the Rock Canyon logo—two hands clasped.

"Your driver will have you back here in two hours, then we'll all take the bus back to the school," I instructed. Then the group broke up, and I hung back with Principal Conway to make sure everyone got into the correct vans and made it off all right.

I felt a pang of jealousy as I waved to April and Claire

as they pulled out of the parking lot with a middle-aged female driver in the last of the vans. My slip of paper said I was supposed to be on van number 8, but there had been only seven vans to begin with, and now everyone but the principal, Chris, and me was gone.

"That's strange," Principal Conway said. "I'll go talk to the director and see what the holdup is with the last van." He pulled out his cell phone and walked inside the rec center.

Chris and I stood alone in the parking lot for a moment. The wind tossed my hair. I rubbed my arms. It had been an exceptionally warm autumn this year, but now I found myself wishing I'd brought a light jacket. Hopefully, the last van wouldn't take too long to get here.

"This is lame," Chris said. "I'm out."

He slung his backpack over his shoulder and started to walk away.

"Um, where do you think you're going?" I called after him.

"I saw an arcade down the street. I'll be back in a couple of hours before the bus leaves."

"But the van is here." I pointed at the white van with dark tinted windows and the clasped-hands logo that was just now pulling into the parking lot.

"Whatever," Chris said, and kept walking.

The white van pulled up just ahead of me. I didn't like the way I couldn't see into the windows. It was one thing to get into a van with a total stranger when at least one other person from school was supposed to be with me, but now that I was alone, I didn't like the idea at all. Goose bumps prickled up my arms, and I hesitated on the curb.

The passenger's-side window of the van rolled down a couple of inches. "You coming?" a deep voice called from inside. I still couldn't see the driver.

I glanced back at the rec center entrance, to see if Principal Conway was coming back anytime soon.

"We gotta get on the road if we want to be back in time for your bus."

I picked up my backpack and walked to the van. I pulled the door open and was about to tell the driver to go on without me.

"Grace Divine?" asked the driver. He smiled at me from under his baseball cap. The sleeves of his flannel shirt were rolled up to his elbows. "I told you I'd be seeing you around."

I almost fell over backward. I grabbed the handle of the door to steady myself. "Nathan Talbot? What on earth are you doing here?"

CHAPTER THIRTEEN

Rescue

HALF A SECOND LATER

"Call me Talbot, please. Nobody but my mom ever called me Nathan."

"Okay, *Talbot*, then . . . seriously, what are you doing here?" I was stalled halfway through the van door.

"Um, my job?" Talbot tipped his baseball cap toward me. It had the clasped-hands logo embroidered on the front. His unbuttoned flannel shirt revealed a T-shirt under it with the words ROCK CANYON FOUNDATION: THE GOOD SAMARITAN PROJECT written on the front. I guessed that was why that guy in the club had called him the Good Samaritan.

Talbot patted the passenger seat. "So you getting in, or what?"

I hesitated again and looked back at the rec center. No sign of Principal Conway or Chris anywhere nearby.

"I don't bite, I swear." Talbot grinned, and his dimples

appeared in his tan cheeks. "Like I said, we gotta hit the road now if we want to make it back in time for the bus."

I couldn't help but stare at Talbot's friendly smile as he spoke. That wave of warm familiarity rolled through me. What was it with him? I mean, he was barely a step up from a stranger, yet *something* about him made me feel like we were old friends. *You can trust him,* a quiet voice whispered inside my head.

"Yeah. Okay." I climbed into the van and sat in the passenger seat. I glanced back at the rec center entrance one last time and figured Principal Conway would know that I'd left with the last van when he came back and I was gone.

"Where's your partner?" Talbot asked.

"He took off. Went to an arcade down the street."

"Good," Talbot said. He gripped the steering wheel with his large, tanned hands and drove the van away from the curb and through the parking lot. "I hate it when I get assigned kids who don't want to do the work." His green-eyed gaze flicked in my direction. "You're up for this, right?"

"Of course." I fastened my seat belt as we pulled from the parking lot onto the street. "Um . . . you're not following me around, right?"

"Self-absorbed much?" Talbot chuckled.

The sound of his laugh again triggered those warm waves through my body. It made me shiver.

"I'm the one who should be asking you that, don't

you think?" Talbot asked. "You going to show up at my dorm room next?"

I blushed. "No, um, it's just weird to see you again."

Talbot stopped at a red light. "Weird creepy, or weird pleasant?"

He smiled at me again, making his dimples super-pronounced. Why did he make me feel like I was curled up in a warm blanket on a cold winter afternoon? And how could the feeling be comforting, yet disturbing at the same time? I looked away so he wouldn't notice the flush of heat in my face.

"Weird pleasant, I guess."

Talbot flipped the blinker on and pulled the van onto the highway. We headed in the direction of the city. I felt a little thrill of anticipation that I might get another chance to look for Jude.

"You saved me some trouble anyway," Talbot said.

"How's that?"

"Now I don't have to try to track down your number. Although I doubt there are many Divines out there."

Crap, I blushed even more now. What was wrong with me? "You were going to look up my number?"

"Your friend dropped her bracelet at the club. I figured she'd want it back, but she didn't tell me her last name. But yours was hard to forget. I've got the bracelet in my bag in the back. Remind me to give it to you before you leave."

"Oh, okay." A little rush of relief calmed the burning

in my cheeks. Of course he hadn't wanted to call me just for the sake of calling me. "So where are we headed anyway?"

"I've got about twenty boxes of donated books in the back of the van. We're taking them to the library on Tidwell Street. Most of their books started falling apart about a decade ago."

"That's it?"

"What, not exciting enough for you?"

"I don't know, I guess I expected something a little more hands-on. I don't really get the point of me being here just to help deliver some books."

"You're here because I'm supposed to teach you the finer points of helping your fellow man. Charity work isn't always glamorous. Yeah, some weeks we get assigned to feed the needy or help build a house in a weekend, but half of what I do is just deliveries." He adjusted his hat. "But don't worry, we'll get pretty hands-on eventually."

I shot a surprised look at him even though my face blazed more than before.

"What?" He smirked. "Don't tell me you're afraid to get your hands dirty? Because if you're one of those kids who gets freaked out by homeless people or is too worried about breaking a nail to swing a hammer, I should just turn this van around right now and ask for a new partner. . . ."

"What? No. First of all, I'm not a kid. I'll be eighteen

in three months. And I am most definitely not afraid to get my hands dirty." I didn't know why, but I felt the urge to justify myself to Talbot—prove myself or something. Maybe it was because Gabriel had made so many assumptions about me after our first meeting, and I didn't want Talbot to do the same. "Charity work isn't exactly new to me. My dad's a pastor. We used to do stuff like this all the time. You know how many hours I used to spend helping out with food drives and volunteering at the shelter?"

"*Used to?* Why do you say *used to?*"

I stared out the window, watching the pedestrians on the street. We were in the city now, so I wanted to keep my eye out for anyone who might look like Jude. "Things have been complicated lately. It's been a while since I've been able to make a difference to anybody."

"Well, now's your chance." Talbot pulled into a deliveries-only parking place outside the library. We each got out, and I met him at the back of the van.

Tidwell Library sat only a few blocks from Markham Street and The Depot. I checked out the faces of every person on the street. I knew Jude could be somewhere nearby, but if this place was anything like Markham, the neighborhood would be deserted by the time the sun went down.

Talbot opened the van's back doors. "Come on, let's get started."

I pulled out a box and almost fell over because of the

weight of the thing. I finally steadied myself and looked over at Talbot. He had three boxes of the same size stacked in his arms.

"You can do better than that, *kid*," he said, with a little goading jab in his voice on that last word.

"Yeah, right."

I thought it would take a million years to unload all those boxes into the library, but Talbot carried in six boxes for every one that I managed to haul in. I hated looking weak in front of him, and I finally got annoyed enough with myself that I managed to muster up a burst of strength that helped me carry in two boxes on my last trip. Considering how much easier it was, I wished I had been able to do that in the first place. But I guess I didn't really want Talbot to notice my disproportionate girl-to-upper-body-strength ratio.

"That's more like it," Talbot said as he held the door open for me on his way out. I carried the last two boxes to the information desk and left them with the librarian.

"So where to now?" I asked when I got back to the van, feeling like I'd gotten a second wind. "Can we go paint over some graffiti or something?"

"Not sure what we have time for, kid." Talbot pulled off his hat. His wavy brown hair all squashed against his head made *him* look like the kid. He reached up to sweep his hand through his hair. But then he dropped his hat and whirled around. "Did you hear that?"

"Hear what?"

I concentrated hard, holding my breath until I felt that stinging irritation in my ears. Then I heard it, too: a woman's scream. It sounded so close in my ears that I thought she must be only a few yards away, but the street was dusky and deserted except for Talbot and me. It could have come from a couple blocks away for all I knew.

"Come on!" Talbot said. "We've got to help."

"What? No. We should call the police!" I reached for my phone in my pocket.

The scream sounded again but suddenly cut off, like someone had covered the woman's mouth. My muscles flared.

"There's no time." Talbot grabbed my wrist. "The police can't help her, but *you* can."

"Me?"

Talbot let go of my arm. "I'm going." He tossed the van keys at me. "Lock yourself in the van if you're too afraid." He took off jogging in the direction of the scream.

"Stop!" I shouted after him. "You're going to get yourself killed!"

"Not if you've got my back," he yelled.

What the hell did he mean by that? I glanced down at the keys in my hand. I'd caught them midair without even realizing it. When I looked up again, Talbot had already disappeared around the corner.

"Crap, he *is* going to get killed," I said to myself. The

tension in my muscles coursed like fire. My body wanted to do *something*, even if my better judgment screamed at me to stay put. Then an explosive bang rattled the sky. *A gunshot!*

Go! a foreign voice shouted in my head. I took off running before I could even stop myself. In a matter of seconds, I rounded the corner where Talbot had turned, and ran smack into a woman who was running the opposite way. Tears streamed down her face, and she held her torn shirt closed in front of her chest.

"I'm sorry. Are you okay?" I tried to grab her arm, but she pulled away from my touch.

"Get away," she cried, and kept running.

But I couldn't leave without Talbot. I took a few more steps and stopped dead at the scene in front of me. Three guys. Two dressed in black with bright red ski masks. I could tell by their slight build that they were probably teenagers. The third person was Talbot. One of the ski-masked guys had him pushed up against a cement wall, a gun pressed to his head—the muzzle lost in the mop of Talbot's hat-head hair.

I tried not to scream. I really did. I choked it back as hard as I could, but a high-pitched squawk escaped from my throat. I threw my hands over my mouth.

The guy pushed his hand against Talbot's sternum, pressing him into the wall. He gestured in my direction. "We've got company."

The second guy turned toward me. He had no face

other than the two dark eyes that glared at me through the holes in the red ski mask.

"Bring her here," the gunman ordered.

The other guy took a step toward me.

"Do something, Grace," Talbot said.

The guy took a second and a third step.

Do what? Run? But I was frozen to that spot. Except, I wasn't technically *frozen*, since every cell in my body seared like Fourth of July sparklers under my skin.

The man had only half a dozen more steps to take to close the gap between us, but I still couldn't move. My stomach clenched into a fiery knot.

"Damn it, Grace!" Talbot shouted. "Do something. I know you can."

"Do what?" I shouted back.

"That feeling in your stomach? That's anger. That's power. Grab on to it and kick that guy's ass!"

How would he know . . . ?

"Shut up." The gunman smacked Talbot on the head with the gun. A trickle of red ran down his forehead. "Grab the girl, now!" he ordered his crony.

Talbot was right. That knot in my stomach had become a flaming rage. Daniel would tell me to push it away. Find balance. But as the large masked thug reached for me, I let that rage wash over me, and my fists went flying. I socked him in the gut, and he went sailing back several feet. I'd had no idea I was capable of hitting that hard.

He hit the brick wall of the adjacent building, but it didn't seem to faze him. He caught himself and charged in my direction. I countered out of his way, but then he swung around and snatched at my shirt. One of his fists had tattoos of the letters *S* and *K* between his knuckles. This guy reeked, and the smell—like two-month-old milk—only aggravated me more. I grabbed his hands and twisted them away from me, then pulled his body down closer as I kneed him in the groin. He grunted with pain. His tongue lolled out of his mouth. I pushed him, and he stumbled back. I kicked him in the left kneecap while he was unstable, and he buckled under his own weight and fell to the ground. I glared down at him, my hands up in fists.

"Hey!" the gunman shouted. "You'll pay for that."

Watch out! I heard inside my head, and I looked up just in time to stare down the barrel of a gun.

"No!" Talbot shouted, and in a lightning-quick move, he wrenched himself out of the guy's hold and then had the man's gun-wielding hand in his. Talbot slammed the guy's arm down and against his knee. I swear I heard the cracking of bones.

The guy dropped the gun and pulled his arm in against his chest, moaning. He took a wild swing at Talbot with his uninjured arm. Talbot blocked the blow and smashed the palm of his hand into the guy's ski mask, presumably where his nose would be. The guy sputtered and coughed.

"What the hell, man?" He gasped and pulled at his ski mask, but before he could even yank it off, Talbot took a running leap, bounced off the cement wall like it was a springboard, and sent a flying kick right into the guy's chest.

The gunman crumpled to the ground. Talbot landed in a crouching position next to him. There was just enough light left in the dim alley to glint off his green eyes, making them look like dazzling emeralds.

I gasped. "You're a . . . You're a . . ."

"An Urbat." Talbot straightened up. He crossed the alley between us, then placed his warm, callused hand against my arm. "Just like you."

BACK AT THE VAN

The thug I'd knocked down got away during the skirmish, and Talbot wanted to make sure the other one didn't escape when he regained full consciousness. I couldn't help watching the large muscles in Talbot's forearms ripple as he used his belt to hog-tie the gunman next to the Dumpster. He did it with such ease I pictured him roping a calf on whatever farm he presumably came from. Talbot then emptied the gun of its bullets and tucked them into the front pocket of his flannel shirt. Then he wiped the gun clean with his shirttail and tossed it next to the semiconscious guy's head. "For evidence," he said.

"Should I call the police now?" I pulled out my phone.

"Let me do it," Talbot said. "My phone's a prepaid, so they won't be able to trace it."

"You mean we're not sticking around?"

"What would we tell them? Besides, I gotta get you back to that bus before they think I've run off with you. I can't afford to lose this job." He pulled out his phone and motioned for me to follow him out of the alley.

"We're just leaving him here like that?" I looked back at the guy, lying on his side, groaning with pain. "It seems a little inhumane."

"That guy tried to kill you, Grace." He flipped open his phone. "Besides, he isn't human. That there is what you call a demon."

At first I thought he was being metaphorical, but then his meaning clicked. "A demon? A living, breathing, bona fide demon?"

"What? Don't tell me you haven't seen one before."

I shrugged. "Well, not really. I met one at a party once. She did this little mind-control trick with her eyes."

"Ah, an Akh. They're a terrible sort." He clucked his tongue. "This one here is a Gelal. They prey on young women. That girl would have gone through all sorts of hell if we hadn't shown up."

"How can you tell?" I asked. The guy still seemed like a person to me. I was itching to go over and take off his mask to see what he really looked liked underneath.

"The smell." Talbot crinkled his nose. "You really are a rookie, aren't you? I bet you haven't even figured out how to track someone yet."

I looked down at the ground. The masked demon let out a loud, angry groan.

"We better go," Talbot said. "I'm just hoping the police get here before he comes to enough to break free."

Talbot hit a button on his phone and put it to his ear.

"You have 911 on speed dial?"

"I told you I make a lot of *deliveries*."

I followed him out of the alley. "Wait, you mean you do *this* a lot?"

But Talbot didn't respond. He was too busy telling the operator on the other end of the line that a young woman had been attacked near Tidwell Library and that they'd find the perpetrator behind a Dumpster near Tidwell and Vine. He hung up before they could ask him any questions.

"You still got the keys?"

"Um, yeah, I hope." I patted down my pockets and found the keys.

Talbot unlocked the passenger's-side door and held it open for me. Sometime between Talbot's shutting my door and his climbing in through the driver's side, the shock of everything that had happened finally hit me. My hands shook so hard I could barely fasten my seat belt.

"Are you okay?" Talbot asked. "You did awesome back there. Just like I knew you would."

"But how . . . how did you know that I could even do anything? How did you know what I am?" I'd already asked how he'd known I was an Urbat earlier, but he'd insisted on taking care of the gunman before we talked about it. But now I wanted answers.

"Your necklace." Talbot reached over and touched the cracked moonstone pendant that hung from my neck. "Kind of a dead giveaway, if you think about it." He brushed one of my curls against my neck with his fingers as he pulled his hand away. "And I saw you fight back at The Depot. Most girls can't pull off a round-house kick like that on a guy that big unless she's packing some serious paranormal heat." He crinkled his nose again. "Plus, you kinda smell, too."

"What?" I sniffed both my arms. I smelled perfectly normal to me—okay, kind of sweaty from fighting, but not at all like those guys in that alley.

Talbot laughed, his cheeks dimpling with his smile.

"You jerk!" I punched him playfully in the arm.

He grabbed my hand. "Hey, watch it, kid. You've got a mean right hook."

Talbot's hand, wrapped around my fist, seemed huge by comparison. I could see the veins stretching along his tendons. He squeezed my fingers, and a pulse of tingling energy ran up my arm and down my spine. It felt like the connection that had passed between Daniel and me when we first held hands in the Garden of Angels. The tingling sensation turned to a shudder. I tugged my hand out of Talbot's grasp. It wasn't right to feel that kind of energy with anyone other than Daniel.

I crossed my arms in front of my chest. Talbot shifted his gaze away from my face. He coughed slightly and started the van. We pulled away from the library. After a moment, I asked the question that had been nagging at the back of my mind.

"If those guys were really demons, then why did they need a gun?"

Talbot shrugged. "I don't know, Grace, but it worries me. Gelals don't even usually come out until well after midnight. They're completely nocturnal, you know? And the fact that they were even here in the city is a mystery. That's the third pair of them I've come across in the last two months, but before that I hadn't even encountered one since I was last on the West Coast." He shook his head. "There's something going down around here. Used to be I had to go looking for demons, track them for months before one came out of hiding, but now the city seems to be crawling with them. And I keep hearing rumors that someone's gathering werewolves, Gelals, Akhs, and all kinds of other paranormal teens into some sort of gang. They supposedly call themselves the Shadow Kings."

"A gang of paranormals?"

"You know those 'invisible bandits' they keep talking about on the news?"

I nodded.

"You don't think humans are behind all that?"

"No. Not at all," I said. "They hit a grocery store in my town. Ransacked the entire place in less than five minutes. My . . . boyfriend and I were saying that a gang of superpowered teens had to be behind it all. And I think my brother may be mixed up with them. He said something to April about finding a new family."

Talbot's eyebrows arched up. "Your brother is like you?"

"Kind of." I didn't know what I should say to Talbot. I mean, we'd known each other only for a total of a few hours—yet in those few hours he'd saved my life twice. And he was the only person I knew like me. Someone who had powers and actually wanted to use them for good. At least from what I could tell. *You can trust him,* that voice whispered in my head. "Jude's turned into a full werewolf. I haven't. He bit me when he first turned, and then he tried to kill his best friend—my, um, boyfriend. I think that's why Jude left home." I breathed out a sigh. It felt good to tell the truth to someone who could really understand.

Talbot nodded. "So who's this boyfriend you keep mentioning? Sounds like your brother dislikes him just as much as I do."

I cocked my head and looked at Talbot. What did he mean by that?

"Sorry." Talbot flashed me a smile. "Just thinking that this *boyfriend* must be pretty special to warrant having a girl like you. But what'd he do to tick off your bro?"

"Oh. Daniel—my boyfriend . . ." Ugh. It was like this conversation couldn't go ten seconds now without one of us dropping the *B* word. Daniel and I didn't even like to call each other boyfriend and girlfriend. It just sounded so trite compared to how we felt about each other. "Daniel, my boy—" I cleared my throat. "He used to be a werewolf. He's the one who infected my brother a few years ago. My brother kind of hates his guts now."

Talbot gave me a quizzical, yet amused look. He shook his head. "What do you mean Daniel *used to be* a werewolf? I was under the impression that being an Urbat is a permanent condition."

"I cured him."

Talbot's eyes widened. He slammed on the breaks just before almost running a red light. "How did you do that?"

Unfortunately, I was too tired to tell that much of the story. "True love's first kill"—I waved my hand in

the air—"yada, yada, yada . . . It's really a story for
another day."

Talbot blinked. He let out a short laugh and then
gazed into my eyes. "I do believe, Miss Grace Divine,
that you get more and more interesting by the minute."

The tone of his voice when he said the words *Miss
Grace* sent another flutter of warm familiarity through
my body. *What is it about him?*

The light turned green, and we drove through the
intersection. I turned my head and stared out the
passenger's-side window. "You should talk. I mean,
I assume this is something you do a lot. Track down
demons and investigate gangs of paranormal thieves? Is
this Good Samaritan job just a front for your vigilante
superhero quest?"

"Guilty as charged," he said.

"Seriously?"

"Got infected when my parents were killed by werewolves, swore I'd use my powers to protect the world
from demons . . . yada, yada, yada . . . It's really a
story for another time."

"Oh, come on, you can't do that to me."

"Yes, I can, because we're here." I followed his pointing finger toward the lit-up bus in front of the rec center.
Students filled the bus, and Principal Conway paced out
in front of it with his cell phone pressed to his ear.

"I guess I gotta go," I said. "Thanks for the . . .
um . . . adventure?"

"I'm glad you were up to it." He grinned at me, all dimply and warm. "Actually, I'm glad you got partnered with me. I'm not sure what I would have done if any other student from your school had been with me today. It kind of feels like fate, don't you think?"

I smiled. "Yeah, I guess it does."

I pulled on the door handle and pushed on the door. I was about to jump out when Talbot said, "Grace?"

"Yeah?" I looked back at him.

He held something silver and sparkly in his hand. At first I thought he was giving me a present—which would have been weird, but sweet—but then he said, "April's bracelet. She dropped it at the club."

"Oh." I took the bracelet from his warm fingers. A narrow slip of paper was wrapped around it.

I looked up into Talbot's glinting emerald eyes.

"That's for you," he said. "Call me if you need anything. Anything at all."

"Okay," I said, and got out of the van.

"Tell April I said hi," Talbot said before I shut the door.

I shoved the slip of paper in my pocket and trucked toward the bus in the dark, wondering how best to explain my lateness when another person fell in right beside me.

"Dude, took you long enough to get back here," Chris said. He had half a sub sandwich in his hand,

and his pockets jangled with what sounded like coins as he walked.

"Where have you two been?" Principal Conway asked when he saw us approaching. "We were scheduled to leave twenty minutes ago. I was beginning to worry that you weren't out in one of the vans at all."

"Sorry, Tom," Chris said to his dad. "I got all hypoglycemic, so I made our driver pull over so I could get something to eat. I don't think this volunteer stuff is good for my health."

"Nice try," Principal Conway said, and led his son up the steps of the bus. "Next time, answer your phone when I call."

I stopped on the top step of the bus and looked back at the parking lot. Talbot flashed the lights of his van and then drove away.

CHAPTER FOURTEEN

A Normal Life

ON THE BUS

"Holy crap!" April slid her silver cuff bracelet onto her wrist. "Number one: I can't believe Talbot found my bracelet at the club—it's supposed to be the feature item in my new fall collection, but there's no way I was going to go back there looking for it. Number two: I cannot believe he's your driver. Number three: I can't believe you guys stopped a freaking mugging together. And number four: The fact that he's an Ur—"

"Shhh!" I tried to throw my hands over her mouth. We sat alone at the back of the bus, but her voice had risen in volume with each number on her list of things she couldn't believe. I suddenly wondered if I'd done the right thing by telling her the truth.

April squealed and wriggled away from my hands. "Number four," she loudly whispered, "the fact that Talbot is a freaking Urbat demon hunter is, like, blowing my mind!" Her voice rose on the last word so it was almost a shout. I pounced on her again, practically knocking her flat on the bus bench, and tried to cover her mouth. She giggled and pushed me off her. "Okay, okay. I'll try to be quiet. But this is, like, too awesome. You have to let me be all girly about your secret rendezvous with Talbot for a moment."

"I know," I whispered. "But if Principal Conway or Gabriel . . . Pastor Saint Moon, I mean, find out that I went out with Talbot alone, don't you think they'll have a problem with that? I don't want them to find out I was working with him one-on-one—let alone what we were doing."

April waggled her eyebrows at me.

"It's not like that . . . ," I said. "Besides, I don't want Chris to get into trouble for ditching out."

"You're a terrible liar. I can see those splotch marks on your neck."

I rubbed my neck. "I'm just hot."

"I'll *bet* you are."

"April, seriously. It's not like that. Talbot's just a new friend. You know how I feel about Daniel." I meant what I said, but my neck still felt all hot and itchy. I pulled a water bottle out of my backpack and took a sip.

"Yeah, but how is *Daniel* going to feel about this? Any boy is going to have a problem with his girlfriend being all *one-on-one* with a hot guy—especially if you're getting all hot and sweaty. Don't you think Daniel will be jealous that he's not the one doing it with you?"

I choked and almost spat water at her.

"I meant *doing it* as in Daniel wanting to kick bad-guy butt with you . . . not . . . you know . . . not you two 'getting it on.'" She made a weird gesture with her hands that I assumed had something to do with "getting it on." "Unless, you and Daniel *are*. You know . . . Um, you're not, right? Because I heard—"

I coughed and cleared my throat. "No, Daniel and I aren't 'getting it on.' No matter what anyone says."

Thanks to my superhearing and all those lovely rumors Lynn Bishop spread last school year, I knew there were plenty of people who thought Daniel and I were "getting it on." But we most definitely weren't. Not that we didn't think about it or want to—just the sight of Daniel most days made my heart race and my legs ache with anticipation.

It was just that, to me, sex was a *big deal*.

I mean, it was a running joke at HTA that if my dad substitute taught one of the religion classes, it was no doubt going to be a lesson on chastity. And let me tell you, having to sit through your dad's lecturing all of your friends about abstinence—not the funfest you'd think it would be. But even though Dad's spiels always made me want to bang my head on my desk, I couldn't help believing the things he was telling us about waiting for marriage. It just seemed to go with the whole package, you know? That if I believed in Jesus, and believed in all those parables he taught, and believed in forgiving people, then what the Bible had to say about sex being sacred and special had to be right, too.

And as much as I wanted *it*—and I knew Daniel was the one I wanted it with—I also wanted to wait. Even if it was one of the hardest choices I've ever had to make.

I'd worried my decision would be a problem for Daniel. We'd lived very different lives during the three years he'd been gone, and he'd, um, *gotten it on*, so to speak, more than once. But one of the things I loved about Daniel was that he'd completely understood.

"You're different from those other girls," Daniel once told me. "We're different. I love you. And I want things to be right with us."

But now with all the lying and fighting and secrets that were suddenly happening between Daniel and me—it almost felt like *nothing* was quite right with us anymore.

"So are you going to tell him?" April asked, pulling me out of my thoughts.

"Tell who what?"

"Are you going to tell Daniel about Talbot and you?"

"I told you, there is no *Talbot and me*."

"But there could be," she crooned.

"Okay, I'm not telling you anything anymore."

"Oh, come on, you know I'm just teasing. I meant, are you going to tell Daniel about Talbot being your driver? You know he's going to be all jealous that he was stuck doing inventory at Day's with Katie Summers instead of being out there fighting side by side with you in the city."

I might have told April way too much lately, but I still hadn't told her the reason I'd been avoiding Daniel all day. As far as she knew, Daniel was just as gung ho about training me to become a superhero. She didn't know how he'd turned his back on me and on the plan that *he'd* come up with in the first place.

"Yeah. I think I will tell him."

My body tingled with the hope of a new idea: when Daniel heard how I took that guy down in the alley, he'd realize that I really could take care of myself out there. He'd change his mind about agreeing with Gabriel. When he heard how I helped save that woman, he'd have to believe in me again.

And then maybe he'd finally tell me whatever secret he was keeping from me.

BACK AT THE SCHOOL

I didn't have to wait long to see Daniel. He was hanging out in the school parking lot when I got off the bus. He leaned against the seat of his red-and-black motorcycle, his hands tucked in the pockets of his hoodie.

"Gotta go," I said to April, and practically skipped over to Daniel through the mostly deserted lot. I was about to throw my arms around his neck and tell him all about what had happened in the alley with the Gelal and Talbot, until I saw the stony look on his face.

It reminded me of Jude. All stoic and cold.

"Hey," I said, stopping short of hugging him. "What're you doing here?"

"Your dad wanted to make sure you had a ride home. I thought you guys were going to be back a while ago, though. I was starting to get concerned."

"Sorry." I gave him an apologetic smile.

Daniel picked up his helmet from the back of the bike and handed it to me. I always thought it was funny that he insisted I be the one who wore it—considering that I had superhuman healing abilities and he didn't. Then again, according to my reading, it seemed like a catastrophic head injury was one of the few things that could kill an Urbat—besides silver and certain demon venom (including werewolf)—if not healed quickly enough. That was probably why when Daniel's monster of a father attacked him when he was only thirteen, he'd tried to smash Daniel's head open with a broken easel.

His father had wanted Daniel dead.

Daniel got on the bike, and I climbed on behind him. He was so quiet and distant I didn't know how he'd feel if I wrapped my arms around his waist like I usually did. I placed my hands lightly on his sides instead. Daniel started the bike, and we pulled out onto Crescent Street. He didn't glance back at me at all while he drove; he just stared straight ahead.

The night air felt so cold and heavy between us, filled with all the things I wanted to tell him but suddenly felt like I couldn't. I shifted back on my seat and let go of his sides, letting my supernatural balance keep me steady on the bike. How could it be that I'd felt perfectly comfortable driving back to the bus alone with Talbot, but now I didn't even know where to put my hands while riding with Daniel?

We pulled up in front of my house. Daniel put his feet down and shifted into neutral, but left the bike idling. He wasn't planning on staying long. "I'll see you tomorrow."

I pulled off the helmet and handed it to him. He didn't touch my fingers as he took it from my hands. I stepped back, ready to walk away.

But I couldn't.

I couldn't run off again without answers. I shouldn't have done that last time—even if that experience had helped me break through the barrier and fully tap into my powers for the first time.

"What on earth is wrong?" I asked Daniel. "Why are you acting like you're so pissed off at me?"

Daniel blinked. He let out a small sigh and then pressed his lips together.

"I'm sorry I ran off yesterday. And I'm sorry I gave you the silent treatment all day today. It's just that I know you're lying about where you were the other night. And on top of that, I couldn't believe how you didn't back me up with Gabriel. But I'm over being angry now. I was done in religion class, but I didn't get a chance to talk to you because of the service project." *And then I spent the next two hours alone with another guy*—but I didn't think now was the best time to tell him about Talbot anymore. "I just want to understand *why* you're acting this way. And I don't want you to be mad at me. I can't handle it anymore."

"I told you already. I'm not mad at you, Gracie. I'm worried."

His words startled me. Hadn't Jude said almost the exact same thing to me once? Back when Daniel first returned to town and Jude had wanted me to stay away from him.

"Worried about what? Tell me, please?"

Daniel gripped the handlebars of his bike. The engine rumbled between us. He leaned his head back and stared up at the crescent moon hanging in the sky, his deep, dark, mud-pie eyes unblinking. The walnut tree—illuminated by the porch light—just beyond him made the perfect background for his silhouette. If this had been any other moment, I would've pulled out my sketch pad to capture the beauty of the image. But now, seeing Daniel this way only made my heart ache for him.

I bit the inside of my lip. "I know something's wrong, Daniel. Beyond lying to me, I can see it in your eyes. You look like you did that night when I kissed you for the first time under the walnut tree. The night I told you I loved you, and you ran away because you thought you could never ask me to save you."

Daniel closed his eyes. I swear sometimes he looked just like an angel.

"But I did save you. In all of this pain we've been through, that's the one thing that's made it worth it." I touched his shoulder. "So what's going on? Why don't you want me to train anymore? And where were you the other night? What happened that you think you can't tell me?"

Daniel shook off my touch. "Do you think I had something to do with hurting that Tyler kid? Is that what you think?"

"No. That thought never once crossed my mind." I held my hands out by my sides. "But I know you weren't home watching TV like you told the police. And I saw a motorcycle just like yours outside a bar downtown when I was on my way home from The Depot. It was a place called Knuckle Grinders, I think."

Daniel flashed a look in my direction. Did he know exactly what I was talking about?

"Why would you tell me you're sick and then go to a bar? Do you have any idea how worried that makes me?" I'd defended him with April—said he wouldn't go back to who he used to be—but I almost didn't know what to think anymore.

"I was looking for information," Daniel said.

"About Jude?" Relief washed through me. "Why wouldn't you just tell me that?"

Daniel bowed his head and closed his eyes again. He looked almost like he was praying. After a moment he let out a long breath and dropped his hands from the handlebars. He looked at me with his dark eyes and swallowed hard. "All I've ever wanted is a normal life, Grace. You know that. I want a normal family. I want Trenton. I want you and me, and a normal future."

"I know, Daniel. . . ."

The only problem was that I didn't know how I fit into Daniel's picture of normalcy. Not anymore, anyway. Not with my messed-up family. Not with my close-to-zero odds of going to college. And especially not with my superpowers, which weren't just going to go away. Daniel could never have a *normal* life with me. He'd need someone like Katie Summers for that.

"Then you can understand why I want you to drop all this nonsense about being a Hound of Heaven," he said.

"But what I don't get is why you wanted me to start training in the first place. You're the one who made me think I *could* be a hero. *You* started me on this path."

"I was just trying to make the best of a bad situation. But I was wrong, Grace. Gabriel is right. It's too dangerous. I couldn't stand losing you to the curse."

"But you're not going to lose me. I'm not going to

change. And even if I did, you could save me. There is a cure—"

"But what if it didn't work? It's not a fail-safe. You can't go about this thinking it isn't a big deal if you change into a werewolf. There might not be a way back from that." Daniel brushed his hand through his shaggy blond hair. "And it's far too dangerous anyway. I don't know what I was thinking. You're no match for a demon. . . .'"

Was that why he'd been acting so weird since the fight with Pete? I wasn't able to fight back then, so now Daniel didn't think I was capable anymore?

I was itching once again to tell him about the alley. About how I took down that Gelal in a matter of seconds. The only problem was that that story also involved a gun being pointed at my head. . . . But he had to know what I was really capable of.

Before I could say anything more, Daniel reached out and took my hand in his. "Gracie, all I want is for us to have a normal future—together. I don't know if that's possible. I don't know if the universe will let me have it. I don't know if I even deserve it." He slipped his fingers between mine. "But I'm sure as hell going to try to get it."

I looked down at our entwined hands. How could I tell him about Talbot now?

"Trenton applications are due in a month," Daniel said. "Have you even looked at yours?"

I shook my head. "No, I've been too busy . . ." *With everything he thought I shouldn't be doing.*

Daniel let go of my hand. He brushed my cheek with his fingers and then drew my face closer to his. He touched our foreheads together. "Will you do this for me, Grace? Can you forget about all this hero stuff before you get hurt? Let your dad and Gabriel be the ones who look for Jude? And let me help you get your Trenton application together?" He shifted his head slightly and brushed his lips against mine. His touch was as intoxicating as always. "Please, Gracie," he whispered against my mouth. "My future means nothing without you."

"Okay," I said. "But you know I don't make promises."

Daniel laughed slightly. "Yes, I know. But I'll settle for your 'okay.'"

I found myself clutching my moonstone necklace as his lips melted against mine. His kiss made my legs ache like they did when I needed a good run. Every tingling cell in my body wanted me to climb onto Daniel's lap on that bike, but he pulled away after a moment.

"I should go," he said. "I've got homework and stuff." He really was taking this college thing seriously. "At least look over that application tonight, okay?"

I nodded. I watched from the porch as he drove away, and then I went into the house.

I sat at the kitchen table with a plate of untouched left-overs pushed aside and my Trenton application spread out in front of me. I'd dug it out of my backpack, where it had been since I'd gotten it from Barlow last week, and broken the seal on the envelope. Mom's evening-news ritual played out in the background as I looked over the requirements: portfolio of twenty-one works in at least three different mediums, two letters of recom-mendation, an application that would span the length of Dad's car if you lined the papers up end to end, and *two* essays.

"Ah, Trenton," Dad said as he came up to the table. "Application time already, huh?"

"Yeah."

Dad picked up a page of the application and scanned through it. He made a low whistling noise. "Tuition has really gone up, hasn't it?"

I nodded. "There's something about financial-aid forms on their website. Daniel for sure qualifies, but I don't think I do."

"Hmm." Dad put down the application. "We'll figure something out. Your mom used to save part of her pay-check each month for you kids. We've had to dip into it a bit lately, but with Jude gone . . ."

Mom clicked up the TV's volume. Apparently, we were being too loud for her.

Dad leaned in close to my ear. "Was she like this the whole time I was gone?"

"On and off," I said. "Worse sometimes. At least she ate some of her dinner tonight."

"Might be time to consult Dr. Connors again."

The TV volume went up another couple of decibels. I rubbed behind one of my ears.

"Make sure you don't leave those essays until the last minute. They're the hardest part, you know."

"Yeah," I said, and picked up the form with the essay questions.

Dad stroked his hand over my hair and then squeezed my shoulder. "Don't know how we'll manage without you here." He picked up his planner from the kitchen counter and headed to his study.

I glanced over the essay questions. The first was the less difficult of the two: "Which artist has influenced your work the most, and why?" I could easily write up an essay on Renoir or Cassatt—if I could pick between the two. But the second question made me pause. Stumped me, actually. "How will you use your talents to make the world a better place?"

I was still mulling over the question when my ears pricked up at the mention of something on TV. I stood up from the table to see the screen better. A reporter interviewed a woman in a torn red shirt who looked vaguely familiar.

"I would have died," the woman said. "The man with the gun said he was going to kill me. But then there was this rush of movement, and this other guy came out of nowhere and pulled the masked man off me. He told me to run, so I did. There may have been a girl there with him. I didn't get a good look at either of them, but they saved my life."

The camera cut back to a reporter standing in front of a news van parked outside that alley on Tidwell Street. "After being saved by an unknown person or persons, Ms. Taylor ran all the way to the police station. When authorities arrived on the scene, they found one of the alleged attackers tied up and unconscious beside a Dumpster. Authorities have not yet been able to identify or question the man, but they hope to interrogate him about a series of similar attacks in the city over the last few weeks. Police think he may have been involved with the murder of Leanne Greenwood, the waitress who was found dead near this same area last month. Although only one of Ms. Taylor's alleged assailants was apprehended, city police are relieved that at least one dangerous criminal is off the streets tonight."

The camera cut to an anchorman—the same one with the poufy hair from the other night. "Thank you, Carlos. And it sounds like we may have a Good Samaritan or two to thank for this arrest?"

"Yes," the reporter in front of the van said. "Captain Morris said that this isn't the first report of an unknown citizen helping to stop a crime in the past few weeks. Perhaps there is hope that the crime wave that has the city gripped by fear has an end in sight."

"That is good news, Carlos," the anchor said, and then the station cut to a commercial.

A warm feeling rushed through me. My fingers trembled as I gathered up my application papers from the table. I looked over the second essay question one more time before I slipped the forms back into the envelope.

How am I going to use my talents to make the world a better place?

I carried the packet up to my room and placed it on my desk next to my more-than-ancient computer. I pulled the khakis I'd been wearing earlier in the day off my chair and stuck my hand in the front pocket. My hands still shook as I dug out the crumpled slip of paper and dialed the number written there into my cell phone.

It rang four times and then someone picked up.

"Hello?" a guy's voice said. My sensitive ears picked up music and what sounded like shouting in the background. He must have been back at The Depot.

"Talbot? This is Grace."

"Hey, kid. What's up?"

I sucked a deep breath in and blew it out and then said, before I could change my mind: "I want you to train me. I want to find my brother—and hopefully take down that gang that's been terrorizing the city in the process."

Talbot laughed. I could hear the smile in his voice when he said, "I thought you'd never ask."

CHAPTER FIFTEEN

Test

"You ready for this?" Talbot asked as I climbed into the van.

"Ready as I'll ever be." I plopped my backpack on the seat between us and pulled out my running shoes from deep inside my bag. I kicked off my school flats and changed into the sneakers.

"So where's your partner? Ditching out again?"

I smirked. "I arranged for him to find twenty dollars in quarters on his bus bench. That should keep him busy at the arcade for a few days."

Talbot laughed. "I like the way you think."

"So what's in store for today? Are we going to have any time for, you know, training?"

"I actually took care of our assignment before I got here. Plus, we've got an extra hour before the bus returns, so we'll have plenty of time for going over the basics."

"What basics?"

"You'll see," he said.

We drove into an area called Glenmore on the outskirts of the city, a neighborhood that had probably been nice in the mid-twentieth century but now was a weird mix of low-income apartments, the original homes of elderly grandparents, and old houses that had been turned into stores. We were only a couple of blocks from the highway when Talbot pulled the van over near a pawnshop called Second Chances. The first thing I noticed about it was the X of police tape across the doorway, and another one over the shattered storefront window.

Talbot grabbed his large backpack from behind his seat and got out of the van. I followed. He walked right up to the storefront. Talbot looked back and forth along the street and then twisted hard on the door handle. I heard a pop as the door unlocked and opened. Talbot pulled the police tape aside and gestured for me to go inside the shop.

"Um, isn't that kind of illegal?" I wasn't exactly big on sneaking into places.

Talbot shrugged. "Sometimes you've got to bend the rules in this line of work."

"What if we get caught?"

Talbot tapped beside his ear. "The place is empty.

The security cameras are still disabled. And we'll be in and out in a matter of minutes. I just want to test something."

"What?"

"You."

I looked into his green eyes and cocked my head, but I didn't say anything.

"Come on, before we lose our chance," he said.

I hesitated for only a second longer and then ducked under the tape and into the store. Broken glass crunched under my shoes as I did a little circle, inspecting the damage around me. All the display cases had been smashed in, and it looked like all the merchandise was missing.

"This place got hit last night," Talbot said. "Whoever did it cleared out the entire inventory and walked off with a six-hundred-pound safe in less than the six minutes it took the police to respond to the silent alarm."

"How do you know all this?"

"It helps to have an in with a detective."

"Oh. So let me guess, no security camera footage?"

"Nope. I questioned my detective friend this morning about it, and he says it's the same as all the other supposedly invisible bandit jobs. No fingerprints, no camera footage, everything gone in a matter of minutes."

"So what are we going to do here?"

"Take a deep breath."

I gave him a quizzical look.

"Go on. Do it."

I sucked in a deep breath. Whatever it was that he wanted me to do must be interesting if he thought I needed to practice deep breathing before he told me. The air tasted sour, like too-old milk, and I let the breath out immediately. I looked around for a water fountain so I could rinse out the nasty taste it left in my mouth. When I couldn't find one, I glanced back at Talbot. "Okay, so what's up?" I asked tentatively. "Why are we here? What kind of test am I supposed to take?"

Talbot raised an eyebrow. "The deep breath was part of your test. You didn't taste anything?"

"Well, yeah. It tastes like sour milk in here, but what does that have to do with anything?"

"Hmmm. We have more work to do than I originally thought. I'd assumed you'd have *some* hunting abilities."

I felt a rush of embarrassment. "No. I get what you mean now." I took in another deep breath and held it in the back of my throat. All I could taste was the sour milk, but I forced myself not to exhale the air. I didn't want to fail in front of Talbot. I didn't want him to think I wasn't up to training. I knew that I was probably getting a bit blue in the face by this point and that made me annoyed with myself. I finally exhaled the air through my nose, and as I did, I caught another scent that I hadn't noticed before. "I taste sour milk, but I smell something else. Like bad meat, maybe? Something rotting."

"Good," Talbot said. "Or bad actually."

"Well, if I didn't do it right, then show me how to do it better. You're supposed to be training me, remember?"

"No training yet. Not until after your test. You did just fine, though. It's just that sour milk means we've got a couple of Gelals on our hands, but the rotting-meat smell means there was at least one Akhkharu here."

"Akh . . . a . . . what?"

"Ahk-hay-roo," he pronounced for me.

I scrunched my nose and didn't even try wrapping my mouth around that word again.

"Yeah," Talbot said. "Just call them Akhs—rhymes with socks. It's much easier to say. Or some people call them vampires."

I could feel my eyes go wide. "Seriously?"

"Except they're not the same as the traditional, I-vant-to-suck-your-blood kind of vamp." Talbot shrugged. "Let's get moving before somebody comes back. We've got another stop to make as part of your test before I get you to your bus."

"And that is?"

"Let's just say it's a good thing you brought your running shoes."

A FEW MINUTES LATER

Talbot hitched his backpack over both of his shoulders and led me to the end of the block. He stopped at the corner with his nose in the air. The street was empty except for an old woman sitting at a bus stop. "You smell that?" Talbot took in a quick breath.

I did the same. "Yeah, it's that same sour-milk, rotting-meat odor."

Talbot nodded with approval. "We're on their trail." He took me by the elbow and we crossed the street, Talbot still testing the air. "Yes, this is the way they went. They were on foot."

"With a six-hundred-pound safe?" My voice held more than just a hint of disbelief.

"Don't underestimate demons, kid. Those Gelals went down easy the other day. Too easy, if you ask me."

My stomach did a little flip-flop. That had been *easy*?

"You ready for the next section of your test?"

"Yeah. Sure. I guess."

Talbot still had me by the elbow, and he pulled me in close to him, our bodies almost touching. He stooped his head so his face nestled close to my neck, and he took in a long, deep breath. When he let the air out, it tickled across my skin, sending tingling goose bumps down my back.

"Did you just smell my hair?" I asked, my voice sounding far too unstable.

"I'm getting your scent. You should get mine, too, in case we get separated."

"Get your scent?" I almost laughed, because I couldn't help thinking of myself as one of those tracking dogs that the police make smell a lost kid's shirt or something before they set out looking for him.

Talbot pulled me closer, my lips practically skimming his neck. His hand squeezed my elbow tight. I took in a deep breath and held it in the back of my throat. Talbot smelled like mint gum, fresh sawdust, and something else that I probably wouldn't have been able to pick up without my developing wolf sense. He smelled like my dog Daisy used to when she'd spent the morning lazing in the sun on the back porch. It was a smell that I'd always found slightly unpleasant in the past— especially when she'd try to nap on my bed smelling like that—but now it made my toes curl with the memory of warm, familiar things.

"You smell like lavender and vanilla," Talbot said. He was so close I could feel his words, warm like sunlight, against my face. He tugged on one of my dark curls.

I took a step back. I'd let him get too close. "It's just my shampoo."

"Well, it's nice and trackable, in case I need to double back to find you. You got my scent?"

I nodded.

"Now that's just plan B in case you lose your way. I want you to focus your concentration on the Gelal and Akh scents. But their trail is old and fading, so don't feel bad if you lose it. My trail will be nice and fresh if we do get separated, so fall back on that." He smiled, all dimly. "And do at least *try* to keep up with me. Won't be any fun if I find them without you."

"Whoa, wait, we're tracking down the thieves . . . right now?"

"Isn't that what you wanted?"

"Yeah, but I thought we'd ease into it. I thought we were going over the basics for a while." That was how Daniel would have handled it. *Take it slow. Stay balanced.* "I mean, you haven't even taught me anything yet."

"These are the basics, Grace. We're demon hunters. No time for taking it easy." Talbot rolled up the sleeves of his red-and-blue flannel shirt.

"So, um, what do we do if we find these demons?"

"We'll figure that out *when* we do."

"*When?*"

Talbot laughed. "This is going to be fun," he said, and took off sprinting down the street.

He was down the block and about to go around a corner before I even realized he was gone. I bolted after him, because I knew I was going to lose him right off if I didn't get a move on. But when I rounded the corner, he was leaning against a tree with his hands in his pockets. When I was about three feet away, he laughed and bolted again. I followed him as he started and stopped like this—a game of cat and mouse—through the lonely neighborhood streets.

Talbot seemed to enjoy himself all too much, which

only annoyed me. He ran in the parkour manner that Daniel had used back when he had powers—taking the easiest passage through, or over, things in his way, rather than going around them. I watched him bound up a flight of concrete stairs to an adjacent building, dive through the railing at the top, land in a head-over-heels roll on the ground, and then pop up again.

"Come on, kid!" he shouted.

I took in a deep breath and followed his lead, shocked and happy with myself when I pulled off the same move. Talbot cheered. A woman walking her dog dropped its leash and stared.

Talbot took off again, running even faster than before. I ran after him, calling on my powers to help me catch up, letting hot, lightning heat push me forward. I was only twenty yards behind him when he veered to the left and then leaped over a six-foot wall and disappeared.

It took all my concentration to change my course. I shifted direction and went careering toward the wall—too fast. But just as I was about to smash face-first into it, my feet kicked off from the ground and I jumped up in the air. My fingers lightly brushed the top of the wall as I leaped over it in half a second flat.

My feet hit the ground with barely a sound, and I slowed to a jog as I approached a three-way intersection. The road stretched out to both the right and left, and a gravel-strewn lane led into a cul-de-sac of dilapidated houses. Talbot was nowhere to be seen, but I could taste his warm scent.

I took a few steps to the left and tested the air. I picked up on the Gelal stench and took another five steps. The Gelal scent faded, as did Talbot's trail. I did the same thing heading right, but that wasn't the correct direction, either. I went back to where I'd started in the intersection and picked up the mixture of scents again. I jogged into the cul-de-sac a little ways. The scent was still strong in the air. Talbot had headed toward one of these houses. But which one?

I turned in a slow circle, breathing in air. Which pretty much made me feel like a dog chasing her own tail. But I picked out a strong path of smells and cautiously followed it to the driveway of what had once been a beautiful Victorian mansion, but now looked as if it should have been condemned at least a decade ago. The smell of rotting meat and sour milk got positively overwhelming as I approached the gravel driveway. Talbot was still missing.

"What now?" I asked out loud with a huff. And then I felt something hard clamp over my mouth and I was pulled behind a tall bush.

I thrashed at my assailant at first, but then I was enveloped in Talbot's warm scent and I heard him whisper, "Shhh. They've got supersenses, too, you know."

He uncovered my mouth, and I turned toward him. "They?" I whispered so softly I was practically just mouthing the words. "So they're here?"

Talbot nodded. "See if you can tell how many." He tapped my ear to indicate that I should listen carefully.

I held my breath, My heart still pounded from running, and I willed it to calm. I listened beyond the crickets chirruping in the bush with us, and pushed away all nearby noises until I could concentrate on the sounds behind the walls of the house. "There are three of them," I whispered. "There's someone snoring, and another two people who sound like they're sitting at a table."

"Four," Talbot said. "There's someone else on the second level. The one sleeping is probably a Gelal. Akhs don't usually sleep." Talbot took off his backpack and opened it. He pulled out what looked like a short sword, the hilt wrapped in black leather cording, and a thick piece of wood, whittled into a point at the end. "You prefer steel or wood?" he asked.

"What?"

"You look as if you like wood," he said with a smirk, and tossed me the stick . . . or stake, I guess I should say.

My hand snapped out and I caught it in midair without even thinking. I could definitely get used to these reflexes. "What are you doing? We're not seriously going in there?"

"Of course we are." Talbot unsheathed the sword. It looked awfully sharp. "Four against two. Those aren't bad odds."

"Okay, no way." My hand shook so hard I almost dropped the stake. "This is a little more than basic training for my first day. I can't go in there."

"Yes, you can, Grace," Talbot whispered. He stared at me with his piercing green eyes. "What if this was your one chance to rescue your brother, and you just walked away? What if he's in there right now? What if they're holding him captive? Maybe that's who's upstairs. For all you know, they've got him chained up in there and they're saving him for their next meal. Don't you want to make them pay for that?"

I could feel that tight, flaming knot forming in my stomach—the same feeling I'd had when I saw that masked Gelal with that gun to Talbot's head. Suddenly, I could picture Jude tied up in that house, bloody and bruised. A monster crouched over him, threatening to tear him apart. I wrapped my fingers around the stake. "Okay, let's do this."

62.5 HEARTBEATS LATER

Talbot kicked in the door, and the two of us burst through the doorway. A man and a woman, who had been sitting at a table playing cards, shouted when they saw us. A third man, who had been asleep on a couch, suddenly shot straight up, looking confused and feral. He lumbered toward us and took a wild swing at me. I easily deflected his blow and pushed him away.

The woman threw the table aside, accidentally knocking over her companion, and lunged at Talbot. Talbot punched her in the gut, and she stumbled back. She snarled and threw herself at him again.

The noxious demon smell in the room made me dizzy and nauseous. The feral man snarled at me. I assumed he was Gelal from his sour-milk stench. He threw another punch toward my face. I ducked and was about to sweep at his legs with a kick when I caught the glint of steel out of the corner of my eye. I turned my head toward the flash as Talbot swung his sword at the woman's throat. It sank deep into her skin with the sound of a knife plunged into a watermelon—and, with a spray of blood, her head separated from her body.

Talbot had *cut off* her head!

I screamed. Like I didn't know I was capable of screaming. *Talbot killed that woman!* I dry heaved, and I scrambled back away from her head as it rolled toward me, an expression of sheer surprise on the face.

What had just happened? What had Talbot done?

He killed her!

I didn't know what I'd expected before we crashed in here. We'd subdue these criminals and leave them for the cops?

But not *murder* them!

The woman's headless body took another step toward Talbot, then crumpled to the ground . . . and shattered into dust before my very eyes. Her head disintegrated, too.

"What did you do?!" I screamed at Talbot.

And then I took a direct blow to the face from the Gelal.

I flew backward and slammed against a picture frame on the wall. I could feel the glass crunch against my shoulder and pain rip into my back. I dropped to my knees. I was stunned, the whole room swimming before my eyes, when the man lunged at me. His fingers elongated into pointed claws, aimed at my throat. Talbot flung his sword at the man. It skewered him through the back and out through his chest. Black ooze spurted from the wound and onto my face. It burned like acid on my skin, and I tried to wipe it away. The man fell over at my feet, clutching frantically at the sword sticking through his chest, but unable to do anything but slice open his own clawed hands.

"Oh, God." I scrambled forward and reached out to help him.

"Don't touch him!" Talbot shouted. He was now in a hand-to-hand struggle with the guy who had been at the table.

The man in front of me shook with agony and then suddenly went rigged. His stiff body rocked back and forth and then exploded into ooze. I jumped to the side just in time to miss the brunt of the burning acid.

I shook as I stumbled as far away from the sour-smelling mess as I could get. I steadied myself against the banister of the stairs that led to the upper level. My breathing came too fast. My stomach lurched. I was about to lose the contents of it when somebody grabbed me from behind. My feet left the ground before I could even react, and whoever had grabbed me flung me toward the couch. I landed half on, half off it, but I had no time to move before someone jumped on top of me. A woman. With pink-and-black hair, and sharp, pointy teeth. She grabbed me by the throat.

Where had she even come from?

She must have been the one who'd been upstairs, I realized, which meant Jude wasn't here at all.

"Don't look her in the eyes!" I heard Talbot shout.

But it was too late. The woman had locked eyes with me, and I couldn't shake the gaze of her coal-black irises. Couldn't will myself to look away or close my eyelids. I could hear the woman chanting something— some other language—but her lips weren't moving. I'd experienced this before, but I suddenly couldn't remember how or when.

"Use your stake, Grace!" Talbot shouted. But he sounded so far away. "Use it, Grace. Kill her!"

You want to give me your stake, the woman said without speaking. *Hand it to me. You know that's what you want to do.*

I gripped the stake in my hand. I'd all but forgotten it was even there. A thick fog swirled in my brain, and all I could think was that I didn't want this terrible weapon. I couldn't kill someone. I wasn't a murderer. I wasn't a monster. If the woman wanted the stake, she could have it.

I slowly lifted my arm and handed it to her.

She clutched it in her talonlike fingers and laughed. *I don't know what Daniel sees in you,* she said inside my head. *You're so weak-minded.*

What? I tried to ask, but my lips wouldn't move. How did she know Daniel's name? How did she know who I was?

But maybe tonight he'll be more fun to party with— she lifted the stake above my heart—*now that you're dead.* She thrust the stake at my chest.

But then she froze as if shocked by something. Her eyes rolled back in her head, breaking the trance she'd held me in. The fog in my mind cleared a bit, and I realized I did know her.

"Mishka?"

"Little bitch," she said, and disintegrated right on top of me.

All that was left of her was a pile of dust. A broken chair leg fell from her back as she disappeared. It rolled off the couch and across the floor, stopping when it hit one of Talbot's sneakers.

"You okay, kid?" he asked, and held out his hand to help me up.

I cowered from his touch and scrambled as far away

from him as I could on the couch while frantically brushing Mishka dust off my pants. "I . . . I . . . knew her," I stammered. "And you killed her." I turned my head from side to side, searching the room for life. It was empty except for two other piles of dust and a pool of acidic ooze that ate away at the carpet. My stomach lurched. I clutched at it with my hand. "You . . . You killed them all."

"Yeah, that's kind of what I do." Talbot brushed his hand through his hair. He'd lost his baseball cap at some point during the fight. "What did you think, we were going to take them all out for ice cream and buy them puppies?"

"No. I thought . . . we'd deliver them to the police. But you *killed* them." It didn't make sense. I'd seen Talbot handle April's silver bracelet without it burning his hand. I'd assumed he was just like me—an Urbat who had powers but who hadn't fallen to the curse. A Hound of Heaven. But if this was the first time he'd killed somebody, shouldn't he have changed into a wolf? Except . . . the way he'd handled that sword, this certainly wasn't his first kill. There had been no hesitation there. "I don't understand. A predatory act . . . if you kill a person, then . . . ."

"These weren't people, Grace. These were straight-up demons. The werewolf curse only affects you if you kill a *human*. The Urbat were created to kill demons. It's what we do."

"But you didn't kill that one with the gun the other day."

"I didn't kill him in front of you because I didn't know if you were ready for that. Apparently, you still aren't. You're far more green than I expected."

"No. It's just that I still don't understand. My brother fell to the curse when he tried to kill Daniel—who was a werewolf at the time. . . ."

"Ah." Talbot sat next to me on the couch. I scooted away from him, not sure if I knew who he was anymore. "You see, werewolves are *still* human. They still have a human heart that coexists with their demon one. That's why killing a werewolf—with malicious intent—counts as a predatory act against a *human*. But true demons are different. Gelals just take on a human-looking appearance. They don't actually have real bodies at all. And Akhs—a species of vampire—take up residence in dead human bodies. Think of them as a demon infestation of a dead human. That's why they smell like rotting meat—at least to someone with a sensitive sense of smell." He tapped the side of his nose. "It's also why they turn to dust when they're killed. The infestation rapidly speeds up the decomposition of the body, so they fall apart when the demon inside them dies."

"Oh."

My mind reeled. Dad had given me books about werewolves, but most of those books just contained myths, no real substantial information at all, and the idea of battling a real demon had always been so far off—and seemed completely unreal—that I hadn't bothered trying to learn much about the enemy. Talbot was right—I really was green.

And it had almost got me killed.

"Thank you for saving me. I would have just laid there and let her kill me." I hugged my knees to my chest on the couch, feeling utterly useless. "I couldn't help doing what she wanted."

"Mind control," Talbot said. "Just remember never to look an Akh in the eyes. That's how they're different from traditional vamps. Akhs are what you call psychic vampires. They feed on your life force, steal your free will. But Gelals and all vamps die the same way. Stake to the heart, or a good old-fashioned beheading."

I shuddered, remembering the sight of the first woman's head being severed from her body. "I was so shocked by everything, I completely forgot that there was one more of them in the house."

"That's my fault. I should have reminded you so you'd have been prepared. But let that be a lesson to the both of us, okay?" He smiled at me. "Rule number one: Never drop your guard."

I half smiled, but then it turned to a frown. Daniel had said that same thing to me time and again. And I hated that I wouldn't be able to tell him about what had happened today.

I'd have to lie to him.

The feeling of utter defeat settled on my shoulders as I surveyed the empty room again. "I just wish you hadn't had to kill them all. I mean, we didn't get to question any of them about Jude. If this is the gang he's been hiding out with, then where the heck is he?"

"Jude was never here," Talbot said. "These creatures were just amateurs. Copycats. They're not the real Shadow Kings. The real gang would have never tripped the silent alarm at that pawnshop."

I stood up and faced Talbot. My hands shook with anger. "Wait, you knew all along they weren't the real gang?"

Talbot nodded.

"Then why did we come here?"

"Because this was a test, Grace. I needed to know if you were ready, and clearly you're not. What you saw here, what happened in that alley on Monday, that was just child's play compared to what we'll eventually face. This little band of amateurs was only four strong. The real gang is probably five times as big."

That thought sent chills down my spine. "So you knew Jude wasn't here before we came busting in?"

"Yes."

"Then why did you say . . . Why did you make me think he was?"

"Because I needed to get you worked up enough to act. Your emotions—that's where your power comes from."

Talbot's words confused me. "But that's not what Daniel says. He always tells me to pull back when I get angry. He says the key to learning to use my powers is balance. He says I should never allow my emotions to get the better of me if I want to learn to use my powers without giving in to the wolf."

"Then you should start asking yourself what reason Daniel has for holding you back."

Heat flashed in my cheeks. *Talbot's right,* a voice said inside my mind. Daniel did want to hold me back.

But that still didn't mean Talbot was right and Daniel was wrong.

Talbot stood up so he was standing right in front of me, only a few inches separating us. He looked into my eyes with his piercing gaze. He reached out and touched my moonstone necklace. I wanted to flinch away from his touch, but I didn't.

"You'll never reach your full potential if you keep wearing this," he said. "I ditched mine a long time ago."

"You threw away your moonstone? Where'd you even get one? I thought they were rare. . . ."

"Old family heirloom. I'm better off without it."

"But Gabriel says the moonstone is the only thing that keeps the wolf at bay. Gabriel—"

"Gabriel?" Talbot pulled his hand away from my necklace and stepped back. "You know Gabriel?"

"Yes." Assuming he meant the same one. "Gabriel Saint Moon?"

Talbot let out a harsh laugh. "He calls himself Saint Moon now? That's ironic."

"You know about Gabriel and the Saint Moons?"

"Gabriel is a notorious coward." Talbot spread his arms out at his sides. "And I *am* a Saint Moon."

I almost gasped. "You are?"

"Or at least my mother was. She was a direct descendant of Katharine and Simon Saint Moon, the first werewolf hunter in my family. By the time my mom was born, the Saint Moons had supposedly retired from the demon-hunting gig, but both my parents were crypto-zoologists. They'd travel around researching local demon mythology—but I imagine they did a little slaying on the side when times called for it. That is, until they had me. They stopped traveling and settled down in a small town in Pennsylvania. The Saint Moons had a truce with Gabriel's pack, which lived in the nearby mountains, but then, on my third birthday, my parents were slaughtered by a rogue band of werewolves from that pack—right in front of me."

This time I did gasp. I covered my mouth with my hand.

"One of the unexpected guests decided to leave me with a special birthday present." Talbot pulled up the bottom of his flannel shirt and showed me the large crescent-shaped scar that looked almost like a tattoo on his well-cut abs.

"I'm sorry." I didn't know what else to say.

Talbot lowered his shirt. "Gabriel is the one who should be sorry. He could have stopped those werewolves, but he didn't. It would have meant getting his hands dirty. And his alpha, Sirhan, barely even punished the wolves that killed my parents. They deserve what's going to happen to their pack when Sirhan dies. . . ." He pursed his lips and looked down at his feet.

"What happened to you after that?" I couldn't imagine being so young and having your parents killed right in front you. He would've been only six months older than Baby James.

"I was sent to live with my grandfather on his farm. He was already caring for my mentally disabled cousin. Our grandfather used to fill the two of us with all these stories of the great Saint Moons. Demon fighters. Brave to the very end. Used to show us this old silver dagger. He died after a stroke when I was only thirteen, and that's when I decided to carry on the legacy. Only I have an advantage over Simon and all the other Saint Moons—I've got superpowers. And unlike cowards like Gabriel, I use them."

"Your cousin, the mentally disabled one, was he the only family you had left?"

Talbot nodded. "I couldn't take care of him, and he couldn't take care of me, even though he was a lot older. I haven't seen him since the day our grandfather died. But we're the last of the family."

"No," I said. "Don's dead. I knew him, and he died

ten months ago. But he'd wanted to be a hero like you."

Talbot lowered his head, and his shoulders slumped. That was why he seemed strangely familiar. Even though none of their specific features were identical, there was still a family resemblance there—that familiarity that struck me so many times before—in the shape of his mouth, the tone of his voice, and the largeness of his hands. Talbot reminded me of a much younger, attractive, mentally and physically sound Don Mooney. There was even a slight resemblance to Gabriel—the two could also be cousins.

"That means *you're* the last real Saint Moon," I said.

Talbot bent down. He'd found his baseball cap. He scooped it up and put it on his head. "I'm going to check the rest of the house for bodies. I doubt those creatures were *welcome* houseguests of whoever used to live here."

He started toward the stairs, then stopped and looked back at me. "You did a decent job here today. We've just got a lot to work on before we start thinking about going after the real gang." He gave me a half smile. "We will find your brother. I promise."

"Thank you," I said.

"Get to work on healing those marks on your face. I bet you can find a towel in one of the bathrooms and wash up a bit. I can't take you back to the bus looking like that."

I found a small bathroom off the kitchen. Yellow rings stained the inside of the sink, and the mirror was cloudy and cracked. An old, stiff towel hung from a tarnished-brass towel ring. I pulled it from the metal loop and used the corner of it to clean a section of the mirror. I stared at the red-rimmed eyes of my reflection and then my pale face and disheveled hair. Red marks shaped like long-taloned fingers painted my neck where Mishka had grabbed me, and three angry, blistering burns welted my face from the Gelal's acid blood.

I closed my eyes and concentrated. Tried to picture my wounds healing over like Daniel had taught me—tried to erase them with the power of my mind. But when I opened my eyes, my reflection appeared exactly the same. My ability to control my superhearing, speed, strength, and agility had increased tenfold since my breakthrough run on Sunday. But the healing power still eluded me. Yes, these wounds would probably heal on their own in a matter of hours—compared to weeks for a regular human—but I should be able to speed up the process even more. Make it take seconds rather than hours, if I concentrated enough.

I didn't have hours to wait, so I closed my eyes and tried again. Healing had been the first power Daniel had developed as a kid—it was how he'd discovered that he had special abilities in the first place. But for some reason it was the hardest one for me. I opened my eyes and frowned at my unchanged appearance—then jumped at the sight of Talbot standing right behind me in the doorway. I gripped the counter to steady myself.

"I'm sorry," Talbot said. "I knocked, but you didn't answer. I was worried. . . ."

"I'm okay. I was just concentrating."

"You better concentrate harder. We've got to get back to the bus, and you're not healed up yet."

"That's because I don't know how to do it."

"Oh." Talbot stepped into the tight room. Only two more steps and we'd be touching. I cursed my heart for beating faster. "I can help you," he said.

"How?"

Talbot took one more step. Closer now. I watched his reflection in the mirror as he reached his hands out and brushed my hair back behind my ears. He cupped both of his hands on my face, pressing his palms into the burns on my cheeks. I winced and tried to pull away from his touch.

"Easy," he said softly. "Don't think about the pain. Think about where the pain came from. Think about how you got these burns. What were you feeling when it happened?"

"Scared." I pictured the sight of the Gelal, skewered

right in front of me. Then the way he'd grabbed at the sword and cut his bare hands. "Horrified."

"Close your eyes."

I let my eyelids drop.

"Concentrate on what you were feeling," he said close to my ear. "Hold those emotions inside of you until they burn."

At first I didn't know what he meant, and it seemed so opposite from what Daniel had told me that I didn't think it would work. But I replayed that horrible scene in my head and let the fear of the moment engulf me. Felt the panic rise in my chest. And then I felt tingling warmth under Talbot's touch. The heat swelled until it felt as hot as white coals, and just when I thought I might faint from the pain, it tingled away into nothing.

I opened my eyes. Talbot pulled his hands away from my face and placed them on my shoulders. The burns were gone.

"Good as new," he said.

I met his gaze in the mirror for a second, then quickly turned my head away.

I didn't know if I could look at Talbot the same way again. He'd changed so much for me in the last few hours. He wasn't just a dimpled-cheeked farm boy who just happened to be another Urbat and reminded me of comforting things. Under that flannel shirt beat the heart of a powerful hunter—one strong enough to kill a demon with a single swing of his steel sword.

Talbot was dangerous.

I had no doubt about that.

But at the same time, I couldn't help picturing him as a little boy, shrieking with fear as his parents died in front of him. It made me want to wrap my arms around him, hold him like Baby James, and tell him everything was going to be okay—that I could help him make the monsters go away.

I pulled out of his grasp and turned to leave. It wasn't right to be this close to Talbot. I loved Daniel.

"Grace."

"Yes?" I glanced back at him.

He stood quiet for a moment. No happiness in his expression at all. "Take that towel and wipe down anything you think you might have touched."

"Why?"

He pulled his cell phone out of his pocket. "I was right. Somebody *did* live here. I need to call the police so they can take care of the body."

CHAPTER SIXTEEN

Beasts of Gevaudan

LATER, BACK AT THE BUS

"Whoa, what the heck happened to you?" April asked when I approached her and Claire in front of the rec center.

"Uh . . ." Did I really still look that bad?

"Ew. Seriously, what's on your shirt?"

I looked down at my white polo. The Gelal acid had apparently eaten away little holes in my shirt, and traces of the black ooze lingered around the edges of each.

"Oh, guts," I said.

Claire made a gagging face. "What did you guys have to do?"

"Oh, um. We were helping out at some old guy's house, and it turns out it was all infested. We had to squash some bugs."

"Sick!" April said. "Dude, I'm so sorry. All we had to

do was help paint a fence behind an elementary school . . . and then we got cookies!" She pulled a cookie wrapped in a napkin out of her purse and handed it to me. "Seriously, I think you deserve it."

"Oh, thanks," I said.

But I didn't know when, or if, I'd ever be able to eat again. Not after what Talbot found in the master bedroom of that run-down house. That old man had never stood a chance against those monsters. At least Talbot had called the police so the old man's body would be found soon and be taken care of. The only thing keeping me from bursting into tears over a total stranger was knowing that I had at least—in a way—been a part of destroying the demons that had killed him.

Claire gave my clothes another once-over. "So what kind of bugs did you have to kill anyway?"

"Really big nasty ones," I said. Then I mouthed the word *demons* to April.

Oh, she mouthed back. She grabbed Claire's arm and pulled her toward the bus. "Let's not make a big deal about Grace's nasty assignment," she said. "You don't want to make people jealous or anything." April laughed uncomfortably.

"But I want to know what . . . ," Claire said as April pushed her up the bus steps.

"Hey, did you know that Jeff Read said you look hot in that sweater?"

I followed them into the bus and sat a row behind

them. I listened as they chattered on about what else Jeff Read had said recently about Claire. I smiled and nodded in all the right places, but I didn't really feel like talking anymore.

When we pulled into the parking lot of the school, I saw Gabriel waiting for us by the front doors. I knew I could fool Claire about the damage to my shirt, but I figured Gabriel would be a harder audience—besides, he could probably smell the Gelal and Akh stench that clung to my hair—so I made a beeline for Dad's Corolla in the parish parking lot.

I pulled from my backpack my set of house keys, which also happened to have a spare to the Corolla on the ring. Hopefully, Dad wouldn't mind if I borrowed it to get home. I even called and left a message on his cell phone, telling him I was doing so. He could always take the parish's truck if he didn't feel like walking.

I parked in the driveway and ran into the house. Mom called my name from the kitchen—followed by the wafting goodness of her pork tenderloin in Marsala sauce—but I pretended not to hear her and dashed up to the bathroom. I pulled off my nasty shirt, wrapped it in the towel I'd used to clean up with at the old man's house, and shoved the bundle deep inside the bathroom trash can. I pulled off the rest of my clothes and stepped into the shower.

I lathered and rinsed my hair three times before I felt like the noxious scents from the afternoon had been washed away. But what were impossible to scrub out were the memories of the day that clung to me now—wiping down a crime scene, watching a demon die right in front of me, the expression on the face of that bodiless head, and Talbot finding that dead old man. I scrubbed and scrubbed. I sat in the shower with my knees pulled up to my chest and let the scalding water rain down on me. But no matter how hard I tried, I couldn't rinse those images out of my mind.

My life had changed in the last few hours.

I'd changed.

I felt like a different person, and part of me longed for Daniel's arms, strong and true, to wrap me in his warm embrace. I wanted to hear him tell me that it was okay for me to be different now. That he still loved me no matter what.

When the water turned cold, I got out and changed into fresh clothes. My plan was to hide in my room for the rest of the night. I still buzzed so much from what had happened this afternoon I worried that if I spent too much time with anyone, they'd be able to tell I was hiding something. They'd be able to see the changes in me. I was just about to start in on homework at my desk when Charity knocked on my door.

"What's up?" I asked.

"Dinner," she said, and gave me a weird look from the doorway.

"I'll just get some leftovers later." I turned away and

gazed down at my book. "I've got a lot of work to do."

"No . . . Mom says everyone has to come. It's a *family* dinner. Mom cooked, and we've got company."

"Really?" Regular family dinner had been a Divine family ritual for the first seventeen years of my life, but now I could hardly remember the last time we'd all sat at the same table together—let alone had company. I guess I should have put two and two together when I smelled good things coming from the kitchen.

"Daniel's here."

"Ooh." I loved that just the mention of his name could make my heart skip a beat.

"And that cute new religion teacher at your school. Pastor Saint Moon."

"Oh." My voice had a very different inflection this time. Gabriel was the last person I wanted to see at the moment. "I really do have a lot of homework. Can you tell Mom that I can't—"

"Yeah, right. Mom's full-on Martha Stewart–ing it down there. She made a four-course meal and pulled out the good china. I wouldn't mess with her if I were you."

"Great," I mumbled.

Mom shouted our names from downstairs. Charity jumped like a frightened cat and yelled, "Coming!"

I got up from my desk and checked my reflection in my full-length mirror, just to reassure myself that there wasn't any *physical* evidence left of what I'd done with

Talbot this afternoon. Charity still stood in my door-way, so I pretended I was checking my makeup—but then I remembered I wasn't wearing any.

"You okay?" she asked.

"Uh, yeah."

I followed Charity down the stairs. Daniel and Gabriel sat at the dining room table with Dad and Baby James. Mom gave us a what-took-you-so-long look as she set a salad bowl on the table.

Gabriel stood up as Charity and I approached, and he bowed his head to me as I sat. I wondered if that had something to do with all of that Divine One stuff he'd been talking about, or if it was just another of his old-fashioned mannerisms. Then Gabriel turned and bowed to Charity.

She totally giggled and blushed.

I totally rolled my eyes.

And Daniel totally snorted.

Charity had no idea just how *too old* Gabriel Saint Moon was for her to have a crush on him.

I sat next to Daniel. "Hey," he said, and squeezed my hand. The edge of the bandage on his arm was all frayed—probably because he kept picking at it.

"Hey," I said back, trying to sound as normal as pos-sible. Because that was what Daniel wanted: normal. Not different, like how I felt now. I smiled casually, or at least I tried to make it seem as casual and natural as I could, but then I worried I was overdoing it. I couldn't look Daniel in the eye, either. What if he could see right through my act? I dropped the awkward smile and turned my attention to Baby James, who attempted to pull a Houdini act with the straps of his booster chair. After I wrestled James back into his seat, Dad blessed the food and Mom dished up salad for everyone.

"This all looks excellent," Gabriel said as Mom handed him back his plate. "I haven't eaten like this since the last time I was in France."

Mom smiled. "Why, thank you, Pastor Saint Moon. We're actually having Italian tonight. Part of my family originates from Rome." She then launched into our more-than-diverse heritage as Gabriel nodded along and asked questions about her family. Listening to Mom engage in a real conversation almost made me like Gabriel for a moment. Almost made me relax.

That is, until Dad turned the conversation in the opposite direction. "So, Gabriel, how is the senior community-service project coming along? I was afraid it would get cancelled altogether when Mr. Shumway quit."

"Quite well," Gabriel said with an ancient smile. "Don't you agree, Daniel?"

Daniel had his cell phone out. "Yeah, I guess." He checked the screen of his phone and then put it on his lap. "We're hoping to have the store up and running again by Halloween. Katie had a great idea to host a holiday street festival outside the store as part of a grand reopening. Games, trunk-or-treating, concessions, fund-raising raffle."

"That sounds fabulous," Mom said. "I should make some caramel apples and popcorn balls to sell for the fund-raising." She almost sounded like her old self. "I can even help with the decorating."

Charity coughed and gave me a look that seemed to say, *Do you think Mom will even remember offering her help by tomorrow?*

I shrugged.

"That would be wonderful, Mrs. Divine," Gabriel said.

Daniel checked his phone again. "Katie will be really excited to have your help. I'll give you her number."

He looked at the screen of his phone one more time. Hopefully, he wasn't expecting a text from Katie or something like that. But then a worse thought crossed my mind. It was hard to remember what had happened while I was in Mishka's mind-control trance, but I suddenly remembered her saying something about partying with Daniel—tonight. But Mishka was dead, so if that was who he was expecting, then surely her text would never come.

"I'll be pulling extra shifts until then to get the store ready," Daniel said. I glanced at his phone, now just as anxious as he was to see if it beeped.

I wondered how I could ask him about what Mishka had said to me without giving away that I'd talked to her. Or the fact that I'd been involved with her death.

"And what about you, Grace?" Gabriel asked. "Are you finding your community-service project worthwhile?"

"Yes," I said. Hopefully, he wouldn't ask me anything too difficult to answer without red lie marks splotching up my neck. "More so than I thought I would."

"Good. I was hoping you'd get into it. See just how much good a person can do in the world. I have a feeling you'll be hooked by the end of the project."

"I think I already am." I didn't have to hide any splotches on my neck—I was speaking the complete and total truth.

"Then perhaps my work here will be easier than I thought." Gabriel stabbed a cucumber with his fork. I realized it was Mom's special gold one, while the rest of us were eating with silverware. I couldn't help staring at it.

Gabriel gave me a funny smile and wiggled his fork. "As you already know, I'm allergic to silver. It was kind of your mother to offer me such a nice alternative. I have to admit food doesn't taste quite as good when eaten with plastic utensils."

"That must be terrible," Charity crooned. She sounded like she was trying to seem older.

Daniel's phone beeped. I jumped. He grabbed it and practically shot out of his chair.

"I'm sorry, but I need to leave."

"Really?" Mom said. "Are you sure? We haven't even had the tenderloin yet." She turned to Gabriel. "It really is magnificent, if I do say so myself. My mother's recipe." She looked back at Daniel with a sweet smile on her face. "It would be a shame for you to miss out, Daniel."

I almost choked on an almond from my salad. That was the second time Mom had been nice to Daniel in one evening. Usually, she just tolerated his presence because Dad said she couldn't forbid Daniel from coming into our house anymore. Mom turned her congenial smile back on Gabriel. Either Pastor Saint Moon was a great mood stabilizer for my mother, or she was trying that hard to impress him. Perhaps there was *some* benefit to having him around.

Daniel's phone beeped in his hand. "Sorry, I really do have to run."

"Where are you going?" I got up from the table. "I'll come with you."

"Grace," Mom snapped. "We have company."

"No." Daniel was already in the foyer. He grabbed his jacket from the coatrack. "I told Mr. Day that if he needed me tonight, I'd come do an extra shift. I'll be working late. Stay here and eat." He went out the door before I had a chance to respond.

Why would he be so anxious about getting a text from Mr. Day?

But at least I knew it wasn't from Mishka.

238

"Tell us more about France," Charity said to Gabriel.

I sat back in my chair and stared at my food.

I suddenly had no appetite again.

AFTER DINNER

I was busy clearing the table while Mom had Charity and Dad helping her dig out all of our Halloween decorations from the basement storage room. She wanted to send them with Gabriel for the fund-raiser. Gabriel had offered his help, but Mom had shooed him off to Dad's study, refusing to let him lift a finger.

I passed the study with an armload of dishes and saw Gabriel sitting in Dad's chair, flipping through one of Dad's many books. He ran his hand through his long, wavy hair. I was right; he and Talbot did look like they could be cousins sometimes—even if most of their features weren't the same. I wondered if Gabriel really had done nothing to stop Talbot's family from being slaughtered. How could he allow that after what had happened to his own sister?

I sighed. *Is there a difference between being a pacifist and being a coward?*

I went to the kitchen and deposited the dishes in the sink. When I came back through the hall toward the dining room, I found Gabriel standing in the study's doorway.

"Did you want to ask me something?" Gabriel stepped

sideways so I could enter the study if I wanted.

I hesitated and almost said no, but I couldn't shake the image of Gabriel standing aside while a mother and father were murdered at a little boy's birthday party. Had he actually been there? Or was it merely something that had been out of his control? I followed Gabriel into Dad's study and sat in one of the chairs in front of the desk.

The only thing was, I had the same problem here as I did with Daniel. How could I ask him the questions I had without revealing how I knew what I knew in the first place?

"Something troubles you," Gabriel said. "Are you still not seeing the merits of your service project? I can assure you, Grace, charity and compassion will provide a much fuller life than any other avenue in front of you."

"But everyone is capable of charity and compassion. What I don't understand is why you don't use your *special* abilities to make a difference. There are a lot of dangerous things out there. Shouldn't we be doing everything *we* can do to stop them?" I couldn't let go of the thought of that old man killed in his house by those demons. *What if Talbot and I had been able to find them earlier? What if we could have saved his life?* "I don't understand you. You have the ability to make a difference, but you just hide up in the mountains with your pack, completely cut off from the world. Why would you turn your back on what the Urbat were originally created to do? Why do you want me to do the same?"

"Because I *am* one of those dangerous things, Grace. And I don't want *you* to become one of them, too."

I looked away from his steel-blue eyes.

"My pack lives in seclusion because we removed ourselves from society for the sake of mankind—and for our own safety." Gabriel picked up the book he'd been looking through. It was one of Dad's werewolf lore books, filled with mostly myth. Gabriel flipped it open to a page with a drawing of a strange hyena-wolf-like creature. "Have you ever heard of the Beast of Gevaudan?"

I nodded. It was one of the more gruesome stories I'd read in the book.

"What do you know about it?"

"I read that a beast terrorized the French countryside in the 1760s or sometime like that. In three years, it killed a hundred and two people. Mostly women and children. Finally, a poor peasant supposedly killed the beast with a single shot to the chest with a silver bullet. He took the body of the beast to the king and was rewarded with a fortune. Scientists claim it must have been some sort of hyena, but many people back then believed it was actually a werewolf that had been responsible for all those deaths."

"They were partially right. It was were*wolves*, actually," Gabriel said. "And there were a hundred and seventeen deaths. This book isn't accurate. Well, actually, none of them ever are, since there're only a handful of us who know what really happened."

"You were there?"

Gabriel nodded. "You see, there was a time when my pack lived close to society. We intermixed like normal people. I even tried my hand at being a priest for a while—not quite the same as a monk. But our alpha at the time—his name was Ulrich—let the werewolves in our pack hunt at will. They were discreet at first, but many of them got out of hand. They believed that we, as superior creatures, should rule the countryside with terror. Ulrich started to believe that he could overthrow the government if the peasants were afraid enough to revolt. Many of the pack took pleasure in attacking women and children and leaving their disemboweled bodies near roads and forest paths for others to find. They'd sit in the town's square and joyfully listen to the wails of the bereaved and the cries of the frightened."

I shifted uncomfortably in my chair. This was worse than the account in the book.

"King Louis XV eventually listened to the concerns of his people and raised a bounty on the head of the supposed beast. He conscripted peasants as soldiers to kill wolves, and sent his greatest noble huntsmen into the surrounding villages and forests. The king's men pillaged many of the peasants' homes for food and supplies, raped their daughters, and decimated their farms—all in the name of finding the beast. It became a very dangerous time for anyone suspected of knowing anything about wolves. Many in my pack were shot by the hunters while in their wolf forms. They all survived, of course, but it was still a very unpleasant way to live. Yet Ulrich and many of the wolves in our pack continued to kill—even at the risk of exposing us all."

"That's terrible. What did you do?"

Gabriel rubbed one of his fingers, which had a lighter band of skin on it than the rest of his hand. "I was concerned for the townsfolk. Heartbroken to see so many innocents die for sport. I was the presiding priest at so many of their funerals. Luckily, I was not the only one who was disgusted by Ulrich's ways. My mentor, Sirhan, who should have been the true alpha of our pack, had not claimed the position out of respect for his father, Ulrich. However, he feared there would be no pack left for him to inherit if he waited too long. He and a couple of other pack mates devised a plan. I refused to take part in it directly, because it involved killing, but as a priest, I did bless a handful of silver bullets for them. Sirhan then waited until Ulrich turned into a wolf, and when he was just about to attack a peasant hunter, Sirhan shot him through the heart with one of my silver bullets. He then told the peasant that if he took the body of the giant wolf to the king and claimed he had killed it, he'd be rewarded handsomely.

"Sirhan became the true alpha of the pack and put

a stop to the killings, and when the time was right, we moved the entire pack to the Americas. We've lived here in seclusion ever since. Sirhan puts the preservation of the pack above all else. And I, as his beta, Keeper of the pack, encourage them to live in peace. Some may call that being a coward. I do not."

"And the pack has been peaceful ever since?" I asked. That didn't jive with what Talbot had told me about wolves from Gabriel's pack attacking his family.

"Many of them still hunt in our territory—animals mostly, but there have been a handful of unfortunate humans who have wandered onto our lands in the past couple hundred years. . . . But we live discreetly. However, a little less than twenty years ago, there was a group of relatively young Urbats in our pack who did not understand the things Sirhan and I tried to teach them. They were a new generation who reveled in the tales of Ulrich and the Beasts of Gevaudan; they thought the pack should return to what they thought of as the 'golden age of the werewolf.' One of them desired to be the new alpha, so they attacked Sirhan, mortally injured his mate, Rachel, and took their killing spree into the nearest town and attacked at least five different households."

The image of a three-year-old watching his parents die flashed in my mind. "And you did nothing to stop them?"

"There was nothing I *could* do." Gabriel slumped

244

his shoulders and again rubbed at that light band of skin on his finger. "When I first turned into a wolf, I went on a killing spree of my own—until I killed my sister, Katharine. When I came to my senses and realized what I'd done, I swore off all forms of violence. I haven't willingly injured anyone since then. I do not raise my hand, no matter the cause."

"So you *did* just step aside and let those rogue wolves kill those families?"

"Sirhan sent men after them. They were captured and dealt with for almost exposing the pack. Their ringleader was banished for injuring Rachel, who eventually died, and for trying to usurp the position of alpha from Sirhan."

"Banished? Why not killed? Where did he go?"

Gabriel pursed his lips and placed the open book on the desk. "Sirhan ran him out of the area. He traveled around a bit, and then decided to start his own pack by marrying a human woman and having a child. He eventually started killing again. I believe you knew him as the Markham Street Monster."

I gasped. "Mr. Kalbi? Daniel's father?" I searched around in my head for his first name—Daniel never ever spoke it.

"Caleb Kalbi," Gabriel said. "Yes."

Now I finally understood why Sirhan hadn't let Caleb's son rejoin his pack last year. Why he seemed to despise Daniel for no fault of his own.

"I am just grateful that Caleb is not a true alpha, or this world may be a very different place. If he'd convinced more than a couple of members of our pack that he should be the leader . . ." Gabriel shook his head. "Caleb did enough damage as the Markham Street Monster, but imagine if he had a whole pack doing his bidding. It'd be Gevaudan all over again. Most likely worse."

I shuddered at that idea. Caleb had killed at least two dozen people on his own before he left town. I couldn't imagine his having an entire pack under his control. "What do you mean by *true alpha?*" I asked Gabriel. "You called Sirhan that before." My head was beginning to spin from absorbing so much information, but I didn't know when I'd get a chance to ask Gabriel questions like this again.

"True alphas are very rare. They are Urbats born with a certain mystical essence that grows in them as they age. They are the true 'chosen' pack leaders, and if a true alpha wants to be the alpha of a pack, usually the rest of the pack will recognize him as such. I don't really know why, perhaps it is some magical phenomenon, or merely pheromones. There have been very few true alphas, and they are even rarer now than before— probably because Urbats tend not to procreate very often. Most packs operate under the leadership of a regular appointed alpha, rather than under the direction of a true alpha. Sirhan is the last remaining true alpha

246

that I know of. I thought there was another at one point, but not anymore. And with Sirhan on his deathbed—"

"Sirhan is dying? Did someone try to kill him again?"

"He's dying of old age, I guess you could say. Sirhan fell to the curse of the werewolf nine hundred and ninety-nine years ago, and he's beginning to feel his age now. He's quite sick. No werewolf has ever lived past a thousand years. I believe it's only a matter of weeks at this point."

"So what will happen when Sirhan dies?" I remembered Talbot saying something about how Gabriel deserved what was going to happen to his pack when Sirhan died.

"According to pack law, when an alpha dies, a new alpha must be called. If there is no true alpha present, then usually the calling of the alpha passes to the beta. That would be me, in this instance. However, before the beta can take charge, he must hold a 'challenging ceremony,' during which any wolf can present himself to contest the beta without anyone prohibiting him. The beta can either step aside and let the challenger become alpha, or the two can fight it out until someone relents—or dies. The winner is named alpha of the pack, even if he is an outsider, or is already the alpha of a different pack. If more than one challenger presents himself—or herself, though that is rare—at the ceremony, then they all must battle it out for the position. It can turn quite deadly."

"And I'm guessing you'll step aside if someone con-
tests you?"

Gabriel sighed. "Usually the beta goes unchallenged
out of respect," he mumbled.

"But what if someone like Caleb challenges you?"

Gabriel blinked.

"You'd fight then, right?" There was more anger in
my voice than I'd anticipated. *Or is he just a coward?* that
voice I sometimes heard growled inside my head.

Gabriel didn't answer. He just tapped his fingers on
the open page of the book.

"What are you two talking about?" Charity said
from the doorway of the study. She balanced a big box
marked HALLOWEEN #3 in her arms.

Gabriel popped up from his chair. "Let me take that
from you," he said, and held his arms out to Charity.

"Thanks," she said as she gave it to him. "Mom's
got like five more of these. Sorry it took so long. Mom
made us reorganize the whole closet before we could
take anything out."

I heard Mom call Charity from the basement stairs,
and she ducked back into the hallway.

Gabriel turned back toward me. "We shall see what
happens when the time comes. But I wouldn't worry
about Caleb Kalbi, Grace. He's a pathetic excuse for a
man or a wolf, and I doubt he'd dare show up alone anywhere near our pack." Gabriel hefted the box out of the

room and said something to my father, who must have been in the kitchen.

I sighed and laid my head down on the table. My brain felt heavy from so much information, and now, on top of my concerns about Daniel and my anxiety over finding Jude, I was bogged down by a whole new set of worries. I glanced over at the book and saw the drawing of the Beast of Gevaudan. Long neck, sharp claws, and teeth dripping with blood. The drawing also depicted a woman lying on the ground, trying in vain to ward off the lunging beast with a long spear. Another question came to my mind, even though it was too late to ask Gabriel now.

What if Caleb Kalbi did *show up to the challenging ceremony—only he wasn't alone?*

CHAPTER SEVENTEEN

Basic Training

I knew Gabriel's stories were supposed to deter me from wanting to develop my powers, but they only made me more determined. There were bad things out there—bad things like Caleb Kalbi (even if, according to Daniel, he was supposedly living in South America now) and bad things like the Shadow Kings, intent on tearing the city apart for who knew what purpose. And I had to be prepared to take them on if people like Gabriel were going to sit back and do nothing. I could barely wait for the school day to pass before I got a chance to see Talbot again.

I tapped my feet with anticipation the whole bus ride to Apple Valley and barely noticed what April was talking about until she asked me how I felt about tiaras.

"Um, what?"

"Tiaras: pro or con? Say pro, because I've been dying

to design a killer tiara. Oh! Maybe it could really *be* killer. Like it could have silver spikes on it that separate into Chinese throwing stars or something." She trembled and wrote something in her notebook.

"What are we talking about again? Why would I need a tiara?" And did I really want to know?

April held up a finger. She wrote one more thing in her notebook. "We were discussing a princess theme for your costume. Like Princess of Wolves. Or Princess Lupine. Princess Puppy . . . no . . ."

"You're kidding, right? No spandex. No tiaras. And certainly no princesses." I tried to grab her notebook to see what the heck she'd been up to while I wasn't paying attention.

She hugged the notebook to her chest to keep it away from me. "How about the B-I-T-C-H Queen?"

"April!" My jaw dropped. She'd never been one for swearing—even the spelling variety.

"Well, you have been really on edge lately," she said.

"I'm not on edge. I'm just, you know, nervous."

I really didn't know what to expect for basic training, since Talbot's idea of testing my skills had been a little more than intense, but I was surprised when he drove us to a run-down Apple Valley strip mall after I met him outside the bus.

"If you think I need to sharpen my shopping skills, I've already got April for that," I joked as I followed Talbot into one of the shops.

"This ain't a pleasure trip," he said, and pointed up to the sign above the shop door. Half the letters were missing, but I could tell it was a kids' karate studio. A dojo—or at least that was what I thought it was called.

I crossed my arms in front of my chest. "If you're thinking of enrolling me in class with a bunch of kindergartners, I can tell you right now that isn't going to happen."

Talbot rolled his eyes. "This place has been closed for the last year. The Rock Canyon Foundation just leased the property. They're planning on fixing it up for one of their youth programs, but I figure we've got the studio to ourselves for a week or so. Perfect place to hone your skills in a controlled environment." He pulled a key from his pocket and unlocked the front door. He held it open for me.

"Controlled environment?" There was a small waiting room in the front of the shop with dusty metal chairs, and then a long dark hallway that supposedly led to the actual studio. "You swear there are no demons waiting inside to jump me?" I could just picture a room full of Gelals with their claws out, ready to pounce on me the second I entered.

Talbot smirked. "Well, I might jump you—but only if you ask for it."

"I'd like to see you try."

Talbot gave his head a small shake. He looked at me with a slightly hopeful glance.

"Bad joke for both of us," I said, feeling embarrassed and guilty at the same time for even responding to his flirting. Daniel and I might not be on the most solid ground at the moment, but that was no excuse. "Sorry." If Talbot was going to be my mentor, then I needed to draw the line between us way before flirtation.

Talbot's cheeks looked a bit pink. "Anyway, I'm just teaching you some new moves today, I promise."

Talbot and I walked down the long hallway and then entered the dojo. It was filled with dusty mats and had a long wall of broken mirrors. Talbot opened his backpack. He pulled out one of those white karate outfits and handed it to me. "There's a bathroom over there. You should change into this *gi* so you don't mess up your school clothes."

I fingered the fabric as I walked into the bathroom. I shut the door tight and pulled off my shirt and pants. I dressed quickly in the *gi* because it felt weird to stand there in just a camisole and underwear when only a thin wall separated Talbot and me. What if he suddenly showed up in the doorway again?

When I padded out of the bathroom, I found Talbot waiting for me, dressed in his own white *gi* tied with a black belt. The white tunic top crossed in front of his otherwise bare chest. He had pecs just as ripped as his forearms. I looked down at his bare feet poking out from the bottom of his lightweight white pants. Why did this whole situation feel more surreal than anything else we'd done so far?

"So you're Mr. Miyagi and I'm the Karate Kid," I said.

"I'm Mr. Who?" Talbot asked.

"You know, Mr. Miyagi. From the movie? Tries to catch flies with chopsticks?"

Talbot gave me a blank stare.

"You know, you have to be all, *'Wax on, wax off!'*" I made the hand gestures that went along with the chant.

Talbot's eyes went wide. He obviously didn't get it.

I made an overly dramatic sigh. I guess kids who grow up on farms with retired demon hunters don't exactly watch a lot of eighties movies. "You're the great karate master, and I'm your student."

"Um, okay." He still looked at me funny. "But I'm not going to teach you karate. I'm actually debating between aikido and wing chun. Both are good for a small-sized fighter. Plus, you need sword training. And then we'll move to crossbows, advanced staking, and maybe even some work with the bow staff."

This time I was the one who made the surprised expression, but not because he was joking. He was dead serious.

SUNDAY AFTERNOON, FOUR DAYS LATER

Training with Talbot was intense, to say the least. He

didn't pull punches, never had to take a breather or nurse a tender knee. Which meant I had to work like hell to keep up with him. And I don't know what it was that made it possible, but I gained more skills in less than a week while working with Talbot than I had in the months of training with Daniel.

Maybe it was the fact that Talbot didn't demand that I hold back at the same time he encouraged me to push forward. He wanted me to grab on to my raw emotions, use them to make me stronger. And I couldn't believe how quickly it worked—how much more powerful I'd become.

Our training sessions were like a drug—fully tapping into my abilities was overwhelming, engulfing, leaving me buzzed with power and wanting more. April always gave me funny looks when I got back to the bus, and she'd ask questions about what Talbot and I did for training, but she never quite understood why I was so excited about sparring.

I'd even contemplated getting together with Talbot on Saturday for an extra training session. But Mom had been in manic overdrive ever since Gabriel had come to dinner and she'd learned about the Halloween fund-raising festival—the same fund-raising festival for which she'd commandeered control of the concessions booths and poured every waking moment into preparing for. And there was no escaping her desire to bake and freeze a zillion pecan tarts all Saturday long for refreshments. We were T-minus six days until Halloween, and I knew that if it weren't for my mandatory service project each afternoon in the coming week, I'd probably never get out of the house to train with Talbot again.

By Sunday afternoon, I felt so positively shaky from having gone so long without training that I could barely think. Which definitely wasn't a good thing, since I was supposed to meet Daniel for a picnic on the parish lawn after services. At Dad's insistence, Mom had granted me a two-hour reprieve to work on my Trenton application with Daniel. Only I still worried he might notice something different about me.

It seemed like the better my training went with Talbot, the harder things got with Daniel. The harder it was to pretend to be normal around him.

I hated keeping things from Daniel. I hated that I couldn't tell him anything about Talbot, or my lessons, or my plans to find Jude, for that matter. But that was just the way it needed to be, because I knew he'd try to stop me.

Daniel wanted me to be normal, but I couldn't be. That wasn't who I was anymore. I had these talents, these abilities. I knew what evil existed in the world, and I couldn't just sit by anymore. I guess that's why in all those comic books, the superheroes have to create an alter ego—the person who pretends to be ordinary so they can still be with the ones they love.

I knew Daniel wanted me to be normal because he wanted to keep me safe. But that was only because he didn't know what I was really capable of. He'd lost his faith in me somewhere, somehow. Lost his faith in the whole concept of my being a Hound of Heaven—but I'd show him; I'd prove to him that I could do this. When the time was right—probably not until after I finished my training with Talbot . . . and maybe not until after I brought Jude home—I'd tell Daniel everything . . . eventually.

So that made what I was doing a surprise. I wasn't technically keeping secrets from the person I loved the most.

Right?

As much as I dreaded trying to pull off "Grace Divine: 100 Percent Normal Pastor's Daughter" for a couple of hours, I longed to be with Daniel. Just that he'd suggested the picnic in the first place made any potential awkwardness worth it. With Mom keeping me busy when I wasn't with Talbot, and Daniel working extra shifts for Mr. Day and helping Katie Summers co-chair the fund-raiser, it felt as if it had been forever since we'd had time to be together outside of school. Or even in school, for that matter—considering he spent most of our lunch breaks planning booths and posters with Katie. And as twitchy as I felt—kind of like power withdrawal—nothing was going to keep me from having lunch with Daniel today.

Except for the fact that Daniel apparently didn't feel the same way.

I sat out on the grass in my knee-length blue dress, soaking up the unseasonably warm October sun, for more than forty-five minutes before I decided he must have forgotten about our lunch. The lunch *he'd* planned. Daniel hadn't been at services. But his church attendance was usually spotty anyway, so I hadn't thought much about it then.

My stomach growled. I was cell-phone-less (Mom forbade me to take it to church), so I went into the parish to use my dad's office phone to call Daniel. Dad wasn't in his office, but the door was unlocked. I went inside and dialed Daniel's number. It went straight to voice mail.

"I hope whatever you're doing is important enough to blow me off," I told the message recorder. "Call my cell when you remember who I am."

I hung up and almost called back immediately to apologize. I hated myself for being so terse. But then again, wasn't the superhero supposed to be the one who was always forgetting about plans last minute, or running off during important dinners? If anyone was going to be standing someone up, shouldn't it be me?

I picked up my application packet from the desk and headed out into the hallway. My muscles twitched, and I was ready to take off on a good run—high heels or no high heels—but as I passed the double doors to the social hall, I heard strange noises coming from inside. Kind of like long, heavy breaths and an occasional grunt.

My curiosity piqued—all of the parishioners should have gone home by now—I pulled open one of the doors and peered inside. Gabriel stood alone in the middle of the room, poised on the tips of his toes, with his arms stretched up high above his head. The palms of his hands were facing each other. He wore a gray linen tunic and pants, like the *gi*'s Talbot and I wore for training, and a long brown robe. I couldn't help thinking he looked like a cross between a monk and a Jedi Knight.

I watched as he very fluidly dropped his arms down so they were parallel in front of his chest, his hands cupped so it looked as if he held an invisible ball. His head turned in my direction. He blinked when he saw me but didn't say anything as he continued with his flowing motions. It reminded me of the martial arts Talbot taught me, yet completely different at the same time. He did another three moves that all melted into one another like a set routine. When he finished with the last one, he turned to me again and gave a slight bow.

"Hello, Miss Grace," he said, and motioned for me to come into the room. "Forgive me for using this space. I'm afraid my room is too small for my exercises."

"I thought you weren't into fighting," I said. "Why are you practicing martial arts?"

"I do not practice for fighting. What I do is for balance and meditation." He rubbed the spot on his finger with the lighter band of skin. "Something I find I need a lot more of these days."

"Is that because you're missing your ring?" I pointed at his hand. It was obvious from how light his skin was there, compared to the rest of his hand, that he must have worn a ring on that finger for many years.

Gabriel gave me an approving nod, like he was pleased by my quick conclusion.

"What happened to it?" I asked. I was surprised he'd come here without his moonstone. It seemed like a great risk for someone who was so obsessed with staying in complete control.

"I gave it to someone who needed it more than I did." He stopped rubbing the light spot on his finger and dropped his hands at his sides. "I just hope it wasn't a wasted sacrifice."

"Jude?" I remembered now that this wasn't the first time Gabriel had come to Rose Crest. I hadn't seen him, but he'd come here on Christmas Eve and had given my dad a moonstone ring for Jude—his very own ring, apparently. "You did that for him? But you'd never even met us."

Gabriel nodded, more solemnly this time. "Daniel talked of you and your family often. I guess I felt like I knew you all. I could tell that you were just like my sister, Katharine, and Jude sounded much like myself back before I joined the church and left for the Crusades. When I got your father's letters about Jude's infection, Sirhan forbade me from getting involved, but I could not help myself. I wanted to prevent your brother from falling to my own fate. But I'm afraid I always seem to be too late." He put his hand on my shoulder. His steel-blue eyes seemed so ancient and sad as he searched my face. "I hope that is not the case with you."

"I'm fine," I said. I didn't know why, but my voice was barely louder than a whisper.

"Nobody is ever as fine as they say they are." Gabriel dropped his hand from my shoulder and stepped back a few paces.

"Well, I am." I felt even shakier than before. I didn't like the idea of his judging me again without knowing me. He'd already made up his mind that I couldn't learn how to use my powers without falling to the wolf, like Jude and him.

"Tell me, Grace, how were you feeling when you thrust that dagger into Daniel's heart?"

The question came out of nowhere, but he sounded so matter-of-fact, like a psychiatrist analyzing a patient lying on a couch, that it left me stunned for a moment.

"I don't know what you mean," I said.

"Were you afraid? Were you angry? What were you hoping to accomplish?"

Is he going to pull out a notebook and start jotting down my answers?

"Why do you want to know?" I asked.

"My pack is quite fascinated with you. Do you realize what a commodity you are to them? A young girl who can save an Urbat's soul. They want me to find out how you did it. But I'm more interested in *why*."

"Because I love Daniel. And I'd promised him I'd save him." It was the only promise I'd ever been able to keep.

Gabriel just stood there, staring at me, as if expecting me to explain more.

"I thought the wolf would take me over for killing him—but saving his soul was more important than anything. I was scared, but only that I wouldn't be able to save him in time. I didn't care what happened to me as long as his soul was preserved."

"Hmm." Gabriel sighed. His forehead creased. Any hint of his ancient smile fell into a frown. He seemed disappointed by my answer. Or maybe it was more that he'd known all along what I was going to say, but he didn't have the first clue what to do with the information. "True love. Few people are capable of that."

"I guess so." I tapped my heel against the hardwood floor. "I think I'm going to go now." I really didn't want to be analyzed anymore.

Gabriel stretched his arms out in one of the poses I'd seen him do before. "You should join me in my exercises. I sense much agitation in you."

"Okay, Master Yoda," I mumbled.

Gabriel gave me a quizzical look.

I rolled my eyes. "Never mind." *Seriously, does nobody else watch movies anymore?*

"It would be good for you to relax. Meditate. Pray. You are letting the wolf have too much control over your emotions. Do you think in your current state you'd be capable of showing the same restraint and love you did the night you saved Daniel?"

"Of course." I looked away from his face, definitely feeling agitated now. He had no business prying into my life—into my head—like this.

"I have my doubts," Gabriel said.

"Whatever. You made up your mind about me the day we met. I'm not going to stand here and try to prove you wrong. I'm not your patient, or your subject, or whatever to be analyzed. Why don't you just go home?"

I turned to walk out.

"I'm here because I care about you."

No he doesn't, that voice said in my head. I used to think of it as foreign, but now it felt comforting. *Gabriel is never going to believe you're capable of becoming a true Hound of Heaven—not in the way Talbot believes you can.*

I was almost through the door when Gabriel called after me. "Remember, Grace. If you let anger into your heart, it will push out your ability to love."

CHAPTER EIGHTEEN

Dances With Wolves

SUNDAY EVENING

Daniel didn't call me back, but *several* hours later he sent a text:

Sorry. Can't talk now. Will call you tonight.

Whatever, I texted back. The longer the hours had stretched without hearing from him, the more I *didn't* want to talk to him. Or so I told myself.

I'm sorry! Okay? Can't explain now. Call you later.

I held my phone for a moment, wondering what to say back. Here I was trying to act normal for him when he was still keeping something from me. It made me feel angry—and like a hypocrite of the worst kind. But most of all, it just made me feel empty. I opened my drawer and was about to drop my phone in when it started ringing in my hand. I answered without looking at the display, expecting it to be Daniel calling, even though he claimed he couldn't.

"Hey, kid. You ready for some real action?" Talbot asked.

A rush of excitement swept my empty feeling away. "Depends on what you have in mind."

"Staking out The Depot. I've got it on good authority that a couple of the Shadow Kings will be there tonight. I think we should follow them and see if they lead us anywhere interesting."

My heart swelled with excitement at the idea, only to deflate two seconds later. "Tonight? I can't. My mom's on the warpath. I told her I had to write a report to get out of hot gluing any more handmade price tags for that festival I told you about. You should have seen the blisters I had to heal on my fingers. I think I'm stuck in my room all night—"

"You mean to tell me that I haven't taught you enough stealth yet to be able to sneak out of your own house?" Talbot asked. "Maybe you aren't ready for a real mission after all."

"No . . . I can do it. I just don't know that I should."

"This is just another part of the superhero gig, Grace. Most crime happens after curfew. If you want to find Jude, then you have to start letting go of the inhibitions that are holding you back."

I stroked my moonstone necklace with my fingers. "I do want to find Jude."

"Good. Meet me outside the club at ten o'clock. That should give us enough time to get into position before anyone of importance shows up."

"But—"

"I want you here with me, Grace."

At least somebody does. "Okay. I'll meet you there."

"Great." I could hear the smile in his voice. "Oh, and Grace?"

"Yeah?"

"*Don't* wear those vinyl pants again. We're trying not to stand out."

THAT NIGHT

At eight forty-five p.m., I went downstairs and got a glass of water, slipped my keys to the Corolla off the kitchen counter, and tucked them in my pocket, all the while making a big deal out of how tired I was, and how I should go to bed early because I had a big test in the morning. Dad snored in his recliner in the family room with a book leaned against his chest, but I said good night to my mom. She barely even acknowledged me over the stack of homemade price tags she'd crafted out of scrapbook paper for the Halloween fund-raiser. I trudged back up to my room, yawning the entire way just for good measure.

At nine p.m., I pulled my hair into a high ponytail and changed into black jeans and a black long-sleeved T-shirt (what else are you supposed to wear on a stake-out?) and then propped a couple of pillows under my comforter to make it look like I was tucked in bed. (Lame, I know. But sneaking out wasn't exactly my forte.) Then I popped open the screen on my second-story window and climbed out on the eave of the roof. I stood on the edge and scanned the street, making sure no one was around. When I was sure the coast was clear, I dove off the roof, did a double flip midair, and landed with hardly a sound near the walnut tree. I felt a thrill of triumphant pride at pulling off the stunt, and almost wished someone had been there to see me.

Luckily, the Corolla was parked in the driveway, and by nine fifteen, I was backing out onto the road. The car rattled and shook the whole way there, and I prayed that it wouldn't stall at each stoplight, but I made it to The Depot just before ten p.m. I stayed put in the car until Talbot pulled up and parked beside me in a pickup truck—blue with rust spots, and looking like it had done plenty of farm hauling in the last couple of decades.

We both got out of our cars and stood on the sidewalk together. Talbot wore a white-and-gray flannel shirt, which actually looked like it had been ironed, tucked into boot-cut jeans. He was without his baseball cap for the first time since I'd met him, and he'd combed his wavy milk-chocolate-brown hair back behind his ears. He hooked his fingers in his belt loops next to his large bronze marshal-star belt buckle.

I rocked back on my heels. "So . . . did you bring treats?"

Talbot scrunched his eyebrows. "For what?"

"Aren't we supposed to sit in a car and eat lots of junk food and guzzle coffee while on a stakeout?"

"You watch way too much TV." He lightly touched my arm. "And besides, why would we sit out here in a car if we can have more fun inside?"

"Fun? Inside?" I gave him an incredulous stare.

"Come on." He slipped his fingers down my arm, grabbed my hand, and pulled me across the street and down the alley between the train station and the old warehouse. He dug a keycard out of his pocket and used it to get us in through the door. We descended the stairs into the cloud of music and fog. I hesitated at the bottom step. I wasn't sure I wanted to go into this place again. Talbot seemed to sense my reason for hanging back. He gave me a reassuring nod and let go of my hand and wrapped his arm around my waist as he steered me through the entrance.

"Just for show," he said, his lips brushing my ear. "No one is going to hassle you this time if they know you're with me." He held me tight against his side and headed deeper into the club. And just like on the night I had come here with April, people seemed to practically jump out of Talbot's way as he headed toward the dance floor. Guys nodded in his direction, and girls gave me envious scowls. I didn't know what it was—his wolf pheromones, perhaps—but he seemed to have a commanding presence in this place. So much so that my breath caught in my chest when he slid his fingers along my arms and entwined his hands with both of mine.

I looked up into his emerald green eyes. "What are you doing?" I whispered.

"Dance with me," he said, and then pulled me into the dancing throng.

It was a quick, pulsating song, the kind of music that swallowed you whole, and I couldn't help being sucked into the gyrating motion of the crowd. Talbot danced with that same sort of commanding energy—not like a farm boy at all, more like he was made for this sort of music. Like he owned this dance floor. His body moved with the pulsing rhythm close to mine, our hands touching, and then not. My heart raced. I couldn't help but stare into his piercing eyes. Almost like he held me in an Akh-like trance.

We danced two songs this way, but then the music shifted into something slower and more sensual. With a smooth, swift movement Talbot wrapped my arms around his neck and then placed his arms around my waist. He pulled me close, his hands pressing against the small of my back. I recognized the hungry glint in his eyes. It was the way Daniel used to look at me.

I felt a sudden tightness in my throat. I turned my head away and surveyed the crowd, wondering who we were supposed to be looking for. When I glanced back at Talbot, he still stared down at me with unblinking intensity.

"Aren't we supposed to be watching out for the Shadow Kings?" I asked.

"We will. But I doubt they'll be here for another hour or two." His voice had a soft growl to it—almost like a contented purr.

"An hour or two? Why did we get here so early, then? And I thought we weren't supposed to stand out."

"What better way to blend in than to pretend we're having fun?" Talbot's large hands slid to my hips. He held me close against him. "You look great tonight, by the way. Kind of 'spy chic' or something. Perfect for kicking some demon butt later on." He sighed and then nuzzled his nose against the top of my head. "Perfect night, don't you think? We may even have time to grab a bite to eat from the bar before the SKs get here."

I shivered, even though it was far from cold on the dance floor. I couldn't help thinking that this *would* seem like the perfect night to someone like Talbot: a little dancing, a little dinner, and a little demon slay-ing for dessert. I thought about his pressed shirt, styled hair, and even the splash of musky cologne I could smell on his neck. I let my arms fall from his shoulders and took a step back. "Talbot, are we on a date?"

Talbot gave me a look like he thought I was totally insane. He dropped his hands from my hips. "Um, no. It's called surveillance. We're blending in." He shoved his thumbs into his belt loops. "I'm sorry if I made you uncomfortable. I thought you'd be up for playing the part." Then he gave me a sheepish, dimpled grin. "But if this *were* a date, would that be so bad? We can make it one if you want."

I sighed. "I have a boyfriend. You know that."

"Then why isn't he the one here with you, helping you?"

"It's more complicated than that. . . . And you're my mentor. I can't cross that line if you're going to be training me."

Talbot's shoulders dropped. He stared over my head.

"I'm sorry. I don't want to upset you. But this isn't going to work if we're not on the same page about—"

Talbot shook his head and laughed. He rocked back on his heels. "Oh, come on, I'm just teasing you, kid. You're so self-absorbed. I'd say it was cute, but you'd probably think I was hitting on you."

"Nice," I said sarcastically, but I couldn't help thinking he was just trying to cover.

Talbot laughed again. "We don't have to dance if you have a problem with that. How about I go get us a couple of drinks and we can wait for the SKs over at one of the tables?"

"I don't drink. Well, I mean, I drink . . . like water and stuff. But you know, I don't *drink*." *Could I seem any more lame this evening?*

"Well, I don't make it a habit to buy alcohol for *minors*." Talbot put an emphasis on that last word, as if reminding me that I was at least three or four years younger than he was. "But I imagine a Coke wouldn't bother your sensibilities."

"Sounds good."

Talbot shook his head and sauntered off toward the bar. I stood on the edge of the dance floor and watched as a couple at the bar moved aside so Talbot could order our drinks before them. He glanced back at me and winked. I blushed and turned away. I rubbed my arms, trying to warm the goose bumps that prickled up on my skin even though it was hot and sticky in the club.

I felt a hand on my shoulder and looked up, surprised that Talbot had returned with our drinks so fast, but the shiver that had caused my goose bumps transformed into a full-on shudder when I saw who stood right next to me.

"So you've finally decided to see what it's like to party with a real man," he said, and tried to wrench me back onto the dance floor.

"Let go, Pete." I yanked my hand out of his grasp. It folded into a tight fist on instinct. Power coursed through my veins. About five different aikido moves that could make him cry like a baby flashed through my mind. He'd deserve it, too, for getting Daniel in trouble with the police. "Get lost before you're sorry."

"I haven't forgotten that you like it rough." Pete gave me a smile that was even smarmier than his ugly goatee. I wanted to claw both of them right off his stupid face. My fingernails bit into the palm of my hand, I was trying so hard not to lash out at him. I could probably take his face off if I wanted to.

Then do it, a voice snarled in my mind. *Teach him never to mess with you again.* I shook my head. Sometimes, lately, my thoughts didn't even sound like me. I backed away from Pete.

My powers tingled under my skin. My muscles tensed, ready to strike. I had to get away from Pete before I actually hurt him. Pete stormed after me. He snarled something, but I concentrated so hard on not lashing out at him that I don't even know what it was. I turned and was about to run when I smacked into Talbot. He jumped back and one of the Cokes in his hands spilled down the front of his white flannel shirt.

"Whoa, what's wrong, Grace?" He tried to wipe at the wet spot on his shirt without spilling his other drink.

I glanced back at Pete. He'd seen Talbot and had retreated a few feet, but the tension in my muscles didn't release. I still wanted to hurt him. "I'm sorry, Talbot. I need to get out of here." I headed toward the exit.

Talbot ditched the drinks on a table and came after me. "Don't leave, please!" He grabbed my hand as I started up the stairs, and whipped me around toward him. His face creased with concern, but then his eyes narrowed with anger. "That guy who was following you, did he hurt you?"

"Not tonight," I said. "But he has before. We kind of have a bad history."

Talbot's hand shook as he grasped my wrist. "I can go back there and talk to him. Make sure he never bothers you again."

"No. Don't. Pete isn't the kind of guy who will listen."

"Then we can *make* him listen. You know we can."

"Please, don't. Pete isn't worth it. That's why I need to leave."

Talbot still shook with anger. I didn't want him to go back and try to start anything with Pete. I slipped my free hand into his and gave it a light squeeze. "Walk me out, okay? I need to go home before it gets too late."

"Stay," he said in a low voice.

"I have a midterm test tomorrow, and you can probably stake out the Shadow Kings better without me. If Pete and his friends try to make a scene because I'm here, they might ruin any chance of us being able to follow the SKs. You can follow them tonight, and then maybe we can figure out what to do with whatever information you get tomorrow."

Talbot sighed. "Fine."

I let him hold my hand, his fingers intertwined with mine, until we got to my car. I pulled my hand out of his and folded my arms in front of my chest. He opened my door for me.

"We're friends, right?" I asked.

"Yes. Of course."

"Good." I gave Talbot a small smile and climbed into the driver's seat of the Corolla. I didn't want to lose Talbot from my life—he'd already helped me so much, changed me—but I also didn't want him thinking there was something between us that couldn't exist. "I like it that way."

LATER

I was worrying what to do about Talbot, and simultaneously hoping he wouldn't get himself into trouble with the Shadow Kings, when the Corolla sputtered and almost died at the light at Markham and Vine. If I'd been paying attention at all to what I had been doing before now, I never would have come this way—especially this late. Markham was definitely the last place I wanted to be alone at any time of the night. I checked my door locks and prayed that I could get the car all the way home. Sure, I could run back to Rose Crest if I needed to, but how would I ever explain how the car got all the way out to the city without my parents knowing I'd snuck off when I was supposedly in bed?

I definitely needed to have Daniel look at the engine before I took the car on another late-night joyride.

Crap. Daniel.

He was supposed to call me tonight, and I'd left my phone in the car. I felt like a jerk for giving him such a hard time for standing me up—and now he probably thought I was avoiding his calls.

The light turned green, and I cautiously eased my sputtering car into the intersection. I turned right and got as far away from Markham Street as I could before I pulled my cell out of the cup holder between the two front seats. I checked the screen.

No messages.

No missed calls.

I dialed Daniel's number. He picked up on the fifth ring.

"Hey, what's up?" he said a little too casually. He sounded like me when I was trying too hard to seem normal.

I could hear faint music and a ticking sound—maybe that cat clock of Maryanne's in his apartment?—in the background. I also heard what sounded like someone else speaking in a hushed tone.

"Where are you?" I asked.

"Home."

"Is somebody there?"

"No. Just watching TV." I heard him cough and then the sounds of the music, and the voice died away.

"You didn't call. You promised you'd call, but you didn't." Never mind the fact that I wouldn't have been there to answer—but still.

"I'm sorry," he said. No explanation offered.

"So where were you this afternoon? I sat there waiting for you for almost an hour. I thought you *wanted* to help me with my application."

"I do, Gracie. But something came up, okay?"

"What? What could possibly come up that you'd forget? You didn't even call."

Daniel sighed. He stayed silent for a moment. "Katie called me this morning. She was freaking out because her little brothers got into her room and trashed all the posters we'd made for the fund-raising booths. She came over so we could make all new ones, and it was so much work . . . I guess I just lost track of time."

"Wait, you're telling me that you stood me up because you were with Katie, alone, in your apartment, and you lost track of time? What the hell were you two really doing?"

Daniel swore under his breath. "It's not like how it sounds. You know me better than that."

"Do I?" I hated myself for getting so mad. I mean, if I told him what I'd been up to this evening, it would sound just as bad. But what I'd done was all in the name of finding Jude. It had a higher purpose behind it—unlike Daniel, who had just blown me off to paint pictures with another girl. Something that used to be *our* thing. "You've been hanging out in bars, lying to me, running out on dinner, and standing me up. I feel like I barely even know you anymore."

"Gracie, please . . ."

"I'm starting to think that your dodging me like this is your way of letting me know you'd rather forget about me and go to Trenton with Katie."

"Don't, Grace," Daniel snapped.

"Don't what?"

"Don't ever think anyone or anything in this world could really make me forget about you."

I sighed. "Then why are you avoiding me?" I remembered that text message that sent him running from dinner. He'd claimed it was from Mr. Day. But did Mr. Day even know how to text? "Is there something else going on? Just tell me, please."

"I can't." He took in a deep breath. "I just need some time. I need you to be patient with me."

"But—"

"I just need some more time. That's all I'm asking for."

He'd all but admitted there was something wrong, and he wanted me just to drop it? But wasn't that what I wanted, too? Just a little more time before I told him about Talbot training me? It felt so different when he was the one keeping secrets.

"How much more time, Daniel? Because I don't know how much longer I can wait."

"I don't know. I really don't know."

My heart ached. I could feel something pulling and straining between us—about to break. It had been only a week and a half since we'd lain together on a bed of grass, watching the stars fall around us, but it suddenly felt like a lifetime ago.

I wanted to be in that place again. Wanted nothing to come between us. Wanted to spill all my secrets so he'd tell me his.

But he doesn't trust you.

"I'll see you tomorrow," I said before I hung up the phone.

CHAPTER NINETEEN

Final Exam

THE NEXT DAY

I barely slept at all after I got home from the club. I regretted leaving before the SKs got there, but at the same time I knew that I had needed to get away from Pete. And I wondered if I'd done the right thing by not just telling Daniel everything.

But I still couldn't do it.

If Talbot had found and followed those SKs last night, then it meant we'd be closer than ever to finding Jude. And I couldn't risk anyone interfering with that.

Daniel and I sat next to each other in AP art like usual. He passed me my pastels when I asked him to, and I nodded when he suggested I use a darker blue than the one I'd selected. But you'd think we were two strangers forced to share the same table, the way our eyes barely met when we talked.

I couldn't help letting out a small growl when Katie

came over to the table to ask Daniel if he still had one of her brushes. I hated the way she looked at him. I hated her shiny hair, her too-cool haircut, and her vintage-style headband with the funky ribbon flower just above her ear.

Daniel opened his bag and pulled out her brush. I wondered if he'd borrowed it while they were working together in his apartment yesterday. And did she just touch his fingers when he handed it her?

"You okay, Grace?" she asked.

I didn't answer.

I welcomed the bell ringing to signify that it was time to move on to the next class, and I could barely wait for the last period of the day, when I could get away from this school and all these *people* and head out to the Good Samaritan project. I wanted to see Talbot. Talk to someone who understood me. But mostly I needed to know if he'd found those SKs last night.

I stopped at my locker on my way to the bus. I couldn't find the stake Talbot had given me, and I wanted to look for it one more time. It wasn't there. I slammed my locker door shut and was about to go when I saw Katie again. She carried a box of poster paints in her arms, headed toward the main hall.

She was probably on her way to make more posters with Daniel.

It seemed like good luck for *her* that her brothers had ruined most of the posters—she'd get more undivided time with my boyfriend. It was convenient, actually, and the timing all too suspicious. She'd been in the art room when Daniel and I had made plans for our picnic, and now I was supposed to believe her little crisis just happened to come at the exact same time?

She's trying to steal him from you.

I clenched my fists as she walked by.

You should teach her a lesson.

My eyes narrowed as I watched her walk. It would take only one hit to send her slamming into the lockers. Paint would spill everywhere. But I could probably get out of there before anyone knew it had been me.

"Grace!"

I whirled at the sound of my name. April came bounding down the hall. I glanced back at Katie. It was too late now to do anything.

"Grace," April said. "Holy crap, you will never believe who just texted me."

I looked back at her.

She shook in that cocker-spaniel way of hers, but the look on her face told me it wasn't out of excitement. It was enough to push all thoughts of Katie out of my mind.

"Who?"

She grabbed my arm and leaned in close. "Jude," she whispered. "Or at least I think it was. The number's blocked, but it has to be him."

She held out her bright pink cell phone. She'd glued

little white gems in the shape of the letter *A* on the back.
My hand shook as I took it from her and read the text:
Tell her to stay away. Time's running out. She's right
where they want her.

"Is this it?" I asked. "Nothing else?" If he was going
to bother to send messages, why the hell was he being
so cryptic? It was almost like he wasn't fully conscious
or something.

"That's all," April said. "But it's him, right?"

"Yes. I think so." *Who else would send this text?*

"But what does it mean?"

"It means we're on the right track." I tossed April
her phone, and we headed straight for the bus. If Jude
was telling me to stay away, then it meant I was getting close. Had he seen me at the club last night? Did
he know Talbot had tracked a couple of the Shadow
Kings—assuming he had? I needed to get to Talbot,
now.

The only problem was that just before the bus pulled
away from the school, Gabriel climbed on board and
announced that he was going to be our chaperone for
the day. This was the first time since the project began
that he'd actually come along with us. I'd wondered if
he had an aversion to the city, but Daniel said it was
because Gabriel wanted to work with the first group for
the first week, and then with the second group for the
last week. But why did he have to choose today of all
days to come along? I needed to find a way to leave with

Talbot without Gabriel sniffing him out.

Gabriel stood at the front of the bus and we drove toward the rec center in Apple Valley. He launched into some speech about today's assignment that sounded more like a sermon. I pulled out my cell phone, switched it to silent, and texted Talbot.

Me: *911! Jude texted April!*

Talbot responded immediately: *?! What did he say?*

I repeated Jude's text to him, then added: *I think we're on the right track. What did you find last night?*

Talbot: *I'll show you when you get here. I have a surprise for you.*

Me: *Problem. Gabriel's on the bus.*

Talbot: *Sh***

Me: *Meet me on the other side of the building. I'll slip away.*

Talbot: *Sounds good.*

Me: *So what's my surprise?*

Talbot: *You'll see . . .*

And then, ten seconds later: *Bring your stake.*

I was still riffling through my backpack when the bus pulled into the Apple Valley rec center parking lot.

"Crap," I said under my breath.

"What're you looking for?" April asked.

"My stake," I whispered, and glanced at Gabriel as he got off the bus. "I swear I left it in my bag on Friday. But I can't find it anywhere."

"Um . . ." April unzipped her bag and stuck her

hand inside. "Okay, don't get mad." She pulled out my stake—or at least something that looked like my stake, only the hilt of it was now covered in bright blue crystals and diamond-like gems.

"You Bedazzled my stake?"

"Um . . . Surprise," April said. "Just because you're hunting nasty stuff doesn't mean you can't do it in style."

LATER

We filed off the bus and down into the parking lot, where the idling vans waited for us—all of them except for Talbot's. The class congregated around Gabriel, who was still going on about something, so it was relatively easy to whisper to Claire and April that I was going to go use the bathroom in the rec center, and then slip away from the crowd. I went inside the building, ducked past the receptionist, and headed out the exit on the other side. Talbot's van waited for me under a large oak tree in the east parking lot. I looked back to make sure no one was watching, and then climbed inside.

Talbot met me with an approving smile. "Looks like my influence is finally rubbing off on you. You're getting good at this sneaking-away thing."

"All part of the job," I said. "So what did you find? And where's this big surprise?"

"I told you, you'll see." Talbot's smile grew twice its

usual size, and he pulled the van out onto the road. He headed in the opposite direction from the dojo, where we usually trained, and drove toward the city. I tried asking him questions about what had happened at the club after I left last night, but he just kept that goofy grin on his face and said, "You'll see," in a singsong voice. Which pretty much made me want to punch him in the arm—and made my heart pound with anticipation.

Talbot pulled the van up to an old apartment building near Tidwell Library. I could see the entrance to the alley where we'd saved that woman from the gun-toting Gelals.

"Soooo?" I asked, tapping my fingers on the dashboard.

"Those SKs showed up just after you left last night. I followed them around at the club, and I distinctly heard one of them say the name Jude."

"They did?" My heart was banging ten times faster now. *Why didn't I stick around last night?* "What did you do after that?"

"I followed them here." He thumbed in the direction of the apartment building. "I think we've found the lead we need to get us to the gang—and your brother."

"So what did you do? Did you question them?"

"Nope. You're going to do it."

"Me?" My heart felt like it had stopped cold in my chest. "I don't think—"

"You're ready. I know we've only been training for a week, but this it, kid. I know you can do it."

Talbot held out his hand. "Where's your stake?"

I pulled it out of my backpack.

Talbot made a choking noise—like he attempted to strangle his laughter—when he saw the jewel-encrusted hilt.

"April," I said.

"Aha." Talbot took my hand and pushed my sleeve up. He gingerly placed my bejeweled stake against my forearm and then tucked my sleeve over it. "Backup. Just in case you need it."

"You mean I'm going in alone?"

Talbot nodded. He held my hand in his for a moment and then let go and moved his hand up to my neck. His fingers tangled with the white-gold chain of my moon-stone necklace. I didn't want his touch to send tingles down my spine, but it did anyway. I was about to ask him to move his hand—to remind him of the line that shouldn't be crossed between us—when I felt a tug and a snap and he yanked my necklace away from my neck.

"What are you doing?" I reached for my pendant in his hand.

He pulled it away. "It's a dead giveaway. You're going to go up there pretending to be a lost little lamb; if those SKs see this, you'll tip them off in two seconds flat."

"But I need it."

"No, you don't, Grace. I've told you before. *This*"—
he held up the moonstone pendant—"is holding you
back just as much as Daniel and Gabriel. They don't
believe in you. They don't know you the way I do. And
you'll never know what you're really capable of without
letting go of the things that hold you back." He tucked
my pendant into the front pocket of my backpack and
then clasped his hands on my shoulders. He stared at
me with his piercing green eyes, seeming to radiate with
that same commanding presence that I'd noticed in the
club. "Consider this as your final test. Show me you're
ready to be a real Hound of Heaven."

UPSTAIRS

I knocked on the apartment door and waited a good
thirty heartbeats before knocking a second time. I
couldn't help feeling somewhat naked and vulnerable
without the moonstone pendant that I hadn't been
without in more than ten months.

"Hello," I called in a sugar-sweet voice that shook
only a tiny bit. "Is anyone home? I need some help."

I knew Talbot was watching. I didn't know from
where, but I could feel his presence close by.

I heard the floorboards creak inside the apartment,
and then the door rattled open. A teenage guy peered
through the crack. He looked just like any other wasted
city kid: stubble dusted his chin, and his eyes were

puffy and red like I'd woken him from a fitful sleep—but I could tell from his distinct sour-milk stench that he was a Gelal.

"Hi," I said, and gave a friendly wave to the guy with my arm that wasn't concealing a weapon. "My car broke down, and my cell's not working." I twirled one of my curls around my finger and snapped my gum. I have to admit I was doing my best impersonation of April. "Do you think I could use your phone? It'll only take a second."

The guy eyed the lock of my hair I had twisted around my finger. He cracked a smile. His teeth were yellow, and one was missing. "Sure thing, little bird." He opened the door wider. "Come right on in."

My muscles tensed, and my stomach clenched into a knot. I recognized that disgusting smile of his. He was the guy who had been harassing April with his friend at The Depot. The one with the iron-hard grip I'd kicked in the gut—the one who could probably crush my bones with his bare hands. I was dressed quite differently than I had been at the club—without the fake tough-girl vinyl pants and smoky makeup—so hopefully he wouldn't recognize me too soon.

I fought off the instinct to run and gave him my best sweet and innocent smile as I crossed the threshold of the doorway into the dank apartment. There was no furniture in the room, only a crumpled mass of blankets in the corner like a nest. No TV, couch, or chairs. Not even a phone on the wall. Talbot had said that he had followed *two* demons here, but that wasn't adding up. As far as I could tell, the guy was alone in the apartment, and it didn't even look like he'd been staying here very long.

"I like your hair," the guy said from behind me.

I pretended not to notice the sound of the bolt in the door locking shut.

"So, um, like, where's your phone?" I asked.

"Oh," he said with a raspy snarl in his voice. He stepped closer behind me. "I forgot. I don't have one." My body jerked as he grabbed me by my hair and pulled my back against his chest. His other hand wrapped around my neck. I could feel his nails elongating into claws as he tapped his fingers against the pulse in my throat.

"That's too bad," I said sweetly, and flexed my wrist. The stake slid out from my sleeve into my hand.

"What?" the guy asked, genuinely confused. I'm sure he'd expected me to scream.

"Now you can't call for help." I felt a burst of power, and I stomped on his bare foot. The bones in his toes popped under my heel.

He screamed and let go of my neck. I grabbed his arm and leveraged his weight against him, flipping him over my shoulder. He landed on his back, a look of pure shock on his face. Then his eyes narrowed, and he snarled at me. "I thought you looked familiar. You're that feisty little bitch from the club." He jumped back up on his feet and came at me with his clawed hands. "Did they send you?"

I dodged his attack and kicked him in the back of the knee. "Did who send me?"

The demon stumbled into the wall and then spun around. "We told them we wanted out, and *he* said we could walk." He lunged at me.

I pushed him aside and then brought my fists up in a defensive position, one hand still gripping the stake. He snarled at the weapon and took a swipe at it with his clawed hand. I dodged his attack and bounced back on my heels.

"But they sent you after us, didn't they?" the guy asked, and lunged at me again.

Is he talking about the gang?

I used three of my new moves to grapple with him until I subdued his attack. "Where are they?" I asked, and slammed my knee into his stomach. "Where's the gang? How do I find them?" I sent a second blow into his gut.

He coughed. "Don't you already know?"

"Tell me where to find them!" I grabbed him by the throat and slammed him against the wall. I held my stake above his chest. "I want to know where to find the Shadow Kings, or whatever the hell they call themselves. Tell me now, and I'll spare your life."

The guy laughed. Black fluid dribbled from the

corner of his mouth. "If you want to find the pack, then why don't you ask their Keeper?"

"What?"

He tried to laugh again, but it ended in a raspy coughing fit. Droplets of black acid landed on my hand, burning my skin, but I didn't let go.

"He's a real grifter, that one. Don't you think?" the demon asked.

"Grifter? Who are you talking about—?"

I heard a cracking noise from behind me, and I turned my head slightly to see Talbot burst through the apartment door, brandishing his sword.

"Tal—?"

"Grace, watch out!"

But it was too late. I'd dropped my guard, and the yellow-teethed guy slashed at me before I could stop him. His claws raked my arm. I howled with pain and anger as blood flowed from the gash. I let go of him and staggered away. I grabbed my arm, trying to stop the bleeding. The guy's eyes went feral with the smell of my blood. He reared his head back and then pounced at me like a lion—claws extended, jaws open for the kill.

Rage pulsed through my veins, gripping my heart. *Kill him!* I swung my injured arm up and impaled him in the chest with my stake. The wood sliced into him all the way to the jeweled hilt I held in my hand.

I pulled the stake out, and black acid blood spurted from his wound. He fell back against the wall. Black ooze smeared down the green peeling wallpaper as the demon slumped to the ground, twitching and groaning, until he went limp. I regained my senses just in time to jump back as he exploded into a smoldering pool of acid and smoke.

I gripped the black-stained stake so hard the fake crystals cut into the palm of my hand. My heart raced like a hummingbird in my chest, and my breath came so fast I was in danger of hyperventilating.

My hands fell to my knees and I gasped for air, only to choke on the acid fumes wafting up from what was left of the demon. I stumbled backward, dizzy, and was about to collapse when warm hands grasped my shoulders.

Talbot turned me around so I was facing him. "You did it, kid! You did it! Come on, we need to celebrate!"

"Celebrate what? I didn't get any information out of him. . . . He's dead. . . . I failed."

"I don't care about information. We'll find the other guy who was supposed to be here and get him to talk. What you should be celebrating is that you killed your first demon. You *are* a true Hound of Heaven now!"

"I am?"

"You are." Talbot squeezed my shoulders. He beamed at me with his dimpled smile. "How does it feel? Wonderful, right?"

Beyond the pain in my bleeding arm, I still felt dizzy and warm and tingly all over—how I could only imagine getting high would feel. I couldn't believe that I'd staked that demon before he could kill me—with my own two hands. "Yeah, it does." I took in a deep breath, and as the shock of what I'd done washed out of me, I realized I was positively trembling from the sheer thrill of it all. I'd never felt so in control. So much exquisite power rushing through my veins.

"I knew you could do it, kid." Talbot squeezed my shoulders again.

If he really thought I could do it all on my own, then why did he come bursting in here? Probably because he'd really thought I couldn't handle it on my own. At least I'd proven him wrong. I was stronger than even he could imagine.

I raised the stake in my shaking hand. "Call me kid one more time, and I'm gonna shove this where it really counts."

Talbot laughed and wrapped his strong arms around me. "You're right. You're hardly a kid." He held me in a tight embrace and stared down at me with his bright, glinting eyes. "You're truly amazing, Grace," he said in a low voice.

The next thing I knew, his hand cradled my cheek, his callused fingers stroking my skin. He tilted my face toward his. His lips hovered only a fingertip's distance away from mine. They vibrated with his breath, as if asking me to be the one to meet him the rest of the way.

I couldn't move.

"Can I?" Talbot whispered.

I gave my head a tiny shake, my lips almost grazing his with the movement.

"Please?" The warmth of his breath made me shudder in his embrace.

"No," I whispered, but I couldn't bring myself to back away. "I already have someone."

"Just once . . . Please. I have to know what it feels like."

I half closed my eyes, imagining getting lost in the intoxicating idea of Talbot's touch, but all that flashed in my mind was the look on Daniel's face if he ever learned I'd kissed someone else. I turned my head as Talbot tried to press his mouth over mine. His lips lightly brushed my cheek instead. He dropped his hand from my face.

I stepped away from him and crossed to the open doorway. "I need to leave," I said, my voice barely working.

"Why?" Talbot asked. "You want this. I can feel it. Stop denying yourself what you want."

Heat flashed through my body. "I just can't."

Talbot's nostrils flared, but then he dropped his gaze. "I'm sorry. I got caught up in the excitement. I'll never do it again." He took a step toward me.

I held my hand up to stop him and shook my head

again. "It's okay. We both got caught up. I need to get back to the bus now."

Talbot reached into his pocket for the van keys. "Let's go, then."

I left the apartment and headed for the van in the parking lot. I could hear Talbot following after me, but I didn't look back.

Chapter Twenty

Need

We both knew I was pretending to be in a hurry to get back to the bus—it was a whole hour earlier than I needed to be there—but neither of us said anything about it. I stared out the window at the side-view mirror, concentrating on healing the burns on my hands and the claw marks on my shoulder. I replayed killing that horrible Gelal in my head, embracing the feeling of exhilarating power—the rush of it all—in order to heal my wounds.

We both stayed silent until we parked under the oak tree where he'd picked me up. I pulled on my jacket to cover up the bloody rip in my shirtsleeve and grabbed my backpack, which I'd left in the van during my little escapade. I slung it over my shoulder and was about to get out without saying good-bye when Talbot grabbed my newly healed hand.

~ 297 ~

"Just tell me one thing, Grace," he said. "Is the idea of you and me being together that terrible to you?"

"I can't do this." I pulled my hand away, my fingers slipping out of his. "You're my mentor. . . ."

"Not anymore. Training's over. We can be together now."

"Please try to understand. We're friends, Tal. And that's all we'll ever be."

He half closed his eyes and sighed. "Don't call me Tal, then," he said. "It sounds too good coming from your lips."

"I'm sorry."

Talbot gave himself a little shake. "Let's forget this ever happened." He found his baseball cap between our seats. He plopped it on his head and gave me a dimpled smile from under its bill. "Friends. That's all."

"Okay," I said, and smiled weakly back at him.

"Hey, don't let this ruin the day for you. You should be proud of what you did back there. Your training's over. You've made it. I'd take you out to celebrate if you'd let me—in a strictly just-friends sort of way, of course."

I gave a slight laugh.

"That's more like it," he said. "You'd better be ready for crackin' some heads tomorrow. We're going to find us a new lead—even if it kills him."

I knew he meant that last part to be a joke—but at the same time I knew it wasn't.

I laughed uneasily and got out of the van. I said good-bye to Talbot and crossed the back parking lot. I went through the building and figured I'd linger at the front entrance of the rec center until it was time to meet the bus, but what I saw out the glass doors in the front parking lot made me stop cold in my tracks.

The bus was there already, and so were all seven of the other Rock Canyon vans—accompanied by a cop car with flashing lights. Students from my religion class sat huddled on the steps to the front entrance, surrounded by people in Good Samaritan polo shirts. A man in a business suit talked to a girl who looked like she was crying. And that girl was April.

I pushed open a glass door and jogged out into the parking lot. As I approached the huddle of students, Claire stood up and pointed at me. "She's here! Grace is here!" she shouted. The rest of the students shot up on the stairs, all staring at me. April came running.

She threw her arms around me. "Oh, my gosh! You're okay. I was so scared." She squeezed me so hard I could barely breathe.

"Whoa! Of course I'm okay." I pried myself out of April's death grip. Her face was splotched with red, and her eyes shone like she was about to burst into tears again. "What's happened to you?"

"What happened to *me*?" she asked incredulously. "What happened to *you*? Everyone's been looking for you! First Pete, and then you not showing up at that karate studio, and then neither you nor Talbot answering your phones. And then I remembered Jude's text, and started thinking you'd been kidnapped. Or worse. Your dad is on his way, and Pastor Saint Moon is totally freaking."

"What are you talking about? I was out on my service project just like everyone else . . . and what about Pete and the karate studio?" *Is she talking about the same dojo where Talbot and I trained?*

"All the groups were supposed to go to this karate studio down the street. Like Gabriel said on the bus. We were supposed to start fixing it up for some youth program. But when we got there, the front windows were all busted out, and inside . . . they found Pete."

"Pete Bradshaw? What do you mean they *found* him?" I'd heard people talked about in that way before— last year when they'd *found* Maryanne Duke and then Jessica Day. Then the other night when the cops told us they'd found that Tyler kid. "Is Pete dead?" I could barely say the words.

April shook her head. "But somebody beat the crap out of him. They probably *thought* he was dead when they left him behind."

"What?" The ground suddenly felt uneven under my feet. "They found him at the dojo?" *Our dojo?* "Did he say who did it?"

"He's totally unconscious. Might even be in a coma. But Julie Pullman is the one who saw Pete first. She said that the letters *S* and *K* were spray painted next to him."

The Shadow Kings! Was this some kind of warning to Talbot and me to back off? Was this why Jude texted me? Had the Shadow Kings been following *us* all along when we thought we were tracking them down? Had they seen me at the club with Pete and decided to use him to send a message? I swung my backpack around in front of me and started digging for my cell phone. I needed to call Talbot and warn him that the SKs were definitely on to us.

"The Rock Canyon people called an ambulance and then sent us all back here," April said. "But when we realized you were missing, Pastor Saint Moon completely freaked out. He called your dad, and the police came, and . . . and . . . I'm sorry. I was really worried about you, so I told him. I'm sorry."

"Told who what?"

"Grace!" It was Gabriel's voice, mixed with reassurance and something else I'd never heard from him—anger. He filled the open doorway of the rec center.

"I'm sorry," April said. "I told him about you and Talbot."

"How could you?" I snarled at April. "I trusted you."

Tears welled in her eyes. "I thought I was helping you."

"Come with me, now," Gabriel demanded.

I followed Gabriel through the lobby and past the receptionist who tried to stop us. But Gabriel just held up his hand to quiet her, and we kept on walking. He opened the door of a room that seemed designed for conference meetings and motioned me inside.

The second the door clicked shut, Gabriel reeled on me. "Are you okay?" he practically yelled.

"Yes."

"Were you kidnapped, threatened, or otherwise coerced into doing something against your will?"

"What? No."

"Then I want you to tell me what your friend meant when she told me that you've been sneaking off alone with some boy during the project. And why, if you weren't even there, was your scent all over the inside of that dojo!" He grabbed my arm. "And then explain to me why I smell demon blood on your clothes"— he wrenched my jacket off my shoulders, exposing the bloody tear in my sleeve and the three bright pink scars on my arm—"and how you got *this*."

You don't have to tell him anything, something said inside my head. It was a mixture of my voice, Talbot's, and the new voice I'd heard before. It was right.

I yanked my arm out of Gabriel's grasp. "I don't have

to tell you anything," I said. "You're not my father. You're certainly not my brother. You're not even really my teacher."

He's nothing compared to you, the voice said.

"I'm your friend, Grace. I may not be your brother, but I care for you like I am."

"You're nothing to me."

"So that's how you regard your friends, as 'nothing'? I understand that boy who was attacked was your *friend*. Is he *nothing* to you, too?"

"Pete Bradshaw isn't my friend!" *He's a son of a bitch who deserves everything that happened to him.* The voice was right; Pete had it coming to him. "He deserved it."

"What?" Gabriel took a step back, rubbing his ringless fingers. "Did you do this, Grace?" He looked afraid, like he thought I was going to pounce on him.

Gabriel is a coward.

"No. I didn't attack Pete. He's not worth my time." I pulled my jacket back up over my shoulders. "I have more important things to do."

"Then why was your scent at that dojo?"

"Because that's where I've been training."

"Training? Daniel told me you two weren't training anymore."

"I wasn't with Daniel. That *boy* I've been sneaking off with, he's a Hound of Heaven . . . and the last of the Saint Moons. At least the *real* Saint Moons. Not a coward like you, who uses the name but does nothing to deserve it."

Gabriel's eyes went wide. "That's impossible, Grace. Don was the last Saint Moon. All the others were killed when—"

"When you stood by and let Caleb Kalbi kill them. Well, you're wrong. Nathan Talbot survived. He was three years old when he watched his parents get slaughtered in front of him—all because you wouldn't act."

Gabriel's mouth hung open for a split second. "I was told the boy died from his injuries. . . ."

"Well, he didn't. And now he's a Hound of Heaven. And he's been teaching me everything he knows. You might be afraid to do anything with your powers, but I'm not a coward like you. I'm a Hound of Heaven now, too. And while you've been hiding out here, afraid to get your hands dirty, I've been hunting demons. I even killed my first one today."

"You did what?" he roared. His body shook. He took another step back, breathing deeply. "No. This can't be happening. You're losing yourself to the wolf."

"I'm not losing myself. I killed a demon, not a human or even an Urbat. I know the difference. I'm not as stupid as you think."

Gabriel winced with pain; he pressed his palms together and closed his eyes, taking a deep breath and then letting it out between his teeth. "You're insanely stupid if you think killing won't change you," he said softly. "Even killing a demon. It gives you a sense of power—the ability to end something's existence, to snuff something out with your own hands. And that sense of power becomes pride, if you leave it unchecked. Soon you start thinking you're better than everyone else. Superior. Or maybe it just makes you feel angry that you can't do more. But those are exactly the feelings that feed the wolf—make it stronger. And before you know what's happening, you'll lose yourself." He reached out to touch my shoulder. "The wolf talks to you. I can sense it. We're losing you already."

I shook off his touch. "Stop saying that! Why can't you believe in me? Why can't you accept that just because you lost yourself to the curse, it doesn't mean every other Hound of Heaven out there is going to, too?"

"You really want to know?" Gabriel asked.

"Yes."

"Because in eight hundred and thirty years, I've yet to meet a single true Urbat who didn't *eventually* fall victim to the wolf."

His words felt like a punch in the gut. I gasped and took a step back, hitting the side of the table.

"Every single one of us falls, Katharine—and so will you."

"I'm not *Katharine*. I'm not your sister. And I'm not weak like you."

Gabriel growled. "I should have just taken you to Sirhan when I got here, like he'd commanded. I thought if I could figure you out, I could spare you the trip. I should have known better. I'm taking you now, so say good-bye to your friends. I don't know when you're coming back."

"Taking me?" *Sirhan commanded Gabriel to take me to him?*

They're coming for you. He makes you think you can trust him but you can't.

"Are you the one Jude tried to warn me about? Are you the one who's after me?" I tried to push past him to get away, but he wouldn't move.

Gabriel put his hands on my shoulders. "No, Grace. That's not what I meant. I'm taking you to Sirhan so we can help you."

I swept my arm out and slammed it against his rib cage. He flew sideways and hit the wall. "You're not taking me anywhere," I said, and bolted out of the room.

LATER

I ran.

Out of the rec center, past the other students on the steps, past the bus and my dad's car, which was just pulling into the parking lot, and out onto the street. I knew Gabriel was perfectly capable of coming after me, but I also knew he wouldn't.

306

He's weak.

He lies.

You're better than him.

I picked up my pace, running harder and faster. My backpack smacked against my back with every step. I dodged pedestrians and cars and leaped over anything that got in my way. I knew people were pointing, stopping slack-jawed to watch the girl who was running like she was being chased by a monster. But I didn't care. I just had to run.

I'd started running because Gabriel said he wanted to take me away. But the monster I ran from now was the words he'd spoken before that. They trailed after me like a demon after its prey: *In eight hundred and thirty years, I've yet to meet a single true Urbat who didn't* eventually *fall victim to the wolf.*

Those words haunted me. Just like the aching, shaking pain inside my muscles that wouldn't ease—no matter how fast I ran. No matter how hard I pounded it out on the pavement, no matter how much I embraced my powers. Nothing eased the pain like before—it only grew stronger and stronger with my raging thoughts.

Gabriel was wrong about me. He couldn't help me. He didn't understand me. He had no right to say I was going to fall. He didn't even know me.

You're better than him!

But I couldn't shake what he'd said, that all the Hounds eventually fell. Gabriel had to be wrong. Falling wasn't inevitable. Why would God have invented the Hounds of Heaven in the first place if all of them failed?

No, you're not like them, the voice said. *You're special. You're the Divine One.*

Yes. Yes, I was different. The Urbat thought that you couldn't receive the cure without dying—but *I'd* saved Daniel. *I'd* cured him.

I was better.

Daniel knew that.

Gabriel had tried to make Daniel forget that—tried to turn Daniel against me. But Daniel had believed in me once.

He loved me.

Yes, Daniel loves you. He's the one who loves you most. Make him remember that.

Go to him.

My body shifted, and my direction veered toward Oak Park. I can't explain it, can't describe it, but every part of me needed to find Daniel, needed to see him, feel him, touch him. Needed to know that he still needed me.

I kept on running until I stumbled down the steps to Daniel's basement apartment and collapsed against his door. I sank to the concrete, quivering like the bright orange aspen leaves surrounding the house. My heart pumped so hard it felt like it was going to burst out of my chest. I'd never run so far, so fast, but still that horrible aching inside of me made my muscles clench with agony.

The door opened, and I heard Daniel say my name as he pulled me up into his arms. "Gracie, what are you doing here? Are you okay?"

I wanted Daniel to ease the pain inside of me, to prove that Gabriel was wrong about me, but hearing his voice and seeing his face weren't enough. I wrapped my arms around his neck and then wove my fingers into his shaggy hair. I kissed the side of his face. Kissed him along his jaw and then behind his ear.

"Well, hello to you, too," he said. "What's gotten into you—?"

I pressed my lips over his mouth and kissed him with such force that he stumbled back into his apartment. I kicked the door closed behind us, dropped my backpack on the ground, and pressed my body against his.

I tasted him with my lips, drew in his almondy scent with every heavy breath, but it still wasn't enough.

Still not enough to ease the pain.

I kissed him harder and ran my hands down his arms, feeling the curves of his muscles under his thin oxford shirt. Daniel's arms tightened around me as he returned my kisses. His hands caressed my back and then pulled my jacket off my shoulders. It fell to the ground at my feet. Then his hands were on my waist, holding me tight by my hips.

I could feel his want for me in his touch, but it still wasn't enough to ease the aching inside. I still needed more. I kissed him harder and used the pressure of my body to propel him toward the sofa bed only a few feet behind us.

Daniel stopped when the backs of his knees hit the side of the mattress. His touch became hesitant as I pressed against him harder. He pulled back from my mouth and whispered against my cheek, "What are you wanting here, Grace? I thought we were waiting."

You can't wait anymore.

"I can't wait anymore." I echoed the voice in my head.

I pushed Daniel. His knees softened, and he sat at the edge of the bed. I climbed onto his lap and kissed him deeply, running my fingers along the buttons of his shirt, tracing his pecs and then his abs beneath the fabric.

The aching in my muscles suddenly surged through my body like some kind of foreign energy. I felt it clutch at my heart, squeezing like a clawed hand. I'd felt that sensation before. I knew what it meant. Something else was in control.

A small part of my brain told me to stop, told me to back off before it was too late—but I couldn't. I wanted Daniel more than anything I'd ever wanted before.

I needed him.

Then devour him! roared that foreign voice inside my head.

And before I knew what was happening, my teeth

were bared in a snarl, and my hands were clawing at Daniel's collar. I ripped his shirt open, sending buttons flying. I could feel Daniel grabbing at my hands, could hear him telling me to calm down, but that only made me claw at him harder. It was like I was watching myself act like a monster from the corner of the room, and I couldn't do anything about it.

"Stop!" Daniel shouted. He grabbed my shoulders and threw me off him sideways onto the bed. He jumped off the mattress. His arms flew up in a defensive position, ready to fight if he needed to. "Easy, Grace. This isn't you. Get ahold of yourself."

I rolled over, panting into his bedspread. My body shuddered and convulsed—like something was trying to tear its way out of my skin. I screamed and clawed at my own neck, searching for my moonstone—but my neck was empty.

"Where is it, Grace?" Daniel asked, urgency bleeding out from his voice. "Where's your moonstone?"

"My backpack," I panted into the sheets.

I heard a rustling noise and then felt pulsing warmth on my back. Daniel sat next to me, pressing the stone against the bare skin at the nape of my neck. I let its calming warmth tingle through me, easing the darkness that had crept into my heart. The deep shudder in my nerves lessened to a tremble.

I looked up at Daniel sitting next to me. His torn shirt hung open, revealing three long red gashes from my fingernails across his collarbone. But it was the expression on his face as he stared down at me that made my eyes fill with tears. He didn't see *me* lying there in his bed.

He saw the wolf.

CHAPTER TWENTY-ONE

Terrible Grace

TEN MINUTES LATER

I perched on the side of the mattress as far away from
Daniel as I could get. I clutched the moonstone in my
hands, rocking back and forth with the rhythm of its
pulse. Daniel started to scoot toward me, his hand outstretched toward the torn sleeve of my shirt.

I shook my head. "No. Don't touch me, please." I
didn't want him near me, didn't want the possibility of
hurting him again.

"How did this happen, Grace?" Daniel's voice
cracked a bit as he spoke. Was he trying to hold back
his anger? "I don't understand how the wolf could have
that much control over you." His voice cracked again.
"This is all my fault. Gabriel was right. I should have
never started training you in the first place. I thought if
I taught you balance, this wouldn't happen. But I did
this to you. I didn't stop your training in time—"

"No," I said. "Don't say that. Don't blame your-self. I did this, not you. I didn't stop training when you asked me to. . . ." My lips trembled, and I couldn't speak anymore. I'd already cried a good amount, but another wave of sobs ripped through me.

"What do you mean? What have you been doing? What happened to your arm? And why the hell . . . ?" He paused, as if dampening his temper. "Why weren't you wearing your moonstone?"

A million lies flashed through my mind—a million excuses I could tell Daniel for why I wasn't wearing my moonstone, my fail-safe. But what was the point of lying anymore?

"I took it off to conceal my identity. I confronted a member of that gang of invisible thieves—they're called the Shadow Kings. I killed him. He was a demon, and I staked him through the heart."

I heard Daniel take in a sharp breath.

"But really, the reason I took off my moonstone was because I wanted to prove that I didn't need it." I shook my head. "But I was wrong."

Gabriel had been right about me.

I was losing myself like the rest of them.

I'd let the wolf inside my head, inside my heart, and it had tried to take me over. Tried to make me harm the person I loved the most. I wasn't stronger. I wasn't bet-ter. I wasn't different.

The mattress shifted as Daniel stood up. I could hear

his footsteps as he paced beside the bed. He stopped a few inches away from me and then went back to pacing. This time he stopped when he was on the opposite side of the room. "Help me understand what you're saying. You went after the gang alone? Why would you do that?"

"Because I wanted to find Jude. I wanted to make my family whole again. Going after the gang was the only way I knew how to find him. But you wouldn't help me. Not you or Gabriel or my father. So I found someone who would. I didn't do this alone. I found someone who believed in me."

"What do you mean you found someone? Who is this person, Grace?"

"His name is Nathan Talbot, and he's a demon hunter—a Hound of Heaven. I met him at The Depot when I went there with April. He saved us from some trouble. . . . But he's been training me. Teaching me the things that you couldn't."

"Why didn't you tell me about this?"

I shook my head. "Because of how you've been acting lately—and demanding that I be normal. And because I knew it would upset you. I knew you'd be worried. I was afraid you'd try to stop—"

"Damn right, I'm worried!" Daniel shouted. "You're keeping secrets from me. Secrets that are more deadly than you could even imagine." He slammed his hand against the wall. "You meet some mysterious guy who *claims* he can train you. How did he even know what you are? How do you know he's not the one Jude was trying to warn you about? The person who's after us? Do you have any idea how stupid you've been?"

"Stop it!" I jumped up from the bed and faced him. "Talbot isn't after me. We've been alone together a dozen times. If he wanted to hurt me, he would have by now. He doesn't want to kill me; he wants to help me. He believes that I can be a hero like *you* used to."

Daniel leaned against the wall, both his fists grabbing the ends of his shaggy hair. "So this *is* my fault. I couldn't give you what you wanted, so you went looking for it somewhere else."

"Don't say that, Daniel . . . I love you."

"But you don't trust me." He let go of his hair and dropped his hands at his sides. "You trust a total stranger more than you do me."

"You're the one who doesn't trust me. What have you been doing for the last week and a half? Katie? Mishka? Drinking at bars? Or something else I can't even imagine? At least Talbot doesn't lie to me!"

Daniel looked right into my eyes. "Tell me something, Grace. Is there something between you and this Talbot person? Something more than just training?"

"No," I whispered, but then the image of Talbot trying to kiss me flashed through my mind, the way it felt when his lips brushed my cheek.

A look of guilt must have crossed my face, because

Daniel dropped his gaze and he put a hand to his forehead. His whole body shuddered like he was holding back a rush of sorrow, and he slumped against the wall.

"No, Daniel. No."

I wanted to rush over to him and throw my arms around his shoulders, but I was afraid he'd just push me away. Any connection I shared with Talbot, whatever bond drew me to him, I realized now that it was skinny and hollow compared to how I felt about Daniel. Nothing compared to how the thought of causing Daniel this pain made me feel.

"It's not like that at all. He tried to kiss me. I told him not to, but he still tried."

"What?" Daniel shot straight up and grabbed his motorcycle keys off the table next to him. "Take me to him. Where is he?"

"No, Daniel. What on earth would that accomplish? It's still not what you think."

"Take me to that bas—"

"So you can do what? He's Urbat. There's nothing you could do."

"I'm capable of doing more damage than you think."

"Daniel, please," I said, trying to calm him down. "Talbot is my friend and my mentor. That's all."

"No, Grace. That's not all. If this guy is the one who told you to take off your moonstone, then he isn't who he claims to be. He should know you're not strong enough without it."

His words stung, but only because they were true. "Well, you don't have to worry about it anymore. I thought I could become a Hound of Heaven. I thought I could take on the Shadow Kings and find Jude. But all I've accomplished is hurting you. You're right. I'm not strong enough. I've failed."

And Gabriel's right, too.

Falling is inevitable.

Daniel sighed. He held the keys dangling from his hand. His shirt hung open from where I'd torn it, and I watched his perfect chest heave as he breathed.

And that was when I noticed it: his perfect, *unmarked* chest.

"Daniel," I said, taking another step toward him, trying to get a better look. "What happened to the gashes on your chest?"

Daniel looked down at his sternum, then hurriedly pulled his torn shirt closed to hide his collarbone, where the three gashes had been only a few minutes ago—the ones I'd given him during my frenzy. "It's nothing," he mumbled, and tried to turn away.

"That's not nothing." I grabbed his hand that held his shirt closed and pulled it away from his chest. I was right—the gashes were gone. The only evidence of them were three faint white scars. "What is this, Daniel? What's going on?"

I grabbed his arm and pulled at the frayed bandage that covered the stitches he'd gotten at the hospital. I expected him to protest, to try to pull out of my grasp, but he only slumped against the wall again—resigned—as I removed the bandage.

Nothing was there. Not even a scar.

"What is going on?" I demanded.

"I don't know," Daniel whispered. He ran his hand over his uninjured arm. "I really don't know."

"But you did know this was happening. You're angry at me for keeping secrets, and yet *this* is what you're keeping from me?"

"I didn't want to tell you yet. . . ."

"Because you don't trust me?" I knew it was a stupid thing to ask. I knew I hadn't been acting very trustworthy as of late—but *this* was too big of a thing to keep from me. "Or because you think I'm too weak to handle it?"

Daniel didn't answer.

"Are all your powers coming back?" I asked.

"Yes. Slowly. But they're developing."

"Oh, God." I stepped back until my knees hit the edge of the bed. "Does that mean you're *not* cured? Does it mean . . . ?"

Falling is inevitable . . . and there is no cure after all?

"I don't know—" Daniel began, but he was interrupted by a loud banging noise on his front door.

"Grace Divine!" an angry voice shouted. "If you're in there, you'd better come out now if you ever want to see the light of day again!"

Dad?

"Get the hell out here now, young lady!" he shouted. "Or I will break down this door if I have to."

I looked at Daniel. He pulled his shirt closed, and his eyes flitted to the rumpled bed. We both knew the door was unlocked.

"Go," he said.

My heart ached like I'd never thought it could. Something was broken between Daniel and me, and I didn't want to leave before I could fix it.

"This isn't over."

I heard the doorknob start to turn. I grabbed my backpack and bolted toward the door, using my super-speed to get there before the knob finished turning. I opened the door, stepped out in front of my livid father, and shut it behind me before he could see anything else.

CHAPTER TWENTY-TWO

The Big Bad Wolf

IN THE CAR

I had no idea my dad could scream that loud—or for
that long. Apparently, Gabriel had filled him in on my
escapades over the last two weeks, and how I'd run
out on him. Dad yelled at me all the way home in the
Corolla, and then we sat in the car in the driveway for
a good long while because he wasn't done. I was tired of
telling my story, so when dad demanded more details,
I rattled off every event that had happened in the last
week like a robot stating facts—well, all the events
except for the ones that involved my lips in any way.
When I was done, I pretty much just shut down and
listened to him yell at me some more. Dad was usually
so even-keeled and forgiving that the whole thing felt
completely surreal.

I could hear the wolf's voice trying to edge its way
into my head. Trying to get me to lash out at Dad with

my words. I hated myself for how easy it had been for the wolf to make me forget everything that was important to me—even if it had been for only a few moments. What if Daniel hadn't been able to stop me from hurting him? I would have lost everything. I clutched my moonstone necklace in both my hands and pushed the wolf away as best as I could. I couldn't afford to let it have *any* control over me again.

I didn't even blink until Dad pulled the car into the garage; he changed his tone to a softer, disappointed almost whisper. "The thing that hurts me most, Grace, is that you thought you had to try to find Jude on your own. If you hadn't been so self-absorbed, you would have known that Gabriel and I have been out scouring the city for your brother. We already knew about the Shadow Kings."

I bit my lip and nodded. *Why does that make me want to cry?* "Are you going to let Gabriel take me away to his pack?"

Dad shook his head. "I'm not letting you out of our sight."

I shuddered with a grateful sob. "I assume I'm grounded, then."

Dad made a scoffing laugh. "If you think you've been grounded before, you aren't prepared for *this* kind of grounding."

Dad wasn't kidding. Not only was I under house arrest, but he escorted me to and from school each day, and every lunch I was required to spend with Gabriel in his classroom, learning the finer points of tai chi and meditation. The Good Samaritan project was cancelled by Gabriel, and the rest of the students were reassigned to helping Day's Market get ready for its grand reopening. I was informed by my father, however, that I'd be helping my mom get ready for the Halloween festival concessions to fulfill the rest of my service project. For good measure, Dad nailed my bedroom window shut and took away my cell phone, because if I couldn't bother to answer it "when it was imperative," then I didn't deserve to have one.

I'd lost the slip of paper with Talbot's number on it, so without my cell I had no way of contacting him to tell him what had happened.

But the part that devastated me the most about being grounded was that, even though it was midterms week, Daniel didn't show up for school the day after our fight. Or the next day. Or the day after that. I called him a few times from our home phone when my parents weren't breathing down my back, but he never answered. And there was no way I was going to be able to stop by his apartment to see if he was okay.

On Wednesday I cornered April after art class and profusely apologized for getting mad at her for ratting me out to Gabriel—she really had done the right thing, after all. She forgave me immediately—but she sounded more than devastated when I told her I wasn't going to be try to be a superhero anymore.

"Are you sure?" she asked. "I've been working on the best costume design."

"I'm sure it would have been fabulous," I said. "But I can't do this anymore. I don't know how to tap into my powers without losing control. I can't risk it again."

I was almost certain Talbot wasn't the one Jude had tried to warn me about. It just didn't make sense. But the longer I was away from him, the more I questioned his methods. Yes, he'd shown me how to tap into my powers, but only by using my anger and fear to do it— the things that made the wolf stronger. Now it felt like I didn't know how to use my powers at all without giving the wolf too much control. And why had he wanted me to take off my moonstone? I wore it twenty-four hours now, even showered with it on, afraid to ever take it off after what I'd done to Daniel.

How had Talbot lasted so long without falling to the wolf while using his methods? Especially without a moonstone of his own?

Was Talbot really that much stronger than I was?

Or had Daniel been right about him—that he wasn't who he claimed to be?

As much as I didn't care for Gabriel's company, I have to admit that I looked forward to our tai chi sessions together. It was one of the few quiet moments in my day, when I could let go of my moonstone and not battle the wolf for free rein over my thoughts. Part of me wished I'd swallowed my pride and let him teach me sooner.

By our Thursday session, I finally broke my vow of silence concerning Gabriel and asked if he knew anything about Daniel's absence. He stood in a T-stance, his arms parallel in front of him. Then he slid into a parting-the-horse's-mane position and said that Daniel was "looking for answers."

"Answers to what?" I asked.

"You know very well to what," Gabriel stated, and then wouldn't say any more. His voice was laced with so much disappointment it made me feel like I was at the bottom of a pit, staring up at an impossible climb.

I turned away, fighting the sudden urge to sweep Gabriel's legs out from under him and send him sprawling across the social hall floor.

I guess he and I weren't going to be friends anytime soon.

By Friday afternoon, Daniel still hadn't shown up

for school, and I learned he apparently wasn't at his apartment, either, when Sheriff Ford and Deputy Marsh showed up on our doorstep asking if I knew where he was.

I shook my head. "I haven't seen him since Monday."

"Do you know where he was Sunday night?" Marsh asked.

"Why?"

"We're looking into possible leads in the Peter Bradshaw attack. We think it's connected to what happened to Tyler, so we're requestioning people."

"I talked to him on the phone that night. He was definitely home," I said, even though I wasn't sure of anything anymore.

Hell, for all I knew these days, I could have been the one who attacked Pete. I could have done it under the influence of the wolf and not even remembered it. Like how Jude had attacked Maryanne's body and didn't even know he was the one who did it.

"Are you sure?" the sheriff asked.

"Yes."

Sheriff Ford asked me a few more questions and then left me with a business card in case I thought of anything else.

But all I could think of was that I wanted Daniel to come home. Gabriel said Daniel was looking for answers, but what if he'd left because of me?

And what if he didn't plan on coming back?

The rest of Friday passed with no word from Daniel, and I would have spent all of Saturday curled up in my bed if it hadn't been for the Halloween festival that evening. It was the last thing in the world I felt like going to, but Mom didn't even blink when I told her I wasn't feeling well.

"Grab that basket of caramel apples and put it in the Corolla," she said. "I'm going over now to supervise the decorating committee. Find a costume, and then I need you to bring over the refreshments for the booth."

"A costume? Seriously, I have to wear a costume?"

"Everybody is dressing up. You'll look silly if you *don't*." Mom was in a kimono that Grandpa Kramer had brought back from their trip to Japan two summers ago. She even had her hair swept up in a perfect Japanese-style bun. She picked up Baby James, who was already dressed in his Max's wolf-suit costume from the *Where the Wild Things Are* book. It was made of white fleece with a bushy brown tail and a hood with long pointed ears. He clapped his hands and crooned, "Wet the Wild Wumpus stawt!"

I laughed, feeling a hint of happiness for the first time in days. It was pretty much the cutest thing I'd ever seen.

"I taught him that," Charity said as she passed me

with a box of orange-and-black tablecloths. She wore an angel costume with glittery wings and a white toga. The whole family dressing up for Halloween had always been kind of a Divine family tradition. One I had apparently been left out of the loop on this year.

"But I don't *have* a costume," I said as they walked out the door.

"Find something," Mom said. "And don't be late with those refreshments."

After she was gone, I tried to find our costumes, but then I remembered that all of the Halloween boxes had been sent to Katie Summers for the festival. After about twenty minutes of digging through the storage room, I gave up and called April for help.

"I am so glad you called," April said when she walked into my bedroom a little while later, with her makeup bag, a small duffel, and a jewelry box. "This is exactly why you need me."

My dad was down in his study working on who knew what, and I figured he couldn't protest my having a friend over if it was technically to help Mom out with the festival.

"I'm at a loss," I said. "I'm thinking of just safety pinning a couple pairs of socks to my sweats and going as 'static cling.'"

April rolled her eyes. She put one hand on her vinyl-clad hip. Her sequined tank sparkled under the light in my room, and her blonde locks were twisted into some weird sort of hair sculpture à la Lady Gaga. I couldn't imagine how many cans of hairspray she'd used to make it stay that way. "Halloween is about releasing your inner she-wolf," she pronounced.

I cringed at her terrible word choice. "I'm not so sure that's a good idea."

"Then at least a little bit of a sex kitten." She unzipped her duffel. "Don't worry, I've got you covered." She pulled out a bundle of red-and-blue fabric. "I've been working on this design for the last few days, but when you said you weren't going to do the superhero thing anymore, I thought I'd never get a chance to see you wear it." She handed me the bundle and then went to her bag for something else.

I held the clothes out in front of me: a tiny blue gingham sheath dress and a solid red hooded cloak. I'd seen these clothes before. In a picture on April's dresser from a daddy-daughter costume party at her elementary school. It was the only picture of her dad in her entire house.

"I'd planned on bedazzling your superhero initials on the back of the cloak, but we hadn't decided on anything, so I left it blank."

"Is this your Little Red Riding Hood costume?" I asked. "And weren't you like ten years old when you wore this? Don't you think it's going to be way too small?"

"Exactly," April said, and grinned like the Cheshire cat.

Seriously, I don't know how April gets me to do these things. I mean, in the picture I'd seen of her wearing this dress, it had hit her midcalf. But as I pulled it over my shoulders, the fabric clung to my chest and hips and barely reached my midthighs. The red hooded cloak that went with it skimmed just above the small of my back. If it weren't for the flesh-colored tights I insisted on wearing with the outfit, I would have felt practically naked.

April pulled a curling iron out of her duffel bag and gave my already naturally curly hair a little more "pow," as she called it. Then she coated all my nails in bright blue polish to match the dress. But the things that almost put the outfit over the top were the tall red-leather high-heeled boots she pulled out of her bag of supplies. The ones I had barely been able to walk in at the club.

I stood in front of the mirror in utter disbelief. "I so can't leave the house in this."

"Yes, you can," April said, standing next to me at the mirror while applying an insane amount of liner around her eyes. "You totally rock that outfit." She flitted over to my desk and dropped her eye pencil in her makeup bag and then picked up two bracelets from her jewelry box. "Do you think Gaga would wear white or yellow gold?" She held up the two bracelets of different colors. One was a gold-beaded bangle, and the other I recognized as the bracelet she'd lost at the club. The image of Talbot holding it out to me in his hand flashed through my mind.

"I thought that bracelet was silver."

"Oh, the ones I sell on my website are silver. But I had the original one made out of white gold just for me. One of the perks of being the designer." She dug into her large jewelry box and pulled out a silver cuff that was almost identical to her bracelet. "You should wear this. It's perfect for your ensemble. But be sure to tell anyone who asks about it that it's one of my fall designs." She flitted back over to me and slipped it on my wrist.

"That's perfect!" she squealed. "Exactly the look I was going for. So innocent, yet so kick-A at the same time. Like Little Red Riding Hood meets Wonder Woman."

"Huh." I stared at myself in the mirror for a second—tiny blue gingham dress, red cloak, long curly hair, high-heeled boots, and silver cuff bracelet. "Well, this is probably the last time I'll be allowed out of my house, so I might as well go out with a bang."

AT THE FESTIVAL, JUST BEFORE SUNSET

Wow. I have to say that Daniel and Katie outdid themselves with the designs for the posters and decorations for the Halloween festival. It was like Tim Burton had swept into Rose Crest and transformed Main Street into the set of one of his movies. All the booths were swathed in bright-colored fabrics, and the posters had been printed with a spidery style of writing that had to be Daniel's doing. I hoped Katie had a whole committee helping her with the actual setup, since Daniel was still nowhere to be found.

Cars, each decorated with a different theme, lined the street for trunk-or-treating. And by the looks of the costume-clad crowd already filling the sidewalks, checking out the concession booths and games, the whole town was probably going to turn out for the event.

Mr. Day stood in front of the market, dressed like an old-timey shopkeeper, passing out coupons in honor of the grand reopening. He beamed at April and me as we walked by with our baskets of refreshments. The store was already packed with customers.

Mom was so busy ordering everyone around that she didn't even notice my costume at first, and by the time she did, April and I were already manning the caramel-apple booth. I could tell by the look on her face that if I hadn't been surrounded at the time by half of the ladies from the Sunday school board, she probably would have thrown a massive fit and sent me home. Luckily, Mrs. Ellsworth, bouncing her fairy-princess baby on her hip, smiled and said, "Don't you look adorable?"

But then again, that comment was probably directed at Baby James in his wolf suit as he pulled on the hem of my dress while begging me to take him through the trunk-or-treat to get some candy.

I scooped him up in one arm and then grabbed a

basket of caramel apples in the other. "I'm going to take James trick-or-treating and try to sell some of these along the way."

"Thank you," Mom said. She patted her forehead with her long kimono sleeve and then counted out change for Amber Clark and her boyfriend. "But don't let him get too much candy."

Baby James and I set out along the street. "Just me and my big bad wolf," I said, and set him down with his trick-or-treat bag. James made a little growling noise and then took off running for the first car in the trunk-or-treat. I followed after him with my basket. We stopped at each car, and everyone fawned over James and his cuteness, and I sold a caramel apple for every third piece of candy he collected. I had only about half a dozen left when we made it to the end of Main Street. We were about to cross and go up the other side when Charity and a couple of her friends came bounding up to me to buy apples.

I handed out three and was counting their money while James pulled on my dress, trying to force me to cross the street toward more candy, when I heard another customer ask, "How much?" from behind me.

"Two dollars each," I said, and handed Angela Leonard three dollars back.

"Thanks," she said.

"But what if I want the whole basket of goodies?" the customer behind me said.

I looked over my shoulder and almost dropped my basket. "Talbot?"

He stood there in a yellow-and-blue flannel shirt and faded blue jeans, but he was without his customary baseball cap. He had a slight smile on his face, but his green eyes seemed serious and concerned.

"What are you doing here?"

"Just checking out the festival," he said, and winked at Charity and her friends. Then he leaned in close to my ear and whispered, "I need you to come with me, Grace. Right now."

"What? I can't. I've got my brother."

James pulled on my hand and pointed in the direction of more candy, making his little growling noise.

"Oh. My. Gosh," Mimi Dutton said. "You guys are so cute. Look, Angela, they're Little Red, the wolf, and the woodsman." She pointed at Talbot last.

Talbot cracked a smile, then cocked his head like he was pointing in the direction that he wanted me to go. *Come now,* he mouthed.

Charity gave me a funny look. "Where's Daniel?"

"I don't know."

Talbot put his hand on my arm. "Excuse us, little ladies," he said to Charity and her friends. "Grace, I need your help with something."

James wailed and started to dart for the street. I bolted forward and caught him by the hood of his wolf suit.

"Whoa," Charity said. "That was fast."

I gave myself a little shake—I hadn't meant to use my powers. I picked up James, and he kicked my legs and whined for candy.

"Charity, will you take him?"

"But Mom said I could hang with my friends. I'm not the one who's grounded."

"Just for a few minutes, okay?" I looked up at Talbot. "We'll be right back, right?"

"Sure," he said, and nodded to Charity. "I just need your sis for a minute."

"Whatever." Charity grabbed James out of my arms and let him drag her across the street toward Gabriel— dressed like a monk—who was handing out Snickers bars from a plastic cauldron.

I slipped around the corner with Talbot before Gabriel could see me with him. "What's going on?"

Talbot grabbed my arm. "We have to get out of here," he said. "You and me. Right now."

"What? Why?"

"There's no time to explain. We just need to go." He grabbed my arm, his hand like a vise over my elbow, and led me into the parking lot behind Lyman's Hardware. The lot was packed with cars, but we were the only people there. "We need to get out of here before they find you."

Talbot pulled me toward his old blue truck, double-parked under a lamppost that shone in the dusky dimness of the evening. I could see from here that the back of his truck was loaded up with what looked like camping gear. I stopped dead, digging the heels of my boots into the asphalt, and pulled my arm out of his grasp. "I'm not going anywhere until you tell me what's going on."

"They're coming for you, Grace," he said. His words sounded just like Jude when he called with his warning. "You're in danger. The Shadow Kings are coming here. Right now. And I can't stop them. They'll tear this town apart until they find you. But maybe we can run. Drive as far away from here as we can get and then maybe hide out in the woods. I don't know. We just need to go."

"They're coming *here*? Right here? I have to warn my family."

"There's no time!"

"My sister's out there with my baby brother, and my parents. Not to mention the whole town. If the Shadow Kings are coming here, then I need to warn them. I need to find Gabriel or my dad." I turned and was about to bolt out of the parking lot.

"Don't!"

Talbot lunged at me. He grabbed my cloak and jerked me back toward him. I yelped and dropped my basket. Caramel apples spilled out around our feet.

"I don't care about them," he said. "You're the only thing that matters."

"They're my family!" *How can he not want me to warn them?* And there was no way I was going to leave Baby James unprotected. I'd promised him that. "I'm not going to leave them in danger."

"Just get in the damn truck," Talbot said, and clamped his hand over my wrist, making my silver bracelet dig into my skin. He started to yank me toward his car, but before he could finish the movement, he yelped and let go of my arm.

I looked at his hand. A red welt the width of my bracelet blistered up on his open palm. The silver had burned him.

"Talbot?" I backed away. I'd thought all along that he was like me. An Urbat who hadn't changed yet. Now it was clear that wasn't true.

Talbot looked at his hand and then back at me. His eyes glinted with light from the streetlamp. A low growl escaped his lips. "Just get in the truck, Grace. I don't want to have to hurt you."

I took another step back. The heel of my boot slipped a bit on the gravel under my feet. "What's going on? Who are you?"

"Someone who can't be trusted," said a familiar voice from somewhere nearby.

I whirled around and watched with disbelief as a tall, broad-shouldered guy stepped out from between two vans in the parking lot. He looked so different, yet so similar at the same time. His once short hair had grown out past his chin, and he had at least three days' worth of stubble on his normally clean-cut face. It gave him the look of a house pet gone feral.

"Jude?"

Talbot let out a sudden curse and clamped his uninjured hand around my elbow. "We have to go, now!"

"Move away from him, Grace." Jude held his hand out to me. "Get as far away from Talbot as you can."

"You know each other?" I looked up at Talbot, who was crouched a bit, with his lips curled back from his teeth in a snarl. He looked like a wolf trying to ward off an intruder from encroaching on his prey. "You said you didn't know him."

"Don't listen to a thing he says," Talbot growled.

Jude laughed. "Talbot lies, Grace. That's his thing. He makes you think you can trust him, but you can't."

Talbot's the one Jude was trying to warn me about when he called? How was that even possible?

"He's a real grifter," Jude said.

My memory flashed to what that Gelal had said just before . . . just before Talbot had burst into the room and interrupted him: *If you want to find the pack, then why don't you ask their Keeper? He's a real grifter, don't you think?*

Grifter? Didn't that mean con artist? And Keeper? I'd heard that word before, too. Gabriel had said it. A Keeper was a beta of a werewolf pack.

My stomach felt like I'd dropped a hundred feet on

338

a roller coaster. "You're one of them," I said to Talbot. "You're one of the Shadow Kings." I tried to pull away from his grasp, but he wouldn't let go of my arm.

"Get in the truck!" He slammed me against the passenger's-side door. "We need to go now, before the rest of them—"

A loud howl ripped through the night—several howls, actually. Talbot looked around frantically for the source of the sound. His grip loosened on my arm.

"Gracie, come here!" Jude shouted.

I kicked Talbot in the shin with my pointed heel, pulled out of his grasp, and ran toward my brother. Jude grabbed me in a quick embrace, then slid open the door to one of the nearby vans and pushed me inside. "You'll be safe in here," he said, and slammed the door closed behind me.

There were two guys in the front seat of the van. I ignored them and crawled to the back so I could see through the rear window. I peeked out just as four guys appeared seemingly out of nowhere and rushed at Talbot. He took a swing at one of them, but then he disappeared from my view as the four guys converged on him at once. I heard him shout with pain. I fell back from the window. A few seconds later the van door slid open. Jude climbed in. Two other guys followed, dragging Talbot's limp body in with them. They dumped him on the floor. His eyes were closed. Blood oozed from a gash in his forehead. I knew I was supposed to be afraid of him, but I still couldn't help being concerned by his shallow breathing.

"What are you doing with him?" I asked Jude. "What's going on?"

"We're delivering him to the alpha." Jude kicked Talbot's prostrate body with his booted foot. Then he looked back at me, his eyes glowing bright. "Along with you, little sis."

"What?"

One of the guys who'd carried Talbot in lunged at me. I tried to back away, but there was nowhere to go. He grabbed me by the throat, and the last thing I remembered seeing were the letters *S* and *K* tattooed on his knuckles right before his fist slammed into my forehead and everything went black.

CHAPTER TWENTY-THREE

The Were-House

IN A DARK, DARK HALLWAY

I woke up with a splitting headache and the sensation of being carried by someone—cradled in his arms like a puppy. Which I imagined was preferable to the way the two burly guys beside me dragged Talbot by his arms along the concrete floor.

I could tell by the faint moaning noise that emanated from his mouth that he was somewhat conscious. But not conscious enough to help heal his wounds, since blood still oozed from the gash in his forehead, matted in his eyebrows, and dripped into his eyes. For some reason it really bothered me that no one wiped the blood from his face.

I was still woozy, and I tried to lift my arms to brush my hair out of my face—and that was when I realized my hands were bound behind my back with some kind of cording. I tried to move my legs, but they were bound, too. I started to struggle against the arms that held me, but they only squeezed me tighter—I wasn't being cradled; I was being held captive.

Faint music vibrated from somewhere nearby—voices, too. I tried to shout, but my tongue felt thick and heavy. I tasted blood in my mouth. I must have bitten my tongue when that Gelal knocked me out. But I could still taste the sourness of Gelal, the distinct smell of dog, and the bile-inducing stench of Akh. The mixture was so foul I almost contemplated biting my tongue harder.

Instead, I mustered up what little human strength I had and screamed, as loud and as long as I could. When I was done, the only reaction I heard was one of the guys next to me laughing.

"They won't hear you over the music," Jude said. I realized now he was the one carrying me. "And even if they did, no one would care. The Shadow Kings own this place."

"Where are we?"

Jude didn't answer. But we were underground—that much I could tell from the weight of the air and the utter lack of natural light. Just a few bare bulbs hung from the ceiling, casting sinister shadows along the corridor. We turned a corner, and the music died away. Then we went through a doorway and into what seemed to be a freight elevator.

Are we in a warehouse?

The elevator jostled to a start and traveled in an upward motion. The gatelike door opened, and Jude carried me out of the elevator. The air felt lighter here but smelled much worse. I blinked at the harsh fluorescent lights, taking in the sounds and sights around me. There was a staircase above us, and as Jude carried me around it, I looked up and saw that the stairs led to a balcony and an upper office with darkened windows.

In front of me was an expansive room that appeared to be part warehouse, part frat house. The center of the room was empty, but a plasma TV about the size of a truck stood in the corner. It was surrounded by sofas and beanbag chairs. Nearby was a pool table, and along the opposite wall was a tall row of warehouse shelving. Four shelves high, and five shelves wide. Each was covered in a thin mattress and blanket—like someone had made bunk beds out of them.

But what startled me most were the fourteen or so teenage guys who filled those sofas and beanbags, lounged on the bunk beds, and played pool. I recognized one of the guys at the pool table as the rough-looking gamer who had gotten into a fight with that Tyler kid over a video game at The Depot. The one who had probably killed him.

Jude shouted something that sounded like a command, and suddenly all the guys in the room dropped what they were doing and jumped up. They stood at attention like soldiers whose captain had just entered their barracks.

My wolfy senses were already tingling, but my whole body shuddered with foreboding as I surveyed the pack of guys. At least four of them were Akhs—I could tell from their talonlike fingernails—and based on the smell, at least five of them were Gelals. I guessed that made the remaining six Urbats.

This was it. I'd found the gang—just not in the way I had intended.

I was a prisoner in the den of the Shadow Kings.

Most of the guys stood stiff like large, tattooed boards, with their heads bowed. Others looked somewhat alarmed at the sight of Talbot and the way the Gelal dragged him to the center of the room. The smallest of the boys, who had been playing a video game on a giant TV, looked like he was barely fourteen. He locked eyes with me for a moment, curiosity painting his expression, but then he turned away when Jude growled at him.

Jude carried me to the center of the warehouse floor and dumped me unceremoniously on the ground. I landed hard, unable to brace myself, next to Talbot, who knelt with his head bowed so low it almost touched the floor.

"We've returned, Father," Jude shouted in the direction of the balcony that overlooked the warehouse floor. "And it was just as I thought. Talbot was trying to help her escape."

I glanced sideways at Talbot, not wanting to take my full sight off the shadowed balcony above us. Had he really been trying to help me?

Talbot's shoulders sagged, but then he lifted his chin and looked up to the balcony. The cut on his forehead had finally started to heal. "Jude was wrong," he called to whomever was up there. "I was bringing the girl to you. It was Jude's interference that almost helped her get away." He pushed himself up as tall as he could on his knees. "I would never fail you, Father. I have served you faithfully for many months. I watched the girl for weeks, as you commanded. Set up this whole charade. Got rid of her original teacher when he started to ask too many questions. Disposed of the van driver she was supposed to work with and took his place. She trusted me, and I had her right where we wanted her." He lifted his chin with pride. "I am your Keeper—your most devoted. How could some worthless girl change that? She is nothing to me."

Talbot's words burned. This situation was horrid enough, but hearing what he really thought about me—realizing all he'd done—felt like pouring acid on a fresh cut. Talbot was probably the one who had tried to kill Pete Bradshaw. But for what purpose, I didn't know. And what had he done with my real driver and poor Mr. Shumway?

The only thing that confused me more than Talbot's betrayal was Jude's involvement in all of this. I'd thought Jude was being held captive by the gang—forced to do their bidding against his will. But according to the scene unfolding before me, Jude wasn't a prisoner here. Talbot was the gang's beta, but Jude definitely had some influence or control. Could I possibly hope that he was just biding his time until he could use that influence to help me escape?

I'd broken rule number one—I'd dropped my guard in so many ways the last couple of weeks. With the wolf. With Talbot. With Jude. And now I was paying the price.

"Talbot lies," Jude said to the person I assumed was up on the balcony. "He cares for her. They were planning on running away."

"What Jude heard me say was only my plan to get the girl to trust me. Which would have worked if he hadn't shown up and made a mess of things. I do not need to be second-guessed in my methods." He turned his glare on Jude. "How bad did you screw this all up? Did you even bother to leave an effective trail behind you?"

Jude glared at Talbot. "Of course I did."

"Enough!" snarled a voice from up above us. It echoed off the warehouse walls. Something about that voice made me want to sink into the ground. Made me feel exposed, ripped open. "Talbot goes free. Jude, take the girl to the room. Then come to me so we can discuss your interference."

Jude ducked his head like a scolded pup. "Yes, Father."

Talbot smirked at Jude as two of the Gelals stepped forward and cut the cording from his wrists and ankles. He stood up and stretched, and the wound on his forehead healed over. He turned to face the teen boys who still watched us with rapt attention.

"I say this calls for a celebration," he said to the boys. "Let's all go to the club."

"But you never let us go," the youngest boy said, his voice cracking with puberty. He indicated himself and the three next smallest of the boys.

"Well, then, today's your lucky day, Ryan. We're all leaving for a while." He glanced at me for the first time since we left Rose Crest. His eyes were void of emotion. "We have to make sure there's ample opportunity."

Ample opportunity? For what?

Talbot looked at Jude. "What are you waiting for, boy? You heard the Father. Take her to the room."

Jude snatched me up in his arms and carried me toward a door marked BREAK ROOM. It must have been a sign left over from when this was an actual warehouse. I thought about struggling, trying to break free of his arms. But where would I go? How could I even run with the cording on my feet? Besides, if I struggled, then they would send someone to help Jude. And that meant I wouldn't have a chance to talk to him alone.

A table and chairs and an old green refrigerator populated the room. From the smell leaking out from the fridge door, I assumed it was packed with takeout boxes and at least a dozen half-eaten pizzas.

Jude dumped me in a chair. He grabbed a coil of rope off the table and started tying me up. I stared at the crown of his dark brown hair as he wrapped the rope around my middle.

"Why are you doing this?" I asked.

Jude didn't answer. He pulled the ropes tighter. I winced.

"Then help me at least understand," I pleaded. "Why would you call and try to warn me about the Shadow Kings if you were working for them all along?"

Jude looked up at me. His eyebrows furrowed with confusion. "What are you talking about? I didn't call you."

"Yes, you did. I'd know your voice anywhere."

Jude shook his head and went back to securing the ropes to the chair.

How can he not remember this?

"You were worried about me. You called me on Daniel's phone from inside his apartment. You said someone was coming for me. You even tried to warn me about Talbot—only I didn't know that's who you were talking about. You said the exact same thing you said in the parking lot behind the hardware store. That he makes you think you can trust him, but you can't."

"Shut up," Jude said. "I didn't call you. Stop trying to confuse me."

"You did call. Which means deep down inside, you still care. My brother's in there somewhere."

"I said, shut up!" Jude raised his hand like he wanted to strike my face. "I would never call to warn you."

"But you did. The night the gang trashed Day's Market. I bet you snuck away just so you could find me." I took a breath. "And you texted April on Monday. And you've even left comments on her blog. Don't you remember that?"

Jude lowered his hand and glanced at my face. A slight look of recognition flashed over his eyes. He shook his head and backed away toward the door. "Be sure to yell real loud if you hear someone coming." He thumbed in the direction of the cracked window. "Wouldn't want Daniel to miss you after all this trouble."

He smirked and closed the break-room door behind him as he left.

This was a trap!

A trap to catch Daniel.

They were counting on his finding me. Hoping he'd follow their trail here. They left the warehouse to make it look like they weren't watching, and now they wanted me to scream for help.

But how were they so sure Daniel would come?

I hadn't seen him in days. I didn't even know if he wanted anything to do with me anymore. Would he even come if he found out I was in trouble?

Simultaneously, my heart filled with hope and dread.

Yes, if Daniel is the person I know him to be—he'll come for me no matter what.

LATER

I rocked back and forth in my chair, trying to loosen my bonds. I needed to get out of here on my own before Daniel found me. Find him before he even got near this place. Now if only I had Baby James's talent for pulling a Houdini out of his booster-seat restraints. That thought made my heart heavy. What if I never saw my family again?

My muscles tensed and ached, bidding me to use my abilities. But I didn't trust my powers anymore. I didn't trust myself. What if I gave the wolf too much leeway again and it completely took over?

But getting out of here before they trapped Daniel was more important. I had to take the risk.

I concentrated on the slight, warm pulse of my moonstone necklace against my chest and siphoned a small amount of power into my arms. I struggled harder against my bonds. The ropes burned my skin, but I didn't have time to devote any power or self-control to healing the tender wounds.

The cording around my arms must have been lined with some kind of metal, because they barely loosened in response to my struggles. If only I could break free of that, the ropes binding me to the chair would be no problem at all. I rocked too hard, and the chair fell backward. It slammed into the ground, and I smacked my head on the concrete—which only made my splitting headache worse—and pinned my arms behind me with my own weight. I used my momentum to turn the chair, and myself, to the side. But now one of my shoulders was pinned; the weight of the chair and my body dug into it with aching force.

The whole situation seemed utterly hopeless, but I didn't stop.

What felt like an hour passed, but for all I really knew, it could have been only a few minutes. The warehouse was still empty—at least from what I could hear. The noises out on the street grew quieter as the night got darker. I had no more feeling in my trapped arm, and I didn't know how much longer I could go before I had no feeling left inside of me at all.

A few more minutes passed, and then I heard the break-room door creak open. I lolled my head in the direction of the noise, expecting to find Jude or Talbot checking on me, but I watched with shock as two people crept into the room. One man was dressed in a brown hooded robe—and the other was Daniel.

"Gracie," he said, and rushed over to me as quietly as he could.

"Run!" I whispered. "It's a trap. Get out of here!"

"I know. You were too easy to find. But we still have

to try." He pulled my chair upright and tugged at the ropes, but they didn't budge.

The man in the hooded robe riffled through the drawers in the counter. He pulled out a serrated knife and approached us. He pushed the hood of his robe off his head and handed the knife to Daniel.

"Gabriel?" I looked at Daniel as he went to work cutting the ropes from the chair. "What the heck is he doing here?" Not that I was ungrateful for his assistance—just surprised, considering our history.

"Gabriel is the one who followed you here."

"Your mother got concerned when she couldn't find you at the festival," Gabriel said as he worked on unwinding the cording that bound my ankles. "Then your sister said she saw you leave Main Street with a boy. I found your basket in the parking lot behind the hardware store and then followed the trail here. I called Daniel as soon as I could."

"Luckily, I was already on my way home," Daniel said. "I wasn't too far from the city." He cut through the last rope and pulled me out of the chair.

"Did you find what you were looking for?" I asked.

"No." He brushed a curling strand of my hair off my face. "But I've found what I need."

I got lost in his deep, dark eyes for a moment.

"We should go," Gabriel said.

"Right." Daniel pulled the cording from my wrists and then locked hands with me. "Stay as close to me as you can. We came in through an entrance in The Depot. There's an underground corridor linking these two buildings together."

"So this is the warehouse next to the club?"

Daniel nodded. "You ready? We're going to make a run for it."

I stretched out my arms and legs, happy for some relief. "They're probably waiting for us."

"We'll just have to see."

Gabriel went out of the break-room door first. Daniel and I followed, hand in hand. We stayed close to the wall, surveying the warehouse. All seemed quiet. The barracks were empty. I looked up at the balcony and the darkened windows of the upper office next to it. There was no sign of whomever had been up there before.

Daniel tightened his grip on my hand. "There's another exit over there. It looks like it's padlocked, but with the three of us working together, I bet we can break it loose. I don't want to risk the corridor. It's too boxed in."

"Sounds good," Gabriel said.

"Ready? Run."

Daniel bolted for the door, and I ran with him. Gabriel followed close behind. We made it to the door, and the warehouse still seemed as empty as before. Were we really going to make it out? Daniel tried yanking on the lock. The metal loop stretched a bit. He shook his head. "Grace, can you do it?"

I felt a rumbling under the heels of my boots. Something was happening inside the building somewhere. I let a small burst of power into my arm as I grabbed the lock and yanked on it. It broke free in my hand. Then I heard a clanking noise from behind us. Daniel went for the doorknob, but I swung around and looked back as the gate of the freight elevator lifted and a pack of boys came rushing in our direction. The door must have still been locked from the outside. It wouldn't open. Daniel put all his energy into kicking at it, over and over again. Then we both kicked together, and I heard the dead bolt crunch through the wood frame. Moonlight flooded in through the crack in the door. But before we could get out, someone was on top of Daniel, pulling him back. I heard Gabriel shout, but I knew he wouldn't fight back. Someone else grabbed me.

I remember screaming. I remember fighting. I remember watching Daniel try to grapple with the person who'd grabbed him. But before I knew what was happening, I'd been seized by three guys who pulled me away from the open door. Another three had Daniel.

Jude led the pack as Daniel, Gabriel, and I were dragged up the stairs and then into the dark upper-level room. It looked like it had once been a large office, but it was now decked out like a luxury hotel room from the Victorian era. Thick, plush curtains covered the windows that would normally look down on the warehouse floor. A large wardrobe was tucked away in one corner, and the only light in the room came from the flickering of a dozen candles on an ornately carved table. A large four-poster bed filled the middle of the room, covered with a lush velvet bedspread and pillows. While the boys downstairs slept on warehouse shelves, whoever occupied this room obviously cared much more for his own comfort.

Talbot stood by one of the bedposts, and I assumed this was his room until he directed our attention to a dark, recessed alcove. With a bowed head, Jude went to stand beside Talbot.

"Now that you're all finally here," Talbot said, "our father wishes to see you."

The boys who held my arms stiffened and exchanged a half-horrified, half-delighted look. Almost as if this was the first time they'd even seen their "father."

"You made it too easy," a voice snarled from the shadows of the alcove. Something body-shaped shifted, and then two yellow glowing eyes appeared in the dark. "It almost ruined the fun."

That voice. What is it about that voice? Something about it makes me feel like I've been ripped open.

Daniel's face went ashy white. He took a step back, but one of his captors pushed him forward. Did the voice sound familiar to him also?

"This is a game to you?" I asked. "Who are you? Tell us what you want with us."

"Oh, you always were a bossy little brat," that eerie

voice said. "I never could stand you and that obnoxious little dog of yours. Do you have any idea how much I enjoyed watching your face when you found her dead on your porch? Almost as much fun as ripping out her throat."

The man laughed and stepped out of the shadows. He had hair so blond it was practically white, a large cleft in his chin, and a crooked, evil smile. He looked almost exactly the same as the few times I'd seen him when I was a kid.

"You," Daniel said under his breath, like he was cursing.

I shot a look at him. His face was so pale I thought he was in danger of passing out. My stomach clenched into a knot.

"Caleb Kalbi," Gabriel said, "what the hell do you think you're doing?"

"Finishing what should have been done the moment Daniel was born." Caleb turned his murderous eyes on his son. "I should have smothered you before you took your first breath." He stepped toward Daniel, his hand outstretched like he wanted to snap his neck.

"Don't you touch him!" I shouted, and pulled against the guys holding my arms.

Caleb laughed. "Oh, you are a tasty treat. I can see why Talbot might hesitate bringing you in. I can imagine that he wanted you for himself."

"Father," Talbot said, "I told you, I was bringing her to you all along."

"I am joking, my son," Caleb said. "Only joking."

My eyes flitted from Talbot to Caleb. Didn't Gabriel tell me that Caleb was the one who was behind the attack on Talbot's parents? Wouldn't Talbot know this? How could he call Caleb Father? Why would he even be helping him? Then again, for all I knew now, Talbot's entire story could have been fabricated. His being the last Saint Moon could be a total lie. Except the way Gabriel stared at him, as if looking at a ghost, made me wonder otherwise.

But before I could say anything, Caleb snapped his fingers, and the guys who held me let go of my arms and pushed me toward Caleb. I stumbled forward. Caleb grabbed my face with one of his hands, cupping my chin with his long fingers. His fingernails jabbed into my skin. I could barely hear Daniel shouting at his father over the pounding of my pulse in my ears. My muscles seared with a burning pain more intense than I'd ever endured before.

"It was nice of you to dress the part. Little Red Riding Hood and the Big Bad Wolf." He looked me over from head to toe. He trailed the fingers of his free hand down my arm, making my skin crawl under his touch. He leaned in, his mouth close to my ear. "My, what nice assets you have, my dear."

"Better to burn you with," I said, and swung my arm up with a flash of power and smashed my silver bracelet against the side of his cheek.

Caleb screamed. He let go of my face and slammed my arm away from him. A large angry burn blistered up along his cheekbone.

My arms went up in a defensive position, but before I could act, three of Caleb's boys were on top of me, binding my arms and legs. I kicked and screamed and tried to flail as they forced me to my knees. Caleb glared down at me, rage burning in his eyes.

"Who let her wear silver in here?" Caleb shouted. "Tell me!"

He scanned the boys in the room. I could hear them all take in a breath. They all feared Caleb—their *father*, so to speak.

Jude stepped forward from beside Talbot, his head still bowed submissively. "I am sorry, Father. I did not realize her bracelet was a danger. I thought it was just a trinket with her costume."

"Well, take it off her now!" Caleb roared.

Jude shot him a look, then ducked his head even lower and approached me. One of my captors held out my arm to him. I stopped struggling and tried to meet my brother's eyes as he stooped in front of me. But he wouldn't look at my face.

"I know there's still good in you, Jude," I whispered.

"You were always such a saint . . . and now you're lost. But you're still my brother. You wouldn't have called to warn me if you didn't still care."

"I am *not* your brother," Jude whispered angrily. "You betrayed me. This is my family now." Jude's hands hesitated over my bracelet, anticipating the burns.

"What kind of father would force you to hurt yourself?"

"*You* hurt me worse than any burn." He snatched my bracelet off my wrist and cast it aside. He shook his hand as little blisters bubbled up on his fingertips.

"I love you," I whispered. "I'm your sister. I want to take you home."

Jude finally looked me in the eyes. His flashed with silver at first, but then softened into the violet eyes that were a mirror image of mine. My brother was in there somewhere. "Just don't pull a stunt like that again, and you'll be fine," he whispered. "It's Daniel he wants."

"I can hear you," Caleb said. "Superhearing, remember?"

"Sorry, Father." Jude lowered his head and stepped aside as Caleb approached.

The welt across Caleb's cheekbone had lessened some, but it was still a bright pink. He sneered in my direction, but then walked past me to Gabriel, who was held by only one guard now.

"I'm impressed," Caleb said. "I set a trap for one

nuisance and ended up with two. It's fitting that you'll see what I'm going to do here. Since ultimately, this all comes down to you and your pack."

"What do you mean?" Gabriel asked.

Caleb's crooked smile danced on his lips. "We both know Sirhan is dying. And when he does, I'll be there for the challenging ceremony."

"You're not wolf enough to show up there alone," Gabriel said. I could practically hear the bluff in his voice. "You weren't even wolf enough to try to kill Sirhan yourself. You made your little friends do it, and they ended up killing Rachel in the process. The pack doesn't forgive easily."

"I'm more wolf than you," Caleb said. "You sit up on your mountain, teaching werewolves to go against their nature, to be peaceful. Thanks to you, they won't be ready for the fight I'm bringing their way. As you've seen, I've been recruiting my own pack. And my boys and me, we're coming to that challenging ceremony, and we're taking over. We've collected enough money to buy off the other challengers, and we're strong enough to fight anyone else. I'll spit on Sirhan's corpse before they lower it into the ground. I'll have everything that should have been mine years ago. And the best part is that you'll just stand by and watch it all happen, won't you?"

Gabriel didn't answer. He just stared at Caleb, as if unmoved by his admission.

So my fear had been right? Caleb wanted to take over Sirhan's pack, and Gabriel was going to do nothing to stop him? If Caleb was capable of practically overrunning the city with fear as the leader of the Shadow Kings, what would happen if he became the alpha of the strongest pack in the country?

It would be Gevaudon all over again.

Caleb's eyes seemed to flash with satisfaction at Gabriel's blank response. "Coward," he said, and cuffed Gabriel across the forehead with his fist.

Gabriel grunted. His eyes rolled back in his head, and he went limp. His captor let go of him, and he crumpled to the ground. The Shadow Kings were apparently good at knocking people out with a single blow. I wondered if that was how they had pulled off so many crimes without eyewitnesses.

"Now, I just have one last thing to take care of." Caleb turned around, smiling like a jackal, and approached Daniel. "I thought you were gone for good until Jude told me where to find you," Caleb said to Daniel. "I was surprised you'd come back. Last I'd heard, you'd split town when I left with your mother. And then you just dropped off the map. I was hoping you were dead. I told your mother you were."

Daniel almost flinched at the mention of his mother. It had been almost four years since she chose Caleb over him. "And where is she? I'm sure you have her on a leash around here somewhere."

"I killed her." Caleb pulled a short knife from a sheath on his belt. "With this."

"What?" Daniel struggled to break free. He always said he didn't have a real mother, but I knew he still cared about her.

"She kept bitching about wanting to come back for you. So I told her you were dead. But that only made her angrier. She wouldn't shut up, so I stabbed her. I guess you can say it's your fault she died."

Daniel's nostrils flared. "So if you didn't want to find me then, why do you want me now? I assume this trap was set for me?"

"Quite right," Caleb said. "I'm glad your friend told us where to find you. Saved me the trouble of doing it myself before the challenging ceremony. Thing is, I thought Jude looked familiar when Talbot brought him home to us. He'd been living on the streets like a stray. Most of my boys were. That's the nice thing about desperate teenagers—they're easy to dominate. You tell them they belong, and they'll do pretty much anything you ask. But I didn't realize who Jude was until one night he decided to entertain us with the story of how he became a werewolf. Seems his sister Grace and her boyfriend, Daniel, had something to do with it. You can imagine how much I enjoyed listening to his story from the balcony, and how badly I wanted to know more.

"He tried to run when he realized who I was and what

I wanted. But then I helped him see we had something in common. We'd both been betrayed by our families. Sirhan would rather leave his pack in the hands of a coward like Gabriel than let me lead it the way it *should* be led. And Jude's family chose the mutt next door over their own son. Once we saw eye to eye, it was only a matter of time before we set our trap."

Caleb's explanation still didn't make sense. Why would he set such an elaborate trap just to see Daniel again? Why did he even care? He'd already replaced Daniel twenty times over with the boys in his pack. Why would he send Talbot to become friends with me, only to kidnap me later and leave a trail for Daniel? I didn't know if these were the workings of a madman, or some genius plot I couldn't comprehend.

"The thing about your friend's story that baffled me," Caleb said, standing right in front of Daniel, "is that he claims you've been cured. I didn't think that was possible. I still don't."

In a lighting-quick movement, Caleb thrust the knife at Daniel. I screamed. The knife plunged into Daniel's upper arm. Caleb pulled it out, and blood spurted from the wound. It slithered down Daniel's arm.

Caleb dabbed at the cut with his fingers. Daniel winced. Caleb brought his bloodstained fingers to his nose and sniffed. I assumed he was testing it to see if it smelled like wolf's blood or like a human's—like Daniel had tested Jude's blood when he found it on our porch, and that was how he knew Jude had been infected. Caleb's eyes squinted with confusion. He tasted the blood with the tip of his tongue. I tried not to gag. His forehead creased, and he seemed even more confused. Then he beckoned Talbot to his side.

Talbot smelled the blood and shook his head. "I don't understand, Father. I can't tell what it smells like. What do you think this means?"

Caleb wiped the blood on Talbot's flannel shirt. "It doesn't matter," he said. His voice sounded like he was trying to cover up his confusion. "Daniel was always going to die, either way. He won't be around to mess up the ceremony. The girl will make the perfect weapon, if she's as strong as you claim."

Talbot's eyes flicked in my direction. But then he nodded and stepped back to where he'd stood before.

Caleb came back over to me. He wrapped a hand around one of my wrists. Every instinct told me to hit him and run, but I was still held by two guys.

"The only problem with killing one's wife is that it gets lonely without a mate," Caleb said. "I think you'll do nicely once we've turned you into a werewolf."

"Don't you touch her!" Daniel shouted. "I'm the one you hate. Kill me and let her go!"

"Oh, I'll let her go all right. Once she turns into a wolf, she won't be able to control herself. Then I'll let her go in a room with you. And then when she's done tearing you apart, I'll let her go back home. Send a message to her precious pastor father for me."

My heart slammed against my chest. That was Caleb's plan? Turn me into a wolf and then get me to kill everyone I loved?

"What?" Jude suddenly stepped forward from beside the bedpost. "Father, you said Grace was just bait. You said—"

"And what do you think happens to bait, boy?" Caleb snarled. "It gets swallowed. And in this case, your sister is going to get swallowed by the wolf. And then she'll be one of us."

Jude looked at me and then at Caleb. I couldn't read the expression on his face.

"Do you have a problem with that?" Caleb asked. "I can always let her at you along with Daniel."

"No. Your plan is perfect." Jude ducked away like a dog anticipating being struck by his master.

I turned my gaze away from Jude. Just when I thought he was still my brother, he proved to be Caleb's lapdog.

"I will never turn," I said. My voice shook too much for it to be convincing, but I tried to hold my head high.

Yes, you will, the wolf whispered inside my head. *There's no escape from me.*

"You will see in the morning, Grace Divine. My methods are quite persuasive. How do you think I came by so many of my boys? Jude and Talbot were rare finds: werewolves already."

My heart suddenly sank for the boys in this warehouse. In this *family*. Some of them were obviously Gelals and Akhs, but most of them had probably been hapless teens, down on their luck—until Talbot and Caleb got their hands . . . or teeth . . . on them.

But my heart also sank for myself, and for Daniel, and for all of my family back home. If so many people had fallen to Caleb's methods, how did I stand a chance?

Caleb made a gesture, and two of his boys picked up Gabriel's limp body and headed for the door. Then Daniel and I were led toward the exit by our captors.

"Why don't you just do it now?" Daniel asked.

"Because anticipation is the best part of the game. Feels just like Christmas Eve, don't you think?"

Chapter Twenty-four

Abide with Me

DOWNSTAIRS

I couldn't even bring myself to struggle as we were hauled off to a new prison. It seemed completely pointless, and listening to Daniel holler and curse as he tried to break free only made every ounce of hope inside of me vanish. Daniel might be slowly getting his powers back, but superhuman strength wasn't fully developed yet.

They brought us to a dank, cold, windowless room. A storage room of some sort on the lower level of the warehouse. A single, dim fluorescent light buzzed and flickered above us. Caleb, or probably one of his boys, had made a couple of slight adjustments to the room—shackles attached to the walls by long, thick steel chains and heavy metal bolts in the concrete, and a security camera in the corner. The boys carrying Gabriel dumped his unconscious body at the far end of the room. They bound his legs and feet with the same kind of cording they'd used before on me. The shackles were apparently designed for Daniel and me, seeing as how our captors chained us by our wrists and ankles on opposite sides of the room.

"I'll take the first watch outside the door," Talbot said as he leaned through the doorway.

"I'll stay with you," one of the boys said, sounding eager to impress Talbot.

"Very well."

Talbot gestured the boys out of the room. I looked up at him, but he closed the thick metal door behind them without even glancing at me. I'd noticed a keypad outside the door like the one at The Depot, and now I heard three distinct thumping noises as three heavy bolts locked into place. There was no doorknob. This door had been specifically designed to be impossible to break through.

I sank to the ground, shuddered, and let out a sob. My wrists felt almost too heavy to lift as I brought my shackled hands up to cover my face.

"Don't." Daniel tried to rush over to me, but the lead on his chains wasn't long enough. He could make it only halfway across the room. He leaned forward as far as he could. "Don't cry, Gracie. Don't give up. We'll find a way out of here. We're going to escape. Even if we have to fight every last one of them."

"But we're nothing, Daniel. That's like twenty

against two. Gabriel won't fight, and you're just getting your powers back. We're no match for them. They'll turn me, and then I'll kill you. And then if they send me home, what will stop me from destroying Baby James and everyone else?"

And the more selfish thought that I didn't voice was that if everyone I loved was gone, there would be no one left to cure me—if the cure even existed. I'd be a monster for all eternity. A Death Dog at the beck and call of a madman.

"You just have to have faith, Grace. Believe in yourself. Don't give up now."

"But I have no more faith, Daniel. No more faith in myself. No more faith in God. He doesn't care about me. He doesn't care about us. It's over. This is the end. Tomorrow I become a monster, and the rest of you die. And God doesn't give a damn."

"I don't believe that. You think you've lost your faith, but I know you well enough to know that isn't true. Deep down, you know you still believe. And I believe in you."

"Then maybe you don't know me as well as you think you do."

"Yes, I do, Grace. And I know exactly what's going on inside your head, because I've been there. That voice you hear—those terrible things that bombard you. Thoughts that make you think God doesn't care about us. Those aren't *your* thoughts. And they don't come from God, either. They're the wolf. The demon. The devil. It's testing you. Tempting you. But if you can push those thoughts away, if you can reach beyond them, then you'll find that there's a true power deep inside of you, a power God has given you to fight the evil, that's greater than anything you can even imagine. You found that power inside of you once."

I shook my head. I didn't know what power he was talking about. The speed, the strength, the agility, they all came from the wolf.

"The night you cured me," Daniel said, "what were you feeling?"

Gabriel had asked me that same question before. I didn't know why it mattered, but I did know the answer.

"Love," I said. "I loved you enough to sacrifice everything for you. I wanted you to be cured no matter what it meant for me. I thought I'd lose my soul, but it was more important to me to save yours."

"Then don't tell me you aren't strong enough, because that's more strength than most people could ever dream of having. There is no greater gift, no greater power than that."

"Than true love?"

"Yes. That's the difference between them and us. We're still capable of love. The wolf tries to destroy love, tries to push it out of your heart, tries to make you destroy everything that you care about. But if you can hold on to that love, and if you can hold on to your faith, then you are stronger than any monster out there. No outside power, no force, no evil can make you turn into the wolf as long as you hold on to that love."

Daniel fell to his knees. His chains clanked against the floor. "I should have never stopped training you," Daniel said. "I should have never stopped believing in your strength. I should have been there supporting you, teaching you the balance that you need. When my powers started to come back, it scared the hell out of me. I thought that meant the cure hadn't worked—and I didn't want to tell you because I didn't want you to think you'd sacrificed everything for me and that it meant nothing."

I moved toward Daniel, closing the distance between us. "But you could have told me. You can tell me anything. Just like I should have told you about Talbot."

"I know, Grace. We were both being stupid. We should have trusted each other no matter what. But I was also scared that my powers coming back meant there'd be no cure for you, either. No safety net. That's why I stopped training you when Gabriel told me to. And then I got so wrapped up in trying to find answers that I neglected you. I pulled away. But I shouldn't have done that. I should have still taught you how to use your powers properly, so you wouldn't have had to turn to someone like Talbot." Daniel held up his shackled hands. "But I'm standing by you now. You and me. We'll fight side by side, and no one will stop us. *Nothing* is going to tear us apart."

I was kneeling in front of Daniel now, at the end of my own lead. I tried to cup his face with my hands, but I couldn't reach him. There was no more give in the chains. Instead, I stared into his deep, dark eyes like I could get lost in them forever.

We weren't going to walk out of here. There was no way the two of us could fight off these demons. No matter how much faith we had. But there was a way to keep the demon inside of me from winning.

I'd been willing to trade my soul for Daniel once because it was the only way to save him. I'd been willing to become the monster for him. And I'd do it now if I thought it would save him again, but Caleb had other plans. He wanted me to turn into the monster so he could use me to destroy Daniel and my family—and I couldn't allow that to happen. No, no matter what happened, I wasn't going to turn. *It's better to die as Grace Divine than to live as a monster.*

I leaned out as far as I could toward Daniel, and Daniel leaned out as far as he could toward me. Our lips could barely meet in the middle. I strained against my chains, feeling like my arms were about to dislocate from their sockets, but I gained another quarter of an inch. I pressed my lips against Daniel's.

I didn't care that Gabriel was unconscious at the end of the room, or that Talbot was outside the door. I didn't care about the security camera in the corner. I kissed Daniel like it was the last time we'd ever kiss.

Because I knew it was.

In the morning, I would die to save the ones I loved.

LAST NIGHT

The next few hours stretched on into the longest night of my life—but it also felt like the shortest. It was the first time and last time Daniel and I would ever spend the night together, and we couldn't even touch. The flickering fluorescent light burned out at some point, so Daniel and I just lay there side by side on the concrete in the dark, able to reach out to each other only with our voices. Sometimes we talked, and other times we fell completely silent, unsure if the other was sleeping until one of us asked a question.

We talked about everything. And nothing. From life's burning questions to the most trivial sorts of things we could think of. At one point I asked Daniel about his portfolio for Trenton, which was due in only a couple of weeks. He described for me in detail how he'd sketched and mapped out a new design for headphones for one of his submissions.

I told him about how one of the Trenton essays had made me want to be a superhero. Daniel laughed. "You'd make a great superhero. Especially if you wore that outfit. What is it, Little Red Riding Hood meets Wonder Woman?"

I giggled. "That's what April said. I'm sure I look

ridiculous." Someone had stripped off my boots before they shackled my ankles, but I was actually grateful for the cloak at the moment. It made a light blanket in this cold, dark room.

"You look amazing," Daniel said.

"You can't even see me."

"I've got the memory of you emblazed in my head. It's keeping me rather warm."

I laughed uneasily and then fell silent for a while. I wondered how long that memory would last in Daniel's head after I was gone.

Gabriel's uneasy, sleeping breaths and moans interrupted the quiet of the room. At least that way I knew he was alive. I couldn't help wondering why he'd come after me if he wasn't going to fight. Why he even cared at all. He'd come to Rose Crest to find out if I was this Divine One who could cure Urbats of the werewolf curse. So why didn't he go back home the moment he heard Daniel's powers were coming back?

Then another thought hit me.

"Don't you worry?" I asked Daniel quietly, not sure if he was asleep.

"Hmm," he said groggily.

"Don't you worry about turning into the wolf again? I mean, I'm wearing a moonstone, so that will at least help me stay balanced for a while. But this is all pretty psycho—aren't you afraid you're the one who's going to change? Maybe you should take the necklace back."

Daniel's chains shifted. I could tell he'd rolled over on his side, facing me.

"That's the thing, Grace. It's totally different than before. I mean, I've got the ability to heal, and my strength and speed are coming back, along with the enhanced senses . . . but I've finally realized over the last few days that even though I've been totally freaked out . . . I don't feel the wolf inside of me at all."

I took in a quick breath. "Then maybe you have been cured."

"I don't know," Daniel said. "I really don't know." He was quiet for a moment. "The fact that Caleb wasn't able to recognize the smell of my blood didn't surprise me. But it makes me wonder . . . makes me wonder if I'm turning into something completely different."

"But what?"

"I wish I knew. I had my blood tested. That's where I was the last few days. I know a guy who works at a research lab in Columbus. He owed me a favor, and I knew he'd be discreet. I drove all the way out there just to find out that he couldn't tell me anything, either."

"Is that what you were doing, all those times you wouldn't tell me where you were? Just looking for answers? I wish you would have told me all along."

"I know. I should have. It's just that sometimes I had to go to some dark places to look for what I wanted."

I swallowed hard. "Like where?"

"That night you saw my motorcycle outside that bar?"

"Yes."

"I wasn't at the bar. I was at the motel behind it . . . with Mishka."

"What?" The wolf snarled terrible things in my head. I pressed my hand against my moonstone, forcing its calming power into my chest. "What do you mean?"

"I wanted her to get inside my head. She has a mind-control power she does with her eyes—steals her victim's free will."

"I know," I said, remembering how she'd almost used it to kill me. And then I remembered what Mishka had said about partying with Daniel. The wolf growled—trying to make me embrace my jealousy. "Why would you want her in your head?"

"She can read thoughts, as well as manipulate them, if she's got you in a deep enough trance. I wanted her to get inside my head to see if she could find the wolf in there. Tell me why I don't hear it or feel it inside of me."

I pictured Daniel lying on a motel bed, Mishka straddling him, staring deep into his eyes. No wonder he hadn't wanted to tell me what he'd been doing that night. "What did she find?"

"Nothing. I didn't go through with it. Her price was too high. I wasn't willing to give her what she wanted in return."

"What did she want?"

"Me."

I gritted my teeth as an angry wave of power passed through me. My eyes stung, and my night vision kicked in for a moment. When I saw Daniel's mud-pie eyes rimmed with sorrow, a rush of reassuring love pushed the wolf away.

"I left, and she was pissed," Daniel said. "But then she texted me the next day and said that she'd changed her mind, that she'd take my bike as payment instead. We were supposed to meet up again—I was waiting for another text from her that night at dinner when I ran out. Only when I got to her place, some house on the outskirts of the city, I discovered the person who texted wasn't Mishka. It was her friend, Veronica. They were in the same coven—like a family—and when Veronica had returned that evening, she'd found that Mishka and the rest of her friends were dead, and that someone had made off with about ten thousand dollars of stolen cash. Veronica wanted me to help her track down whoever killed her friends and get the money back. She said she'd help me if I did—get into my head for me. I tried. I wasn't even with Katie on Sunday like I told you. I was trying to follow a lead that turned out to be nothing." He groaned. "And I can't believe I made up that lie about being with Katie at my place. It was the first plausible thing that popped into my head. But it was also the dumbest thing I could have said."

I almost laughed. "No, the alone-in-a-motel-room-with-Mishka thing tops it. But I did almost take Katie's face off the other day. I'm just glad I didn't act on the urge."

Daniel's eyes went wide. He rolled over flat on his back, I guess deciding not to pursue that line of conversation. "The lead I followed was a total dead end. I never did figure out who attacked that coven."

"Um . . . Well, I've got good news and bad . . . ," I said, and then I told him the story about what happened at that house that day. How terrified I'd been the first time I saw Talbot cut off someone's head, and then how he had staked Mishka with a chair leg just before she almost killed me. And then, in an effort to be truly honest, I told Daniel about how Talbot had taught me to heal the burns on my face.

"I can see why you were attracted to him," Daniel said. "You always go for the dangerous guys."

"Yes, but I only love *you*," I said.

And then we fell silent for a long, long while.

I must have drifted off to sleep at some point, because my eyes popped open when I heard a shout and a scuffle outside the door. The first thought I had was that Jude must have come to his senses and was trying to rescue us. I sat bolt upright, but then I realized there was no noise at all.

"Are you okay?" Daniel asked. His voice cracked a

bit. If he was like me, he was probably getting parched. It had been several hours since I'd had anything to eat or drink.

"Yeah, it must have just been a dream."

"I had one, too," Daniel said. He was quiet for a minute. "Do you think after Trenton, we could get married and settle down in an apartment in New York City or somewhere? I could be an industrial designer, and you could fight crime like a part-time ninja assassin."

I almost laughed, but then I stopped myself, because I knew it would come out as a sob. I was quiet for a while as I composed myself. "Yeah," I said. "Yeah, that would be awesome."

I heard Daniel's chains rattle as he changed positions. I took a deep breath and concentrated some power into my eyes until my night vision returned. I found Daniel kneeling on the concrete in front of me. I didn't know if he could see me in the dark, but he had one of his special smiles—the one that said he was truly happy—on his lips.

"So you'll do it?" he asked.

"Do what?"

Daniel shifted so he was on only one knee now.

"What the hell are you doing?"

"Grace Divine, when all this crap is over, and we're out of college, and you take some time off from kicking bad-guy butt, will you marry me?"

He might as well have just kicked me in the chest

the way all my breath seeped out of me and my heart seemed to stop beating. "You can't be serious."

"I'm as serious as I've ever been."

I laid my head against the concrete floor, unable to respond. What did he think he was doing? How could he ask me to make promises for a future we had no chance of having? Didn't he know how this ripped my heart in two?

"Yes," I finally whispered, because even though I knew our getting married would never happen now, I wanted him to be happy—if only for a moment.

I rolled over and closed my eyes. I willed myself not to fall asleep again. I didn't want to dream about rescue again. No more fantasizing about *my* life beyond the next few hours. Instead, I pictured Daniel going off to Trenton, then moving into that apartment on his own and becoming a designer.

I wasn't leaving here, but if I could help it, Daniel would. Maybe I could create enough of a diversion to give Daniel a chance to escape. Maybe Caleb would be thrown off guard enough by my choice to die that Daniel could find a chance to get away. Maybe someone could be bribed to help us—if only we had something to bribe him with.

I reached my hand out toward Daniel, still unable to touch him. "Will you promise me something? A real promise. Not the kind that gets broken."

"Okay," Daniel said hesitantly.

"Promise me that if you get a chance to escape, you'll take it. No matter what."

"There's no way in hell I'm going to leave you behind."

"But what if it's too late for me—"

"That's not going to happen."

"But what if it does? If it's too late for me, and you get a chance to run, promise me you'll get away from here as fast as you can? You won't hesitate, or look back? You'll run to my family and take them someplace safe?"

"Yes," Daniel said. "But only—"

A loud clanking noise cut him off, and the door slid open. Eight of Caleb's boys entered the room.

CHAPTER TWENTY-FIVE

In the Lion's Den

A MOMENT LATER

They were all shirtless, Caleb's pack. I didn't know why. Maybe just to show off their impressive muscles or the SK tattoos on their shoulders or biceps. Three came to me, and another three went to Daniel. The last two yanked Gabriel up from where he lay.

One unlocked my shackles while the others held me tight. I kicked and flailed, as did Daniel, but Gabriel didn't resist as they dragged us out of the dungeonlike room. They walked us up a flight of stairs. I went limp and refused to move, hoping my resistance might create some type of distraction for the others, but one of my captors merely grabbed me and threw me over his shoulder like a sack of potatoes. I could see the rippling muscles down his back, but I still knew where he was vulnerable. I was about to slam my fists into his kidneys when another guy grabbed my hands and held them in an iron-tight grip.

Gelal, I thought, sizing him up. This one I could kill if I needed to. But the one holding me was most definitely Urbat. He stank like a rabid dog.

My ride flipped me over when we got to the top of the stairs, and tossed me to the ground. I didn't hesitate and scrambled to my feet, but then two of the guys were holding me again. Jude stood there watching the whole thing, unmoved. Caleb stepped out of his room and met us on the balcony overlooking the warehouse floor. An evil grin spread across his face.

"I hope you two enjoyed your time together. I know we enjoyed watching it."

One of the guys holding me laughed.

The security camera. Of course, they had been watching.

"It was quite touching, watching you two blather on about true love and all that rot. Although perhaps we should have made your chains longer. Some of us were hoping for a little skin after that kiss." He gave me a once-over with his eyes that made me want to vomit. His gaze lingered on my legs, making me wish my dress were about four feet longer. "Although I'll have more time for exploring that later."

Three more of the guys laughed. They sounded like sick hyenas.

Daniel thrashed in his captors' hands. "Don't you dare touch her!" he shouted at his father.

"Oh, don't worry. We'll be gentle—at first. It's been a while since we've had a girl in our home."

"Probably because they don't last long once you get your paws on them," Talbot growled from the shadows just beyond Caleb. I noticed him there for the first time, his hands tied with cording and two of Caleb's Akhs holding him. The last time I'd seen Talbot, he'd been the guard at our door. Why was he tied up now?

"That's why I wouldn't bring her to you," Talbot said. "You don't deserve to have her."

Caleb snapped his long fingers, and one of Talbot's captors punched him in the gut. Talbot doubled over and coughed.

"Talbot was supposed to turn you during the last couple weeks. He usually has a talent for it. But apparently you have more influence over him than he had over you. That's one of the reasons I decided to wait until this morning to turn you myself. Not only is anticipation one of the best parts of the game, but I also wanted to see who was still loyal to me. I expected one of them to try to free you last night, only I'd expected it to be your brother, not my own beta."

So that was why Talbot was tied up again. He'd tried to rescue us. Perhaps that commotion I'd heard at the door hadn't been a dream after all. Yet my own brother stood by Caleb's side, unrestrained, unwilling, unwanting to do anything. Maybe I'd been wrong about there still being good in him.

"There is something special about you." Caleb stepped close enough so I could smell his scent of alcohol and wolf. He ran one of his fingers down my cheek and then along the vein pulsing in my neck. "It's like you inspire devotion in the most unlikely places. I was right to choose you. You'll be an excellent alpha female when I make you my mate."

"That will never happen," I said as if stating scientific fact. I wouldn't give Caleb the satisfaction of my sounding angry or scared. I'd be dead before he could touch me again anyway. "And you are no *true alpha*. But Daniel is."

Or was: the realization dawned on me. Now it all made sense, the reason Caleb would go through all this trouble to find and destroy him before the challenging ceremony. It was the same reason Caleb had hated Daniel from the moment he was born. Daniel had been born with the essence of the true alpha. He was the person Gabriel had been talking about when he said he'd thought there had been another true alpha besides Sirhan—only he wasn't so sure Daniel still had that potential now that he was cured . . . or, er, everything was confused. But Caleb wasn't taking any chances. If Daniel was a true alpha, then he was the one person who could ruin Caleb's opportunity to take over Sirhan's pack.

"Daniel's got more potential for being an alpha in his little finger than you'll ever have. That's why you hate him, isn't it? Because he's everything you're not."

Caleb shoved his face into mine, his nostrils flaring, his yellow eyes squinted. He spread out his fingers in front of my throat, like he wanted to strangle me with his bare hand. But then he grabbed my moonstone pendant and ripped it from my neck with such force it made my head jut forward and then snap back.

He threw the pendant against the concrete wall, and I watched it burst into black bits of shattered hope. I tried to scramble for one of the pieces, but I couldn't break free from the arms that held me. I'd been counting on the moonstone buying me a few minutes of balance.

"It's time to finish the game." He snapped at the two guys holding me like they were trained mutts. "Throw her in the pit."

I didn't kick or scream or thrash this time when the two guys picked me up. Without my moonstone necklace, I couldn't risk getting worked up at all.

My time was over.

I held perfectly still and let them carry me to the edge of the balcony. I looked at Daniel one last time. He was thrashing, with four guys holding him back. But he stopped for a moment, like he could feel my gaze on him. He looked up at me with tears flowing from his eyes.

"I'll love you always," I said to him as the two guys pitched me headfirst over the side of the balcony.

"No!" I heard Daniel shout.

I'd wanted to fall. Just let my head crack against the concrete floor twenty feet below. But my instincts kicked in, and my body twisted midair. I landed with a head-over-heels roll and bounced back up on my feet. My left ankle faltered a bit under me, but I pretended not to notice.

I stood alone on the warehouse floor.

"You're going to have to do better than that," I shouted back at Caleb.

He leaned out over the balcony railing. "Oh, we're just getting started, girl."

The ground rumbled under my feet, sending a shooting pain through my tender ankle. A large garage-type door slowly opened on the far side of the warehouse. The rumbling groan of the door was accompanied by a chorus of growls.

"You see, Grace Divine, the wolf has quite the instinct for self-preservation. Threaten it enough, and you won't be able to stop it from breaking through."

The door continued to rise, revealing a line of six growling werewolves. Their eyes rolling and their teeth bared, they crouched, ready to pounce into action. They looked like the only thing holding them back was a signal from Caleb. He held his finger up, as if he had more to say before he sicced his Dogs of Death on me.

"Do your worst," I shouted at Caleb. "But this I promise you: I'll die before I'll fall."

"You'll fall, girl," Caleb snarled at me. "You'll fall so hard and so far, *I'll* be the only thing you'll be able to see when you look up from the glorious hole you've made out of your life. And then you'll belong to me."

He made a swift movement with his hand. The pack of wolves burst through the door. I fought the urge to pass out or run, or even scream. They ran in two lines and then fanned out, forming a circle around me. No escape now. My body shook. Pain mounted under my skin, and my muscles threatened to explode. The demon in my head demanded I let it free.

I couldn't let that happen.

I couldn't lose control.

One of the wolves lunged at me. My leg shot out in a side kick, and I sent him flying. He whined with pain when he hit the ground with a crack. *Not so hard, Grace*, I told myself. I really didn't know if self-defense counted as a "predatory act," but I couldn't risk killing one of these beasts. I couldn't even *want* to kill them. They had human hearts behind their wolf ones.

A second wolf attacked. I kicked him away. He was barely affected by the blow and came charging again. I punched him across his snout. Blood burst from my knuckles as I busted one of his razor-sharp fangs. The other wolves must have smelled the blood, sending them into a frenzy.

Two wolves came at me at once now. I deflected one, but the other tore at my leg with his claws before I could kick him away. Blood flowed from the wound, soaking the fabric of my ripped tights.

I had no time even to think about healing the gashes, because a third wolf pounced on my back, almost doubling me over. He sank his teeth into my shoulder. Burning venom shot through my arm and back. I couldn't take the weight of the wolf much longer, so I reared my head back and slammed it into the wolf's head. He yelped and slid off, his claws shredding the back of my cloak as he fell.

Another wolf lunged and sank his teeth into my side, piercing my abdomen. I felt something burst inside my back. A kidney? I screamed with agony and used all my remaining strength to throw that wolf off me.

I grabbed at my side, slick with blood, just as another wolf rammed into my leg with his head. My injured ankle snapped. I howled and toppled onto the concrete floor.

The six wolves circled around me, snapping and growling. I waited for a deathblow, but none of them broke from their holding pattern. Caleb must have given them a signal to wait. He probably took pleasure in the sight of my lying there in a pool of my own blood.

Get up, that horrible voice howled inside my head. *Get up. Kill them! You want them to die. Get up and kill them all!*

"No!" I shouted back at the voice. I tried to push myself up on the concrete, but my arms shook so hard I fell flat on my face. My body convulsed like there was something fighting to get out from inside of me. A burning inner flame engulfed me, lapping at my soul. *Kill them! Kill them!* the wolf's voice chanted in my head. *They deserve to die! Get up and kill them before they kill you!* I curled into a ball. Tears streamed down my face. *Let me kill them. It's the only way! Embrace me, and we'll destroy them all.*

I shrieked in agony as my muscles clenched, and my head and body jerked uncontrollably in a seizure.

"This is it!" Caleb leaned over the balcony railing. "You want to kill me, don't you? Here I am, girl, come and get me!"

Yes, kill Caleb. Kill him, and all of this stops!

"No," I whispered. There had to be another way. I believed that. I really did.

I rolled on my back and stared up at the ceiling, imagining I could see the sky outside. "Dear God," I whispered. "Please, spare Daniel and my family. I know you can. You can let me die, but do not let me fall to the curse. Save them."

"Do it!" Caleb shouted at the wolves.

They stopped circling me and backed up in crouching positions, ready to attack.

A wave of fire ripped through me, and the demon in my head screamed for me to act. The werewolves reared back, about to lunge at me. I rolled on my side and whispered good-bye to Daniel, even though I knew he'd never be able to hear me.

"*No!*" Daniel shrieked, followed by a shout from one of Caleb's men as Daniel broke free from his grasp and pushed him aside. The others were too distracted by the wolves and me to react quickly enough.

Yes, I thought. *Yes, Daniel has a chance to get away!*

Then Daniel threw himself over the balcony.

No, he's supposed to run away! I watched in horror as he fell toward me, but instead of crashing to the ground, Daniel did a twisting flip in the air and began to . . . transform.

Shift.

Change.

His clothes burst from his body.

I blinked, and when I opened my eyes, instead of Daniel, a large white wolf had landed on all fours only a few feet from where I lay.

The wolves who had been about to attack me turned their growls on the white wolf, warning him away from their prey. The white wolf seemed to stare at me. I noticed a diamond patch of black fur across his sternum as he crouched. His lips pulled back in a snarl, and he pounced in my direction.

I closed my eyes and prepared to die.

A rush of movement exploded around me. I heard snapping and snarling and whining, and when I opened my eyes again, the white wolf was on top of me—standing over me in a protective stance.

The white wolf threw his head back and let out the most ear-piercing howl I'd ever heard. It echoed off the walls of the warehouse, shattering glass in the windows above. Shaking my body down to my broken bones.

When the noise died, there was nothing but silence.

Nothing but the white wolf standing over me, glaring out beyond us, as if daring anyone to make a move in our direction.

I could barely keep my eyes open as I tilted my head to see what had happened. Two of the wolves lay bleeding on the ground, one had retreated to the garage door, but the other three looked as if they were bowing, heads lowered in supplication, to the white wolf.

"No! No! Kill him!" Caleb shrieked at his wolves. "Kill them both!"

But the three wolves lay on their bellies and refused to move.

"Then I'll kill you myself!" Caleb started to climb over the balcony railing.

"Not if I have anything to say about it," another voice shouted, and someone hit Caleb across the back of the head with a metal bar. It may have been my vision failing, but I could have sworn it was Gabriel.

Caleb crumpled in a heap behind the railing, and there was a rush of chaos as one of Caleb's Gelals lunged at Gabriel, and another one went running in their direction. I heard Talbot scream something. He jumped on the Gelal's back and threw his bound arms over the Gelal's head and around its neck. The two went falling over the balcony and landed hard.

Talbot pushed back on his knees and pulled the Gelal up with him. He jerked his bound arms, which were hooked around the Gelal's throat, and snapped its neck. The Gelal crumpled and Talbot pulled his arms over its lolling head. Before he could move, an Akh flew at Talbot, and the two fell into a grappling match.

But where was Jude? Why couldn't I see him anywhere?

The entire warehouse erupted in an all-out brawl as I scanned it for any sign of my brother. Two more werewolves came charging in our direction, ready to attack the white wolf. But the wolf didn't move from his protective stance over me. I must have slipped out of consciousness for a moment, because the next thing I knew, the two wolves were bowing in front of the great white wolf. One of them was smaller than all the other wolves—*Ryan?* I couldn't help wondering.

I coughed and tasted blood. The white wolf leaned down and nuzzled the side of my face. I stared into his deep, dark, mud-pie eyes—Daniel's eyes.

But how?

And why, if Daniel had been a black wolf before he was cured, was he a white wolf now?

I heard a great howl and used all my energy to turn

my head and watched as Gabriel crumpled against the railing of the balcony, his arm hanging over the side in an unnatural way. Caleb, looking fully recovered from the blow to the head, roared and launched himself over the railing. He landed on his feet on the warehouse floor.

"Watch out," I whispered to Daniel.

The white wolf's head snapped up, and he crouched back and growled at Caleb, who came charging at us with a vicious snarl. "You die now!" he shouted.

The Daniel wolf barked, and the five wolves who bowed in front of us jumped up and turned, snarling at Caleb. They reared back, ready to attack him.

Caleb slowed his charge, sizing up the pack in front of him. *Six against one*, I could almost see him thinking. Calculating his odds behind those yellow eyes.

Then Talbot stood beside us. The cording around his wrists dripped with Gelal acid. He yanked hard, and the corroded binding fell from his hands. He clenched his fists in front of him and glared at Caleb. Three dead Gelals littered the ground in his wake.

Seven against one.

"Looks like we've got you surrounded," Gabriel shouted from the balcony. He held his injured arm against his chest, but he brandished the metal bar in his other hand. Two Akh teens lay moaning at his feet.

Caleb took a step back.

Eight against one.

But where were the rest of Caleb's boys?

And where was Jude?!

"Here!" I heard my brother shout. At first, I didn't know where his voice came from, but then I tilted my head back as far as I could and saw him standing by the open freight-elevator gate. The elevator was packed with Caleb's remaining boys. They must have fled from the upper level through the shaft. "Here, Father! Hurry. This way." Jude waved at Caleb, offering him a way to escape.

"No," Caleb said. "We finish this." He glanced back at what remained of his Shadow Kings. "Come!" he shouted at them, like they were a bunch of his lapdogs.

Not a single one of his boys moved from the safety of the elevator.

"Come!"

"No, Father," Jude said. "We're leaving. Now."

Caleb furrowed his brows. A snarl marred his face. Had Jude ever dared to speak to his master this way before?

"Come now, Father," Jude said.

Caleb glared at the white wolf for a moment longer. His gaze flicked to Talbot and then Gabriel up above. I wasn't sure which of the three he wanted to kill the most.

He turned and bolted toward the elevator.

The white wolf made a motion as if to go after Caleb, but then hesitated, staring down at me as if he was afraid to leave his protective stance over my body.

"Go," I said. "You have to stop them."

The white wolf grunted, and he and the five other wolves bounded after Caleb, leaving me alone in a pool of my own blood on the cold concrete floor. I didn't have the energy to keep my head tilted back to watch them in their pursuit.

I felt warm arms scoop me up, and someone cradled me against his chest. "Talbot?" I asked, recognizing his scent.

He turned me toward the commotion just in time to see Caleb lunge for the elevator, the six wolves close on his heels—but not close enough. Caleb slipped through the narrowly opened gate into the elevator with his boys. The white wolf pounced after him, but Jude threw himself between Caleb and the white Daniel wolf, blocking the opening of the elevator.

The white wolf pulled up short, skidding to a stop in front of Jude. The other five wolves halted behind the white wolf, snapping and howling. The white Daniel wolf growled at Jude, but my brother didn't move—only glared at Daniel, as if daring him to tear through him in order to get to Caleb.

Daniel took a step back with a frustrated whine. Jude had just done the one thing that would stop Daniel from catching his father. Daniel wouldn't willingly harm my brother again.

Caleb slammed the elevator gate shut, leaving Jude

on the outside. Caleb rammed his fists against the gate, rattling the cage and roaring with anger. "When Sirhan dies, so will the rest of you," he shouted as the elevator started to lower.

Jude shouted at Caleb not to leave him behind.

"You're on your own, boy," Caleb snarled. He and the rest of his lost boys disappeared into the basement of the warehouse.

The Daniel wolf howled.

Caleb and his pack would be gone, out the corridor and through The Depot, before anyone could stop him.

Talbot hitched me up in his arms and started to carry me away, his shoulder blocking the scene by the elevator from my view. And blocking me from *their* view. Talbot could run off with me at this very moment, and no one else would even notice.

"Put me down," I tried to shout, but it came out as an airy whisper. "Where . . . Where . . . are you taking me?"

"I'm just trying to help," Talbot said.

"Why?"

My head felt so heavy, and the world started to turn dark and splotchy all around me. I don't know how fully with it I was when I thought I heard Talbot answer: "Because I love you."

"No . . . you don't," I tried to say, but I don't think the words actually left my mouth. *Does Talbot even understand love?*

Talbot said something I was too groggy to understand. I strained what was left of my superpowers to listen to him. ". . . because you reminded me of who I wanted to be . . . a long time ago. Like my ancestors—the Saint Moons. But I've been alone with only the wolf in my head since I was thirteen . . . I'd lost sight of everything I once believed in." Talbot held me closer to his chest. He leaned in to whisper—or shout, for all I could tell—into my ear. "Caleb offered me a family, but you offered me something worth so much more: myself."

"Jude?" I whispered, unable to process Talbot's confession. My brain was far too fuzzy. "What . . . happened . . . ?" I couldn't even think straight enough to finish the question.

Talbot grunted. He turned me back toward the freight elevator. My vision was hazy and spotted, but I could see the white wolf and the five other wolves surrounding Jude, who had been abandoned by his so-called father—thrown, quite literally, to the wolves. The Daniel wolf stood steady, but the other five scratched their paws at the ground and growled at Jude, looking eager to attack.

My brother dropped to his knees in the midst of the pack. He threw his hands over his face. "Please . . . I just want to go home now," I thought I heard Jude say as I slipped from consciousness and my mind faded to black.

CHAPTER TWENTY-SIX

Stuck

HOW MUCH LATER, I DON'T KNOW FOR SURE

I awoke to something warm and wet brushing my face.
I swatted it away and rolled over on my side to find a
mound of soft white fur acting as my pillow. It smelled
wonderfully of almonds, and in my half dream–like state
I was ready to snuggle up with it and go back to sleep.
But that was when I noticed the blanket lying under me.
It was the plush velvet bedspread—on Caleb Kalbi's
bed.

I sat up quickly—too quickly—and was about to bolt
when little white spots started dancing in front of my
eyes. I lay back down against the soft pillow.

"It's okay," I heard a familiar voice say from somewhere nearby. "You're safe. We just brought you to the
most comfortable place we could think of."

"Daniel?" I asked. My vision was still a little weird,
and I couldn't place the voice.

"No, it's me, Talbot." He turned to someone else in the room. "Do you think she has amnesia?"

The other person apparently ignored him. "I'm here, too," he said.

"Gabriel?"

I shook my head, and my vision cleared up a bit. Gabriel and Talbot stood at either side of the bed, looking fuzzy in my vision—but almost like brothers—and also quite concerned. They weren't the only ones in the room with us. Five teenage boys sat on the floor just beyond the foot of the bed. They bowed their heads almost to the ground when I looked at them.

"What's going on?" I asked. Why did my ankle throb so badly and a knot in my back feel like it was on fire? Why were my dress ripped open and my abdomen wrapped in what looked like makeshift bandages torn from bedsheets?

"You gave us quite a scare there," Talbot said. "We weren't sure you were going to make it." He took a step toward me, but suddenly, my pillow growled and Talbot took two paces back. "Whoa, easy there," he said, with his hands up, as if afraid my pillow might bite him. I knew I wasn't completely with it, but this whole situation seemed incredibly surreal.

"What happened?"

"You'd better get to work healing yourself. Your body can only do so much with wounds this bad without your help—especially with how much werewolf venom you've probably got in your system. We tried to use our own powers to help speed up your healing, but I'm afraid that kind of transfer only works on superficial injuries."

I squinted at Talbot, noting the genuinely concerned look on his face. I didn't understand him at all. He was evil, yet he *wasn't*? And had he said something about being in love with me?

"He's right, Grace." Gabriel sat on the edge of the bed. Apparently, my pillow didn't have a problem with that. "There will be time for explanations later. Right now we need to make sure you're okay." His arm was supported in a sling made of scraps from his monk's robes.

"Why wouldn't I be okay?" I lifted my arm. A bandage around it was soaked with reddish-brown sticky, congealing liquid. Blood. My blood. Then the fight with the wolves suddenly came back to me. "What happened? Where's Caleb? Where's Jude?" I scanned all the vaguely familiar faces in the room. "Where's Daniel?" I practically shouted.

My pillow whined and pushed me up as it shifted. I turned, kneeling on the bed, and discovered the pillow was actually a white wolf. He whined with agitation, shaking his head back and forth. It almost seemed like he was trying to tell me something.

"Caleb got away," Gabriel said.

"But you fought him?" I shook my head. "I thought you didn't fight, no matter the cause."

"Let's just say someone inspired me. Showed me it was possible to fight for what's important without losing yourself. You're a very brave girl." He patted his arm through its sling. "Not sure I'll be doing anything like that again soon, though."

I tried to smile at him, but I think it came across as a grimace.

Talbot cleared his throat. "Jude's here."

He pointed to the alcove where Caleb had been lurking the first time we'd been brought to this room. I blinked, and my eyes focused on Jude, who sat in a high-backed chair, staring at his empty hands.

"He says he wants to come home," Gabriel said.

"Really?" *Finally?* A pressure I'd felt in my heart for the last ten months suddenly eased. "Jude, I can't tell you how happy that makes me."

Jude shook his head and looked up at me. I was surprised at how blank his face appeared—even more stoic and stonelike than I'd ever seen him look before. His eyes weren't rimmed with concern like those of everyone else who stared at me in this room. No, Jude's eyes seemed completely empty.

Suddenly, the memory of Jude's helping Caleb escape flashed in my mind. Then the sight of his falling to his knees in front of the angry wolf pack, begging to come home. Was that really what he wanted, or was it the only way he could think to get out of the situation alive?

That heavy pressure settled back in my chest. My

brother sat here right in front of me—but it was like he wasn't my brother at all.

But at least he's coming home, I told myself. He'd been lost, but now he was found. And we'd figure out how to help him, whether he knew he wanted help or not.

"As for Daniel," Gabriel said, grabbing my attention again, "he's . . ." Gabriel indicated the large white wolf.

I stared into the beast's eyes. Yes, those were Daniel's eyes. The wolf started to rock back and forth, yipping and whining, growing more and more agitated. I didn't sense any malice in him like any other newly turned werewolf, but he was definitely troubled. I petted his back, trying to calm him.

"I don't understand," I said. "How long has it been? How long was I out?"

"A *long* time."

I glanced back at the teens at the foot of the bed. They'd shifted to their knees, their heads still bowed in what seemed like reverence.

"I don't get it. Are these the wolves . . . the boys . . . who bowed to Daniel and then turned on Caleb? Why would they do that? I thought they wanted to kill me."

"Daniel is their alpha now," Gabriel said. "Although their devotion to him is greater than I've usually seen. It must be his true alpha nature. He saved you by exerting his dominance over them—choosing to embrace his true alpha essence—and, in turn, became their new leader."

But why were *they* all changed back to human form, and not Daniel?

"I don't get it," I said, growing as frantic as the white wolf. "Why hasn't he changed back? Why hasn't Daniel changed back into a human?"

The white wolf yelped and shook his large head. I wrapped my arms around his neck. My blood had matted in his white fur. I leaned my head against his chest. I could hear only one heart beating—not two, like when he'd been a werewolf before. Did his true alpha–ness *do* something to him?

"What the hell is going on?" I asked Daniel.

"I think . . . ," said Gabriel. "I think he's stuck."

"No," I said, clinging to the white wolf's neck. "No, that can't be."

The wolf arched his head back and let out the most mournful howl I'd ever heard. It sounded almost like a scream.

Acknowledgments

So many people deserve my immense gratitude for helping make this book a reality—and for keeping me from losing it during the process:

You, my awesome readers, because without your enthusiasm this book wouldn't have had a chance to exist. Thank you for all the love.

The agents at Upstart Crow Literary, namely Ted Malawer and Michael Stearns. Thank you for believing in me and helping to share my books with the world.

The amazing folks at Egmont USA. I am often surprised by how many people think I'm responsible for everything that goes into creating my books, from the cover design, the editing, and even all the way down to the choice of the typeface. This couldn't be further from the truth. I write the stories, but an entire team helps turn those stories into books: Doug Pocock, Elizabeth Law, Mary Albi, Regina Griffin, Nico Medina, Robert Guzman, Alison Weiss, Katie Halata. And especially my intrepid editor Greg Ferguson, who not only puts up with, but embraces, my crazy antics and the "Jimmy Olsen" nickname I've inflicted upon him. And who also isn't afraid to push me until things are as great as they can be—or to whip out his super-editor cape and come to the rescue of a hopelessly stranded author on the streets of NYC. This one's for you, Greg: Spunkgate! (Yep, I just worked that reference into a book.)

JDRIFT DESIGN, I didn't know it was possible to create a cover even more beautiful than the one for *The Dark Divine*. Wow, just, wow.

My enthusiastic publicist, Virginia Anagnos.

Noreen Gibbons, for never failing to offer help—even when it's completely inconvenient to her.

Whitney, for being an eager mother's helper.

My mom, Nancy Biesinger, for bringing over bags of groceries on the deadline days, and for helping out in hundreds of other ways.

Sara Zarr, who gave me just the right advice at just the moment I needed to hear it.

Mathew J. Kirby, for his ongoing friendship and support—and free psychological guidance, of course.

The SIX—the best critique group and posse of friends an author could have: Brodi Ashton, Emily Wing Smith, Valynne Maetani Nagamatsu, Kimberly Webb Reid, and Sara Bolton. If it weren't for the suggestion of adding a "Bedazzled stake" to this book by Brodi Ashton at a hilarious lunch on an otherwise no good, very bad day—*The Lost Saint* may have never come together the way it did. And if it weren't for the daily input and understanding of The SIX, I may have succumbed to the writer crazies a long time ago. (Or more so than I already have!)

The rest of my friends, siblings, nieces, nephews, in-laws, and Dad, who help out in so many ways, from entertaining my boys, to just being a listening ear, or a shoulder to lean on. I feel way too lucky to have so many wonderful people in my life.

My boys, who I couldn't love more—even when they're jumping on top of me and pretending to fire-bend lightning bolts at my laptop while I'm working. Nothing makes me prouder than when they ask if they can tell me a story. (Just you wait, publishing world, these boys have got it going on!)

And most especially Brick, who held on tight during the insane roller coaster that was this last year. Thank you for never letting go. You are my inspiration, my love, my saint. I know you're not perfect, but you're the perfect man for me. I.L.Y.R.U.T.T.M.A.B.A.

EGMONT PRESS: ETHICAL PUBLISHING

Egmont Press is about turning writers into successful authors and children into passionate readers – producing books that enrich and entertain. As a responsible children's publisher, we go even further, considering the world in which our consumers are growing up.

Safety First
Naturally, all of our books meet legal safety requirements. But we go further than this; every book with play value is tested to the highest standards – if it fails, it's back to the drawing-board.

Made Fairly
We are working to ensure that the workers involved in our supply chain – the people that make our books – are treated with fairness and respect.

Responsible Forestry
We are committed to ensuring all our papers come from environmentally and socially responsible forest sources.

For more information, please visit our website at www.egmont.co.uk/ethical

Mixed Sources
Product group from well-managed forests and other controlled sources
www.fsc.org Cert no. TT-COC-002332
© 1996 Forest Stewardship Council

Egmont is passionate about helping to preserve the world's remaining ancient forests. We only use paper from legal and sustainable forest sources, so we know where every single tree comes from that goes into every paper that makes up every book.

This book is made from paper certified by the Forestry Stewardship Council (FSC), an organisation dedicated to promoting responsible management of forest resources. For more information on the FSC, please visit **www.fsc.org**. To learn more about Egmont's sustainable paper policy, please visit **www.egmont.co.uk/ethical**.